Glass Tiger

Also by Joe Gores

A Time of Predators
Dead Skip
Full Notice
Interface
Hammett
Gone, No Forwarding
Come Morning
Wolf Time
32 Cadillacs
Dead Man
Menaced Assassin
Contract Null and Void
Cases
Stakeout on Page Street: and other DKA Files
Cons, Scams and Grifts

Joe Gores

GLASS TIGER

AN OTTO PENZLER BOOK

Quercus

First published in Great Britain in 2006 by

Quercus Publishing
46 Dorset Street
London
W1U 7NB

A CIP catalogue reference for this book is available from the British Library

ISBN (HB) 1 905204 54 X
ISBN (TPB) 1 905204 55 8

Printed in Great Britain by
Clays Ltd, St Ives plc

10 9 8 7 6 5 4 3 2 1

For Dori
The Dream Dreaming Me
Now and Forever
Here and Hereafter

Separation from its fellows appears to increase both cunning and ferocity. These solitary beasts, exasperated by chronic pain or widowhood, are occasionally found among all the larger carnivores.

Geoffrey Household
Rogue Male

The ferocity is gone. I don't have it in me any more. I can't even kill the bugs in my house.

'Iron Mike' Tyson, ex prize-fighter

PART ONE

Corwin

If men had wings and bore black
feathers, few of them would be
clever enough to be crows.
Henry Ward Beecher

Prologue

New Year's Eve

Tsavo Game Park, Kenya

THE BLACK RHINO stopped browsing to throw back its massive head and snort. His scimitar horns, the front one five feet long, gleamed like dull carbon under the gibbous moon. He was big as a boulder, a ton-and-a-half of living fossil plunked down on the wet-season savanna. Since the devastating horn and ivory raids by Somali *shifta* poachers in the 1970s and '80s, only this lone bull survived outside the game park's pitifully small rhino recovery reserve.

The compact man three feet from the rhino's left flank froze with one foot raised above the calf-high grass, one arm still outstretched. He was downwind, but his scent must have been carried by a vagrant night breeze. Rhinos' keen sense of smell, coupled with dim eyesight, made them unpredictable and even deadly if you couldn't get out of their way in time. The rhino snorted again, satisfied that all was well, and returned to stripping tender twigs and new leaves off the acacia bush with his delicate, beak-like mouth.

The man lowered his foot, put weight on it gradually so no twig would crackle. He laid his palm on the rhino's rounded back as gently as a falling leaf. It was his fifth New Year's Eve to do this, but he was always surprised by the softness and warmth of the hide. Explorers' tales from previous centuries made rhinos out to be great armored beasts with skin three inches thick, but they were surprisingly vulnerable to ticks and black flies and disease.

The rhino stopped munching to begin moving his back slightly under the human hand. After five minutes, the man moved silently away, out of the brush and out of danger and into the open veldt.

As he did each year he whispered, 'Happy New Year, *Bwana Kifaru*'

– Swahili for Big Boss Rhinocerous. Getting away unscathed from petting Bwana Kifaru was his New Year's Eve ritual. Only Morengaru, the other guard at Sikuzuri Safari Camp, understood it as a stab at needed danger. The man started the four-mile trot back to the Galana River's south bank. Almost 40, five-ten and built like an Olympic gymnast, hard of body, with coal-black hair and bitter-chocolate eyes, he was the only white camp guard in the country. And since big game hunting had been banned in Kenya, the closest to a white hunter the wealthy guests at the luxury resort would ever get. So he was obliged to attend Sikuzuri's official New Year's Eve party, even though he only wanted to return to his thatch-roof banda and reread one of the halfdozen paperback mysteries left behind by departing guests.

When he got to the ford across the Galana, he stopped abruptly, remembering the New Year's Eve seven years ago, after which everything had gone dead in him. Tonight he felt like a bear coming out of hibernation. What was going on? As he crossed the Galana, he could feel numbness disappearing, feel a return of something like that fierce adrenaline rush he once had lived for as the junkie lives for the needle.

Not killing. No, never again killing. A quest. A vital, necessary trackdown of… what? Or of whom? For whom?

Minnetonka, Minnesota

Sleeves rolled up and tie pulled awry, the former governor of Minnesota stood at his thermopaned study window, drink in hand, looking out over frozen Lake Minnetonka with glacial blue eyes. At fifty-five, he had a strong jaw and good cheekbones and the thick, slightly unruly hair Jack Kennedy had made de rigueur for serious national contenders.

'Thinking of how far you've come, darling?' He turned. After their return from the big New Year's Eve blast at Olaf Gavle's multi-million-dollar house, Edith had gone up to bed. Yet here she was back down again, wearing her shapeless flannel nightgown and green chenille robe.

'Thinking of how far I have to go. Can't sleep?'

'I get lonely when you're not next to me.'

Edith was forty-nine, the only wife he'd ever had, short, slightly plump, with the bright inquisitive eyes of a chickadee. He had been unfaithful to her with only one woman, who was now gone, and had never been able to decide whether Edith had known or not.

Looking down, he told her, not for the first time, 'If chickadees weighed a pound apiece, they'd rule the world.' She bumped him with a well-upholstered hip. He added, 'Twenty days, love. How often have I doubted this time would ever come?'

'I never doubted,' she said, suddenly fierce. 'Never for an instant. You're a man of destiny. Nothing can stop you now.'

The Great North Woods

Outside, it was thirty-six degrees below zero. Winter's icy hand gripped this northern land by the balls. Inside, the 56-year-old man started up from his sleep with a muffled 'Whompf!' The embers of the hearth fire dug harsh shadows into his lean face, seamed and nut-brown from exposure to a lifetime of bad weather.

He loved it all. Or once had. Now, he leaned against the wall behind his bunk in the one-room log cabin, deep-set hazel eyes staring through the moonlight from the window and into the familiar, already fading image:

Nisa, pounded back up against the bulkhead beside the houseboat's couch by the heavy .357 Magnum slugs...

Two months ago. He had dropped the gun like it was red hot. He had been shot the year before, turning it all sour. And tonight, along with Nisa, was an image from that earlier night:

Two yards away was a gaunt timberwolf, tongue lolling, ears pricked. Real? Or hallucination? The man had been shot three times from ambush and had to crawl a thousand feet to the cabin and a telephone before he went into shock.

His racing heart began to slow. The nightsweat of terror began drying on his face. Anger replaced it. Once he had been a trapper and a hunter: now he ate out of cans. Now he had a limp and a damaged lung and missing fingers, and couldn't even bring himself to bow-hunt whitetails for food.

And now, a visitation of the Nisa nightmare again, a month since the last one. His nightmares after his wife Terry's death, of her fleeing him, had prevented him from tracking down the drunken fool who had killed her. The Nisa dreams were different, guilt-filled – what had he done? With tonight, the wolf and a strange, palette-knife swirl of other images. Some stalking beast, dark and lithe and lean and tireless. Stalking him...

His bitterness became rage: having been made prey, he could no longer be predator. But because of what he had done, the nightmares of his daughter's death left him no choice. He had to atone, even while telling himself he never really would.

Never could. But now...

The gray wolf was easy. Himself, being urged to hunt again. But who – or what – would be hunting him? Easy surface analysis: if he hunted, he would be hunted by his own guilt.

Deeper analysis: literally hunted?

'Are you good enough?' he demanded of the faded image.

Unfairly, he would have to call Janet after convincing himself he would never put her in danger again. Ask her to meet him some-where, tell her he needed her help, remind her that two months ago she had been urging him to be a predator...

As he slid back down under the covers, he wondered if she still had old Charlie's bearskin.

The Sierra Foothills, Northern California

The 26-year-old woman stood looking out the open door of her cabin three miles from the Casa Loma general store. Her eyes were a startling blue in a tawny face with a strong nose and high cheek-bones; utterly straight raven hair flowed down to the middle of her back. This had been her parents' cabin under her father's long-since discarded name of Roanhorse: now it was hers. Pale blue moonlight showed her a muledeer doe and a yearling fawn browsing at the edge of the snow-clad clearing. She raised a steaming cup of coffee to salute them.

'Happy New Year, guys,' she said aloud. They ignored her, as was right between old and trusted friends.

Her bare feet were frigid on the pine planks, but she stood there a moment longer, feeling the night. A New Year, a year of change. She would write the letter, first step toward building a new life. After all, there had been nothing from Hal since he had left her hospital room on the eve of the elections. What had he done since? What might he still do?

She shivered, stepped back, shut the cabin door, and crawled into her bunkbed under the bearskin he had given her.

Rockville, Maryland

A cigar smouldered in an ashtray on the bedside table. The motel had a king-size bed and a dirty movie channel on the TV for nine bucks a night. Pale moonlight filtering through gauzy curtains showed a burly bear of a man in his late thirties, sitting on the edge of the bed with his pants off. Dense black hair covered his head, back, chest, belly, groin.

The platinum-haired black whore crouched between his thighs had long limbs, dangly breasts and very full lips and white teeth. She drew back her head momentarily to speak.

'It's starting to get there, baby,' she crooned. 'Oooh, baby, it's gonna be sooo good!'

But it wasn't. He had thought, after that night two months ago, that this would never happen again. One thing he knew for sure: it was all this ugly black bitch's fault.

'Aw hell, lady, this ain't working.'

He stood. His big fisted right hand struck her in the face, breaking her nose and mashing the suddenly hateful lying red lips flat against her teeth. She scrambled backwards away across the threadbare rug like a frightened spider, platinum wig down over one eye. But he followed, relentless, kicking her in face, belly, breasts.

Panting, spent, he stared down at the sobbing woman. There would be no repercussions: just in case, he had prepaid Sharkey out in L.A. enough to assure her silence here in D.C. In just twenty more days he would start to savor the power he had worked so hard to get. Then he wouldn't need bitches like this one any more.

He wiped himself with a handful of Kleenex, put on his pants and left.

Happy New Year.

Arlington, Virginia

Happy New Year? The upscale tract house occupied a half-acre of prime real estate on a twisty, winding blacktop road off the George Washington Memorial Parkway. The tall, very fit African-American saw the last of their party guests out into the winter night. When he turned back to ruefully survey the damage, Cora was giving him her patented dissatisfied look.

'We'll clean this mess up in the morning,' he told her.

Cora's gleaming hair was artfully styled; in her heels, she was just three inches shorter than his six-one. She had cool eyes and the haughty, brown, fine-boned face of that Ethiopian fashion model who had married the rock star a dozen years before.

'We'll get the cleaning service to do it in the morning.'

At double or triple rates, of course. He stifled his irritated response. His crack FBI Hostage Rescue/Sniper team had been out in the boondocks on special assignment for all of November and December. He seriously needed to get laid. He put an arm around his wife's waist to guide her toward the stairs.

'Sure thing, baby. But tonight we got some lovin' to do.'

She went with him, but might not have heard him.

'Now you're going to be home more, I think we should start looking for a bigger house, further out.'

Translation: an acre of land where they could keep a horse and pretend to be landed gentry. Was that any different from ten acres and a mule? Cora didn't want kids to ruin her figure; she was all about appearances, as ambitious for money and social position as he was for power and political access. Now if something would just happen in the next twenty days to keep him and his team on that same detached duty to the Chief of Staff for the foreseeable future, that would make it a Happy New Year for sure.

Something did.

1

JANUARY NINETEENTH. HAL Corwin crossed the Truckee Post Office parking lot with the slightest of limps, gingerly, as if not sure of his footing on the just-plowed surface. Here, at nearly 6,000 feet of elevation on the Cal-Nev border, the frigid air bit hard at his bullet-damaged lung.

Janet Kestrel stepped down from the driver's side of her old dark-green 4-Runner facing out from a far corner of the lot. Its motor was running as if for a quick getaway. Her tawny face was as brown as his, but from genetics, not weather. Today her ebony hair was piled on top of her head under a furlined cap.

Hal put his left hand on her arm, tenderly. The hand was missing two fingers. 'Delivery tomorrow morning, guaranteed.'

'Know why that doesn't make me happy? Tomorrow afternoon he'll have all of the world's resources at his command.'

'Doesn't matter. He has to feel it coming.'

Before that night last November she had been avid, urging him on. She knew little about the deaths and was afraid to ask. Afraid to know what she might have helped drive him to.

They hugged. He was a rangy six feet, the top of her head fit just under his chin. Her blue eyes were tight shut. During four months last year, he had become the father she had lost, she had become the daughter he had... oh God, what had he done?

She had driven up here as he had asked, would go home and wait for his call. But she had written the letter. She stepped back from his embrace, schooling all emotion from her voice.

'Page my cellphone when you need the 4-Runner.'

'I will. Just bring it back here and catch the first bus down the mountain. Don't tell anyone what you're doing.' He laid a gentle palm on her cheek. 'I'll call you afterwards.'

She climbed into the 4-Runner. He bowed slightly and swept a courtly arm to usher her away. Any chance of seeing her again was probably nil, but setting it up now meant there could be no possible danger to her later.

Gustave Wallberg didn't have George W.'s little-boy smiley-eyes, nor Clinton's testosterone-drenched good-old-boy appeal. Instead, he had the rugged good looks of, say, a retired pro quarterback, just right for this 300-channel sound-bite era.

Protocol demanded that he wear a diplomat's gray cutaway, but he had wanted a snap-on bowtie. Emily had insisted on hand-tied. Once in a lifetime, after all.

He pulled the offending tie apart yet again and said, 'Dammit anyway,' without turning from the mirror. Emily appeared behind him in her Bill Blass original.

'Yes, dear,' she said gaily. 'Turn around.'

The anteroom door banged open and Kurt Jaeger surged in like a charging bear, bigger than life. He had an unlit cigar in one hand, a flat blue and white Post Office EXPRESS MAIL envelope in the other. Seeing Emily, he slowed, found a grin.

'So, Emily. Ready for the big moment?'

'Yes, if this man would only stand still long enough for me to' – she gave her husband's tie a final jerk – 'get this right…'

Wallberg was slanting a look at the envelope. 'Something?'

'The usual suspects – their undying love and devotion so they can be riding the gravy train as it leaves the station.'

Wallberg knew his man too well to believe this. It was in Jaeger's heavy voice, in the small, hard eyes that dominated the meaty face. He waited patiently until the door to the suite's bedroom closed behind his wife, then snatched the envelope from the hand of his Chief of Staff.

'Now let's see what's so damned important you had to…'

He ran down. One line, laser-printed on standard letter-size paper so it had no identifying characteristics the FBI lab could analyze. Mailed yesterday from Truckee, California.

'Who has seen this?'

'Me. As one of the new boys in town, I was being shown how the White House mailroom guys X-ray all incoming for poisons and explosives and biohazards and all that crap. I saw his name on it and snagged it unopened after they ran it through.'

'What's the temperature going to be for the ceremony?'

'Twenty above. With wind-chill, five above.'

'Tell Shayne O'Hara I agree with his Secret Service lads. At five above, it is more prudent to go with the closed limo.'

An hour later, Wallberg was standing before Chief Justice Alvin Carruthers, his right hand raised, his left hand flat on an open Bible. He was hatless, the icy wind ruffled his hair as he recited the oath of office after the aged jurist.

'I, Gustave Wallberg... Do solemnly swear... That I will faithfully execute... The Office of President of the United States... And will to the best of my ability... Preserve, protect and defend... The Constitution of the United States...'

As he repeated the sacred words, that mad message burned in his brain: CONGRATULATIONS TO A DEAD PRESIDENT. CORWIN. Dear God. Would he have to shift priorities for his first weeks – months? – in office to accomodate the nearly unthinkable fact that Hal Corwin might still be alive?

The late March air was icy. Hal Corwin shivered as he crawled out of his sleeping bag to restart his fire. His campsite was a calculated quarter-mile off the ridge trail above California's King's Canyon National Park, at the edge of the sub-alpine zone where ponderosa pines crept up to mingle with old-growth Douglas firs and Engelmann spruce.

He sat on the hollow fir log that dominated the clearing as he waited for snow-melt to heat for instant coffee. The log was six feet in circumference and twenty-five feet long. It had been rotting there for four hundred years. The scattered droppings of countless generations of tiny deer mice, shrews and voles living in its depths had nourished the root fungi that laced its open end.

As he breathed the icy air as deep as his damaged lung would allow, he massaged his bad leg.

He stepped away from the tree and was struck a terrific blow below the left knee...

The stalking beast of his dreams didn't exist, but he knew in his gut that tomorrow the searchers, lesser men, would come.

At two minutes after midnight, a red Chevy Tracker turned off California 180 to stop in the puddle of pale light by the antique gas pumps fronting Parker's Resort. Two men got out to walk toward the rustic bar-cafe. One was six feet and hard-bitten, the other short, round, red of face. Both wore insulated coats and hunting caps with the earflaps down.

Seth-Parker had just finished scraping the grease into the trap underneath the grill. He was a tall, stooped, skinny man, with wary brown eyes and a drooping ginger mustache. The rolled-up sleeves of his long-johns showed tattooed forearms. He stepped into the open doorway, his shadow cast long before him. His 12-gauge leaned against the wall two feet away.

'No gas tonight, guys,' he called. 'Sorry.'

Except for the cafe, he and Mae weren't really open for the season until the weekend, yet here were these two showing up at midnight on this lonely stretch of highway.

Big Guy stopped, said disarmingly, 'How about a cabin?'

'That we might be able to do. Depends on—'

'How about something to eat?' said Short and Round.

'Just closed down the grill.' But Seth's wariness was gone. Obviously, for Short and Round, munchies were more important than mayhem. 'Toasted cheese sandwiches?'

'With bacon in 'em? And fries?'

'Bacon we got. No fries tonight. Potato chips, pickles.'

While Seth grilled the sandwiches, they wandered around the old chinked-log building, drinking Miller Lite and looking at the deer and elk heads over the bar, the Chinook salmon mounted above the wide stone fireplace with its still-glowing hardwood embers.

Seth joined them at the table to have a beer himself. He never could get to sleep much before two a.m. anyway.

Short and Round, washing down his sandwich with his beer, said primly, 'No private facilities are allowed in national parks, but this place sure as hell looks private to me.'

'Run down, you mean?' Seth chuckled. 'My granddaddy built it before the park went in. Sure you guys wouldn't be happier at Grant Grove Center? It's official, open all year. New cabins, a lodge, gift shop, grocery store – and you can get gas there.'

Big Guy shoved his plate aside, shook out a Marlboro, slightly raised it and his eyebrows. Seth nodded. He lit up.

'Walter and I were trying to hook up with an old friend back at Cedarbrook, somehow we missed connections.' He took a photo out of his shirt pocket. 'Maybe he stopped by here?'

Seth studied the proffered picture, said reluctantly, 'Feller come by ten, twelve days ago. I ain't sure, but it could be him.' He felt them tense up while trying to hide it. He returned the photo. 'He come back three days ago.'

'What for?'

'Stock up. Instant coffee, Granola bars, Cup of Noodles, like that. And beef jerky. Lots of beef jerky.'

Big Guy asked, 'Where's he camped?'

'Said he's been bivouacked up off the ridge trail.'

'Sounds like we'd better get an early start to catch him in case he's thinking of moving on.'

Seth stood up to pull on his wool shirt and anorak. In the mountains in late March, the outside nighttime temperature was still in the 'teens, with snow still deep under the ponderosas.

'Breakfast's seven to nine, but Mae'll open up at six.'

As he crossed the dimly-lit gravel drive to fire up the propane heater in cabin six, he thought, Friend my ass. Heat, most likely Feds. He could smell a cop like a bean fart at a girls'-school social.

Another dawn. Corwin sat beside his final fragrant spruce fire, drinking coffee. The searchers would be coming up the ridge trail from Parker's place, moving slowly, silently. They'd be good. He knew that he was better.

A winter wren gave a sleepy cheep in the juniper thicket at one edge of the clearing. A pygmy nuthatch made tiny scraping sounds on its first upside-down journey of the day down one of the ponderosas. High above, in the tree's crown, the band of resident crows was waking up with muted, grumpy squawks.

Soon they would head out to the lower-elevation meadows to forage, drift back up here to their roost at dusk. He would miss them. His name, Corwin, meant 'friend of crows' in Old English.

He kicked the fire to embers, got out the last of the beef jerky. As he had done every morning since coming here, he scattered pieces of it over the log. Several choice morsels he squashed with a thumb down into the deepest furrows of the bark.

When three quick, light caws identified him as Crow Three, eight sooty birds floated silently down through the branches. The breeding male, big as Poe's raven and shiny as a stovepipe, landed on the log itself. In high school, Corwin had ended up as Bird Crow, and had passed the name on to the breeding male.

He had begun by scattering the jerky on the log. Had worked his way closer until he could sit on the end of the log while they ate. He knew he didn't look like another crow to them, but he always furnished them with beef jerky. Crow Three.

Bird Crow began digging at the choice bits of jerky buried deep in the bark. His cohort hopped up to gobble the easy ones. No jostling, no shoving. A clan. A family.

Seven minutes later, the sentinel left in the top of the ponderosa sounded the alarm. The searchers had arrived.

'Shit,' said Ray in a low voice. His FBI I.D. was strung on a lanyard around his neck and his Sig Sauer was in his right hand, held low at his side. 'Crows. They'll alert him. C'mon!'

The crows barely had time to flap up from the log. One, huge and shiny as a raven, stayed to rip out bits of bark and throw them in all directions with savage sideways flings of its head, somehow always keeping one beady eye on the intruders. Then it was gone with a final fat morsel in its beak.

Walt sat down on the log, winded by his sprint to the clearing. His feet didn't quite reach the ground.

'I get it, Ray. Since the crows are here, he can't be.'

'Smart fella, Walt.'

Ray held an ungloved hand above the embers of the fire before letting himself sit down and light up. The harsh smell of burning tobacco drifted through the clearing.

'Twenty minutes,' he said. 'Maybe thirty. That close. That's the bad news.' He feathered out smoke. 'The good news is that he can't be more than forty minutes ahead of us.' He smeared out his just-lit Marlboro against the log. 'Let's move. Let's show those Secret Service fucks how to take down a suspect – we'll have this guy's ass in custody before noon.'

'Unless he resists,' said Walter piously. He was an asshole, but he loved mortal shooting and was good at it.

'Unless he resists,' Ray agreed.

The crows were back at the beef jerky when Corwin crawled out of the log dragging his pack and sleeping bag behind him.

FBI. He even recognized their voices: they had smoked a cigarette above his hiding place back in the Delta in November. As expected, they had been told that he was armed and dangerous. Well, he once had been. He'd lost track of the men he'd killed over the years. These two were no threat.

He trotted unevenly away down his backtrail, leaving Bird Crow's gang of ruffians to savage the last of the jerky. He'd call Janet from Cedarbrook, she'd leave the 4-Runner for him at Truckee as planned, he'd pick it up with no contact between them. She would be safe, he would have a clean vehicle to drive now that he was clear of the searchers. In two or three weeks their masters would surely find someone better to send after him – the shadowy tireless tracker of his nightmares?

By then he would be hidden away. In plain sight.

2

ON AN EARLY April dawn two weeks later, an unmarked G400 Gulfstream jet circled Nairobi International Airport preparatory to landing. Terrill Hatfield stared almost gloomily down at the flat brown earth rushing up to meet them. He had his New Year's Eve wish: he and his FBI Rescue/Sniper Team were on detached duty to the President's Chief of Staff for the foreseeable future. But they had failed to catch Corwin at King's Canyon, as they had failed to catch him in the Delta in November. And now this.

After he deplaned, a government car took Hatfield from a far corner of the field to the far side of Kenya passport control and customs check. He had read the file of the man he had been sent here to bring back. Impressive. Too impressive. He and his men could get the job done without the help of this outsider. But Hatfield had been told to bring him: bring him he would. He would wait for an enabling incident, grab his man, and fly him back to D.C. In custody. It would exceed his authority, yes, but the stakes were high and he had Kurt Jaeger behind him.

What if the man succeeded where Hatfield had failed? There was a way around that. Use him, then step in to seize the power and glory of success for himself alone. Step on the son of a bitch hard, right away. Keep stepping on him. Control him, use him, obstruct him if necessary, then find a way to discard him.

Brendan Thorne began bucking hard under Ellie, the 23-year-old blonde straddling him at Sikuzuri Safari Camp in Tsavo East. Eleanor's groom, 59-year-old Squire Pierpont III, was paying eight hundred bucks a night, not the usual $600, because his new trophy wife, after glimpsing Thorne on their arrival, had insisted on an extra-spacious banda with two private bedrooms.

Hemingway's randy white hunters with their double-wide sleeping bags were no more, so two or three times a year Thorne, lowly camp guard, got seduced by women like Ellie: bored wives dragged to darkest Africa by wealthy husbands. It was the only social life he got, and as much as he could handle.

Ellie started panting, open-mouthed. Her eyes rolled up. Thorne flipped her onto her back and pumped hard. She came again in synch with him. Vocally. He was glad she had put all that Halcyon in her husband's final whiskey-soda last night; his job was the only thing that held Thorne together. Since New Year's Eve, no worthy stalk had yet appeared to rouse him from the somnolence of his narrow days. But he kept hoping.

Thorne emerged into cool pre-dawn darkness to find the other camp guard, a Wanderobo-Masai named Morengaru, squatting beneath an African toothbrush tree. The shotgun that he used for everything from buck to buff rested buttdown on the ground between his knees, the muzzle pointing up past his left ear.

'Na kwenda wapi?' Thorne asked. Morengaru stood, swung an arm to the east. Down river. 'Kwa nini?' Why?

Gathering dawnlight picked out the high cheekbones on the African's deadpan ebony face. 'Lori,' he said.

Morengaru was going downriver because he had heard a lorry. It must have come from Somalia, three hundred miles to the north. In the 1970s and '80s, Somali ivory and horn poachers had been the reason Sikuzuri Camp needed armed guards. They had wiped out Tsavo's rhinos and had reduced its six thousand elephants to a few hundred, then had started killing tourists until Richard Leakey's Kenyan Wildlife Service rangers started shooting them on sight.

Now Thorne and Morengaru mostly protected the resort's guests against Tsavo's notoriously uncivil lions. Tsavo's males were sparsely maned and much bigger than Africa's other lions – four feet at the shoulder, five hundred pounds in weight, a feline 'missing link' between Africa's modern lions and the hulking extinct unmaned cave lions of the Pleistocene. Occasionally they ate careless people, even well-heeled wazungu on photo safari.

'Na piga minge sana,' said Morengaru.

He had heard the sound of many 'blows' – which Thorne knew meant in context the pounding of automatic rifles.

'Namna mbali?' How far away?

Morengaru held up five fingers: five kilometers. Since he could hear a car engine starting up twenty kilometers off, on a moonless night could see the moons of Jupiter with his naked eyes, Morengaru's five clicks absolutely meant five clicks.

A superb starling with a metallic-blue back and chestnut belly swooped down on green-tinged blue wings to the rim of the water pan left out for Yankee, the camp watchdog. He checked right, then left, then plunged his whole jet-crowned head underwater and shook it violently. Came up, sent spray in every direction, repeated, again, yet again, then flew off. As always, the two men watched this morning ritual with great respect.

A kilometer downriver a leopard bitched about his empty gut with a frustrated, rasping, two-note cry. Morengaru said with a sly look and in passable English, 'Since we two landless rogues, maybe we go hunting now.'

'You cheeky bastard,' said Thorne. They both laughed.

Could the leopard kill himself a shifta? A gratifying thought, but unlikely. The shifta's specialty was spraying their prey with AK47 assault rifles from a safe distance away.

So why was Thorne leaving the camp Uzi at home, starting on his first manhunt in seven years with only his Randall Survivor and his 9mm Beretta? Was it his pathetic bow to a time when he had been a fighting man instead of a glorified babysitter? Or because his killing days were gone forever?

Sikuzuri Safari Camp was strung out along a quarter-mile of the Galana River's south bank. Bar and lounge, dining hall as big as a posh restaurant, good china, chairs and tables of native hardwoods, buffalo horns and animal skulls on the walls.

The two men trotted down one of the resort's well-marked paths. Golden pipits hurled themselves from bush to bush like tiny gold coins. The watumishi boys were stirring: strong coffee wooed their nostrils, but they had no time for a mug of it. An agama lizard popped up from behind an exposed acacia root to eye them icily, then ducked down again, like an infantryman checking out enemy troops from his foxhole.

They went silently down river on game paths twisting through saltbrush and doum palm, wary of ambush. Saltbrush, thick and bushy like dense groves of cedar, could conceal the leopard they had heard, a pride of lions, even a herd of elephant. All could kill the unwary, and often did.

The long rains were gone. Northeast across the Galana, thickets of spiked wait-a-bit comiphora shrubs – *ngoja kidoga* locally – blanketed the plains with nasty curved thorns that could claw the skin off a man's back as neatly as an attacking leopard. Seven Grant's zebras foraging the dried grasses looked car-wash fresh. Their kick could break a lion's jaw.

Beyond was the flat-topped Yatta Escarpment, the longest lava ridge in the world, black and forbidding in the early morning light. Tsavo was the size of Massachusetts, still untamed and essentially untouristed.

A six-foot russet-necked Goliath heron, Africa's largest bird, fished the sedges along the shore beside a shady grove of tamarind trees loaded with rattly brown seedpods. The tree trunks were polished red by mud-covered elephants rubbing against them. Morengaru stopped abruptly.

'One click more.'

Ten minutes further on, across the river and below a small ridge, three maneless male lions were feeding on the massive body of a bull buffalo. A fresh kill, an hour old, not ripe yet.

The old bull, alone on a ridge above one of the small dry stream beds called luggas, fearless because he weighed as much as a VW Beetle, hadn't had a chance. The three lions, each the size of a small grizzly bear, had been lying in wait. Each lion would eat seventy-five pounds of the buff's meat before midday, then would not feed again for several days.

Another two hundred yards brought the dull telltale glint of metal in the saltbrush, also on the far side of the river. A decrepit British lorry of incredible vintage, camouflaged with branches.

Morengaru jerked his head downstream, whispered, 'Kiboko.'

The hippos' telltale protruding eyes showed above the water. They killed more Africans each year in panic than any other animal did on purpose. But they posed no real threat as long as the men didn't try to cross near them.

Back upriver, the way they'd come, a fish eagle swooped low over a large eddy of russet water where half a dozen fifteen-foot logs drifted in slow, aimless circles.

Thorne chuckled and said in English, 'Hippos and crocs.'

Crocodiles were Africa's second deadliest animal. On purpose. A sudden lunge, a three thousand-pound snap of massive jaws, and a tribal woman washing clothes in the river, facing the shore as always, would be dragged backwards screaming from the bank. Then she would be stuck in the mud at the bottom of the river until ripe enough to be torn into bite-size pieces and eaten.

The two men could cross in only gut-deep water right where they were, but the crocs made such a crossing a race with death. Lose their footing, lose the race. Don't try, and the shifta would be free to do whatever bloody work they were about.

Thorne trotted down the bank, went in, churning ahead, bent forward, straining against the weight of water, looking neither back nor to the sides. Morengaru would be behind him. The stolid hippos would be watching. The crocs would be coming; coming like half-ton cigarette boats, heads up, jaws gaping, casting spreading wakes behind them. The men splashed up the far bank with six feet to spare, the crocs lunging halfway out of the water before sliding back with frustrated jaw-clacks.

A brace of startled waterbucks bounded off across the savanna like outsized jackrabbits. Dense clouds of flies rose from the truck bed. Thorne approached with massive foreboding.

'Cocksuckers!' he exclaimed involuntarily.

Tossed carelessly into the back of the lorry was a pair of black rhino horns, matted hair use-polished into the hardness of bone, the curved front one five feet long. Hacked off with pangas after the nearly extinct animal had been killed by the burst of automatic weapon fire Morengaru had heard. Bits of skin and flesh still clung to them, pink but darkening rapidly.

Just over three months ago, Thorne had laid his hand on Bwana Kifaru's back. He had considered the ugly, endearing, grumpy, near-sighted beast a friend: now he was dead and left to rot, slaughtered for hacked-off horns that would be carved into status-symbol handles for the decorative daggers of petro-rich Yemeni Arab young-bloods. Left-over bits would be ground into aphrodisiac powder for Asians who didn't trust Viagra.

Just a bonus for the shifta. In 1989, the Conference on International Trade in Endangered Species had imposed a world-wide ban on the sale of elephant tusks. But now Zimbabwe and Botswana, overpopulated with elephant, were lobbying to lift the ban, again sparking demand for ivory in Japan and China.

So the shifta were after the last two of the Galana's old bull elephants who carried 175 kilos of ivory that would sell for $6,000 a kilo. The tusks would be worth a million dollars to a black market buyer: the raiders had not come hunting on spec.

'Not today, you fuckers,' Thorne whispered to himself.

Nobody had been left to guard the lorry. Keys in the ignition. Thorne dropped them into his pocket. Morengaru moved slowly forward, bent at the waist. He put gentle fingertips into several shallow, barely-discernable depressions in the dust. Came erect displaying three splayed fingers.

'Tatu.'

Three shifta. Catch the bastards, hand them over to the Kenyan Wildlife Service, rough fuckers who would work them over until they gave up their buyer. A very good day's work indeed.

Thorne swung an arm, breathed, 'Sisi endelea. Upesi.'

Let us go quickly. They trotted along the edge of the savanna for silent movement, detouring through the saltbrush only to avoid the scavengers squabbling over Bwana Kifaru.

It was a Hieronymus Bosch painting come to life. Snapping jackals, snarling spotted hyenas, spindly-legged marabout storks with bald heads already red from being thrust into the rhino's guts. Leaping, yelling, fighting. Overhead circled a pair of tawny, muscular bataleur eagles, disdainful of the scene below.

A kilometer on, they passed a score of elephant skulls as big as boulders, left by the poachers of fifteen years ago. Every gaping eye-socket held a nest of spur-winged plovers.

Half a click, and they came upon still slightly-steaming cannon-ball-size piles of fresh elephant dung. Getting close. A Hemprich's hornbill foraging the strawy brown mounds for seeds and grasses flapped away, indignantly clacking his dusky red downturned beak. Later his own droppings would spread the seeds over the savanna to complete the cycle of death and rebirth.

Silent as ghosts, the two men moved downriver and upwind. Stopped. Ten yards ahead, facing away from them, were the shifta, three scruffy men in kepis and cast-off military uniforms with sandals made of truck tires.

Thirty yards further on in a small clearing were the two old bull elephants. The larger was thirteen feet at the shoulder and weighed seven tons. Thorne had named him Tantor after Tarzan's elephant friend. Tantor had just curled his sinuous trunk around a bunch of browse like a cook's hand around a pound of uncooked spaghetti, was shoving it into his curiously delicate mouth and chewing, rumbling with pleasure. His massive forehead was braced against a doum palm to temporarily ease the weight of ten-foot tusks that almost touched the ground.

The younger bull, Dumbo, with only slightly smaller ivory, was shielded by Tantor's bulk. The shifta were waiting until they could kill both animals with one sustained magazine-emptying burst of rifle fire. If only wounded, they would disappear into the saltbrush in seconds, taking their ivory with them.

A drab little bulbul, unconcerned with the drama below, sang its beguiling song in the foliage overhead. Thorne slid to his right, knowing Morengaru would go left. No twig crackled underfoot, no branch rustled.

The man in front of Thorne raised his AK47 to shoot Tantor in the spine. Thorne tapped him on the shoulder.

'Don't do that,' he said in English.

The Somali whirled, bringing around his automatic weapon. Thorne had been thinking capture, but everything became liquid quicksilver as training and temperament overcame resolve. His left hand whipped his knife across the man's jugular with a powerful backhand slash. Bright arterial blood gushed.

The one in the center got off an errant burst into the sky as Morengaru's 12-gauge dissolved the top of his head in a spray of brain and bone. He fell, a sack of bloody flour.

The third tried to fire from the hip, but Thorne's Beretta slammed four glazer rounds into his chest in a silver-dollar cluster. His gaunt, aristocratic face went gray with death.

Five seconds.

The elephants had whirled to face them, huge as houses, ears flaring, trumpeting. Then they were gone with that lovely gliding silent stride that always took Thorne's breath away.

On his thirtieth birthday, Thorne was killing men in Panama as a sometime assassin for a CIA front. On his thirty-fifth, he became a Tsavo camp guard because belatedly he had sworn to his dead Alison's memory that he would never again kill another human being.

Today, on his fortieth birthday, he had killed two of them. He had betrayed Alison's memory because he had been betrayed by his New Year's Eve feeling that a worthy stalk of worthy prey would appear. No killing, just the stalk. But two men were dead by his hand. Killing them, he had again felt that wondrous cleansing adrenalin rush. But also nausea.

The bulbul resumed its beguiling song as Thorne threw up into the saltbush.

3

THEY LEFT THE shifta's lorry a mile downwind so the stink of death would not accompany them across the shallow ford to the camp. Sikuzuri, after all, was strictly for the diamonds-and-Ferrari set. You paid big money to sit on your veranda facing the Galana and listen to real lions roar and real elephants trumpet with no bars between you and them. And, because of Thorne and Morengaru, with no real danger to yourself.

A pale goshawk chanted at them from a phone pole. A black-shouldered kite kweee-e-e-ed at them from the wire. Thorne sometimes made photo ops for the tourists by putting a cube of raw meat on his palm so a kite could swoop down and snatch it.

Eight black-headed sacred ibises pecked wih curved beaks in the mud beside the ford. To the ancient Egyptians these birds symbolized Thoth, who totted up your good and evil deeds in the Book of the Dead. Today Thorne, betraying himself and Alison's memory, had killed two men to save two elephants and avenge a dead rhino. Where did that fall in Thoth's scales of justice?

Morengaru went off to clean his shotgun, Thorne went into the office. Steven Livingston, manager of Sikuzuri for three years, looked up from his computer. He was a ruddy-faced Brit with round glasses and a bristling ginger mustache and a degree in hotel management. Inevitably, he was called Stanley Livingston instead of Steve. He held out an envelope to Thorne.

'Eleanor Pierpont left this for you before they went off, Brendan. It will be a bloody nice tip, I daresay.'

Thorne laid the envelope unopened on the desk.

'Give it to Morengaru for his 401K.'

He dialled the Kenyan Wildlife Service at Voi to get Jehovah Muthengi, a Kamba under whom he had served as a tracker and guide for two years before moving on to Sikuzuri. At odd times they had drunk a good bit of Tusker beer together.

'Jehovah, we ran across three shifta this morning, trying to poach those bull elephants. We stopped 'em, but Bwana Kifa—, but that old lone bull rhino's horns are in the back of their lorry a mile below camp.' He listened, frowning at Muthengi's words, then shrugged. 'Sure, call Nairobi. I suppose the Kenya National Police will want to see what's left of 'em in situ.'

When he hung up, Stanley Livingston was drawing up his well-fed body and staring at him with goggle-eyed outrage.

'Now see here, Thorne, this bloody well isn't on, killing Somalis. These high-handed tactics—'

Thorne shut the screen door behind him with exaggerated care, went down to the modest banda he had built himself in the thorn-fence-enclosed boma where the workers lived. He cleaned the Beretta with a toothbrush and Hoppe's No. 9, ran cleaning disks down the barrel to clear away the powder residue. Sitting in his canvas safari chair outside his hut, he read a book left behind by a guest, *Dante in Love*, Harriet Rubin's contemplation on the writing of the Divine Comedy. Two men dead by his hand. In which ring of the Inferno would Dante place him for that?

Three hours later a cloud of red dust chased the Wildlife Service Land Rover into camp. Muthengi was behind the wheel, Sergeant Hassim and Corporal Abdulla were with him. Livingston had the wind up, was jittering around as if trying to dodge an angry wasp. Looking on, fascinated, were guests waiting to go on photo safari when a lowering sun made the animals active.

Thorne advanced with a smile. 'Jehovah.'

'Mr. Thorne, sah.' Whoops. No Brendan. Way too formal.

Muthengi was a short, square, very black man, so black the inside of his mouth was purple. He wore a safari jacket, khaki shorts, knee socks, desert boots, and a ripoff U.S. Army .45 in a hip-holster like a Western gunslinger. He couldn't hit anything with it, but it had seemed an innocent affectation. Until today.

The rangers were Cushite Borani tribesmen from the Northern

Frontier District where it bordered Ethiopia. They were over six feet tall, wiry, with beautiful, disdainful faces. They wore the green camise and beret of the Kenyan Wildlife Service.

Thorne greeted them cheerily in Swahili; they answered with distant nods. He tensed up even more. Livingston's jitters. Muthengi's formal greeting. The rangers' embarrassment. Damn. He hadn't even been to the capitol in six months, but any non-citizen working in Kenya for local pay was on shaky ground.

'What did Nairobi have to say about my little *shauri*?'

My little affair. Responding, Muthengi did not meet his eyes. 'They said you must be, ah, placed under arrest, sah.'

In an obviously rehearsed move, Hassan and Abdulla brought up their rifles to point at Thorne's chest. He stood very still. Rangers were notoriously nervy behind the gun, and these were serious weapons, G3 semiautomatics in 7.62mm NATO caliber.

'What's the charge, Jehovah?'

'Ah… poaching rhinocerous horn, sah.'

'I see.' He almost did. Someone in Nairobi must have been waiting for any excuse. 'Shauri ya Mungu, Jehovah?'

'Ndio.' Muthengi, embarrassed by his own betrayal, nodded solemnly. 'Yes. It is indeed God's affair, sah.'

Morengaru had drifted up silently through the tourists, unnoticed by anyone save Thorne, carrying his shotgun. To Morengaru, killing men was nothing. Thorne pecked two hooked fingers toward his own eyes, then turned his hand to peck the same fingers toward Morengaru's eyes.

'Tatuona tena,' he said, low-voiced. 'Uso kwa uso.'

We shall see each other again. Face to face.

Morengaru nodded solemnly and faded away, still unseen. But Muthengi, thinking Thorne was speaking to him, took it as a challenge. His moment of embarrassment turned to anger.

'Cuff him,' he said brusquely to his rangers.

Thorne put his hands behind his back to feel the cold bite of steel around his wrists, not for the first time.

'We will go to Manyani to meet the plane,' Muthengi said.

'Thirty miles of bad road,' said Thorne. When he looked over at Stanley Livingston, he realized the camp manager had been privy to the bust, but had told him nothing. So Thorne added to him, 'Keep my Land-Rover here until I come back. Give the keys to Morengaru – and send my things home to Mum.'

Livingston colored and went quickly into the office and slammed the door. Thorne could read his mind: bloody Africa.

In Nairobi hours later, Muthengi and the other two stooges delivered Thorne to the dark and deserted-looking sandstone-block Department of Justice building on Jomo Kenyatta Boulevard. They climbed three flights of stairs past uniformed guards to an open door spilling light across the hallway.

A lone black man, light-skinned for a Kenyan, was sitting on one of the hard benches outside the enclosed receptionist's area. He did not turn his head to look at them as they passed. The hairs on the nape of Thorne's neck rose. Muthengi knocked on the door to the magistrate's inner office.

'Come.'

Arthur Kemoli, a Luhya from up around Kakamega way, had a single official-looking document squared upon his desk. The lamp laddered harsh shadows up his underlit features. He was Thorne's age, wearing heavy-rimmed glasses, his tight-curled black hair cropped close against his skull.

During Thorne's brief stint as a Kenya Wildlife Service ranger, he had caught Kemoli's son trying to smuggle out protected bushbabies. Instead of busting him, Thorne cuffed him around the ears and kicked him loose. Kemoli, not satisfied with such banal punishment, took a club to the bare soles of his son's feet. The boy had been unable to walk for three weeks.

'Why is this man cuffed?' Kemoli demanded.

'He is a dangerous prisoner, sah,' said Muthengi piously.

Kemoli gestured. The cuffs were unlocked. Thorne rubbed his wrists. Kemoli's hand made a shooing motion.

'Outside, the three of you. And shut the door behind you.'

The three stooges departed, hesitantly. When they were gone, Kemoli came around the desk for an embrace, solemn-faced.

Thorne paraphrased, "All animals are equal. Some are just more equal than others."

'You remembered!' Kemoli exclaimed with real pleasure.

As a student at Kakamega Boys Secondary School, Kemoli had read Orwell's *Animal Farm* and had loved Squealer, the pig who ran the place. He took the name as his own, and until entering politics was known as Squealer Kemoli.

Thorne sat down across from him. His wrists were raw from the shackles. Kemoli shoved the document around with his ballpoint pen. There was regret on his face.

'Do you know the Swahili proverb about the elephants?'

'When two elephants fight, it is the grass that is hurt.'

'Just so. This is an order for your immediate deportation. You are the grass. One elephant is our quite new Kenyan government after four decades of corrupt rule by KANU under Arap Moi, which was preceded by another decade of corrupt rule by KANU under Jomo Kenyatta. The other elephant—'

'Is the American in your anteroom. He's too light-skinned for an African and he is used to waiting. A U.S. cop or federal agent. The hairs on the back of my neck tell me he's no friend.'

Kemoli nodded and sighed. 'Indeed not. Since all of the embassy bombings and threats of embassy bombings, your country has been a very large bull elephant in East Africa. They request, we agree. They demand, we comply. They demanded.'

'Sign the bloody thing, Arthur. If they'd wanted me dead, I'd have been persuaded to jump out of the plane on the flight from Manyani. Somebody wants me to do something nasty for them.'

Terrill Hatfield drove the Kenyan government Land-Rover himself, the two rangers in the back with the muzzles of their rifles screwed into Thorne's neck. Thorne got a last look at Nairobi Game Park by moonlight. Leopards and hyenas from the park sometimes wandered adjacent housing developments at night.

Hatfield searched him totally before shoving him up the stairway into the interior of the Gulfstream. In three of the nine leather club chairs were armed men dressed in suits. Not Secret Service. Not Marines. They almost stunk of Agency, but not quite. Most likely FBI, operating illegally overseas.

'What's it all about, Alfie?' asked Thorne.

'Shut the fuck up,' Hatfield explained. 'You're getting a free ride in a thirty-eight-million-buck plane. Be grateful.'

With no book to read, he feigned sleep during the flight from Nairobi west across Africa. Wondered why the guy who had grabbed him was so hostile. It seemed a lot more than just keeping Thorne down, but he couldn't worry about that now.

After the fueling stop in Dakar, he sat upright during the crossing of the Atlantic to D.C. He had just killed two men; he knew from bitter experience that if he slept his nightmare of seven years before would return. Just as well. Something truly rotten was brewing. He had to prepare his refusals for it.

It was sometime in the wee hours when the jet landed on a secluded corner of Reagan National across the Potomac from D.C. An icy rain was falling as they left the jet for the waiting unmarked government van. Where were the cherry blossoms?

Thorne was dressed in khaki pants and a short-sleeved shirt of fabric as thin as his blood after his years in the tropics. But as they crossed the Key Bridge, he was damned if he would shiver, or let his teeth chatter, or ask for a coat.

At the northeast guard booth, he caught just a glimpse of spot-lit lawns and the unmistakable white, pillared building just beyond. The uniformed officer inside the booth activated a switch to raise the car-blocking iron beams in front of the van, and lower them behind. Around behind the White House, they went down a narrow ramp with high concrete walls on either side. The van stopped, they got out into the drizzle.

A steel-armored door opened, a guard in uniform, one of the fifty-man detachment of Secret Service agents who worked three eight- hour shifts 24/7, checked their credentials. He kept his light in Thorne's eyes the whole time because Thorne didn't have any credentials.

Hatfield and yet another uniform took Thorne down a long basement corridor to a chamber with another steel door. They went in, Hatfield shut the door in the Secret Service agent's face. It was a carpeted, windowless room with doors in all four walls, a conference table and eight chairs and a portable sideboard. There was the low hum of hidden air-conditioners.

Three men were staring at Thorne as if he were a bug on a pin. Two of them were young – twenty-five, twenty-six, one darkly good-looking, like Montgomery Clift before the bad times, the second chubby, friendly-looking, nondescript. The third man was burly, chomping an expensive cigar, exuding power. Small hard eyes dominated a meaty face Thorne recognized from BBC telecasts in Kenya.

'Any trouble, Terrill?' the cigar-chomper asked.

Hatfield sneered at Thorne. 'From this hunk of shit?'

'Okay, okay, we all know you're a tough guy.' Without offering to shake hands he said to Thorne, 'My name is—'

'Kurt Jaeger. President Wallberg's Chief of Staff.'

Jaeger shot a quick, hard, angry look at Hatfield, who put his hands up in the universal palms out not-me gesture.

'We can cut across, then.' Jaeger gestured at the handsome one. 'Hastings Crandall, Presidential Press Secretary.' At the chubby blond one. 'Peter Quarles, Presidential Aide.' At Thorne's captor, 'Terrill Hatfield is—'

'A Feeb,' said Thorne.

Jaeger chuckled. 'He's good, Terrill. Yes, Mr. Hatfield's FBI Hostage Rescue/Sniper Team is on special assignment to me.'

So the suits on the Gulfstream would be part of Hatfield's handpicked team of ball-busters, thinking of themselves as the saviors of the non-Muslim world.

'Okay, that tells me who. Now one of you tell me why.'

Nondescript, round-faced Peter Quarles spoke up.

'Chief-of-Staff Jaeger tasked us with a computer search. The computer picked you from several hundred possibles.'

'Picked me to do what?'

Jaeger said smoothly, almost soothingly, 'To figure out a foolproof way to assassinate Gustave Wallberg, the President of the United States.'

4

'FUCK YOU AND the whore you rode in on,' snapped Thorne, shaken. He'd known it would be bad; just not this bad. 'I'm nobody's fucking assassin.' Hatfield said, 'At Tsavo—'

'Kill or be killed, Jack. Not like this.' He wouldn't do it, no matter what. 'I believe Wallberg will be a hell of a president. I even voted absentee for him, the first time since 1988. I won't figure out a way to kill him for you assholes.'

'I really do hope you'll reconsider.' Thorne turned. Advancing with outstretched hand from the door in the far wall was President Gustave Wallberg, heavyweight charisma in his grin. 'Out of curiosity, who did you vote for in eighty-eight?'

'Bush. The first one. He and Nixon are the only statesmen we've had in my lifetime. And maybe Gorbachev.'

'Not of my party, but a wise choice,' said Wallberg.

Brendan Thorne sat on the President's right, Jaeger on his left, Hatfield across from him. The two kids were just there. A third mid-twenties man, redheaded and with shrewd blue eyes in a round ruddy drinker's face, came in from the far wall door. The shrewd eyes took them in with a single bitter sweep.

'Could you bring us some coffee, Johnny?'

'Coming right up, Mr. President,' Johnny said moodily.

Obviously part of the original team along with Hastings and Crandall, reduced to a gofer, and not liking it. Had he gotten aced out by them? Or by Jaeger? Or by the booze?

Wallberg said, 'When I was in high school in Rochester, Minnesota, my best friend was a kid named Hal Corwin. We played football and hockey together. After graduation I went to the U of Minnesota, he went to Rochester JC. After four months, Hal quit college to join the army. I have not seen him since. Just last year I learned he had been a sniper behind enemy lines in 'Nam. An assassin. Apparently, on his return, like many Vietnam vets, he had a hard time adjusting to civilian life.'

Jaeger took over. 'He reputedly became a foreign mercenary – this gun for hire. His wife was killed by a drunk driver when he was out of the country. In some round-about way his daughter, Nisa, blamed him for the death of her mother. I guess he accepted that guilt; in any event, he became a recluse in the forests of northern Minnesota.'

Thorne felt as if all the air had been driven out of his body by the parallel with himself. Did they know about Alison and Eden? No. They couldn't. No one in government knew.

Hatfield said, 'A year ago last November, Corwin was wounded in a hunting accident. In retrospect, we believe that while recovering he developed some sort of bizarre paranoid fantasy that his son-in-law had shot him. Deliberately.'

Jaeger cleared his throat, his heavy face solemn.

'At the time, President Wallberg was Governor of Minnesota and was developing... what should I say?'

'Presidential ambitions,' said Wallberg. He added with a grin, 'God, Brendan, did I have presidential ambitions!'

'The Governor was assembling a campaign evaluation team. Myself, Hastings, Peter...' Jaeger gestured at the redhead just returning with a carafe of hot coffee and accessories, 'Johnny Doyle here. Nisa, Corwin's daughter. When we committed to the campaign, she said she was worn out and resigned. Her husband, Damon Mather, stayed on.'

'She volunteered for my first gubernatorial campaign when she was in college,' explained Wallberg, 'and worked on my second campaign as an adult. She came back aboard when I won the Democratic party nomination. She had a fine political mind. But in the last weeks of the campaign, both she and her husband resigned from my staff without telling us why.'

Jaeger said, 'We believe now that Corwin had started stalking them, and they went to hide out on a houseboat in the California Delta. Nisa called on election day in a panic. Somehow Corwin had learned where they were. I grabbed a couple of private guards at campaign headquarters, but we had to drive up from L.A. because the tule fog had grounded air traffic in the valley. A seven-car crash on 1-5 north of Stockton tied traffic up all the way back to Manteca. We didn't get to the Delta until two a.m. By then Corwin had already murdered them both.'

Murdered his own daughter? God, if Eden was still alive...

'There was gunfire,' said Hatfield. 'The local cops went in, but he was gone. Since they had resigned from the campaign, the Secret Service couldn't investigate. Mr. Jaeger asked my FBI team to look for Corwin's body in the Delta. After six days, we decided that he had either drowned or died of his wounds.'

'So why am I here?' demanded Thorne. 'Get the charges against me dropped and fly me back to Kenya with no hard fee—'

'Charges?' demanded Wallberg, suddenly icy.

Hatfield looked uneasy. 'Thorne has been, ah, deported from Kenya on a poaching charge.'

'I told you to ask him if he would come. *Ask* him.'

Jaeger scaled a sheet of paper in a plastic sleeve across the table.

'It came the morning of the President's swearing-in.'

Thorne read: CONGRATULATIONS TO A DEAD PRESIDENT. CORWIN.

He objected mildly, 'Anybody could have sent this.'

'Nobody outside this room knows it was Corwin at the Delta. Not even the Secret Service.'

'My men traced someone we think is Corwin to King's Canyon National Park in California,' said Hatfield. 'Two of my Hostage Rescue/Sniper team members, Ray Franklin and Walt Greene, showed his picture around, got a maybe identification. They got to his campsite up on the ridge trail just twenty minutes too late.'

Wallberg blurted, 'It's all crazy! I haven't thought about Hal in years, but apparently he thinks I put Damon up to shooting him. He murdered Damon. He murdered Nisa.' His voice rose. 'Now he wants to murder me. He has to be stopped.'

Hastings Crandall, the Press Secretary, said, 'I had Pete run a computer search to evaluate hundreds of ex-servicemen. You're a generation behind Corwin, but you were a close match. The parallels are amazing. He grew up in Minnesota, you in Alaska, you both hunted all your lives. He was Special Forces in 'Nam, then a mercenary. You were a Ranger in Panama, then did classified stuff for a CIA front. After some unknown trauma in your life, you became a recluse in Kenya as he did in Minnesota.'

'I did some killing in Panama, yeah, but I don't do that any more. I resigned because I shot a couple of innocents by mistake.'

'I'm not asking you to kill,' said Wallberg. 'I just want you to come up with scenarios of how you might kill me. The FBI Hostage Rescue/Sniper team will do the rest. Right, Terrill?'

'Right. He won't have to get his lily-white hands dirty.'

'I'm not going to force you to accept.' Wallberg glared balefully around the table. 'I am ordering your full exoneration in Kenya if you take the job or not. But – I need you.'

They wanted him to play a chess game where you never saw your opponent's board, he never saw yours. Neither of you could be sure the other existed. The greatest stalk a hunter could have, of the most dangerous game on earth, and he wasn't expected to kill anyone. All he had to do was find an ex-sniper who had become a foreign mercenary and had murdered his own daughter. Hatfield and his goons would do the rest. A worthy stalk of a worthy opponent, without personally facing that dreadful enticing moment of kill or not kill.

'Let's do it, Mr. President.'

Watching Wallberg, Thorne saw a not-so-subtle release of tension. The squared shoulders relaxed, the hard knots of muscle at the corners of the mouth softened.

'I feel in my heart that you're going to stop this man.'

Jaeger said, 'A major's pay and perks. In the morning, go to the Mayflower Hotel shops and pick up a wardrobe more suited to the climate. Hastings and Peter will be logistical support.'

Hatfield said, 'I'll schedule your psychiatric interview and psy tests. You've been through it before with the CIA, but your records are ten years old.'

The Mayflower Hotel. First cabin. And he could ace the psychological tests – he always had.

The general exodus left Jaeger and Hatfield alone. Hatfield said, 'He's more of a liability than an asset.'

'What's your problem with this man, Terrill? That's what psy tests are for. I know you regard your team highly, but they didn't do shit in the Delta or at King's Canyon. What we need are results.' He added, with a shrug that came out almost as a shiver, 'Maybe Thorne can stop that psychotic son of a bitch.'

That psychotic son of a bitch wound his way through the raspberry and prickly ash that had replaced the white pine and balsam destroyed by a lightning fire years before. He went quickly past the fire-blasted spruce a thousand feet down the burn before pausing to strip off the glove that kept his maimed hand from aching on this chilly April day.

His left hand was jerked sideways by a hurtling slug. A spray of salty blood splattered across his lips...

At the cabin, he added a log to the embers in the stone fireplace, started cleaning his rifle. Post 9/11 there were many new hi-tec sniper rifles, laser sights and all the rest, but for him, the Winchester Model 70 he had carried ever since 'Nam.

An hour later, he poured coffee from the tin pot on the hearth, booted up his computer, and used Google to confirm that, as usual, the President's Press Secretary was not making a lot of announcements about Wallberg's movements outside Washington. His inaugural-day letter? Good. Let those bastards sweat a little.

'Should I be doing a little sweating myself?' he asked the sometime pursuer in his dreaming mind. No answer. He never got any response from Nisa when he spoke aloud to her, either.

At 1:45 p.m. he remembered breakfast and heated up a can of the spicy chili that Janet Kestrel had gotten him addicted to.

5

THORNE WALKED OUT Connecticut Ave from the Mayflower for his 3:30 appointment in Georgetown. He needed the time to think things through.

His first problem was Hatfield's hostility. Where did it come from? What did it mean? It was like the man really didn't want him to find Corwin, which made no sense. When the CIA had run their tests on him ten years ago, they had choppered him to Langley. But instead of sending him to the FBI's pros at Quantico, Hatfield was farming him out to some supposedly independent psychiatrist who might be in Hatfield's pocket.

If he misread Hatfield, could he end up rotting in a Kenyan jail on the phony poaching charge despite the president's assurances of immunity?

Second problem. What if he actually found Corwin? He knew from Tsavo that he still could be seduced by violence, by the adrenaline rush. Could he break his vow again to save the president's life, and again face his nightmare, maybe forever? Would it be better to just slip back into the easy, morally safe life at Sikuzuri, and let Hatfield find Corwin – if he could?

No. He might end up in jail instead of Tsavo. He had to get a read on Hatfield's motivations from the shrink while the shrink was trying to get a read on his.

Three names, all M.D.s, were etched into the discreet brass plaque beside the front door of the mellow weathered brick house just off Wisconsin Avenue. There was a security camera above the door. The airy waiting room would have once been a living room, probably wall-to-wall then. Now, gleaming hardwood, a tube-aluminum and nubble-fabric couch and half a dozen chairs along the side walls, tables with lamps and magazines between, framed hunting prints above, flowery freshener on the air. Three identical doors set into the far wall. A den of shrinks.

On the couch, a frosty-haired woman looked straight ahead with a combat veteran's thousand-yard stare. In one of the chairs, a middle-aged man with dense eyebrows and hairy ears and a big nose was almost surreptitiously reading a magazine.

The middle door opened. A white-coated, worried-looking man with a Sigmund Freud beard peered out. 'Mr. Hedges?'

Hairy-Ears jerked so violently that the *New Yorker* shot off his lap onto the floor like a tossed frisbee.

'Yes, I, um, here, ah… present…'

He went through the door. The shrink closed it behind both of them. Thorne went over to pick up the magazine and put it on a table. The frostyhaired woman winked at him. Three minutes went by. The right hand door opened, she entered, it closed.

Out in Hopland, on northern California's Redwood Highway, Janet Kestrel turned from the Sho-Ka-Wah Casino cafeteria's pick-up counter with her order of chili and coffee. From beyond the plain partition walls came the ringing of bells, the whirr of slotmachine wheels, the cries of winners, groans of losers, the calls of blackjack dealers, amplified announcements of jackpots.

She took an empty table. The reply to her letter had said she should be here for a twelve-thirty interview with Charlie Quickfox, president of the tribal council. She was deliberately early, uneasy because she had denied this half of her heritage for the past decade and felt like a fraud by coming here now.

At 12:15, a stocky, elderly man sat down across from her with a mug of steaming black coffee. He had a seamed lived-in face as brown as hers, but his eyes were a piercing black to her blue. Grey hair made a long ponytail down his back. His cowboy boots were muddy, his jeans pale with washing. His tie was a leather string held in place by a beaten silver clasp in the stylized shape of a perching hawk.

He pointed at her water glass with its Sho-Ka-Wah logo that included the same stylized perching hawk, this one pink and gold.

'The kestrel. Our tribe's symbol. There is no Hopland clan name of Kestrel, yet that's what you're calling yourself.'

'Better than my mother's name – Jones. She was white. She's dead. My father's name was Roanhorse. He's dead too.'

Quickfox's stern face softened. 'Roanhorse. We played football together at Santa Rosa High School.'

'He drowned in a pool of his own vomit.'

'You reject his name because he was a drunk? Many of our people despair and become drunkards.' His swung arm encompassed the casino. 'Fighting that despair is what this is all about.'

'When he was drunk he beat on my mom. He was drunk a lot. My sister Edie got out quick and married a Mexican.'

'You reject your name, now you want to be recognized as a member of the Hopland tribe. And share in our gaming revenues.'

'Recognized, yes. Revenues, no. But I'm hoping to get a job in the casino. I've dealt blackjack in Reno.'

The old man pushed back his chair. 'We will take up your petition at the next tribal council.'

He stood up, leaving his coffee behind. Janet spooned her chili. Almost cold, but still with some bite to it. Hal had her 4-Runner and was out doing whatever it was he felt he had to do. And she had made her first move to build a real life for herself.

At exactly three-thirty, a cute blonde receptionist with a short nose and big round blue eyes stuck a head full of tight ringlets out of the left-hand door. She was petite and shapely and a dead ringer for randy young bride Ellie in far-off Tsavo.

'Brendan Thorne?' she asked with bland neutrality.

He nodded, followed her into a small orderly office, watching her hips work under her tight skirt. She turned and fixed him with an icy stare. Her voice was cold, professional.

'I am Doctor Sharon Dorst.'

'I am Mister Brendan Thorne.'

Two leather loungers and a leather couch formed a casual grouping off to one side, but Dorst strode to her desk and sat in the swivel chair behind it. This left him with the straight-backed chair facing her across this bastion. No psychiatrist's couch for the likes of Brendan Thorne.

He let the silence build. It was her office. She finally asked, 'What do you see as our main issue here, Mr. Thorne?'

'That I don't get to have the shit scared out of me in the waiting room like poor old Mr. Hedges.'

She couldn't quite hide her smile.

'That's because you drew me instead of Dr. Benson.'

'Benson? And Hedges? You've got to be kidding.'

'Actually, he's Doctor Martin.' She checked the wall clock. 'You have already wasted five of your session minutes, Mr. Thorne. As you have been told, I am a contract therapist for the FBI who will administer certain tests and make certain evaluations of you for the Bureau. They will get my written and verbal reports. No one will ever see my session notes.'

Thorne scrubbed his hands. 'Then let the healing begin! Word games to probe my vocabulary. Photos of faces and later a whole bunch of new photos to see how many I recognize from the first batch. Identifying the logic of series of symbols. Remembering and repeating lists of things that don't go together, like clown and broccoli. How many details I can recall from the four quadrants of a scene you show me or from a story you read to me. How fast I can click a key with my forefinger.'

'You tell me, Mr. Thorne, what should we do with our hour?'

'Look at ink blots that remind me of naked women?' Then he held up his hands in surrender. 'Okay, it's in the file, but – background. I was an Army Ranger stationed in Panama. Until we handed over the Canal to the locals in 1999, SOUTHCOM – that's the U.S. Army's Southern Command – was in charge of security for the Canal. Panama borders on Colombia, and the Colombian government gave control of an area the size of Switzerland to the Revolutionary Armed Forces of Colombia – FARC. They were really rebels running drug-manufacturing plants in the area. They supplied seventy percent of the cocaine entering the States.'

'Your job was… what? To stop them?'

'Impede would be a better word. We'd go into the jungle for weeks at a time to destroy the manufacturing plants. After the Rangers, I couldn't settle down into civilian life, so—'

'Were you using cocaine yourself?' He answered with a surprised but stony silence. She quickly asked, 'Why did you resign from the Rangers?'

'Because killing didn't bother me, and I felt that it should. But I missed the action in the field. When a CIA front asked me to go back to Panama clandestinely for the same sort of work, their shrinks told me I was in the two percent of military men who can kill repeatedly, without hesitation and without bad dreams afterwards. So I accepted that maybe that's who I was.'

'You said to yourself, Okay, I'm an adrenaline freak, an apostle of the gun, seeking the perfect kill-shot, da-dah, da-dah. And shooting at people for the CIA doesn't bother me.'

'Right. Only when I missed. I imagine Corwin, the guy I'm supposed to find, was the same way – until his wife died.'

'So why quit to bury yourself in Kenya?'

'I killed a woman and her infant by mistake.'

'I know that's what the file says, but I don't buy it.' She wasn't a dead ringer for randy young Ellie in Tsavo after all: too damned smart. She added, 'Collateral damage is always part of warfare.'

'Not of my kind of warfare. They died, I quit. Finis.'

'But you just recently killed two men in Kenya.'

'Somali shifta raiders. Poaching rhino and elephant.'

'Yet you were deported by the Kenya government for poaching protected animals yourself.'

He said defensively, knowing it sounded lame even as he did, 'Hatfield set me up as a poacher so Kenya would deport me.'

She said almost derisively, 'And then asked me to evaluate you as a manhunter for his own Hostage Rescue/Sniper team?'

'Yeah! Exactly. After Wallberg took office in January, Jaeger, his Chief-of-Staff, tasked Hatfield with finding a psycho who is gunning for the president. A computer chose me to do it. The president wants me on board. Hatfield doesn't.'

'Why doesn't he?'

'You tell me. You work for the FBI. His guys came up short a couple of times, sure, but if I find the stalker, Hatfield's the guy who'll nail him. You know him, he's obviously used your profession-al services before.' He waggled his fingers at her. 'C'mon – what do you think his agenda is?'

'Asking me that is so far outside the box—'

'That you're aching to do it?'

Again, that quick smile she couldn't quite hide.

'All right. Just a personal assessment, not professional. Hatfield is ambitious. From your file, killing without hesitation was once easy for you. You were the sort of man he wishes he was. So he's worried that you'll find Corwin and just take him out on your own to get the credit for saving Wallberg.'

'That doesn't explain the hostility. He can have the glory, believe me.'

'Maybe I do. But he doesn't. Which is enough about Hatfield. This is your hour, not his. I can help you, but not if you hold things back. You have to tell me everything.'

He liked her, and she was asking him to trust her. But what if he was wrong? Or what if Hatfield came after her and she caved? Thorne would have to take the hit. Could he? Yeah.

'I made up the woman and child who got killed in Panama because there was a woman and child who got killed here in the States. Alison and Eden. Nobody knew about them. We weren't married and Alison hated what I did, but she loved me. She had Eden just after I went back to Panama for the CIA. I wasn't even around for the birth. I had my fucking mission.'

He stopped for a moment, cleared his throat. It was much harder to talk about it than he had expected.

'Seven years ago, when Eden was two, we planned to take her to a children's afternoon New Year's Eve party. But I got a call to go back to Panama. Alison begged me not to go. We had a big blowup, I stalked out and just – left. Alison took Eden to the party anyway. Driving home at five in the afternoon, her car was hit by a drunk driver and they both were killed. I didn't hear about it from her folks until a month later. They blamed me for it. Even today her mother won't tell me where they're buried.'

She said, frowning, 'Corwin's wife gets killed by a drunk driver while he's away being a mercenary and he runs off to the great north woods. Your woman and infant daughter get killed by a drunk driver while you're away in Panama for the CIA, and you run off to Kenya. Have I got this right?'

'Yeah. After they died I told myself that was that, and just went back to Panama like nothing had happened. Then I started having the nightmare. Every night.'

'The nightmare? Always the same one?'

'Yeah. My assignment is to take out a drug dealer who will pass through a certain tract of forest with a briefcase full of papers vital to the CIA. It is dawn, wet, misty. Visibility is bad. The target appears, dressed in cammo. I fire, a spine shot, high up, between the shoulder blades. At the moment I fire, I realize the target is a woman. I feel bad, I've never killed a woman before – but we need those documents.'

He stopped, shivered. It was real, absolute, immediate.

'She is lying face down on the path. I turn her over. She is Alison. Dead. Underneath her is Eden. Dead. She was carrying our daughter, not papers. My shot killed them both.'

'You got so desperate that you quit your contract—'

'And swore to Alison's memory I would never kill again.'

She said slowly, thoughtfully, 'And after a few weeks, the nightmare stopped. And you went to Kenya and ended up in Tsavo as a camp guard, protecting people, not shooting them.'

'Until seven years later, when I killed two shiftas. The nightmare came back. That's what I don't want Hatfield to know about. The nightmare.'

'The nightmare makes you too vulnerable.'

'Not just vulnerable. At risk.' He paused, thought for a moment.

'How can I explain it to you?' He leaned forward intently. 'Okay, many years ago I read a book by a man who trained big cats. Lions, tigers, like that. He said that tigers in captivity, unlike lions, have hearts of glass. They are prone to depression, can get discouraged, can... shatter. As if they themselves were made of glass.'

'You're afraid that facing Corwin you'd be a glass tiger?'

'Good way to put it. But I'm afraid I wouldn't be one. Most of what you call glass tigers give up, die. But some go rogue, like the one that tried to kill that guy, Roy, in Las Vegas. All it had left was instinct. And by instinct, a tiger kills. By instinct, what does an assassin do?'

Her hands on the desk were restless, moving. They stopped.

'Two dead shifta.'

He nodded, stood. 'What do you guys say? Our time is up?'

She might not have heard him.

'You can't just walk away here, Thorne. You need to find Corwin, need to act, one way or the other. That's the only way you can face down your demons.' She realized she was almost panting as she said, 'I'm passing you for this assignment.'

He was caught off-guard. She was tough. He said bitterly, 'You've been ordered to pass me. I'll survive – or I'll shatter like... like that glass tiger of yours. While you and asshole Hatfield play Russian roulette with my life.'

After he left, she sat in her big chair behind her big desk and stared at the wall. She had another client to prepare for, but she just sat there. She knew, deep down, that she was expected to pass Thorne for the assignment. If not by Hatfield, by Kurt Jaeger, maybe even by the President himself.

What if she was wrong in her analysis? Then she was indeed playing Russian roulette with Thorne's life. But what could she do about it now?

6

THORNE WANDERED, ENDED up on the Georgetown Dock at 31st and K Streets. A Coast Guard patrol boat slapped bow-wash against the sides of expensive anchored private yachts. A military helicopter whup-whup-whupped by overhead.

Set back from the walkway behind several levels of outdoor tables was a sparkling glass-clad restaurant three stories high. He got a beer in a plastic glass from the awning-covered drinks kiosk at street level, sat down, sipped it, stared out over the Potomac toward the Pentagon.

He wanted to be pissed off at Dorst, but couldn't be. She had her job, as he had his. And she was very good at it, very tough-minded, willing to roll the dice – he grinned sourly – with his life. On New Year's he'd wished for a quest, a hunt, a vital, necessary trackdown. Now he had it. Could it be that she was right? Could finding Corwin be his salvation?

He finished his beer and wandered, restless. Behind the kitchen entrance to the restaurant a cook in a white apron was smoking a cigarette. An echoing, not-yet completed galleria brought Thorne out above a bowl-shaped mall area. He stood watching the massive fountain spout water high into the air.

According to Dorst, Hatfield could never have access to what he had told her about his nightmare; forget about Hatfield.

Hatfield's coat hung over the back of his chair, his tie was loosened, his coffee mug squatted on the right front corner of his blotter. He could smell his armpits. His floor of the J. Edgar Hoover Building was after-hours silent. He tossed aside Dorst's written report and rubbed his eyes. He sighed.

He and his team had been trained to use the gun to rescue

hostages. Thorne had been trained to use the gun to kill people. He had not only the sniper's eye, he had the assassin's mind. So was killing a woman and child in Panama by mistake enough to make him disintegrate the way he had? Or was he faking it? Angling for the chance to take Corwin out himself, beat Hatfield to the power and the glory? Nothing in fucking Dorst's report answered that vital question about Thorne's emotional state. She'd blown it. Jaeger wanted Thorne aboard, Hatfield didn't. Dorst should have found him unfit because he'd run off to Kenya.

Right now, without consultation, Thorne was flying off to California to 'get into Corwin's mind' before coming up with a scenario. Or was he really serving notice that he was one independent son of a bitch with balls the size of grapefruit? When Thorne came back to D.C., Hatfield would put men on the fucker to monitor his movements and contacts.

Meanwhile, he needed a hell of a lot more than Dorst's official report on Thorne. He needed her session notes. Better schedule an appointment with her out of the office.

He checked the clock. Christ, ten. He speed-dialed.

'Hatfield residence.'

Cora. Trying to make people think they had a maid. He put all the warmth he could into his voice. 'Hi, sweetheart. It's me. We had a meeting that just broke up. I'll bring takeout. Chinese? Thai? Whatever you—'

'I'll be in bed when you get here. Asleep.' She hung up.

'Well, shit!' he snarled at the dead phone. He blamed his troubles with Cora in D.C. on Thorne out in California.

It was dawn when the red-eye dropped Thorne at Oakland International. Long-eared jackrabbits hopped in the grass beside the runway, ignoring the lumbering jetliners. His 'undercover' car turned out to be a souped-up Police Interceptor Crown Victoria with the extra-capacity gas tank that Ford made only for law-enforcement agencies. Fucking FBI. The Crown Vic would make him as inconspicuous as a dancing bear at a ballet class.

He threaded his way through East Bay traffic toward the Delta's sprawling Medusa-head of twisting, intersecting sloughs, its thousand miles of waterways, its hundreds of miles of levees, its islands reachable only by boat.

The Sunset Bar and Grill where he had his appointment with a San Joaquin County Sheriff's deputy was attached to the Tower Park Marina near a place called, appropriately enough, Terminous. Thorne reached it by a blacktop access road across California 12 from the tiny Terminous General Store. There was a tall black watertower, a trailer park as big as a suburb, and a guard shack with nobody in it.

Thorne parked near the foot of the marina's boat ramp next to a Sheriff's cruiser with a light bar on top. It was a beautiful California spring day with drifting white puffs of cumulus cloud; even this early in the season there were tourists in shorts and t-shirts, boaters in light windbreakers they'd need out on the water.

The cafe was built right on the dock. Inside, dust motes danced in the late-morning sunlight. To his left, a family of four was eating a late breakfast in front of one of the wide windows that overlooked the guest boat-docking slips. Powerboats and sailboats could be lowered right off the dock into sparkling but cold-looking Little Potato Slough.

At the round table closest to the door was a husky early-thirties Latino in a tan Sheriff's uniform. The creases of his sleeves and pantlegs could cut paper. A miniature purple heart and mid-East service bar were pinned above his ESCOBAR nametag.

He stood. 'Special Agent Thorne?' His voice was ice.

'Just Brendan Thorne. Forget the Special Agent tag.'

'Just Escobar.' After a pause, he grudgingly took Thorne's hand. They sat down. 'Okay, so why are the Feebs sucking around now, five months after the fact?'

'Routine. The Bureau likes to see if anything—'

'I wasn't on it long enough to screw anything up.' Escobar was an obviously tough, brainy Latino cop with an even more obviously built-in shit detector. 'The sheriff's department got the call, me and my partner were in the barrel that night, we got to the crime scene just after the shootout with the suspect. He was long gone, you Feebs showed up, took over. End of story.'

'Please, relax. I'm a day-tripper, not a lifer.'

After almost thirty seconds, Escobar settled back into his chair. Thorne regarded him thoughtfully.

'Iraq?' he asked casually.

Escobar's sudden change of expression transformed his hard, bony face. 'Afghanistan. Thirteen months, Army Reserve – I wanted to make a few extra bucks to supplement my cop's pay and look what it got me. A Purple Heart. I loved it. And unless I miss my guess, you've been in the shit somewhere yourself.'

'Rangers, then a contract killer for the CIA in Panama.'

'Okay, no more bullshit. Why are you here? Really?'

'Really? The federales aren't really sure the guy who did it died that night. They're afraid he might be a political with a personal hard-on against somebody in the new administration.'

'I can guess who, us getting called in by the guy who's now Wallberg's Chief of Staff. Who then slams the door in our face.'

'I'm surprised you're even talking to me.'

'You're not like those regular FBI fucks. You and me, we can do a trade: what I know for what you know.'

'Okay,' said Thorne instantly, 'what do you know?'

Escobar grinned, stuck with it. 'Yeah. Well, me and my partner got the call-out at two-thirty a.m. Lots of fog. Jaeger had two plain-clothes black security guys with him, said the suspect started shooting as they approached the houseboat. His guys returned fire – Jaeger didn't have a weapon. No shots were fired at us. We worked the bullhorn, no response, so we put in teargas, went in. Two dead vics. White male, mid-thirties. White female, late twenties. Multiple gunshots. A Python .357 Magnum was on the floor near the bodies. Empty. I presume it was the murder weapon. I was afraid the civilians might corrupt my crime scene, so I took blood and fluid and tissue samples before I went back up on the levee to call it in.'

'Presume? What about ballistics?'

'Before I could call SIU, two carloads of feds showed up. I told them the perp must have slithered off the stern of the houseboat while Jaeger's guys were shooting the shit out of the front of it. Told 'em he'd be bottled up in the slough – his car was half a mile away at the levee gate.' His mouth twisted bitterly. 'That's when the Big G. dropped the hammer on us.'

'Do you think the perp was wounded?'

'There was a blood trail to the stern, but was it his blood? We never even got a courtesy call afterwards. Never got any DNA, never saw the results of the autopsies or tox screens, never were given any possible I.D. of the suspect, never learned the names of the vics. Never learned why a guy like Jaeger was out there. Never learned if the Magnum was the murder weapon or who it was registered to. All we got was a big load of national security bullshit. I've got the blood and fluid samples I didn't tell the Feebs about, and nothing to compare 'em with.'

'Victims, Nisa and Damon Mather,' said Thorne. 'Husband and wife. They'd been staffers on Wallberg's election campaign until they quit and hid out here in the Delta because they were being stalked by someone. Wallberg's people didn't know anything about it until Jaeger got a phone call from Nisa on election evening. That's why the FBI is on it instead of the Secret Service – the vics were no longer on Wallberg's staff.' Thorne told his lie smoothly. 'The perp's name died with the victims.'

Escobar nodded. 'Thanks for telling me. I'll drive you to the scene and bring you back afterwards.' At his Crown Vic, he paused, then handed Thorne a three-ring binder from the back seat. 'I always keep a personal Murder Book. Better read it on the way. Whoever the perp is, he's one sick son of a bitch.'

'How do you mean?' asked Thorne, surprised.

'Just read the Murder Book.'

As they went east on gun-barrel Cal 12, Thorne read. Damon Mather was found lying on his back in the middle of the room in the classic death pose, arms and legs splayed. Loosened bowels and bladder.

A single shot to the chest with a heavy-caliber slug consistent with the .357 Magnum on the scene.

Escobar slowed the Crown Vic, put on his right blinker.

'It's a half-mile walk from the White Slough Wildlife Area gate on Guard Road to where their houseboat was moored on Disappointment Slough. We can climb over the gate.' Nisa had been pounded up against the bulkhead by the other five rounds. Unlike Damon, she had fought for her life: broken nails, dermis under two of them, head at an angle, eyes open and glazing, tongue out one corner of her mouth. Blouse ripped down.

Contact wounds, powder burns around each of them. One in the stomach, one into each breast, the final two rounds into her mons veneris. Her clothing was soaked in blood and urine. And something else. Corwin had masturbated on her body after he had killed her. The first, heaviest spurt into her face, the rest onto her bared breasts like some obscene pornographic film.

His own daughter. Thorne felt a wave of nausea. Nisa was long dead, but he still wanted to protect her from Corwin.

'One sick son of a bitch,' he agreed.

They walked along the raised levee road. Grass grew between the ruts. To their left was Disappointment Slough. To their right, sunken stubble fields waited for spring planting. A jackrabbit hopped up on the levee in front of them, afternoon sunshine turning his long erect ears red, almost translucent.

'When you see a rabbit with light shining through his ears, you've entered the land of enchantment,' said Thorne.

'I could use a little enchantment.'

A cold breeze had risen, rustling the thistles flanking the track.

Herring-bone clouds stretched across the sky. A brace of mallard whistled by overhead. Across the channel was a brushy oval unin-habited land mass called King Island. Escober stopped beside a knee-high thick-stemmed bush with a single white four-petal flower.

'I used this bush as a landmark to come back after the feds left.' He gave an embarrassed chuckle. 'I was really pissed.'

'You find anything?'

'No place to hide with searchers just minutes behind you.'

Across the channel a two-trunked dead tree lifted stark, naked arms to the sky as if in prayer. For the souls of the dead Nisa and Damon?

'I see what you mean,' said Thorne. 'Nothing to find. I'm through here.'

7

SHARON DORST ENTERED the Department of Commerce building from 15th Street. An American flag hung over the entrance. She was wearing her black power suit with a string of pearls around her neck and a small gold American flag pinned to her lapel. Without government I.D. she was meat for the scanner, her purse and briefcase meat for the x-ray machine. Nothing beeped.

In the echoing, nearly-deserted basement cafeteria, she doctored decaf with Equal and milk, paid the cashier, and carried her coffee out to the south-side courtyard. She sat down at a wrought-iron table near the big stone fountain. Right on time. Hatfield wasn't, but she was glad of the time alone.

She had done three evaluations for him before Thorne's, but when he had said he wanted to meet her here, all her alarm bells had gone off. Why here? She could give him her evaluation, all that he was entitled to by law, in her office. Did he want her out of the way so he could send in a black-bag team to rifle her files for her private session notes on Thorne? She knew the FBI sometimes did things like that. So, at the last minute, she stuck the sessions notes in her briefcase. She was being irrational, but she felt better having them safely out of the office.

When a scowling Hatfield finally arrived, twenty minutes late, he plunked down across the little table from her. He wore the standard FBI uniform: white shirt, Brooks Brothers suit, dull tie. He slammed his cup of coffee down in front of him, slopping some into the saucer. She tried to read his face. Had he searched her office or not?

'Okay, let's have it.' She stared at him in astonishment. He snapped his fingers. 'Your evaluation. Of Thorne. Let's have it. I'm on a tight schedule here and I'm running late.'

She ostentatiously checked her watch. 'I noticed.'

'Don't give me any crap, lady.' He took a gulp of coffee. 'Okay, we'll play it your way. What did the tests suggest about Thorne's mental and emotional states?'

'I didn't run any tests. We just talked.'

'Talked? Jesus H. Christ, get serious.'

She took a sip of coffee, trying to mask her dismay. She hadn't run the standard neurological and psychological tests on Thorne because they had been run several times before, by the Army and then by the CIA, and the results had been consistent every time. She didn't need a battery of tests to tell her who Thorne was, psychologically.

But she couldn't say that to Hatfield. She had been commissioned to run the tests, and she hadn't run them. She had made herself vulnerable.

'I felt the standard battery of tests would be counter-productive with this subject. He's been down that road before.'

'Is he a burned-out case or what?'

She groped for something that would not betray confidentiality, and remembered Thorne talking about tigers with hearts of glass. And her calling them glass tigers.

'It's not that easy. He used an analogy. In captivity, tigers often have hearts of glass. Under pressure, they can shatter. The deaths of the innocent woman and child in Panama put such pressure on him that I think of him as a glass tiger.'

Hatfield was staring at her, rage suffusing his features.

'A glass tiger? Are you nuts? He's a fucking assassin, the sort of bastard our Hostage Rescue/Sniper teams are supposed to put down. Now, goddammit, what made him run off to Africa?'

This was a disaster. But she found a calm, steady voice to say, 'I've told you as much as I'm at liberty to discuss.'

'Fuck that, lady! I need your session notes on him.'

Her heart was pounding, but her face was icy and aloof.

'By contract, I'm not required to show you anything.'

'Shit, lady, you broke the contract when you didn't run the tests. Under the Patriot Act I can have you stuck in a mental institution for a couple of months as a possible security risk – and justify it with paperwork.'

She stared at him, loathing him, fearing him, knowing he could make good on his illegal National Security threat. But she said, 'The client–doctor privilege protects therapists and their patients from people like you.'

He might not have heard her.

'Your notes weren't at your office, my people looked. So give them to me now or suffer the consequences.'

Her hand automatically went to the briefcase beside her chair. How had she been so stupid as to bring the folder with her? But if she'd left it at her office…

Her gesture was enough for him. His hand shot out, grabbed the briefcase. She tried to jerk it back, but he fended her off with an elbow while rifling through it. She grabbed again, her nails scored long red lines down the back of his hand.

He half-raised the hand as if to strike her, but then, a triumphant look on his face, held up her session notes on Thorne with his other hand.

'You'll have these back first thing tomorrow morning.'

'Im going to report you to—'

But he was already gone, crossing the courtyard with long strides. She stared after him, numb, on the edge of tears. All she could do was leave a cryptic warning message for Thorne at the Mayflower Hotel, and hope he called in to get it. And that he would understand it.

The little general store was white clapboard, two-story, raised six feet above the ground on pillars against the Delta's winter floods. Out behind, two house trailers were settled down comfortably on their blocks like regulars on their barstools. A battered white TERMINOUS MARKET sign creaked on guy-wires from the store's old-fashioned false front.

Thorne sat in his car next to a new red Beetle convertible, rereading the FBI file. The investigation had been incredibly sloppy, or else

Hatfield had deleted anything useful. But Nisa's phone call had been traced to the payphone here at this run-down market he had barely noted when he had passed it on his way to Tower Park Marina.

Inside it was cluttered and comfortable, with fishing lures and candy bars and postcards and cold beer and sodas and bottled water. It smelled of live bait and microwaved burritos. The proprietor was in his late sixties, with a lot of white tousled hair and a tobacco-stained gunfighter's mustache. He nodded twice to himself when Thorne showed his FBI credentials, like a robin checking out worm-sounds.

'Wondered when you guys would be around again.'

'Well, the phone company records show the woman who was killed made a call from your payphone here that afternoon.'

'Yep. Reco'nized her right off from the pichurs they showed me.' He looked as if he wanted to spit the juice from his chaw of tobacco into the spitoon, but instead just worked his jaw around. 'Her and her husband bought supplies here, said they was on vacation in a rented houseboat. Damn shame, I say. She was a mighty nice lady. Pretty, too. Got to know her, her coming in to get them calls every Tuesday an' Thursday, two 'clock, straight up, reg'lar as clockwork.'

Nothing in the file about her receiving a series of calls.

'Ah… know who they were from?'

'Nope. But they was all of 'em long-distance calls.' He chuckled. 'Now I think of it, most anywhere you'd call from here would be long-distance, wouldn't it?'

'Sure would. Could you hear her end of things?'

He winked at Thorne. 'Little place like this, couldn't help hearing, could I?' His face fell. 'All she ever said was something like, "Everything's fine" and "Thanks" and she'd hang up.' Then he brightened again. 'Got one two hours early on 'lection day, 'bout noon, thereabouts, an' it shook her up real good. Soon's she heard the voice, she yelled, "You!" an slammed down the receiver. Then she made a buncha calls of her own.'

Got an unexpected call that panicked her, started trying to reach Jaeger. She finally did, but too late to save them. Had this all been deleted from the file? Or had the FBI just never found out about all of those calls? The old man was going on.

'Waitin' for them Tuesday an' Thursday calls, she'd listen to my tales 'bout the old days when Terminous was the railhead for produce comin' out of the Delta. A real nice lady.'

The Delta. A synapse fired in Thorne's brain. Below that dead tree reaching imploring arms to the sky had been a messy waist-high mound of interwoven twigs and branches and reeds some eight feet in diameter. He checked his watch. He was in a sudden hurry to get out of there. Dusk would soon fall.

'You got any of that black electrician's tape for sale?'

The old man cackled. 'Course I do! It's a damn general store, ain't it?'

At the White Slough Wildlife Area gate on Guard Road, Thorne wrapped his flashlight with electrician's tape and rummaged through his suitcase for a heavy turtleneck sweater. The sun was low, a cold wind had kicked up, swirling dust. The rabbit was gone. No enchantment this time around. Just icy water and a half-assed idea.

Across the channel, a sentry muskrat, its segmented rat-like tail wound around behind it, was sitting on top of the messy mound of interwoven twigs and branches and reeds Thorne belatedly had recognized as a muskrat house. He had also remembered a Michael Gilbert story that mentioned ancient Britons hiding in underground burrows called dene holes to let the Saxon invaders overrun their positions. Hide in plain sight.

He stripped naked, leaving his clothes folded in the track like a suicide going to drown himself. Flashlight in hand, he slid down the steep side of the levee to the water. A lesser grebe popped up in midchannel, swam for a moment, dove under again. Thorne shivered in the cold wind. He was at least as tough as a helldiver, wasn't he?

As he dove in himself, the sentry scrambled off the muskrat house. Thorne swam underwater as long as he could, surfaced a few feet from the house, numb with cold. He was used to African waters, warm and sunlit. And full of parasitic bilharzia worms. And hippos. And crocodiles.

Corwin, a generation older and a sicko at that, had been doing this in November. If he could take it, by God so could Thorne. On his next dive, he used his temporarily waterproofed flashlight to find the underwater entrance. Fighting irrational fears of an icy tomb with his face buried in mud, he rammed and wiggled his way up through glutinous mud and water and rotted reeds to burst into air rank with the smell of rodents.

He rested there inside the house, panting, just his eyes and nose above water. No muskrats. His light died, but not before he had seen the proof he sought: a partially obliterated handprint next to his own in the mud beside the entry hole.

Corwin must have been able to disappear into himself as Morengaru could, so animals no longer sensed his presence. Because according to the FBI file, a sentry muskrat had been sitting on top of the house that morning until scared off by two searchers who sat down to smoke a cigarette.

Was he Corwin's equal? Thorne remembered laying his hand on Bwana Kifaru's warm flank in the African moonlight. Damn right he was Corwin's equal.

He surfaced outside the muskrat house, crossed the channel. Now the water felt warm, but the wind was numbing on the levee. He pulled on the heavy sweater, jogged back to the car carrying his other clothes in one hand, his shoes and socks in the other.

He had passed a motel off the cloverleaf where east-west 12 intersected with north-south I-5. Microtec Inn and Suites. This time of year they'd have plenty of vacancies. And across the interchange, Rocky's Restaurant. Check in, grab a hot shower and something to eat, try to sleep, in the morning call the Mayflower just in case they had found Corwin and he could quit looking.

Who was he kidding? He was hooked on the hunt.

8

DORST WALKED THE 45-year-old Library of Congress research librarian to the door. Her husband had dumped her for a twenty-something grad student. Dorst's phone, turned down during sessions, started clicking. She caught Thorne in mid-sentence.

'... got your message, I'll try again in an hour—'

She picked up quickly. 'Thanks for calling back.' She felt like crying. It had been so easy to assure him that his deepest secrets were safe with her. 'Hatfield... grabbed my session notes right out of my briefcase. He threatened me with National Security if I said anything. I... I caved in.'

'Don't sweat it, Doc. You done fine. You called it right. He went after you because he's afraid to go after me.' Thorne chuckled. 'No glass tiger problems. Right now I'm in California, on my way to King's Canyon. My hunt is starting to feel like German intelligence chess during World War Two. A three-dimensional board, players unknown – and everybody blindfolded.'

Seth Parker ambled over, wiping his hands on his apron. His rolled-up sleeves showed the crude prison tats on his forearms. The deeply tanned, compact man who had taken the Parkers' last unrented cabin the night before was sitting at the bar under the mounted elk's head. He moved his own head slightly.

'Join me?'

Seth's wary brown eyes reflexively darted around the old chinked-log building that smelled faintly of breakfast even though mid-morning deserted. Third week of April, the tourists were off hiking or driving through the natural wonders of King's Canyon. He ran a finger along his drooping ginger mustache.

'Don't mind if I do.'

Seth got two Miller Lites from the cooler and twisted off the caps. They tinked long-neck bottles, drank. The stranger laid a hundred-dollar bill on the bar. Obviously, no tourist.

'Guy passed through last month, planned to camp up off the ridge trail. Ten, twelve days later a couple of other gents came looking. Said they were his friends. Remember any of them?'

Seth remembered all of them. Because he was always curious about things, he had been around the corner from three murders during his years in stir. Because he was also always cautious, he was alive today. But because of those prison years, Mae hated him getting involved in anything beyond running the resort. He reluctantly snapped the bill away with his forefinger. It landed in the puddle left by Thorne's bottle. Thorne shook his head.

'I'm on expenses, you aren't. Start at the beginning.'

What the hell, Mae was off doing up the cabins. So he told Thorne about the lanky fiftyish hard-bitten man who had walked into his not-yet-open resort at noon on mid-March day...

'Walked.' A statement from Thorne, not a question.

'With his camping gear. Reckon he come on the Greyhound stops at Cedarbrook, some miles down the canyon, walked from there. Stocked up on camp grub real good. Knew just what he wanted.' He shut an eye for a moment, recollecting. 'A dozen Cup of Noodles for soup, freeze-dried veggies, big block of sharp cheddar, instant coffee, Granola bars, trail mix. Beef jerky.'

'Anything strike you as odd? Out of proportion?'

'Way too much beef jerky.' Contempt entered his voice. 'Hell, them guys claiming they was his friends never even picked up on that. I think they was Feds, after him. Had his pichur.'

'This one?'

Seth bent to look at the photo Thorne laid on the bar.

'Yep. Reco'nized him right off, acted like I wasn't sure.'

Thorne put the photo away. 'Tell 'em where he was camped?'

'Just said up on the ridge trail. Guess they didn't find 'im – I ain't heard nothing more about none of them since.'

From the FBI report, Thorne knew Ray and Johnny had missed Corwin by only twenty minutes: they scared up a flock of crows when they burst into the clearing, and the embers of the campfire were still warm. He slid off his stool, leaving the $100-bill.

'How about you sell me way too much beef jerky?'

Meanwhile, up in Minnesota, Corwin had gone ninety feet in thirty minutes in his totally silent stalk across a wet, crackly surface. Up by his cabin, three miles away, the snow was gone except under the densest stands of pine and there was the constant tinkling of ice-melt. Down here in the silent river bottom, receding floodwaters had laid down a springy foot-deep bed of driftwood under the leafless hardwoods.

Three yards away, oblivious to his presence, a sly-faced red fox nosed at something on the ground. Twenty feet above his head, a brilliantly-colored wood duck sat on a limb of a leafing oak that until the week before had been standing in flood water.

Corwin crackled driftwood, the duck shot indignantly away, jinking through the branches like a maneuvering jet fighter. The fox fled. Corwin went to see what it had been sniffing. A snowy owl and another wood duck, both dead. He gingerly picked up the owl: still warm. The duck came with it, clutched in the spasmodic death grip of the owl's curved, needle-sharp talons.

He stood holding the two dead birds for a full minute, motionless except for almost minuscule movements of his eyes. The owl was big – four-foot wingspan, weight about five pounds, grey-brown banding in her feathers. A female. In Alaska he had seen a female hit a man who threatened her nest so hard she had knocked him right off his feet. So what could have killed this one? Not the fox: snowies often hunted foxes for food.

He looked up. Directly overhead was a high-tension electric line strung through openings cut in the branches by the power company. The duck waddling around on the driftwood, the owl's sudden swoop – snowies hunted both day and night. Wings beating, she rose through the trees – and hit the power line rubbed bare of insulation. Instant electrocution for them both.

Corwin laid the dead birds back on the driftwood for the fox to feed on. He was ready. Ready to seek, rend, destroy...

A giant fist shattered his chest. He felt bone and muscle and meat give inward, snap, tear...

Once predator, now only prey... Shot from ambush. Then, Nisa's betrayal...

Nisa, wet with blood and semen, him standing over her, all passion spent, looking at her with dazed, horrified eyes...

Goddammit, he would continue to search the Internet for the president's travel plans. Couldn't quit anyway. By now, he was sure, someone would be working out the puzzle of his carefully obliterated backtrail.

'Come and get me, you bastard,' Corwin said aloud.

Thorne knew, when he saw the clearing a quarter-mile off the ridge trail in King's Canyon, that this was where Corwin had been bivouacked. The perfect place to melt into the trees and be gone if pursuers appeared. But Corwin had wanted them out in front of him, so he could double back and be free of them. Hide in plain sight. It was what Thorne would have done.

Ray and Johnny. The same members of Hatfield's Hostage Rescue/ Sniper team who had sat on the muskrat house in the Delta smoking cigarettes while Corwin hid right below them. He wondered if either of them had been aboard the Gulfstream jet that had taken him from Nairobi to Washington and the White House.

Corwin's campfire had been banked against a huge old hollow fir log, its open end laced with root fungi. The bark on the upper side had been pecked or literally torn away.

A flock of crows. Way too much beef jerky.

Thorne sat down with his back against the sun-warmed curve of the log. He let himself melt into the forest sights and sounds and smells. At dusk, the far-off calling of the crows coming up from the meadows where they had been feeding roused him from a reverie close to sleep. He ripped off pieces of beef jerky and thumbed them down into the bark of the ancient log as yelling crows swept unseen into the top of a ponderosa.

Thorne gave a single rusty caw. He hadn't mimicked a crow's call in a lot of years. The noises above stopped abruptly. He tried two caws. Nothing. But three caws brought a huge black shape sweeping down to circle the clearing and settle on the nearest tree. Big as a raven, black and shiny as the phony lead Maltese falcon Gutman had hacked at with his pocketknife. The breeding male. The dominant bird of the flock.

As Thorne knelt and backed into the open end of the log, the big crow gave the feeding call: a dozen more black silent shadows drifted down to the log.

After ten minutes, Thorne crawled back out of the log through the veil of root fungi. The crows were gone. The jerky was gone. In the morning, he would leave them the rest of it.

Thorne slept well that night, in the log. No nightmare.

9

GELSON HENNINGS WAS a big, balding man with cold eyes and a hook nose, a retired four-star Army general who had been teaching military strategy at the Command and General Staff College when tapped by Wallberg for National Security Advisor.

'How about you come up with a new set of options for the President on our current Iran strategy?' demanded Jaeger. At these daily security meetings, his job was to keep the confrontations between Hennings and the President to a minimum.

'How can I come up with options when I'm still not sure just what our present Iran strategy is?' Hennings said bluntly.

'The American people are sick of terrorist plots and nuclear scare tactics,' Wallberg snapped. 'Iran is not America's problem. Iran is the world's problem. Let the U.N.—'

'Keep sucking its collective thumb, as usual?' Hennings leaned across the table. 'I have to tell you, Mr. President, that if we don't act, the Israelis will. Unilaterally. They've done it before. The Entebbe Raid in the eighties, their strike on the Iraqi nuclear facility a few years later. The U.N. says Iran will have a nuke within four to ten years. The Israelis are giving it a year. We need to elucidate our policy now.'

Wallberg covertly glanced at Hastings Crandall, who said immediately, 'Ah, I'm sorry, Mr. President, but the delegation of school children from Chicago…'

'Damn!' said Wallberg. 'I forgot.' He stood up. 'Sorry, gentlemen, but that's all the time we have for this right now.'

Jaeger stayed behind. Wallberg sat down again, heavily. There was no meeting with school children from Chicago, but he had been having trouble keeping focussed.

'I'm coming to feel Hennings was a mistake. Too abrasive. No rounded edges. Not a team player. He doesn't get what this administration is all about.'

'He's the best we're going to get for the job.'

'I know, I know,' he said petulantly. He leaned forward suddenly in the big executive chair he had brought to Washington from his governor's mansion in Minneapolis. 'The polls show I need to get out of D.C., let the people see their President…'

'That's dangerous until we have a fix on Corwin.'

'I thought you were going to end the Corwin problem,' he said shrilly. He softened his tone. 'What is Thorne doing?'

'He's in California, where Corwin eluded Hatfield's people. Twice. He says he's trying to find out how Corwin thinks.'

'That sounds like B.S. to me, but maybe not. Have him report directly to me here immediately he gets back.'

Thorne made Jaeger uneasy: no give in him. Thorne closeted with the President made him even more uneasy. As long as Hatfield kept Thorne away from the President, Jaeger would help Hatfield with his as-yet unstated but obvious ambitions.

'You got it, Chief,' Jaeger said.

Thorne phoned ahead to set a meeting with Wallberg's aides for seven-thirty in the morning, then caught the redeye out of Oakland. Hastings Crandall, Peter Quarles, and Johnny Doyle had all been with Wallberg since his days as Minnesota governor: they had to know a lot that Thorne needed to know.

As usual, he stayed awake during the flight, fearing public nightmares, so he was first off the plane at Reagan National. In the same basement conference room where he had been recruited to look for Corwin, Crandall and Quarles shook hands with him, then took places at the conference table. Doyle wasn't there. Aced out again? Or too hungover to make it?

But then Doyle's ruddy drinker's face appeared over a tray with two coffee carafes, regular and decaf, milk, sugar, pink, blue and yellow sugar substitutes, croissants.

'A few too many at the Hard Times Cafe last night?' sniggered Crandall.

'I live in Old Town, so that's where I drink,' said Doyle.

'Just pour our coffee, we'll buzz you if we need anything.'

But Thorne said, 'Mr. Doyle, why don't you join us?'

Whichever way the other two jumped, Doyle might just be Thorne's go-to guy. Crandall made a show of checking his watch.

'I have a briefing with the President in twenty minutes.'

'This won't take long. First, I need everything the White House has on Corwin, from the day he was born up to the present.'

'No problem there,' said Quarles.

'Second, I need the phone records from the Terminous Market in Terminous, California, for the day of the killings, and the... oh, say, the two weeks before that.'

'I can do that,' said Doyle.

'Third, the sheriff's deputy first at the crime-scene found a .357 Magnum handgun in close proximity to the bodies. Was it the murder weapon, and who was it registered to?'

'The cop didn't know?' asked Doyle, surprised.

But Crandall was on his feet, checking his watch again.

'I have to tell you, Mr. Thorne, that this is very sensitive National Security material you are asking for here. You should have checked with Agent Hatfield before talking with any local hayseed law enforcement.'

Inside, Thorne was amused. Hayseed? Escobar had a subtlety of mind that Crandall, who had just unwittingly confirmed the .357 as the murder weapon, could only wish for.

'I'll check with Agent Hatfield and get back to you with anything he clears for your eyes,' Crandall said.

He nodded and left, Quarles scrambling to his feet behind him to leave also, with no mention of the promised Corwin background material. Doyle was still in his chair, looking hungover. Thorne went to the sideboard, refilled their cups.

'They're gonna give you jack-shit, you know,' Doyle said.

'I know.' Then Thorne added, 'I'm at the Mayflower.'

*

It was a nice day, so Hatfield walked the half-dozen long downtown blocks to the White House. He would shape his report so it seemed he had suggested Thorne go to California, because the bastard actually had figured out how Corwin had eluded his men in the Delta and in King's Canyon.

He stopped so abruptly in the middle of the sidewalk that pedestrian traffic had to flow around his immobile form like running water around a boulder.

He would have to authorize Crandall to give Thorne selected information on Corwin's background. But no on the phone records. Absolutely no on the .357 Magnum. There was too much about that night that he himself didn't know, and wished he did.

According to Dorst's session notes, killing now supposedly was instant aversion therapy for Thorne because of his dead shackrat and their brat. Excellent intelligence to have. But what about those two dead shifta? Under pressure, Dorst would tell him how they fit into the equation. And tell him how best to use Thorne's recurring nightmare to keep the man in line.

He turned into the recently-opened Pennsylvania Avenue foot-traffic mall in front of the White House.

Whatever Dorst came up with, he definitely would put people on Thorne here in D.C., and monitor him electronically out into the field. Keep him under control.

He lengthened his stride, suddenly eager. He hadn't told Thorne about today's meeting, and would tell the President that Thorne had been reluctant to interrupt his work on Corwin for a talk session. Admirable.

But he was sure that subconsciously, Wallberg would be pissed at Thorne for ignoring a presidential summons.

10

THORNE DID A quick circuit of the weight machines in the Mayflower's fitness facility, showered, took fifty laps in the pool, had another shower because of the luxury of unlimited water.

At the front desk was a sealed manila folder from Crandall, delivered by messenger. Something substantial? Or a brush-off? Suspecting the latter, he walked back to the only quiet place in D.C. he knew, the Georgetown Dock. He chose a table on the second level above the drinks kiosk, and ordered iced tea.

To his left, traffic grumbled and complained on the Key Bridge leading to the Washington Parkway. A white tour boat with brown trim was just ducking under it, cringing as the flat awning over its superstructure barely cleared the bridge's under-arch.

He opened the folder on Corwin. As he had expected, a stripped file. Grade and high school – indifferent grades – a semester of junior college, Vietnam. Unsubstantiated speculation about a possible career as a merc, his wife's death while he was gone, his retreat to the great north woods. But they'd forgotten to remove – or hadn't thought it important – that Corwin'd had a drunken, abusive father, and a submissive mother. It could be assumed he'd be a kid heading for trouble. No phone records. No ballistics report. No crime scene evidence.

The tour boat glided into a mooring spot at the end of the dock far to Thorne's right, under a sign, 'See Alexandria by Water.' Tourists disembarked and wandered away as the four-person crew began preparing for the return trip.

On his own, Thorne had ferreted out that Corwin had twice eluded pursuers by hiding in plain sight. But he needed to know how good a long-range sniper Corwin had been in 'Nam. During those purported mercenary years afterwards, what had he been doing?

Where had he been doing it? In cities? In jungles? In deserts? Long-range kills with long guns, or short-range kills with hand guns? With explosives? The knife? The garrotte? Or up close and dirty, the way he'd done his daughter?

He couldn't even begin to speculate on where and how Corwin might try for Wallberg – or on how hard he might try – until he had more background, more history. Which he wasn't going to get sitting here drinking iced tea.

Thorne looked around for the waiter and a sturdy athletic blonde sitting one level above him, wearing hiking shorts that showed a lot of inner thigh, casually lowered her head to talk to the collar of her shirt. Probably just out of training at Quantico, on her first big assignment. Alerting the tail-car that would be a couple of streets over from the dock to advise the other on-foot trackers via two-way miniaturized radios.

Out in the jungle, the rainforest, the savanna, tells might be a leaf overturned so its pale side was up; a tuft of grass slowly springing back to its original position; a branch stirring when there was no wind. Here, he looked for inconsistencies of dress or action.

A girl in hiking clothes talking to her collar. Two very tanned mid-twenties jocks standing just below the kiosk, gesturing at the moored yachts – with tiny receivers in their ears. A middle-aged, dispirited, vacant-eyed homeless man with a stolen shopping cart. But the derelict's unkempt hair down to his shoulders wasn't quite filthy enough, and his shoes were too new, not run-over enough. Hatfield had strong-armed Dorst's session notes out of her, but obviously didn't trust them.

Thorne paid his check and went back along the dock toward Georgetown University. The tails might become a problem eventually, but for now their presence would unwittingly furnish visual white noise to mask his actions.

He couldn't use his room phone to tap his intelligence sources outside official channels. Cellphone? Not unless he got a one-use he threw away afterwards, or stole someone else's, or bought a phonecard. Anyway, all of those could eventually be traced, and the act of procuring them would alert Hatfield to the fact that Thorne knew he was under surveillance.

He wandered around the sprawling Georgetown campus until he found the library, old and almost spooky, and went around behind to go inside. In the computer room, he logged onto the internet. Called up the *New York Times* and the *Washington Post* coverage of the president's recent successful campaign, starting with the Democratic Convention. Paused at the front-page picture of Wallberg with his wife Edith and their grown children after he accepted the nomination. Their son, 30, a lawyer in St. Paul; their daughter, 27, finishing a psych PhD from University of Chicago. The nuclear family intact. Hiding what secrets?

Thorne chose an array of stories to make it look convincing, and started printing. Getting more background on Corwin would make sense to Hatfield. As they printed, he quickly and surreptitiously sent an e-mail to an old Ranger buddy named Victor Blackburn who had lost part of one hand in Panama and until retirement was riding out his career behind a desk. His job gave him access to many of the Army's most sensitive files.

He and Victor had seen – and done – some shit in Panama that had welded iron bonds of friendship between them. They had been half crazed from weeks under the pressure-cooker canopy. Sitting back to back, getting eaten alive by whatever insects were flying around or mooching over them from the leaf-litter in which they squatted, the rain coming in bursts like rifle fire. And Thorne once had arrived while Victor was being tortured for intel and had ended the torturers before they could end Victor.

His e-mail to Victor was short and to the point:

Victor: Anything you can dig up on a Halden Corwin (?NMI?) who maybe had a troubled childhood and suddenly quit junior college in 1966 to go into Special Forces and volunteer for a crack sniper team in Vietnam. Why he volunteered for service, how good he was, what he did after he got out. Word is he became a mercenary, but I need

confirmation and as many details from as many places as
you can find.

Thorne.

He sent it, deleted it, then left the work station for the men's room
so a studious-looking woman with big hornrim glasses could stroll
by his table and note the printouts.

He carried them back to his hotel in the gathering dusk, stopping
in the lounge for a drink and surreptitiously watched the Feebs drop
visual on him for mobile surveillance outside the hotel in case he
went out again. Which told him that his room phone was bugged by
this time, also.

Only then, unobserved as far as he could tell, did he go to the desk
to ask for any other mail. There was another manila envelope, this
one hand-delivered. No sender's name on it.

Was it from Johnny Doyle? In his room he tore open the envelope
with an urgency that surprised him. He realized that he just had to
know whether his go-to guy had come through or not.

It was from Doyle: photocopies of the Terminous Market phone records for the day of the murders and the two weeks preceding. Obviously conned out of a phone-company employee so there would be no telltale paperwork. Probably a drinking buddy. Social engineering.

Several local calls either to or from the Tower Park Marina, the attached Sunset Bar and Grill, and the adjoining trailer park. Three outgoing long-distance calls to suppliers, four incoming from them. Paydirt was calls from various cities in the western states each Tuesday and Thursday at two p.m., the last three from the same L.A. phone booth. The calls to Nisa.

At noon on November third, election day, a call had come from an unknown number in L.A. two hours early. The instant Nisa heard the voice, according to the Terminous Market proprietor, she had cried, 'You!' and slammed down the receiver. Corwin, telling his daughter he had found them?

Had to be. She 'real quick' made several calls of her own – starting at 12:04 p.m. – trying to track down someone, who was hard to reach, at the elegant Marquis Hotel in Beverly Hills. Obviously Jaeger, who had said that when she got him, he grabbed two private security guards and tried to get to her. Because of bad weather, they arrived too late to save her and her husband.

How had Corwin known where to find them? And once he knew, why call her? He was maybe psychotic, but not demented and not dismissable. He had withdrawn when he had suffered the loss of his wife, had brooded, alone, in the great north woods until someone shot him. Deliberately, he came to believe. Finally, that it was his son-in-law. So he went looking.

Revenge. Revenge within Corwin's own moral code. Totally understandable to Thorne. A moral code that could explain the phone call he never got a chance to complete. Almost chivalric.

But then why murder Nisa with such sadistic rage? And why, if the man he thought was his attacker was now dead, was he threatening Wallberg? Going back further, why would Mather try to kill Corwin? How could Corwin's death advance his career?

More likely, as everyone believed, it had been just a random hunting accident, not Damon Mather at all. Corwin had acted on a paranoid obsession devoid of any basis in fact. His stalk of the president was just more delusional behavior.

Stymied, Thorne went back to those calls every Tuesday and Thursday. From Arizona, New Mexico, Utah, Colorado, Nevada, finally California. Reassurance calls from someone on Wallberg's staff? But until Nisa's panicked calls, nobody had known why they resigned from the campaign, let alone where they were.

Maybe a way to check on that? Thorne huddled over the news reports from the Georgetown library's computer, laboriously checking the whereabouts of Wallberg's campaign party against the city of origin of each of those Tuesday and Thursday phone calls.

Huddled around a table in an isolated corner of the Hoover Building's cafeteria were Hatfield, the bogus homeless man, the two jocks who had been discussing yachts on the Georgetown dock, and the dark-haired woman with studious hornrims who had checked out what Thorne was doing at the library. The rest of the crew, including the bogus hiker with the splendid thighs, was patrolling the streets around the Mayflower. None of them was from Hatfield's crack Hostage/Rescue team; but these were eager, competent agents or trainees unaware that their surveillance of Thorne was unsanctioned, arguably illegal.

Hatfield pointed across the table at the homeless man.

'Gary. Has he burned you people?'

'No way, Boss.' Gary, really into his dumpster-diving persona, smelled bad. 'He's clueless.'

'He might be hot stuff out in the boonies,' smirked Jock Number One, who had a rather patrician nose. 'But in an urban environment he doesn't know where to look or who to look for.'

Hatfield pointed at blond Jock Number Two, who looked something like a very young Jack Nicklaus. 'Nutshell his day.'

'Breakfast at the Mayflower. Up to the fitness facility, worked out, swam. Checked at the desk, got the file on Corwin.'

Back to Jock Number One. 'Michael?'

'Walked down to the Georgetown dock, had iced tea and read Corwin's file. Thought for a while, then left.'

Gary, the homeless man, took it up. 'Wandered around the Georgetown campus. As soon as he headed for the library, I alerted Charlene so she could be inside ahead of him.'

'He went to the computer room and logged on to the internet,' said Hornrims. 'When he went to the men's room, I was able to ascertain that he was accessing presidential campaign coverage in the *New York Times* and the *Washington Post*.'

Trying to find a pattern of movement that Corwin might also find, thought Hatfield, hoping to get to the intersection of President and assassin before the assassin did. Correct, conventional stuff. Good. Thorne was being predictable.

Jock Number One said, 'He went back to the Mayflower, ordered room service.'

Jock Number Two said eagerly, 'Should we access his room to make copies of the articles he abstracted from the newspapers?'

'Too risky. We have the tap on his phone.' Hatfield leaned back, feeling smug. 'Good work, people. Stay on him. Remember, if he takes a crap...'

'We're there to hand him the toilet paper,' said Gary.

When panic struck, Nisa had called Jaeger for help. All of the Tuesday/Thursday calls had originated in cities where Wallberg's campaign was on that day. So the calls had to be reassurance calls from Jaeger. Who had lied when he said no one knew where they had gone. Acting on his own, helping them hide? Or...

What if Wallberg had come to believe that Mather had tried to murder Corwin? He would have had to drop Nisa and Damon from the campaign and its safety net of Secret Service agents: an assassination attempt stemming from his campaign team, rather than directed at it, would have been disastrous. In that case, Jaeger's help would have been damage control, keeping Nisa and Damon from the media.

Thorne wished he had a photo of Nisa. He wished he knew whose .357 Magnum it was. He wished he could reconstruct the sequence of events aboard the houseboat that night. He wished, he wished... But none of it was going to happen easily, not with Hatfield's people following him around like ducklings that had imprinted on him.

He bedded down at 2:30 a.m. and tossed and turned for an hour, almost afraid to seek sleep. But when it did come, no nightmare rode it. His subconscious must have thought he was doing something right.

Gustave Wallberg stood at a window in the Oval Office as if watching, through the lace curtains, the small army of gardeners making the wide expanse of White House grounds bright with spring flower borders. Actually, he was seeing last night.

Edith, his chickadee-quick wife, sitting on the edge of the bed in one of her usual shapeless nightgowns, watching him remove the fancy brocaded robe she had given him for Christmas.

'What's bothering you, darling?'

He said, 'Politics and polls, sweetheart, inspired by our friends across the aisle, hinting that I'm staying inside the Beltway because of terrorist threats, implying that I'm afraid.'

'Polls! Politics!' She put her arms around him. 'You aren't afraid of anything on earth! You are my fearless lion.'

That's when he made his decision.

'I'm meeting with Kurt and the staff tomorrow to announce that we will be making a swing through the top red states with a major domestic or foreign policy announcement at each stop. Shake 'em up a bit.'

He turned from the window: suddenly he had seen, reflected there, not Edith, but Nisa. Nisa, waiting for him in the little motel out by the Minneapolis airport with the grotesque faded pink fake-flock wallpaper, naked in the bed that brayed and banged the wall in delight at their passion...

But Nisa was gone. Dead and gone. And he was alive.

12

Doing laps in the hotel pool, Thorne decided he'd ditch the Feebs following him. Their surveillance was almost insulting, it was so slipshod. He hit the shower, stood under pounding water that was first boiling, then icy, towelled off, dressed.

Yes, ditch them, but in such a way that they couldn't be sure it had been deliberate. Then what? A movie? A bar? Until Wallberg ventured beyond his iron ring of security inside the Beltway, he could only wait. As he was sure Corwin also waited.

Then he had it. Ditch his minders, meet Johnny Doyle as if by chance, hint about his need for the murder-scene forensics.

Wallberg met his people at noon in the basement conference room. Jaeger, Hatfield, Crandall, and Quarles, with Johnny Doyle bringing people things they wanted. No official record of the meeting: the audio and visual recorders were turned off.

It had been put out to staff that it was a housekeeping, not a security, briefing. These were done every morning by the National Security Council: National Security Advisor Gelson Hennings, head of the White House Secret Service detail Shayne O'Hara, and the heads of Homeland Security, FBI, CIA, and NSA.

'You have two weeks,' Wallberg told the people assembled in the room. This had been his style as governor. People did their best work under pressure. 'Then we make a major swing through the top red states. I need input from all of you on where to go and what to say when we get there. At the end of it, I want the themes of this administration's first term in office succinctly spelled out for all to see.'

'Two weeks! That doesn't give us time to—'

'That is all the time you have, Kurt. Inform the cabinet and the Secret Service. Keep the speech-writers busy. Get out the front-men to set up the press arrangements. Have O'Hara coordinate with local police, Homeland Security, and the FBI.' He grinned his famous grin at Hatfield. 'The rest of the FBI.'

'This is about Corwin,' Hatfield exclaimed.

'Yes. Corwin. I need your assessment. Is it safe for us to make public appearances outside the Beltline?'

Now was not the time to hesitate. 'I and my men now know how he escaped in the California Delta in November, Mr. President, and how he eluded us in California's King's Canyon in March.' Hatfield did not say that it was Thorne who had worked out Corwin's methods. 'With what we now know, he will be unable to mount any viable assassination attempt.'

Doyle was behind the wet bar, unnoticed by anyone, a ghost of times past. When the President ordered them to get front men out, he felt his own surge of emotion. He would get his old job back! As of this instant, Thorne was gone from his radar.

Jaeger was intense. 'You are saying, Terrill, that Hal Corwin is still alive and active in his desire to assassinate the President. So the danger from him is still very real.'

'Real, but assessable, like that posed by foreign terrorists and white supremacists and anti-abortion activists and other right-wing kooks. Once we know the sites, Mr. President, I and my men will evaluate the potential danger at each stop.'

'Get to it, people, said Wallberg. 'I want twice daily briefings from everyone involved, starting this afternoon.'

He lingered after the others had left. He hadn't consulted Jaeger beforehand, though the bond between them went back to that shared decision on election day. A decision that gave Kurt a lot of power. But not even Jaeger knew everything. No one did.

'Ah... Mr. President...' He turned quickly. It was Johnny Doyle. 'You said, sir, that you would be needing front men to go out before your trip. I thought maybe...'

'Out of the question,' Wallberg snapped. Crandall and Quarles had keyed him in on Doyle's drinking problem. He strode out, stopping just short of adding, 'You fool.'

*

Halden Corwin drank black coffee as bitter as his thoughts, and clicked the president's official website on his laptop to make his daily check on any travel plans by Wallberg, and rubbed his aching knee. Who was he fooling? He was half-crippled. Despite daily practice, he might miss his shot even if he got it. Maybe he should just fold his hand, rot here in this one-room cabin where he lived his narrowed life…

He came erect with a jerk, self-loathing forgotten. A travel itinerary! Ten stops in five states in six days, starting two weeks from today. One site leaped out at him from all the towns and cities and rural areas listed. Years ago, unwinding between overseas jobs, he'd gone on a hiking trip near that spot.

Leaving Terry home to mind baby. Memory wrenched an unexpected sob from him. After Terry's death, he had gone to the site of the hit-and-run on Hennepin Avenue in Minneapolis. Terry was crossing with the green light when a Mercury Cougar knocked her catty-corner across the intersection and smashed her against the second-story window of an office building sixty feet away.

They caught up with the hit-and-run driver a week later. He lost his license for a year. Corwin took a vow to stalk him and take him from his wife as the man had taken Terry from him.

That same night the nightmare started. The THUD of impact, he was running hard across the intersection to catch Terry before she hit the sidewalk. He was too late. As he knelt beside her broken body, she floated to her feet and began to glide away.

He ran after her, calling her name, pursuing her through the hot, devastated landscapes of his mercenary assignments, dead bodies strewn about. She paused to look back at him with great sadness, then disappeared into a grove of mortar-shredded palm trees and was gone. That was when he awoke. Every time.

The nightmare continued during two more years of mercenary jobs before he finally understood what Terry was telling him: No more killing. No more dealing out death in hot countries. No more thoughts of killing the man who had killed her.

He deeded their house to Nisa, went into the north woods to become a trapper and a hunter of animals, not men. The nightmare stopped. The years went by. Then he was shot himself, his attacker's slugs taking him down, ripping his flesh, leaving him half-crippled, distorted of mind and emotion. He couldn't hunt even animals any more. His life was over.

But Nisa began driving up to visit him at Whitby Hernild's little clinic in Portage. As he healed, she invited him down to St. Paul for Christmas. When he tried to find out who had shot him, and why, she had helped him look…

Back to the site of Wallberg's speech. It would work. He would make it work. Energized, he limped aross the little cabin to get his fleece-lined jacket from its peg on the wall beside the fireplace. He went to the wardrobe he had built to hold his clothes and meager possessions, and got out his gun case.

The rifle, the scope, the ammo that he would use on that day. There was so much newer, better sniper hardware now. The M-40A3 rifle, and the newest night scope, the AN/PVS-10. But it wasn't the hardware that counted: it was the software, the wiring inside the brain and body that made the great sniper.

From now until he left for the Bitterroot Wilderness Area, all of his practice shots would be made at a thousand yards out, out beyond any imaginable security perimeter, out where even now only a few shooters could go. If he really existed, was the dangerous tracking beast of his dreams one of them? Anyway, no way could he divine where and when Hal Corwin would strike.

Corwin took his rifle out into the cold northern spring day. A vivid flash of memory: going deer-hunting for the first time with his dad so many years before. The thud of hunters' shots, thirteen of them, and his father saying, there'll be blood on the snow tonight…

The president and all of the president's men were going to western Montana. Waiting there for them, rifle in hand, would be Halden Corwin. There'd be blood on the snow that night, too.

*

Brendan Thorne sauntered across the opulent Mayflower lobby, a man at loose ends. Jock Number One yawned, folded his newspaper while standing up from his lobby chair. Outside the revolving door to Connecticut Avenue, Thorne set off toward the Georgetown Dock, knowing the invisible net surrounded him.

He strolled through the gathering dusk to the three-story, glass-clad restaurant. No awning-covered drinks kiosk at street level for him tonight, no beer in a plastic glass. He chose a table on the second outside level, set for dinner.

Hornrims from the library and the lady hiker with the thighs – tonight demurely covered by a mid-calf dress – took a nearby table to chat animatedly about their non-existent jobs at Georgetown University. When the waitress brought water and a menu, he spoke loudly enough for the Feebs to overhear.

'I'd like a glass of the house chardonnay and an appetiser of fried clams to start. And a slice of lemon in my water.'

She wrote on her pad. 'Very good, sir.'

She detoured by the Feebs' table to leave menus. Thorne watched the brightly-lit parkway traffic on the Virginia side of the Potomac. As she returned with his wine, he saw the white tour boat line up to begin its transverse under Key Bridge.

'Your clams will be right up, sir.' She had a Georgia accent and mahogany skin and an elaborate corn-row hairdo.

'Thank you. And, oh, miss, where are the rest rooms?'

'Inside, sir, on the third floor.'

He slipped two twenties under his water glass where the two Feebs couldn't see them, then went up the stairs to the sparkling ornate indoor restaurant. Neither stood to follow him. Past the stairs, through the kitchen to the narrow garbage-pail-lined alley behind, through the deserted not-yet completed galleria behind the bowl-shaped mall enclosing the massive fountain.

Tourists were still disembarking from the tour boat to the dock beyond the little park beyond the mall. Thorne stepped aboard four minutes after leaving his table at the restaurant.

13

INSIDE THE ENCLOSED cabin were a dozen rows of unoccupied benches and a steep narrow stairway leading up to the bridge. Aft, between the doors to the rear observation deck, an acned teenager in the tall paper hat was pouring hot fresh corn from the popper. The aroma filled the cabin.

Thorne chose a bench well forward where he could see the stubby gangplank. No more riders came aboard after him. The pilot climbed the stairs to the bridge. He was not over twenty years old, with a great shock of unruly blond hair.

They cast off to slide away from the dock, then turned down river toward Alexandria. A canned commentary pointed out the sights on either side of the river, but in the dark, little could be seen except moving headlights on the flanking parkways.

A mother and her ten-year old son chose the bench ahead of Thorne's. The boy got up on his knees to shoot through the window glass with a palmsize video camera, then sat down and pushed buttons to review his footage.

Two teenage girls sat down on the far side of the cabin, giggling and gossiping. Four more teens joined them. All wore leather jackets and jeans. One girl held up her hand and made baby-bird-opening-its-beak gestures with it. A boy bought popcorn, and shoved a handful of it into her mouth while the others laughed. They all were speaking Russian. Only in D.C.

The tour boat slid into its berth at the Cameron and Union Street Dock in Old Town Alexandria at seven-thirty. A Dixieland band was playing with large enthusiasm and small talent in front of the Torpedo Factory, left over from World War II and converted into an

Art Center. The smell of broiling steaks from a fancy restaurant on the dock made Thorne's mouth water. He hadn't gotten to eat his fried clams.

Way up at the very far end of King Street glittered the George Washington Masonic Memorial. Thorne walked up toward it past Market Square and the Apothecary Museum. There were cobbles underfoot, and the old houses and office buildings of weathered and painted brick were lovingly cared for.

The foot traffic was mostly local folks out for an evening stroll. He stopped to pet a black and white springer spaniel.

'His name is Tuxie,' said the zaftig blonde with the dog. 'Because his white chest is like a tuxedo.'

'Nice name,' said Thorne. 'Nice dog.'

She nodded, making golden curls jump. 'Dogs are the best people there are,' she said seriously.

The Hard Times Cafe was halfway up King Street from the dock. Inside, booths flanked the heavy door along the front wall, none of them occupied. Behind a deserted reception desk was a bar half-filled with drinkers on this weekday evening.

Thorne took a booth and asked for a draft beer, a bacon cheese-burger, and fries. If Johnny Doyle didn't show, at least he'd get a chance to eat. He'd just leaned back on his bench with a sigh of repletion when a shadow loomed over him. Doyle, red-faced and disheveled, with a slight slurring of his words.

'Thorne! What the hell are you doing here?'

Thorne got to his feet and stuck out his hand. Johnny took it. His palm was moist.

'I was at the Georgetown Dock and saw the Old Town tour boat and jumped aboard. Let my buy you a drink.'

'Let me get mine from the bar. I was in the can.'

He came back, half-empty glass in hand, sat down across from Thorne, and leaned confidentially across the table.

'No crap now, Thorne, how'd you end up at the Hard Times?'

Even high, he was no fool.

'I wanted to thank you for those phone logs.'

'What phone logs?' Doyle dead-panned. He motioned with his empty glass.

'I'm shelebrating the end of my career.'

Thorne caught the waiter's eye, made a circular gesture for refills. 'I guess I'm not following.'

'You heard about the president'sh barnstorming tour?'

'It was on Fox News Channel.'

'Full-court press. Front men out an' everything.'

'Hey, that's great! Since you were a front man during—'

'No, it's shitty. I pissed the Old Man off just suggesting I be one of them.' He downed half his new drink, lifted his eyes to meet Thorne's gaze. 'I know I drink too much, but it'sh never interfered with my work. It'sh those two pricks, Crandall and Quarles. They're ass-lickers an' they're probably queer for each other an' they're always tellin' the Prez I'm unreliable.'

'I thought all three of you were with the president in Minnesota during his years as governor.'

'Yeah. Good times. Me an' Jaeger an' Crandall an' Quarles an' Nisa…'

He shook his head. 'Beau'ful, shmart p'litically. She an' me usta be buds. Tol each other things.'

'Why didn't she join Wallberg's presidential campaign?'

'He was bangin her while he was gov'nor, 'fore an' after she married Mather. Was Wallberg broke it off, when he shtarted his run for president. Y'know, knight errant, sittin' up over 'is armor, regain his purity, all that shit. She was cryin' an' let it shlip when I asked her wha' was wrong…'

Regaining his purity might have been what he told Nisa, but the truth would have been different: fear that the affair might be discovered under the intense, minute scrutiny any presidential candidate was subjected to by the media. Thorne realized he hadn't been listening; Doyle was staring a him, blear-eyed.

'Was 'nother reason, too. Our wunnerful Chief of Staff, Kurt fuckin' Jaeger, had th' hotsh for her. She turn'd 'm down cold, he started goin' af'er campaign workers, lottsa complaints. Sho…' Doyle chortled. 'Early days o' th' campaign, black pimp in L.A.

named Sharkey shtarted findin 'im black local hookersh anywhere, any time, din't mind gettin' beat on.'

Nothing in any of that for Thorne. He asked, 'Why'd Nisa rejoin the campaign after Wallberg got the nomination?'

'Couldn' shtay 'way. Pol'tics in her blood. Draf'ed his speeshes, worked out th' campaign shtrategy...' He shook his head sadly. 'Ol' Wallberg, he foun' out Corwin was after 'em, he dumped 'em both. Cold. C'n you b'lieve 'at? An' they got dead. 'Coursh mosta Wallberg's big idealsh jus' bullshit. While he was shtill th' Guv he tole us he was shcared some guy knew somethin' could do him outta the pres'dental nomination...'

Couldn't have been Corwin. He and Wallberg, kids in high school together, sure. But Wallberg's father was the mayor of Rochester – those early years were an open book. Still, if Mather heard Wallberg's remark and thought Corwin was that threat, he might have thought Wallberg would owe him if he...

'Was Damon Mather there the day he said that?'

'Can't 'member. Whatta fuck differensh it make now?' He lurched to his feet, staggered unsteadily toward the men's room.

Was there anything useful in all these drunken character assassinations? Yeah. Something was hidden in Wallberg's past.

When Doyle shambled back, Thorne said, 'Y'know, Johnny, that FBI guy, Hatfield, is sure making my job a lot harder by denying me access to the documents I need.'

'Yeah. I 'memeber you ashkin' bout th' forensicsh an' provenance on the murder weapon. Crime schene. Gun.' Doyle put a finger alongside his nose. 'Jush leave it to ol' Johnny.'

Thorne walked him home to his apartment on Cameron Street two blocks from the Hard Times Cafe, caught the last tour boat to Georgetown at ten o'clock. He walked back to his hotel.

The watchers were on duty outside. He could almost hear their collective sigh of relief when he showed up. They hadn't tossed his room and they probably wouldn't tell Hatfield he'd been in the wind for almost six hours.

14

THE NEXT MORNING, Thorne got an e-mail message from Victor Blackburn on one of the hotel computers maintained for guests.

Where the hell you been the last six years or so? I'm still at Benning, getting fat and lazy. Last physical, I could muster only 75 pushups. Remember when we could do 200 of those mothers without breaking wind?

Halden Corwin. In certain circles, that pussy is a sort of legend. I would have liked to go up against him in his prime. Came from a dysfunctional family, drunken father, submissive mom. Between the lines, his old man probably beat on the boy when he was drunk.

Rochester High School, always in trouble, good at sports. He and Wallberg played hockey for a local amateur team called the Mustangs. Both graduated in June, 1965. Wallberg went to the University of Minnesota, Corwin started Rochester junior college in September, wild-ass kid just turned 18.

New Year's Eve, 1966, Corwin had a fatal drunken stolen-car hit-and-run accident. Judge gave him a choice: volunteer for Vietnam or serve a stiff jail-sentence for vehicular manslaughter.

He chose 'Nam. Married a girl named Terry Prescott the day before he left. Did three tours in country, the last two as a long-range sniper behind enemy lines. Exceptional behind the gun. At various times, he took out four gook officers with 1,000 yard shots.

When Vietnam ended, he came home to Terry and in '73

they had a daughter, Nisa. But peace-time Army couldn't
hold him. In the mid-'70s he went the soldier-of-fortune
route. The records are sketchy. Maybe Nigeria. Maybe
Angola. Maybe the Sudan. Maybe Biafra. Maybe all of
them. Maybe none. Maybe yes, maybe no, maybe bullshit.
State department tried to pull his passport, but, no proof.
Dropped off the screen. No other official records I can
access without other agencies knowing someone is
looking. If you're after Corwin, cream his ass. Fucker
hadn't ought to be that good. Buy me a drink sometime
and tell me how it turned out.

So Corwin's wife, Terry, had been his girlfriend when he and
Wallberg were playing hockey together. Wallberg knew the wife,
years later had an affair with the daughter. Creepy, but that's all:
Corwin never saw Wallberg again after he went to Vietnam.

Hide in plain sight. Thorne felt a tingle. He wouldn't wait for
Doyle to come through. He'd tell Hatfield he was going into the field
again, and fly out the next day.

Janet Kestrel waved her thanks to the grizzled rancher who had given
her the ten-mile lift on California 120 from Groveland to the River
Store at Casa Loma. The River Store was a brown rustic wooden
one-story building with a steepled shingled roof covering the store, a
deli, and the AQUA River Trips office and store room in back.

Above the roofed and railed porch was a wooden coffee cup and
saucer painted light blue, and a big blue sign with ESPRESSO DELI
– River Store in blue and gold lettering. An American flag was angled
out from one of the porch's support pillars. The only vehicle in the
parking area was a threeyear old Suzuki SUV that belonged to the
store's proprietor, Sam Arness.

'Hey, Janet.' Arness was a bulky man with a gray handlebar mustache, long hair in a ponytail, jeans and boots and a faded mackinaw.
'Jessie's at the Pine Mountain Lake Campgrounds, Flo's on her way
in. She'll give you a lift to the Put-In Spot.'

She missed her 4-Runner's four-wheel drive that could take her down five miles of incredible dirt track to the Tuolemne River thousands of feet below. Riding sedately down with Flo just wasn't the same.

'So I've got time for a cup of coffee.'

'And a Danish,' grinned Arness.

Janet had missed last year's stint as a white-water guide on the Tuolemne, and she was glad to be back. She loved going down the narrow, fast, twisting river in a rubber raft. It was a level 4 ride, which took great skill to keep from coming to grief on submerged rocks. But she would abandon the river for good if she heard from Charlie Quickfox at the Sho-Ka-Wah Casino.

What they would be talking about skirted the illegal, and since Hatfield could never quite escape the paranoid suspicion that the Justice Department's internal security bugged their own agents' offices, he arranged to meet Ray Franklin at the Lincoln Memorial. Beltliners wouldn't be found dead there unless they were squiring around out-of-town visitors. It was crowded with shrieking, running school kids from shit-kicker towns like East Jesus, Nebraska, and Dismal Seepage, Arkansas. Small chance of anyone seeing or overhearing them anywhere near there.

They stood side-by-side overlooking the long skinny Reflecting Pool that fronted the Memorial: two random strangers contemplating the placid water. Roy Franklin was a field man, plain and simple, six-foot, hard-bitten, in his element behind the sights in a hostage situation, almost ill-at-ease in a suit and tie. Hatfield spoke without looking at him.

'Your buddy Thorne is flying to Minneapolis tomorrow, then driving north to Portage where Corwin had his cabin.'

Ray shook out a Marlboro, lit it, sucked smoke greedily into his lungs. He didn't appreciate Hatfield's ironic coment about buddies. Without ever having met him, he hated Thorne's guts. The bastard had made him and Walt Greene look bad by finding the way Corwin had eluded them in the Delta and in King's Canyon. By making them look bad, he had made their whole Hostage Rescue/Sniper team look bad.

'That asshole. He's not going to find anything there. In November we were all over that place like flies on shit. Even checked for hollowed-out logs and loose stones in the fireplace. Talked to that hick doctor with his one-man clinic who patched Corwin up, talked to the bank manager, the Catholic priest, the protestant minister... Nobody knew anything, except the bank manager. He said that when Corwin left, the doctor bought the cabin to fix up and rent out this spring. End of story.'

'Even so, go to Minneapolis and put a GPS transmitter on the car the AIC Minneapolis will give Thorne to drive.'

'Why don't I try to get audio on his interviews as well?'

'We don't want to alert him to the surveillance, Ray. I just want to know where he goes. Anyway, what's he going to learn? You've already talked to the same people he'll see.'

Corwin never tried to anticipate his shot, it had to just sort of... happen. Through the scope he could see, a thousand yards away, the white cambium where his round had hit the oak tree. If it had been a man, it would have been dead.

He maneuvered himself to his feet, worked his left leg for the three-mile walk back to the cabin. Tonight he would e-mail Whitby Hernild that he would be leaving. Driving the seven miles into town was a needless risk. Around here, people knew him.

Within ten days, Gustave Wallberg would be standing at a podium on a platform in a mountain meadow, his minions about him, beginning his speech. What odds that he would finish it?

The clerk gave Thorne a nine-by-twelve envelope when he stopped at the Mayflower's massive front desk to say he'd be away for a few days. He stuck it into a topcoat pocket so the watchers outside wouldn't see it, opened it in the taxi on the way across the Potomac to Reagan National. From Doyle, obviously.

The Delta crime scene data. The .357 Magnum had been purchased by Damon Mather in a St. Paul gunstore in mid-March of the previous year, probably for self-defense when Corwin turned up alive. Which greatly increased the odds that Corwin had been right, Mather had shot him. So why hadn't Damon shot when Corwin stormed the houseboat? The only fingerprints on the weapon were Corwin's. The ultimate irony: Mather and Nisa had been murdered with their own firearm. How had Corwin gotten it away from them?

Thorne put the report away. From the doctor at Portage, he hoped to learn how debilitating Corwin's injuries had been. In 'Nam Corwin had been a thousand-yard assassin. Would those injuries prevent him from going for the sniper's shot against Wallberg?

15

Since Hatfield couldn't resist peering over his shoulder, Brendan Thorne didn't check the vehicle awaiting him at the Minneapolis airport – a Crown Vic, of course – for the GPS transmitter he knew would be hidden on the car's underbody. Without visual surveillance the GPS tracker was useless anyway. He would just be going exactly where they expected him to go. He just hoped to learn things they didn't expect him to learn. Things they hadn't learned in their own interviews.

On the drive north, Minnesota 169 reminded him of the Alcan Highway with its flanking muskegs on the way to Fairbanks. A flat landscape broken by dark green evergreens growing thicker with every passing mile. To his right lay the vast expanse of Lake Mille Lacs. It was a clear day: blue water and bright sun, fishermen in motorboats trolling for walleyes, or plug-casting along the lake's weedy edges for northern pike and pickerel.

During the winter, the frozen lake would be dotted with ice-fishermen's shacks on runners, smoke coming from their stovepipes. Kids, as he and his buddies had done in Alaska, would be making ice rinks by shovelling away the snow, piling up backpacks at either end to make impromptu goals for afterschool hockey games.

Portage. Three bars. Two churches. Cafe, Italian restaurant, pizza joint, shops, supermarket, drug store, hardware store, bank, three-story granite City Hall and sheriff's office on the town square. Wilmot's General Store with handmade crepe-paper Easter cutouts fading in the windows. The Chateau Theater with FOR RENT FOR PARTIES OR MEETINGS on the marquee in black capital letters that once had spelled out current movie titles.

Thorne drove through on Main Street to the Bide-A-Wee, one of the town's two motels, asked for the furthest corner room from habit, said he'd be one night, maybe two. The wide-hipped woman checking him in had faded blue eyes and a stingy chin and the midwest twang most Minnesotans didn't even know they had.

'You've got your pick right now, but there's good walleye fishing all summer long, so from Memorial Day on we'll be full as a tick right on through Labor Day. During deer season, full up on week-ends. The bucks run big up in these parts.'

'I'll remember,' promised Thorne. 'Where's good to eat?'

'Breakfast, the Good Eats Cafe. Alfred's, that's a nice steakhouse a couple of miles out of town near the airport. And there's the Pizza Palace and Dominic's Italian.'

He dumped his overnighter on the bed and walked into town. The local branch office of Marquette Bank had the ground floor of a two-story red brick building on Oak and Main.

Arlie Carlson, the bank manager, was in his forties, a stocky man with graying blond air. False front teeth and faint scars beside his shrewd blue eyes suggested he had played hockey in the days before protective masks. Thorne flashed his temporary FBI credentials, and was led into an inner office. Carlson closed the door. They could see the tellers and customers through the interior window. Carlson's high tenor voice didn't go with his build or his hockey scars.

'Special agents were up here from Minneapolis last November, asking some pretty pointed questions about Halden Corwin. Never did say what it was all about...'

'Sorry, I wasn't involved in the original investigation.'

Carlson's blue eyes said he didn't believe a word of it. Thorne took out a notebook and consulted a page that from across the desk Carlson couldn't see was blank.

'I understand that Corwin sold his cabin before he left.'

'To his best friend, Whitby Hernild, the local doctor in these parts. I guess you can demand to know the selling price and I guess I'd have to tell you, but…' His eyes hardened. 'It's confidential bank information and we always protect our customers.'

Thorne winked. 'Need-to-know – just like the Bureau. But can you confirm that Corwin left town right after the sale?'

'Sure can. Next day.'

Thorne made a check-mark on his blank notebook page.

'Is there anything else that you might have learned since we were here in November?'

Carlson started to shake his head, then frowned. 'Wait a minute. When we sent out the tax documents in mid-February, we found that Doc Hernild had never transferred title.'

'Doesn't sound too important.' Thorne stood up. Carlson was on his feet, hand out, affable now that Thorne was leaving.

The April afternoon sun was hot; on impulse, Thorne turned in at Dutch's Tavern. He needed to think about what Carlson had let drop at the very end of the interview. Only two drinkers at the bar, heavy, hard farmers in bib overalls, holding glasses of draft Hamms in calloused hands. They turned in unison when Thorne entered, then turned back to their conversation.

He took a stool near a fishbowl full of hard-boiled eggs with a hand-lettered sign, 'Toofer a buck.' The thick-bodied bartender was sprinkling salt in draft beer glasses, sloshing them in hot soapy water, then setting them upside down on a rubber mat to drain. He had bright blue eyes and a heavy jaw; his thinning blond hair was going silver and was parted down the very center of his square Teutonic head. Obviously Dutch himself. He came down toward Thorne automatically drying his hands on a wet-grayed apron.

'What'll it be there, mister?'

'Draft beer. And…' He picked a hard-boiled egg out of the bowl, tapped it on the stick hard enough to crack the shell.

'You betcha.'

Hernild had bought the cabin off Corwin and Corwin had left town the next day. Okay, getting shot had ended his life as a recluse in the big woods, he needed traveling money, so the quick sale to his best friend made sense. But why had Hernild never registered the transfer of title? He was paying property taxes on a cabin that on the books still belonged to Corwin.

Down the bar, Dutch had drawn the beer, was slushing away the head with a wooden tongue-depressor, then topping it again from the spigot. He returned to set down the wet-beaded glass. Thorne raised it in salute.

'You cut the clouds off 'em, my friend.'

'Two other bars here in town, local folks wouldn't let me get away with a short fill.' He leaned heavy forearms on the mahogany. 'Just passing through?'

'Looking for a cabin I could maybe rent for the summer.' Thorne took a bite of egg, sipped beer. 'The bank said the local doctor had one for rent.'

'Doc Hernild. But I heard he rented it out a month back.'

A month. March. Just about the time Corwin had disappeared after ditching Franklin and Greene in California's King's Canyon National Park. Thorne feigned disappointment, then brightened his face.

'Hey, maybe it's short term.'

'Maybe. You can find the doc down at the river end of Hemlock, can't miss his place. Real old-timey private practice, even does house calls. He's got a little clinic where he treats patients right there at the house, flies his own plane. A couple of times he flew into the deep woods and landed on country roads to pick up injured hunters.'

Hernild's clinic was a one-story wood frame add-on in front of a two-story white frame house with green shutters. The house overlooked the river through a stand of just-leafing willows. On the clinic door was a brass plaque:

WHITBY HERNILD, M.D. Underneath in smaller letters was, Nine—Five, Monday—Friday and beneath that in smaller letters still, Ring Bell for Emergencies.

Just-budding, not yet fragrant lilac bushes flanked the walk. The reception room was deserted, but a tall handsome blonde with her

hair done up in a bun at the back of her head came through the door ,
behind the desk.

'Hi. I'm Ingrid, Dr. Hernild's nurse-receptionist.' She was very
Nordic, strong-bodied and large-boned, with big white teeth. A grin
lit up her face. 'His wife, too. Unless this is an emergency I'd like to
take a little history first…'

'No emergency. Not even a patient.' He opened his FBI credentials,
showed badge and commission card. She made a little face when she
saw them.

'You guys again? You know everything we know about Hal.'

Whitby Hernild was a lanky-legged heron of a man, also
Scandinavian, six-foot-six and skinny, as pleasantly ugly as his wife
was pleasantly attractive. Together they made a striking pair. He was
wearing a white doctor's smock over street clothes.

Ingrid went away, they faced one another in a room with a chair, a
stool, a counter with a sink, cabinets, and a table covered with fresh
white tucked-in sheets.

'What can I tell you that Arlie Carlson couldn't?'

'Arlie sent up a smoke signal, huh?' Thorne took out his notebook.

'Carlson couldn't give me details of Corwin's injuries in that
hunting accident.'

'Extensive. Varied.'

'Oh, come on,' said Thorne good-naturedly.

Hernild stared at him with glacial blue eyes.

'Nowdays you probably could force me to tell you anyway, so okay,
he was hit three times. Left knee, left hand, chest. The knee shot
carried away the inferior genicular branch of the popliteal artery and
vein, the biceps femoris tendon, part of the gastrocnemius muscle,
and part of the head of the fibula. That the sort of thing you need,
Agent Thorne?'

'Why the hard-on? I'm just doing my job here.'

'And I'm just a doctor doing his. I hate to invade any patient's
privacy no matter who's asking.'

'And here I thought it was maybe because he was shot three times.
That's a deer-hunter very persistent in his mistake.'

Hernild shrugged. 'He was semaphoring his arms to show the hunter that he was a man, not a whitetail buck. It didn't work.' He pointed to the little finger and ring finger of his own left hand. 'The second shot carried away the fourth and fifth fingers of his left hand, counting from the thumb.'

'Okay. In English this time, how bad was the knee wound?'

'Bad enough. It was a long process. We put a drain in Hal's leg, and removed it gradually as the tissue knit and the possibility of infection lessened. Because the head of the fibula was fractured, we had to insert the tendon just below the damaged area. Which means Hal now walks with a limp – his left leg is slightly shorter.'

Ingrid thrust in her blonde head.

'Whit, you've got patients waiting…'

'Just one little minute more,' said Thorne quickly. She made a face at him and withdrew. 'And the chest wound?'

'Ah, the chest wound.' Hernild didn't seem worried about waiting patients. 'The bullet fragmented the seventh rib, but glanced off rather than penetrated. Before the cold stopped it, couple of hundred cc's of bleeding, mostly internal. He had an open fracture, with splintered ends of rib bone driven out through the skin and also into the chest cavity.'

'But not into the lungs themselves?'

Hernild gave him a sharp, appraising look.

'No, but Hal was afraid that a cough, even a deep breath, could collapse his lungs by compressing them with outside air being drawn in through the open chest wound.'

Thorne mused, 'He needed a compress, a bandage, something to make the chest reasonably airtight…'

'One of his mittens, fastened with his belt.' Thorne realized he had gotten Hernild's attention with his informed musings. 'Crawled a thousand feet to his cabin, crawled inside, used his bow – he'd been bow-hunting a big whitetail buck when he was hit – to knock the phone to the floor. He dialled 911.'

'He saved his own life,' said Thorne, almost in admiration.

Again, that look. Hernild said, 'It healed clean, without infection, but it left him with what we call 'splinting.' The inability to take a really deep breath because of pain in the chest wall.'

'How do I get to Corwin's cabin and why didn't you—'

'I've got patients waiting. If you have some more questions, come back at eight o'clock tomorrow morning.'

16

CORWIN HIKED BACK toward his cabin, his rifle cradled in the crook of his left arm, muzzle angled up and away from him. He was ready. He paused, went into an awkward half-crouch over a dug-up meat cache beside the trail. A fox, for sure.

He had a sudden vivid memory of the first time Nisa had visited him at the cabin after Hernild had released him from the clinic. He had taken her tramping through the still snowy woods to show her the first fox she had ever seen in the wild. The memory of that moment was filled with incredible sweetness, like biting into a honeycomb.

Then, too, he had squatted beside the path, pointing out the tracks. A gray: thicker tail, smaller pads but bigger toes than a red. Then he took her to the fox's den in the base of a dead oak tree, showed her the tuft of reddish-gray fox fur caught on a bit of protruding bark at the mouth of the hole. Pointed out scattered bits of bone, a patch of down-soft rabbit fur, three bright wood duck feathers.

Then he put his lips against the back of his hand and sucked sharply to mimic the thin squeaking of a mouse. A sharp nose was suddenly raised against the leafless hardwood boles on a small rise at the far end of the burn. The fox, lying up on his backtrail, gray brush over paws, all senses alert.

And Nisa, eyes shining, hair sleek and shiny as the fox's pelt, exclaimed in sheer delight, 'Oh, how beautiful!'

Nisa. Dead. The thought thumped his chest like a heart attack. What had he done? He tried to cling to the fox memory. Couldn't. He virtually fled back up the burn to the cabin, cleaned his rifle, added a log to the embers of the fire, and fired up his laptop to send Hernild the message that he would be leaving in two days. But waiting was an e-mail from Hernild:

Another one. Different from the others. This one is good.
He wants to see the cabin. I stalled him until morning, but
he is watching me.

It just hurried Corwin's departure by a day. He sent:

Thanks. Forewarned is forearmed. I'm off tomorrow..

He ate, then stowed everything he would need in Janet's 1990 4-
Runner, hid it three miles away in a thick stand of spruce on the
other side of the creek. He would leave before dawn.

A fingernail crescent of new moon gave scant light, but he knew
every tree, every bush, every turn in the trail on the way back. This
cabin, before he was shot, had been his home since Terry's senseless
death. He had come back to it after King's Canyon because they had
already searched for him here. Walking softly through the dark-
shadowed woods, hearing the questing whoo, whoo, whoo-whoo of
a great horned owl, he found himself intensely curious about the
new FBI man.

Different from the others. This one is good.

Who was he? How old? What did he look like? How did he move?
How clever in the woods? How observant of sign? No man could
match Corwin here on his home ground, no matter how good he
was, but still… was this the questing beast of his nightmares?

At 7:45 in the morning, even fortified with eggs and bacon and hash-
browns and toast, Thorne yawned as he pushed the buzzer on the
door of Hernild's clinic. He had been in his car a half mile down the
road until three a.m. Hernild had gone nowhere. Thorne hadn't
really expected him to, but he had learned to be methodical and
cover all contingencies when on the hunt.

Hernild opened the door himself, crisp in his doctor's whites, a
steaming cup of coffee in one hand. Ingrid was not in evidence.
Hernild raised the cup in a question.

'No thanks. I just had breakfast.'

Hernild nodded and leaned his butt against the edge of the reception desk. He extended a sheet of paper.

'I drew you a map of the way to Hal's cabin. In winter you'd need four-wheel, but this time of year you can make it.'

Thorne studied the sketch. Corwin's cabin, deep in the woods, was a simple rectangle. A dotted line marked the logging-trace in to it from the quarter-section gravel road.

'Isolated.'

'Hal built it himself. Cut down the trees, peeled the logs – therapy after Terry's death. He sliced his leg with an axe and drove to my clinic one-handed, holding it closed with the other hand so he wouldn't bleed to death. That's how we met.'

'How did he make a living during his years here?'

'Trapping, hunting – after the shooting all that stopped.'

'Why didn't you transfer the title to yourself after you paid Corwin for the cabin?'

'He needed money to get away from all of the associations this area evoked after he was wounded.' He paused for emphasis. 'Hal Corwin is my best friend. If he ever wants the cabin back, it's here for him. Meanwhile, I rent it out to cover the taxes. There's someone living there now, in fact. I hope you won't bother him unduly.'

Thorne nodded. 'Sure not. Are you in touch with Corwin?'

Hernild hulked over him, suddenly hostile. 'What do you idiots think Hal has done?' It was a good intimidation tactic, just being used on the wrong man: Thorne never backed down from anyone. 'Why can't you leave the poor bastard in peace?'

Thorne thought: Because the poor bastard is planning to assassinate the president of the United States. He said: 'You know Corwin spent several years as a paid mercenary in some of the world's nastiest civil wars…'

'Maybe. But whatever Hal did before Terry was killed, he left it all behind when he came up here. After he was shot he couldn't even kill animals any more.'

'Still,' said Thorne, deliberately provocative, 'there are some questions about the deaths of his daughter and her husband we believe he could help us with.'

'His daughter? If I read you right, you bastard, and I think I do, he adored his daughter. For Chrissake, after he was shot, she tried to help him find whoever had done it.'

Which was news to Thorne. He felt as if the trail had just become more twisted, more convoluted: she helped him look, but Corwin still blew her away and beat off on her body. At least he now had a chance to ask the question he'd been leading up to.

'What if Mather was the one who shot him? Deliberately?'

'That's crazy. Crazy! After Hal and Nisa patched things up between them, Damon came up here a time or two with her. That was it. Good God, man, he and Mather barely knew each other...' He stopped, his long, almost ascetic face totally devoid of emotion. 'I have to go make house-calls.'

It was a real old-timey log cabin like the maple syrup tins that Vermont Country Store still sold out of its nostalgia catalogue. Peaked roof with hand-hewn shingles, peeled log walls. Built to last, perhaps a lifetime. A lot of effort for a man working alone.

No smoke wisped from the chimney of the hand-laid stone fireplace. The April-wet ground showed a variety of sign: birds, rabbits, squirrels, two, no three different whitetail deer, fox galore, a muddle of porcupine tracks, then a track that sent Thorne's mind backward in time. A wolverine! He hadn't seen a wolverine's spoor in over twenty years.

Plenty of game around here for a man bent on making his living from hunting and trapping. Until getting shot ended it for him. According to Hernild.

Thorne walked boldly up to the door, then checked. He had picked up another Randall Survivor in D.C., but his 9mm Beretta had been left behind at Tsavo. Well, too late now.

'Talk to me,' he said aloud to the cabin.

I'm empty. Come in and find what you are looking for.

'I don't believe you. I can smell coffee.'

Last night's.

'This morning's.'

The door had a simple push-up latch that would stop no one except porcupines in search of the salt they loved. Porkies after salt once had eaten the handle off an axe his dad had left in the woodpile overnight.

Thorne took a deep breath, pushed up the latch, opened the door a foot, called loudly, 'Anybody home?' The coffee smell was stronger with the door open, that was all. 'Coming in.'

He laid a hand on the big speckled blue and white enamel pot on the kerosene stove, jerked it away again. Still hot. And – a nice touch – there was a clean heavy white ceramic mug on the counter beside it.

He poured, sipped. Good coffee, too. It would be.

An obvious challenge. I was here, I made coffee, I even left some for you. Now I am gone. And I won't be hiding in plain sight next time. After Thorne had left the clinic yesterday, Whitby Hernild must have warned him of Thorne's arrival. How? Not the phone. Phones, land or cell, left records. But under the table he found a power-surge strip, the kind you plugged a computer into to protect against burn-outs.

Of course. E-mail. Corwin would have it to check the president's travel itineraries on the White House website.

Thorne relatched the door behind him. Didn't want the porkies partying in there, even though Corwin would not be back. But he'd been living here for a month. Hiding in plain sight, but he'd also wanted to be on familiar ground. To train for a presidential assault? If so, Thorne was sure the woods would tell him what sort of assault Corwin was planning.

He started down the burn in front of the cabin, then checked himself once again. He was being observed. Birds and small animals were always intensely interested in anyone invading their domain, but maybe something bigger? Something potentially threatening? A bear? Or a man? If a bear, a mother with cubs.

If a man, Corwin. Thorne went on down the burn.

17

THE COATED LENSES of Corwin's binocs reflected no light. No telltale glint to alert his pursuer.

This was no ordinary Feeb. He wasn't armed. He'd checked out the animal and bird sign around the cabin, circled it in the bush, then went in boldly. Now, starting down the burn, he seemed to sense observation.

Through the intervening foliage, Corwin tracked him with the binoculars. Totally at home in the woods. A man who had never been a desk jockey. A hunter. Highly trained in the same ways Corwin himself had once been trained, then had further trained himself. As Corwin had.

Who was the hunter here, who the prey?

Thorne's eye was caught by the gnawed ends of toppled finger-thick saplings. A cottontail's bite, not the single hatchetlike chop of a snowshoe rabbit. Not twenty minutes old. Under the nearest evergreen, a little bundle of concealed fur.

Then a flash of red on a fire-blasted spruce twenty feet away caught his eye. A black bird, the size of a crow, with a prominent red crest and white flashes on the wings and neck. A pileated woodpecker, arrowing away from the far side of the tree with a ringing cyk cuk-cyk of irritation.

The trunk of the dead spruce bore waist-high gouges. Not bullet scars. Knife scars, but not to gouge initials into the trunk: to dig out… what? Rifle slugs? His pulse elevated, he did a slow 360, eyes probing. To the west, beyond an intervening narrow slough, was the crown of a low hill partially screened by the bushes gradually reclaiming the fire-denuded burn.

If a non-hunter, an amateur, was planning to shoot someone – his wife's father, for example – who habitually walked up a fire-cleared burn on his way to his cabin, what would he have to do before attempting to commit murder?

Sight in his rifle ahead of time, using that lone dead spruce tree as a marker. Maybe from that low hill to the west?

The dead spruce was visible from the hill's false crown, maybe 150 yards away as the crow flies, five hundred yards laboring up the way Thorne had come: across the strip of marsh, then up the hill through the ash and hickory saplings gradually replacing the oaks and elms logged off many years before.

He began moving out in a slow, ever-widening gyre. An hour later and maybe fifty yards from where he had started, absorbed and eyes searching the ground, he was startled by a pair of pine siskins tit-titting angrily at him as they flew out of a just-flowering dogwood six feet ahead of him.

His eyes automatically followed their flashing flight, passing over cut brush a few yards up the hillside, registering it as the work of cottontails, then snapping back to it.

Behind the brush, half-hidden in the burgeoning squaw grass, was a form never found in nature: a rough platform, six feet long by three feet wide. He squatted beside it. Ash saplings, six inches in diameter, laid out side-by-side. Another sapling, the same size, laid at a right angle across the uphill end of them, lashed into place with thin nylon cord. A larger log, a foot in diameter, lashed in place across the downhill end. Except for the thick undergrowth on the hillside below it, it looked like an impromptu bench-rest laid out for prone shooting.

Thorne laid down on it, facing downhill as if taking up a prone firing position on a rifle range. Now the cut brush that had first caught his eye was in front of him. It formed a perfect keyhole though which he could stare directly down at that dead, distant, knife-gouged spruce tree.

Corwin had been right, everyone else wrong. He had been a tin bird in a shooting gallery, victim of a deliberate, can't-miss shot by an amateur killer. But after years as a hermit, living off the land, he just would not have been a man to anger anyone, be in anyone's way, threaten anyone. Not a man anyone could conceivably want dead.

He would have cast about for anyone who might deliberately want to shoot him. And for some unknown reason of his own, he had fixed upon his son-in-law, Damon Mather. Maybe he was wrong, but probably he was right. But even if right, why, when he had killed her husband, had he killed Nisa in such a savage manner?

During the next six hours, having found the evidence of Corwin's stalker, Thorne found five different places where a professional shooter had fired at targets of opportunity: rock outcroppings that would scar easily, so the bullet-strikes could be checked out with binoculars. Trees where the pale flesh of the trunk would show the bark had been blown away by direct hits.

Shots taken at ranges of 750 to 1,000 yards, from elevation wherever possible, in every sort of terrain. Hellish long shots that few shooters could make. Oh, misses, too, but shockingly few in relation to the rounds fired. Sniper rounds, high velocity, heavy weight. Sent on their way by a wonderful rifle shot, they would dissolve a man's head like a dropped watermelon.

He had learned what he had come to learn. Time to head back to his Crown Vic. Down here in the lowlands, the light was fading. Then he realized he was staring at the eight-foot stump of a dead oak hollowed out by the years. Around it the grass had sprung up so vigorously that it was already chest-high.

With two broken-off branches angling out at shoulder-height, it evoked a man giving a speech at a podium. At chest-level it was riddled and ripped by Corwin's high-velocity rounds.

Here, now, at the end of this day, Thorne knew with certainty what he had only intuited before: Corwin would go for an open-country stalk, not a city stalk, and would try to make a long-range kill from an elevated position. Which narrowed down the sort of presidential stop Thorne had to look for.

Thorne had been stopped by this realization a scant two yards away from the bullet-blasted oak stump, one foot raised for the next step, just as he had stood at Bwana Kifaru's flank, unnoticed. And at that same moment, he had the overwhelming feeling of being observed. He tensed. Could Corwin possibly have been tracking him all day? Could the man be that good?

Then a big brown blunt-nosed woodchuck came thrusting up out of the opening at the top of the stump. Not Corwin, just the wood-chuck, somehow sensing his presence and being made uneasy by it. He chuckled and deliberately shook himself like a dog coming from water. Her worst fears confirmed, the woodchuck scrabbled back down into her hollow stump as if pursued by a lynx.

Thorne thought, with not unjustified pride, that the years of training, the years of Morengaru's coaching, had not been wasted. All in one day, he had walked up unnoticed on a woodpecker, a rabbit, and a groundhog. His skills were intact. Now he was eager to get back to his motel and check out the president's trip against what he had learned this day. He knew how: next, he had to figure out where Corwin would strike.

An hour after the tracker had gone, Corwin stirred. It was darkening rapidly now: dusk in another thirty minutes. His various wounds ached. His own fault. He had been following the tracker too closely, too interested in seeing the terrain and his own shooting areas through another man's eyes, in knowing what the tracker was finding out. He had gotten careless.

He'd just had time to drop silently into the high grass on the far side of the woodchuck's tree stump and huddle there, motionless, barely breathing, seeking a state of non-existence so the sense of threat would pass. Even so, it was the woodchuck who saved him from discovery. Luckily, the FBI tracker had thought his feelings of being observed had come from her, not a man, and had left without checking behind the stump.

His off-hand challenge with the hot coffee pot had not been such a clever idea after all, Corwin realized. He had been hard-pressed to keep tabs on his pursuer unseen during the long afternoon stalk. And this was his home territory. The man had even picked up on the site from which Corwin had been ambushed.

How had the FBI come up with such a person, almost a shadow figure of Corwin himself? He was a new, disturbing factor in the equation. That he had even thought to check out the cabin and surrounding area meant that time was running out for Corwin.

He almost surely had confirmed for himself that Corwin had been shot from ambush. Probably now was coming to believe that Mather had done it, maybe even that Corwin had been justified in going after Mather.

All of that was irrelevant. What was relevant was that the tracker almost surely now knew how Corwin planned to make his assassination attempt: a long range sniper shot, from elevation. Also, he had almost surely figured out that Corwin would do it sometime in the next ten days, during the presidential barn-storming tour.

The one thing he didn't know, couldn't know, was where Corwin would make the attempt. That was Corwin's edge. Corwin decided to retrieve Janet's 4-Runner from its hiding place, and tonight drive west non-stop to the Bitterroot Wilderness Area on the Montana-Idaho border. This would buy him the time he needed to establish his base of operations and study the terrain and conditions and find his one perfect place of ambush.

He felt a surge of his old confidence. When he found the right spot, he would know. And when the right moment came, he would take his shot. One shot was all he would need.

He was that good.

18

THORNE SPENT THE night in the Bide-A-Wee in Portage, working his computer for the president's trip. Too charged to sleep, he left before dawn to drive back down to the Twin Cities. He now knew when, where, and how Corwin would try to kill the president. But he would have to convince all the president's men that he was right on all counts, because Hatfield would be out to discredit him in subtle ways. Hatfield needed Thorne's input, but wanted him far away when Corwin was taken down.

Thorne's Northwest flight from Minneapolis to D.C. was at nine the next morning, so he had time for one final information probe he didn't want Hatfield to know anything about. If he got a lead the Feebs hadn't gotten, he could keep it to himself by seeming to do the plodding, the predictable.

Minneapolis/St.Paul International was near the Minnesota River and Fort Snelling, a few miles west and south of downtown. He checked into an airport motel nearby that had frequent shuttle-service to Northwest departures.

He left the Crown Vic in the parking garage under the downtown FBI Field Office, rode the elevator up, went through the security checkpoint, and turned the keys over to the Agent in Charge. He was a stern-faced dark-haired man named Breen who resembled the late Robert Ryan in one of his tough-guy roles.

'You could keep it, drop it at the airport in the morning.'

'I want to stroll around town this afternoon. It's easier to just catch a shuttle to Northwest tomorrow a.m. But thanks.'

The SAC obviously had been briefed. He dropped any pretense of being helpful. 'Knock yourself out, Thorne.'

When Thorne was on the elevator down, Ray Franklin, whom

Thorne knew only by name, not by sight, came out of the field agents' bullpen where he had been skulking.

'I'll get the GPS transmitter off the car.'

'You want us to put a tag on him?' asked the AIC.

Franklin knew Hatfield wouldn't want anyone in Minneapolis in the loop. He just shook his head.

'Who's he gonna talk to, what's he gonna learn during an after-noon in Minneapolis, that we don't already know?'

Thorne rode inter-city buses out to the old rambling house on Marshall Avenue in St. Paul where Corwin and Terry had lived and Nisa had grown up. The FBI file said that Corwin had deeded it to Nisa when he had gone off to become a hermit. Her best friend, Jewel Bemel, and her husband, Nate, a clinical psychiatrist, had bought the house from the estate.

Thorne didn't know what – if any – of Nisa's papers the Feebs might have left behind. But he hoped they might have missed, or considered unimportant, something that might give him a clue, however slight, as to whether Mather had shot Corwin. Or maybe the Bemels themselves might have some ideas. It was better than spending the afternoon at a movie.

The evergreens dotting the well-tended lawn towered over the two-story house. At a guess, planted when the place had been built, probably in the 1920s. He paused before he committed himself, then, feeling almost guilty, took out the temporary FBI credentials he had been given when he was approved for the assignment by Dorst's report. There was a shiny badge, and a commission card with the red, white and blue FBI seal on it.

He rang the bell. The door was opened without hesitation by a handsome late-thirties blonde with big blue eyes and big hair and a full-lipped mouth that looked ready to smile merrily in the right cir-cumstances.

'May I help…' She saw his FBI credentials, and grabbed his arm with surprising strength. 'Oh my God! Come on in!'

A slightly bewildered Thorne was led into a spacious living room with a hardwood floor partially covered by an ancient Karistan rug that had retained its deep, rich colors. She kept on talking over her shoulder as she led him to a leather couch behind an oak-burl coffee table so polished it gleamed with subdued inner fires.

'Nate will be home in a few minutes! Do you want some coffee? Of course you do! I'm Jewel.' By this time, somehow, she had him seated on the couch. 'I'm just glad that someone is still looking into the terrible tragedy that befell Nisa!' He noted she had mentioned only Nisa, not Damon. 'If you would prefer tea...'

'Coffee is fine.' He knew he had lucked out here, so he added, 'And yes, their tragedy is why I am here.'

'There you are!' she said, departing for the kitchen.

In the corner a stately grandfather clock as tall as a man leisurely tock-tock-tocked off the seconds. Above the smoke-blackened stone fireplace was an oil painting of a cavalier in a stiff ruffled collar and wearing a swash hat with a long plume in it. His right hand rested on the gleaming pommel of a sheathed sword. He looked half-pugnacious, half-confused.

The top of the baby-grand piano was covered with framed photographs. There were four featuring Nisa, moving her through the years, starting with her wedding day – she blonde and beautiful, intense, Damon young and handsome and virile-looking. Hairstyles changed, but not her face: heart-shaped, sensual, with a short nose and intelligent liquid-blue eyes. Nor her figure: a laughing swim-suit shot showed she was taut-waisted, long-legged, full-busted. Which of her attributes had captivated at least three men – Wallberg, Jaeger, and her husband? Four, if he counted her own father's obsession with her.

He heard a key in the front door lock and turned just as Jewel came from the rear of the house carrying an ornate silver tray with a plate of shortbread cookies and a silver coffee urn and Meissen cups and saucers on it.

'Here's Nate now!' She talked in exclamation points.

Nate Bemel was a slight gentle-faced man in his sixties, six inches shorter than his wife, wearing an expensive wool suit, conservative tie, and gleaming shoes. Jewel briefly hugged him.

'Nate, this is Mr…' She trailed off. 'Oh dear, I didn't even get your name!'

'Brendan Thorne.'

'Mr. Thorne is from the FBI. They're finally doing something about Nisa's death!' She turned to Thorne. 'Don't think I'm callous, we liked Damon. But he just rode her coattails! Rode her coattails.'

Thorne and Nate shook hands. When they were all seated and coffee had been poured, Thorne made an almost placating gesture.

'I hope my coming here today doesn't raise false hopes. We are still investigating their deaths, but the case is ongoing so I can't really…'

'Can't talk about it.' Nate gave little bird-like nods of his head, a sweet smile illuminating his face. 'Just what I tell the authorities when they come around asking questions about my patients. I don't keep notes of my sessions, so I tell them, Go get a court order, and we'll talk again. They never do. Verbal reports without written back-up are hearsay. When you go to a shrink you should get confidentiality.'

Unless the FBI invokes National Security, Thorne thought. Then even the shrink didn't get confidentiality.

He said, 'How did you and Nisa meet, Mrs. Bem… Jewel?'

'She was running Gus Wallberg's campaign for governor—'

'Hardly running it, Jewel love.'

'Well, she was too! In everything except title! I was publicity director for Dayton's, Minneapolis, and she was looking for contributions to Gus's campaign. We hit it off right away!'

'Jewel raised a lot of money for the governor,' Nate said fondly. 'She knows how to work public companies for donations.'

Jewel gave a wide-open laugh. 'I grew up on a ranch in Texas, and got my fill of the outdoors early on! The only wide-open space I like is the main floor at Nieman-Marcus. Hiking is what you do between Saks Fifth Avenue and Lord & Taylor!'

'Have you spoken with Nisa's dad?' asked Nate, doing Thorne's work for him. 'We met him only once, but we liked him a lot and sort of hoped he'd come to see us here after they were murdered. But…' He shrugged.

'That's actually one of the questions I came to ask, where is Mr. Corwin? Also, although I don't have a court order, I'm hoping you might be willing to let me see any diaries, notebooks, memos, calendars, things like that – anything Nisa kept when she worked on the president's election campaign. I'm sure the other special agents took most of it away with them, but—'

'They took nothing! Just asked a few questions and left!'

Even though Johnny Doyle had given him the probable answer, Thorne wanted their take on a final question.

'Do you know why Nisa didn't join Wallberg's camapign at first, then signed on just before he was nominated?'

'She wanted to get pregnant,' said Jewel promptly. 'She felt the clock was ticking! But Damon had a low sperm count, and wouldn't hear of artificial insemination. So she went back to the campaign. Just couldn't stay away from politics!'

Nate started to remonstrate, 'Jewel, that's just—'

'That's what she told me. And what difference does it make now, anyway? They're both dead.'

'Did you notice anything in her papers that might—'

'Oh, we never looked at them!' said Jewel. 'Just too sad!'

'They're in my workroom in the garage,' said Nate. 'I restore antique clocks as a hobby.' He gestured at the man-high clock in the corner. 'A work of art, that one. Pine-faced grandfather, roller-pinion, eight-day wooden movement. American, not German. Early American clockworks were made of wood because they couldn't get iron, and the brass industry hadn't started yet.' Again that shy, sweet smile that Thorne had come to find endearing. Nate got carefully out of his chair. 'Come on, I'll give you those papers.' He added almost wistfully, 'You can fix a damaged clock a lot easier than you can a damaged psyche.'

'Just too sad!' exclaimed Jewel Bemel.

19

NISA HAD NOT kept a diary as such, but Thorne found her note-book had served much the same function: shopping lists, notes to herself, strategies for Wallberg's campaign all jumbled together. There was also a manila folder with two pages of hand-written notes confirming that she had helped Corwin look for the shooter. Thorne went there first.

> January 20th. Damon in Des Moines with the campaign
> for the Iowa caucus. I knew Dad was looking for the man
> who had shot him, so I said I wanted in. He finally
> agreed.

As Thorne had surmised, Corwin had dug slugs out of the spruce from the sighting-in of the shooter's rifle. Then he had found eight spent cartridge cases at the ambush site up on the hillside that Thorne had uncovered the day before. He took the brass to a hand-loader for analysis and anything distinctive, then canvassed Portage for info on the shooter.

> Nothing on the cartidges. But a nervous-acting hunter
> used the payphone in Dutch's Tavern the night of the
> shooting. Dark hair, dark glassses, mustache, goatee.
> 'Actorish'.

On February 25th, the day after the first Democratic primary in New Hampshire, Corwin learned at the Portage airfield that All-Weather Charter Tours of Robbinsdale had flown in a man on the day he had been shot, had flown him back out after dark.

Some sort of real-estate deal. No name, but the same
description of the nervous drinker we got from Dutch's
Tavern. It's a start.

Corwin talked to the ex-bush pilot who owned All-Weather. The
Portage client's name was Hopkins and he had paid with a credit
card from Primary Power, Inc.

Primary Power, Inc., is a Democratic fund-raising entity to
help Gus Wallberg win the nomination! Gerard Hopkins
has to be someone associated with the campaign!

Gerard Hopkins? As in Gerard Manley Hopkins, the poet? Thorne
thought, reading the notes, an obvious ringer. But Corwin dismissed
Hopkins out of hand. Corwin hadn't seen or spoken with Wallberg
for forty years, why would anyone attached to Wallberg's campaign
want to kill him? But Nisa wasn't giving up. Somebody thought that
killing Corwin was the way to money, power and leverage if
Wallberg became president. And why had he come disguised, unless
he was known in Portage from before the shooting? Corwin finally
agreed to try and get the number the man had called from Dutch's
Tavern, but Dutch didn't have it.

The last entry in her slim folder was made by Nisa on her return
from what must have been her final stay at Corwin's cabin.

Check on bush pilot.
Check on drama costume houses.
Check on shooting ranges.

The first, the bush pilot, had a check-mark beside it. All-Weather
Tours. Been there, done that.

Next, drama costume houses. Try to find where the shooter
bought the mustache and goatee. No check mark.

Last, shooting ranges. Someone probably had coached the
shooter, not knowing what he was planning. No check mark.

Mather fit on all counts. He was not ex-military, would have been an amateur, would have needed a disguise – no matter what Hernild said, he had to have been known in Portage. But in their search for the shooter, it never occurred to either Nisa or Corwin that the man they sought might be Nisa's husband.

Frustrated, Thorne put the folder aside and turned to her pocket-book-size notebook. Shopping lists, appointments, ideas for Wallberg's campaign strategies to give to her husband since she was not with the entourage. The ideas looked extremely sound to Thorne. Then, among voluminous political notes on Wallberg's Florida win, a note handwritten, underlined, in caps: OH MY GOD! IT'S DAMON!!!

Finally! Two solid FACTS in a morass of speculation.

One. Damon Mather was indeed the shooter.

Two. Until this entry, Nisa had no idea that he was.

The following entries started almost three months later, shortly before the Democratic convention chose Wallberg as their presidential candidate. Once again they were totally political in nature: Nisa had thrown herself into the camapign.

Not a word about Corwin. Not a word about how she reacted to her husband's guilt, or about how she had discovered it. Obviously, she had let Mather know she had found him out: the day after the OH MY GOD! IT'S DAMON!!! notebook entry he had bought the .357 Magnum. Just as obviously, she had not told Corwin that it was Mather who tried to kill him. If she had, she would not have been killed along with Damon. Maybe. Perhaps.

Which left Thorne out of the loop, reporting his movements to a man who hated his guts for reasons really not clear, and being lied to besides. Well, the first thing you learned as a Ranger scout/sniper was to always give yourself a back door. He got a cab and told the driver to take him downtown.

The Oasis was a no-frills drinkers' joint, the back-bar mirror clouded, the usual stale beer smell mixed with stale smoke, the varnish worn down to the bare wood along the rolled edge of the bar where drinkers had rested their forearms and elbows. A backwards neon Bud Light sign was in the front window; a faded HAMM'S, THE BEER REFRESHING! banner was scrolled along the top of the backbar. The TV above the bar showed an NBA elimination game with the sound turned down.

From a quick look around, Thorne knew that none of the three drinkers was the kind of man he was looking for. But then the door opened, outside light laying someone's entering shadow across the front of the bar. This man was a definite prospect. Thorne immediately took a stool and laid down a twenty.

'Shot and a beer,' he said to the bartender.

In the mirror he watched the newcomer look around appraisingly. Then he sidled up beside Thorne as the bartender came back with Thorne's beer and shot.

'Benny the Boozer,' the bartender said to Thorne in a flat voice, and left.

Benny eyed Thorne's shot, licked his lips. Borderline alcoholic but not yet homeless. Fifty-five, maybe, with a too-lined face and a tattered gray cardigan three sizes too big. Vietnam vet, tiny military disability pension, sleeping in the back seat of a beater or in a rented room somewhere.

'How goes the battle, Benny?'

'I lost.'

Thorne slid his untouched shot Benny's way. Benny's hand shook picking it up. He drank. Thorne gestured for another.

Benny cast him a shrewd eye. 'Why?'

'I know a Vietnam vet down on his luck when I see one.'

Benny laid the second shot down. His hand no longer shook.

'First Combat Infantry Division. We saw some shit.'

'The Big Red One,' Thorne agreed. He slid off his stool, leaving his beer and the twenty. 'I'm hungry. You coming?'

They sat at the high counter in a gleaming, white-tile, glass and chrome White Castle, Thorne drinking coffee and Benny gobbling little yellow-wrapped hamburgers. Finally Benny leaned back and

belched with his mouth open. His teeth were bad. His eyes were not
so far back in his head.

'So whadda ya want? My fair white body?'

'Your wallet.'

'You think I got the crown jools in there?' But he took out the
worn leather and flopped it almost defiantly on the counter. Thorne
fingered through it, took what he wanted, held the items up for
Benny's appraisal, gave the wallet back.

'You can get replacements.' He laid two hundred-dollar bills on
the counter. 'This'll buy you a couple months rent, groceries. Maybe
even let you get off the sauce. Who knows?'

He shook Benny's hand and walked out into the night.

Benny, staring after him, said softly, 'Who knows indeed?'

Thorne made one more stop, at a bank's all-night teller machine to
start what he had decided would be his daily routine: drawing out
his debit card's maximum daily amount of cash for the moneybelt
around his waist. His back door should he need one.

After clearing airport security at 7:15 a.m., he stopped at a bank of
payphones before going on to the gate for his flight to D.C. A tinny
computer-generated voice gave him the long-distance charges.
He shoved coins into the slot. The phone was picked up on the
second ring.

'Doctor's office.'

'You're up bright and early, Ingrid. This is Thorne.'

'Oh. You.' Her tone was scolding, but with a hint of amusement.
'He's free, but don't keep him too long. He's got to go make house
calls at eight o'clock.'

After a pause, Hernild's voice came on. 'The bad penny.'

'I know Corwin was living in his cabin until you warned him off
the night before I went out there. I need to ask you—'

'I don't know where he went.'

'I know. I need to ask you why he sold the cabin and took off. I
know Mather shot him. I know he killed Mather and Nisa. Now he

plans to kill the president of the United States. I can't let that happen. Can you help me out on any of this?'

'Apart from Ingrid, Hal Corwin is the best friend I've ever had.' A long silence. 'Okay, he told me he couldn't get the phone number the shooter called from Dutch's payphone. But being the old country doctor type, I could. It was an unlisted Minneapolis number. I told Hal. The next day he sold the cabin and left for good.'

'Why did you think it was for good? He came back.'

'Because he took his bearskin. Old John, the Indian who trained him to be a hunter and woodsman, gave it to him when he was a kid.' Corwin's mentor, as Morengaru was Thorne's. 'When I saw it was gone, I called the number.' Another pause. 'Nisa answered. I hope I don't live to regret this.'

'Nisa didn't,' said Thorne, irritated, and hung up.

All the work and time he would have been saved if Hernild had told him this the first time they had talked! Hernild had known all along that Mather was the shooter. Mather had called Nisa after shooting her father, using her as an alibi – 'Hi, honey, I'll be home late…'

A betrayal. Despite it, she had sided with him. In June, Corwin got Nisa's unlisted number from Hernild. He left Portage the next day, obviously thinking it was for good. But then he kept stewing about it. Mather shooting him, Nisa hiding that fact from him. Then five months later, in the Delta, he murdered them both.

Corwin must have done awful things as a merc – they all did. Things he couldn't forgive himself for. The kind of things Thorne had never had to stew about, because he was still working for the government after he left the Rangers.

Even so, Corwin had been able to live with those things, because Terry and Nisa had always been behind him, his core, his center, his anchor, his Ground Zero.

Then Terry was killed. Nisa blamed him. Guilt, no longer suppressed, washed over him like blood. Bad dreams, too, Thorne was sure, much like his own after Alison and Eden were killed.

After Corwin himself had been shot, and partially crippled, Nisa came back into his life. She even started helping him on his hunt for his attacker. Redemption! A second chance! Then she turned on him again, turned instead to the man who had tried to kill him.

Love and hate were like the tusks of fossil mammoths curving back on themselves so completely that their tips touched. Perhaps love and hate had touched in Corwin. He killed them because together they had taken his last chance at redemption.

It almost explained everything. Except where he was and what he was doing during those five months between his flight from Portage and his reappearance in the California Delta. Except why Mather had tried to kill him in the first place.

And then, the jackpot question: why Corwin, after Nisa and Damon were dead, decided to go after Gustave Wallberg, soon to be President of the United States.

20

CARRYING ONLY AN old WWII .38 revolver, his survival knife, and his rangefinder for a final check of distance, range, and elevation, Corwin left the Motel Deluxe in Salmon, Idaho. He had rented his room there for two weeks under somebody else's name. His tripod was hidden up on the mountain, on site. He had zeroed-in on his first day there, so as usual, he left his rifle, ammo and scope in the room. No need to bring them back to the sniper nest until That Day.

A maze of narrow, unimproved roads lay west of 10,757-foot Trapper Peak, still mostly white-clad, framed by shorter peaks that had not retained their winter snow. Some ten miles north of Trapper, Corwin turned on to a minor national-park road, then a dirt road, then turned again into an abandoned logging trace. After half a mile on that, he bounced the 4-Runner off the track, covered it with fir branches cut the first day, and left the ignition key in front of the left rear tire as always.

He hiked with his slightly-limping gait five miles back to a sub-alpine valley on the near side of a range of granite peaks from the meadow where the president would soon speak. His way led him past a small mountain pond rimmed with ice and up around the northern edge of the massif. That was the only exposed rock he had to cross. He came back south on the far side in the cover of a mixed conifer-hardwood forest to follow a narrow, black, icy, rushing melt water torrent down the slope.

He was totally focussed on his hunt, giving no thought to whoever might be hunting him. He felt he'd covered his backtrail too well for anyone to decipher it.

Camp David, Maryland, was a U.S. Navy facility, maintained solely for presidential recreation and occasional meetings where the press was barred. It was inside a camouflaged electrified fence; thirty remote-operated, all-128 weather scanning cameras were hidden in the trees. In camouflaged bunkers around the grounds was a platoon of forty highly-trained and attack-alert Marine sentries equipped with night-vision glasses.

Kurt Jaeger had arranged for Terrill Hatfield to drive him from the helipad to the Presidential cabin in a golf cart, the camp's usual mode of transport. He wanted to have a totally private conversation with the FBI man.

'I gather you don't think much of Thorne, Terrill.'

Surprisingly, Hatfield said, 'If anybody is going to find Corwin, it'll be Thorne. I want him to do that, but I want to take Corwin down. Myself. I want to be Director of the FBI.'

'I want to be Secretary of State in Wallberg's next term.'

After this exchange of confidences, unexpected on both sides, they rode in silence for two minutes. Then Hatfield said, 'We use Thorne to find him, then we send Thorne back to Kenya to rot in jail as a poacher. Out of sight, out of mind.'

'Out of the President's mind at any rate,' agreed Jaeger. 'Whom meanwhile we will have saved from a mad stalker.'

Corwin was facing east, the sun at his back, forty-five minutes before the president would be scheduled to arrive on speech-day. They would be in light, he would be in shadow, in a narrow V-shaped slot between two granite walls that were flanked by stunted pine shrubs. Not like the succession of cramped spider holes he'd worked out of in Vietnam.

He would be firing from the prone, the most stable of positions, with a tripod. The pines would make the opening invisible to scanning binoculars directed up the cliff-face from the meadow far below. The floor was dry packed earth. Where the slot came to a point a dozen yards behind him, the torrent he had followed down the cliff face would be his escape route.

Corwin pointed the Barr & Stroud prismatic optical rangefinder like a camera at the only place in the meadow where they could put a podium. It was 1,210 yards. A hellacious long shot: nobody would be looking up here before he pulled the trigger, and after he fired, it would be an hour of confusion before they scoped out exactly where the shot had come from.

By then he would be long gone, in the stream to confuse the inevitable bloodhounds. And instead of riding it down, he would climb uphill through the icy water to emerge into shielding trees, cut diagonally up across the face of the mountain below the tree line, go back around to the western side. No exposure, not even to choppers. Back to Janet's 4-Runner by dark, start driving long before they could get their perimeter check-point system operational, be hundreds of miles to the west by dawn.

Not even the unknown tracker, even if he somehow got the location right, could know where Corwin was planning his ambush. He would have dozens of square miles of meadow, forest, and precipitous rock face to comb for shooting sites, with nothing to indicate that Corwin had ever been in any of them.

When Thorne stepped off the helicoptor at Camp David, he was picked up by a six-foot, hard-bitten man in a golf cart who said he was Ray Franklin, Hatfield's hot-shot who had been outfoxed by Corwin not once, but twice. And, concomitantly, embarrassed by Thorne not once, but twice. Franklin was from a crack FBI field unit, and Thorne had made them all look foolish.

Flanking the narrow blacktop was dense forest; beyond were Maryland's Catoctin Mountains. Camouflage tarps covered the Secret Service Command Post and the roof of the comm center.

'Were they already in place before 9/11?'

Franklin sucked hard on a Marlboro. He was just as hostile as his boss. 'Yeah. Towel-heads aren't the only ones gunning for the President besides your shit-heel buddy Corwin.'

They didn't speak again until Franklin swerved into the woods to stop at a one-story 3,000-square-foot rustic cabin with a half-log exterior. Reverence entered his voice.

'Behind those logs is a solid-concrete inner shell with Kevlar plugs. Bomb and weapon resistant. The basement is stocked with supplies and reinforced to ground-zero specifications in case of a nuclear attack.'

The door opened and Hatfield gestured at them impatiently.

'Thanks for the ride,' Thorne said.

'Fuck you,' said Franklin.

Dominating the big informal room was a burnished dining table with a halfdozen chairs around it. Framed cowboy art, landscape photographs, and western-motif tapestries covered the walls. Two overstuffed sofas were covered with textured pillows.

The president, Jaeger, Hatfield, and the Bobbsy Twins, Crandall and Quarles, were already at the table. For the moment, no Johnny Doyle. When Thorne began his presentation he realized that he didn't have many friends in the room. Hatfield's play obviously was to get Thorne's input, downgrade it in the president's eyes, then present it as his own.

Thorne began, 'Mr. President, in your website announcement of locations where you will be giving speeches on your trip, I noted one in the Bitterroot Mountains of western Montana.'

'Yes, the U.S. Fish and Wildlife Service is releasing two young grizzly bears back into the wild there. It's an experiment, not popular with everyone, to show my support for the environmental movement.'

'Corwin will be there,' said Thorne.

'The Secret Service will be there too,' said Hatfield. 'In force. The local ranchers claim the grizzlies will attack their livestock, and Montana and Idaho are loaded with anti-government militia and survivalist groups. Security will be very tight. A fucking squirrel won't be able to get close to the President.'

'Corwin doesn't have to get close. He's a sniper.'

'Was a sniper – forty years ago. We're talking about a mountain meadow surrounded by mixed hardwood and conifer stands. In the forest, Corwin has no shooting lanes. The surrounding peaks are too far back for a sniper shot, and he can't get close enough for a knife or a bomb or a grenade. So it has to be a handgun, and a snap shot at that, from the crowd. Forget it.'

Thorne made his voice incredulous, though it was what he had expected from Hatfield.

'We're talking about the life of the president of the United States here! I was brought in because the computer told you that the scenario I worked out would probably be the one Corwin will use. Well, this is where I would strike. A sniper shot from outside the Secret Service security perimeter.'

Hatfield had come prepared. He snapped his fingers; Johnny Doyle appeared with a topographical map to spread out on the table. All carefully choreographed. Had Hatfield's hostility blinded him to the dangers of this site? If he had considered it in private, he now was rejecting it in public.

'The closest places from which he could get a clear shot are seven-hundred-fifty yards out.' Hatfield jabbed his finger at the map. 'There and there and there. Corwin wouldn't waste his chance on a shot he'd be sure to miss.'

'I agree. But he will be using a high-powered rifle with a sniper scope from an elevated rock-face beyond seven-hundred-fifty yards out.' Thorne was doing his own finger-jabbing. 'Here, say, or here. It's what I would do if I had his skills.'

'What the hell do you know about his skills? After he left Vietnam, we have no hard facts about—'

'But *in* Vietnam,' said Thorne quickly.

When Corwin was in a bodybag he'd file a report with the facts he'd dug out, but not before. They knew nothing about his Victor Blackburns' intel, nothing about Corwin hiding out in his old cabin near Portage, nothing about about those thousand-yard practice shooting sites. Thorne wanted to keep it that way.

'He's fifty-six fucking years old,' sneered Hatfield, 'and half-crippled. His hand and eye coordination have to be going.'

'Do you want to take that chance? Let the Secret Service handle the upclose and personal. It's essential that your men set up at seven-hundredfifty yards, looking out and up, not down and in. I can be on site, monitoring—'

'Like hell you can! You're here in an advisory capacity only – your own request. No field work. Well, you've advised. Ray Franklin is waiting outside to take you back to the chopper. You will return to D.C. forthwith to await further instructions.'

Thorne looked to Wallberg for support. It was the man's own life that was at stake here. The president wavered, then looked away. Hatfield had convinced them that he had it under control. None of them understood how formidable Corwin was.

Jaeger said, 'Thank you for your input, Mr. Thorne.'

Thorne walked out. It was up to him to go to Montana and assess the site in person rather than on paper.

'I say we ship his sorry ass back to Kenya,' said Hatfield when he was gone. 'His usefulness here is ended.'

'What if, just what if, he's right?' asked Wallberg. 'What if Corwin is there and does try to shoot me when I—'

'Then my men will tag him before he can fire. This is my game, Mr. President. I know that nobody can make a thousand-yard down-angle shot while dealing with those mountain updrafts.'

'With the Secret Service and the FBI's hostage rescue men on site,' Jaeger added unctuously, 'we will have security, and containment of the fact that there's a lone gunman from the President's past stalking him with murderous intent. That he's a deluded psycho is irrelevant. If the fact that he's out there became known, the political fallout would be unthinkable.'

21

THORNE TOLD THE Mayflower's front desk that he could be reached c/o Victor Blackburn at Fort Benning, Georgia, then sent Victor an e-mail.

> Victor: Check me into the BOQ, then make yourself scarce
> for a few days. We're out in the woods getting drunk like
> all good Rangers should. Details later. Thorne.

He back-doored his minders, walked out to the depot on L Street, and caught a through bus to Atlantic City. From there he flew commercial to Missoula, Montana, rented a car, drove to Hamilton, and checked into the Super 8 Motel under his own name. The risk was small: officially, he was at Fort Benning.

The next morning he drove south on 93, turned onto narrow 473 well short of towering white-clad Trapper Peak so he could approach the meadow the way the presidental party would enter. Using his temporary FBI credentials for site access, he spent the day working his way up and down the granite rockface, and through the tumbled massive boulders on the slope overlooking the meadow. Hatfield was right: no ambush sites up to 750 yards out.

The next day, he drove south of Trapper on 93, went west into Idaho on narrow unmarked dirt tracks, then north again seeking a way up to the western side of the Bitterroot ridge whose eastern slope facing the meadow he'd combed the day before. He found a subalpine valley and hiked up it, looking for man sign. None. But this was the way Corwin would have to have come to prep his shot. If he was here at all.

For the next two mornings, Thorne, seeking sniper sites, worked his way up over the ridge and down the far side toward the meadow.

The more acute the downward angle, the harder the shot. By the last day he could safely work the mountain before Hatfield's Feebs arrived, he had three maybes: 950 yards out, 1,095 yards out, and a literal long shot at 1,210 yards out.

The last was a sniper's dream, a narrow V-shaped slot between two granite walls camouflaged by stunted pines. The floor was dry packed dirt. Behind, a narrow mountain torrent rushed down slope from the melting snow lingering in shaded areas far above. Good escape route for Corwin after the shot.

But the distance: over 1,200 yards! Twelve football fields laid end to end down the mountain face. Your slug would drop some twenty-five feet while the swirling, unpredictable winds of the 7,500 foot elevation played games with it. Utterly impossible.

Still, this was Corwin...

Day after tomorrow, Thorne was quite sure, both he and Corwin would be working their way over the summit and going down the far side toward the meadow. Two reluctant killers, one bent on murder, the other bent on stopping him. Stopping him how, if it actually came to that? With his Randall Survivor?

Reluctant as he was, Thorne had no choice: Hatfield had mesmerized himself and all the president's men with the idea that if Corwin showed at all, he would try wet work, up close and personal. He also remembered Sean Connery's scorn-filled line in *The Untouchables* about bringing a knife to a gunfight.

In a downtown Hamilton gun store, Thorne professed total ignorance so the clerk could sell him a bolt-action Winchester Standard Model 70 in .30-06 caliber with a Weaver K-4 scope. Thousands were sold every year. No waiting period, no papers to sign. Just another guy who liked to go out in the woods and blast away. Nothing to alert Hatfield's men if they even bothered to check.

At four-thirty a.m. on speech day, Corwin checked out of his motel. He needed time to hide the 4-Runner and walk back. Afterwards, he'd call Janet's cell to find out where to leave it. He'd be in everybody's cross-hairs until they figured he had died or disappeared for good, but she would be well and truly out of it. As long as he was in her life, she would never find a man of her own.

For a moment, his resolve flickered. Today, he planned to commit murder. All those countless nights full of grotesque dreams and memories came back to him full-force. Would he have the seeds for any more killing?

Two rangers from the U.S. Fish and Wildlife Service were working with two college students from the Wildlife Biology Program of the University Of Montana's School of Forestry at Missoula to release a young male grizzly named Smokey, and a female, gender-misnamed Winnie the Pooh, into the wild. Not that the bears knew they had names. They were wild, and wanted to be.

'Just two lousy bears being released,' groused Laura Givens. She was twenty and earnest.

'It's a start,' objected Ranger Rick mildly – yeah, his name really was Ranger Rick, Rick Tandy. He was twenty-two, and more interested in getting into Laura's pants than arguing with her.

Sam Jones, the other ranger, was thirty-five and secretly sided with the ranchers on this one, as did many in Fish and Wildlife. More grizzlies they didn't need to pull down and maul their livestock.

'Just two-hundred and seventy-eight bears to go,' he said.

'It should be six-hundred and twenty-eight bears to go,' exclaimed Laura, eyes flashing. 'That's how many we need for a full recovery of the population.'

Sean McLean was twenty-five and completing his PhD. He said in support, 'There are sixteen-thousand square miles of virgin territory here – just a couple of highways and a few unimproved roads through. Enough land for our bears to reproduce, and eventually bridge the gap between the existing populations. But you Feds are giving us only the area north of U.S. Highway 12 to work with.'

'So two bears is a great sufficiency,' said Sam. 'What do you say to that, everyone?'

Neither Laura or Sean spoke. The bears, stalking their cages, growled in unison.

*

The press was in the back of Air Force One, the players were in the front. Wallberg distractedly riffled the pages of his speech. He and his entourage would be choppered from the Air Force base near Missoula, to an LZ near the speech site, and then motorcaded in armored limos to the meadow where the grizzlies would be released.

'The grizzly bear is a keystone species, with stringent habitat requirements. They serve as a natural barometer of ecosystem health for hundreds of other species…'

The pages fell to his lap. Corwin had assumed mythic proportions in his mind. Thorne said Corwin would be here. He believed Thorne. He raised the speech, tried to concentrate.

'Grizzlies cannot survive if their remaining habitat is broken up into small chunks through reduction and isolation…'

Superimposed on the pages was Corwin's face from The Desert Palms Resort last fall. If only the Secret Service had been a few seconds quicker, had shot a little straighter…

'Since the pockets of grizzlies in Yellowstone and the surrounding wilderness areas are not contiguous, they are not enough to maintain the population at a viable level…'

That night in the California desert, Corwin had no idea why Mather had tried to kill him. But before election night he must have found out: Mather was dead, and now he wanted Gus Wallberg.

Looking down at the distracted President, Jaeger felt only contempt. A man fearing for his life would hide that fact.

'Mr. President.' Wallberg looked up, startled. 'Before you mount to the podium, you will shake hands and trade quips with the college kids who worked with the bears. Then you will move over to the cages, talk knowledgeably with the rangers…'

'Uh… what sort of crowd will we have?'

'Small, probably vocal, maybe hostile – they don't see it as an environmental issue, they see it as a land-use issue. But with half the Washington Press Corps and all four networks right there, your speech will be on everybody's dinner-time news.'

Wallberg rubbed his eyes. 'That's what counts.'

'Hatfield and O'Hara have the site sewn up tight. If Corwin should be there and somehow got a shot, your Kevlar vest would stop the bullet cold. Any danger is minimal—'

'I don't care anything about any on-site danger,' Wallberg blustered. 'I'm trying to concentrate here.'

The man didn't even try to hide his fear. 'Sorry, sir.'

Wallberg pulled himself together enough to read aloud:

'By releasing these two symbolic bears, Pooh and Smokey, into the wild, we will provide a biological corridor to link our nation's last grizzly populations for genetic interchange…'

He lowered the speech. 'I see the cage doors opening, the bears hesitating, then ambling forth, touching noses, maybe, then, realizing they are free, trotting off into the forest…'

'It will bring down the house, Mr. President.'

Walking down the aisle, Jaeger remembered his first sexual humiliation after Nisa Mather had turned him down following Wallberg's exploratory fund-raiser at Olaf Gavle's house. Jaeger had pulled Nisa into a bedroom, started groping her. She slapped his face, hard, and stalked away with blazing eyes.

How different it all would have been if she had succumbed to his advances! She hadn't, so, frustrated and vengeful, he had sought out a campaign worker named Kirsten who had milkmaid breasts, rounded hips, strong thighs, and was blonde all the way down. Then he couldn't get it up, not even with her naked on a motel room bed. It had never happened to him before. After that night, it started happening to him a lot.

L.A. was their last stop on this trip: maybe give Sharkey a call. Get a blonde who looked a little like Nisa Mather…

He felt himself stiffen slightly at the thought. His mind was miles away from presidential security concerns.

Shayne O'Hara's mind was filled with presidential security concerns. He was a russet-faced fifty-year old who looked as if he should be leading the parade on St. Paddy's Day clad all in green, shillelagh in hand. But under that bluff good-guy exterior was a shrewd, ambitious man who brooked absolutely no fuck-ups.

Terrill Hatfield said, 'My men are in place, seven-hundred-fifty yards out, ready to do the necessary.'

'Seven-hundred-and-fifty yards? Jaysus, Terrill, Al-Qaeda has no expertise at long-distance assassination.'

'But some survivalist who hates the President might,' said Hatfield. It sounded weak to his ears, but O'Hara nodded.

'Well, with your men covering distant threats, and my boys covering for close work, we'll be fine. I've kept four-and-a-half Presidents alive, starting with the elder Bush and counting our newly-elected Wallberg, and haven't lost one yet.' He checked his watch. 'Home Plate's speech starts at three p.m.'

You won't lose one today, Hatfield thought as he walked away. Not with his own boys 750 yards out, all the hardware and all the jargon of the trade in place. In his ear receiver, he could hear their pre-op adrenaline-charged chatter. To him, they sounded like a pack of coyotes warming up for the hunt.

Franklin's voice. 'Ray One to TOC. Request Compromise Authority and permission to move to Code Yellow.'

Yellow: the penultimate position of cover and concealment before Code Green, which meant, in this case, if they got visual on Corwin. Green was the moment of truth. Hatfield, Tactical Operations Commander for this operation, spoke into his bone microphone – called a 'mic' by the troops.

'Copy, Ray One, stand by.'

Walt, ever eager to use his weapon, broke in, 'Walter Two. Is that an affirmative on Compromise Authority?'

Compromise Authority was a euphemism for permission to open up with their MP5 machine guns, their snipe rifles, their flash bangs, their .40 Glock semiautomatics. All the toys. This was what his boys lived for, and he loved them for it.

'Copy, Walter Two. Affirmative on Compromise Authority if the situation moves to Code Green.'

They would protect the president, all right. But not from threats by the towel-heads and survivalists O'Hara was worried about. From the Halden Corwin whom Thorne had warned them would be there. Like Wallberg, Hatfield believed Thorne.

But his men were not facing out and up, as Thorne wanted, but in and down. If Corwin was fool enough to show, he wasn't fool enough to set up beyond five hundred yards out. Hatfield's men would nail him. Hatfield would rub Thorne's nose in the take-down – before he had the bastard deported back to Kenya to rot in prison while Jaeger made sure that the President thought Thorne was in Tsavo.

Hal Corwin would be dead. Thorne would be out of the picture. With the man who would be next Secretary of State as his ally, Terrill Hatfield would be the next Director of the FBI.

22

THORNE WENT IN light: his scope-mounted rifle slung across his back, his binocs hung around his neck, a handful of shells in his coat pocket, his knife and canteen on his belt. He also went in slow. Working his way up the valley between flanking stands of blue spruce, he began to feel that maybe Hatfield was right. No vehicle hidden under the trees. No tire tracks, no footprint, no broken branch. If Corwin wasn't here now, he wasn't coming.

Maybe Thorne could relax a bit. Hatfield, despite all of his obstructionist bullshit, would have his men 750 yards out, scanning the tall crags behind them.

Thorne briefly checked out the bird and animal sign under the reeds edging the pond. Soft-padded mink tracks, pattering mouse tracks, a dozen long-toed coyote tracks beside the cattails with their brown heads just starting to form. Tiny coins of duckweed floating on the surface with their filaments of root trailing down into the water. Pondweed, punched down into the mud by sharp-edged mule deer hoofs…

He stopped dead.

Among the deer tracks, a single human boot print, water seeping into it. The track pointed north, toward that edge of the massif. The direction he had always thought Corwin would take, the direction he had taken himself when scouting sniper sites on the other side of the ridge.

Thorne came erect, scanning the massif. Movement caught his eye, right at the edge of the open ridge face. He fumbled out his binoculars, raised them, adjusted them.

Too late. Nothing. Had there been? Bighorn? Elk? Man?

He began trotting up the rising terrain toward the northern edge of the ridge.

*

Corwin had come in an hour before, also light. Binocs around his neck, canteen and old Smith and Wesson .38 revolver on his hip, cased and loaded rifle over his shoulder, in his pockets his cellphone in a waterproof case to call Janet when it was all over, an empty plastic water bottle, and a roll of masking tape.

Above to his right, the sheer rise of granite; below to his left, a sheer thousand feet of freefall. Out of habit, he checked his backtrial before rounding the northern edge of the massif on those few yards of exposed bare rock.

Someone! He slithered behind a plate of stone, jammed his binoculars to his eyes. The figure by the pond sprang into tight focus, just coming erect, staring up at the rock face, raising his own binocs. Scanning. Now moving. Starting up from the valley floor, coming fast. It was the hunter who had uncovered his practice sites, who had ferreted out Mather's ambush site.

Corwin belly-crawled around to the other side of the ridge, into the cover of the pines, shrubs, and broken expanses of rock, adrenaline pumping. The tracker was at least fifteen years younger than he, hard and fit and fearless. No way to outrun him. He cursed his shortened leg, damaged knee, splinting in his chest.

Corwin took the revolver from his belt, from his anorak pocket took the empty plastic water bottle and the masking tape. He taped the mouth of the bottle over the gun's muzzle.

An unmuffled shot might just carry too far in this thin mountain air despite the fact that his pistol fired a .38 short, a relatively low-powered round without a lot of punch or noise. The plastic bottle would trap the escaping gases of his shot, muffle the sound without impeding the bullet's flight in any way. It was a home-made silencer, good for only one shot, up close.

Thorne went around the end of the massif in a rush, dropped to the ground in thick cover. Waited, panting, for his pulse to slow. The worst kind of a stalk, where you weren't sure the prey was even out there. The movement he had seen from below could have been a deer, a bighorn sheep, a chimera.

But he knew it was Corwin. Dorst had been right. Alison and Eden receded in his interior ladscape, replaced by the need to match himself against this master woodsman, whatever the outcome. He went down through the scattered tree-growth, slowly, silently. Whenever he passed anything that might conceal a man, he scouted the possible ambush from the side before moving on.

Corwin climbed up on a ledge and stood there for two minutes, pistol in hand. Caught a glimpse of distant movement, no shot possible. He had to push it, make it happen. He crossed the stream on a fallen log, deliberately leaving wet footprints on the decaying wood. From the end he leaped into the brush beyond, snapping twigs, rustling leaves, setting up his ambush.

Thorne heard muted snapping and rustling and froze. Moved on downstream. Wet tracks where Corwin had crossed a fallen log to the lower side. Thick growth over there where Corwin would wait for Thorne to cross the log. Still hiding in plain sight.

Thorne crawled away upstream, slowly, silently on splayed elbows and knees. Found a place well out of sight of the log that was narrow enough so he could leap over the rushing water.

He went back downstream on the lower side, moving with the silence of his years in Tsavo, expecting every moment to see some darker shadow in the undergrowth, his Randall Survivor in hand. Bring on the nightmare. But he saw no shadow. No Corwin.

Out-thought again. Anger stifled angst. Boldly he leaped up onto the log to examine the tracks. Yes. They went both ways. Corwin had recrossed to the uphill side, had gotten into the water to wade upstream while Thorne went downstream, the sound of his passage masked by water rattling over pebbles.

Corwin came out of the thigh-deep water in a rush. Rolled into a clump of willows on the down-side bank, crushing them slightly, but not enough, he hoped, to attract notice. He let himself relax, became at one with pale stems and pale leaves. His silenced revolver was ready. A quick shadow flitted by overhead and a Steller's jay landed on a nodding branch over the water, head cocked, staring at him.

Across the stream, the tracker stepped partway out of cover, eyes searching uphill – in the wrong direction. Didn't realize Corwin had recrossed the stream. The ambush had worked.

Corwin pulled the trigger as the jay yelled and fled. The tracker's arms flew wide and his cap flew off as he fell in that unmistakable bag-of-bones way that meant a mortal hit, his rifle clattering on the rocks a dozen feet away.

Corwin had seen it a hundred times: a man couldn't fake a fall like that. He started to wade into the stream to make sure the man was dead. But there was blood on the waxen face, on the rocks under the head, and he was out of time. He melted into the cover on the down-hill side of the noisy torrent.

Thorne came out of it slowly. Shooting pain in his head. He didn't know where he was, had no memory of anything. But his lizard brain down at the base of his skull knew movement might mean death, so he just opened his eyes without moving his head. Above him, sunlight through hardwood branches, pine boughs. Not Panama. Not Africa. Not the desert. The sound of an endless freight train rolling by was a rushing torrent. The mountains.

It was coming back, in fragments. A muted POP like a breaking twig. Ambushed. A home-made silencer, empty soda bottle, water bottle, one shot only. Corwin! How long had he been out? Fifteen, twenty minutes? Why had he been unconscious?

He sat up, slowly. Abominably aching head. His cap was a yard away, his rifle a dozen feet away. Must have thrown his arms wide as he went down. Blood on the rocks. Carefully probing fingers found a flap of loose skin on his forehead. Hit his head as he fell. He looked across the rushing stream. A crushed clump of willows on the other side.

How had Corwin missed at a range of six yards?

Then he heard again the Squawk! and midnight flash of Steller's jay and Yes! More pieces slipped into place. Alerted, he had been letting himself go limp and fall like a dead body even as the slug snatched away his cap. His head hit the rocks, knocked him unconscious. Blood flowed, so he really did look dead. And Corwin hadn't wanted to risk a second, unmuffled shot.

Thorne stood up, dreadfully dizzy, squinched his eyes at his watch. One-eleven. The speech was scheduled for three p.m. Follow the stream down the slope. Hurry!

Corwin dropped awkwardly into his spider hole, unslung the rifle from his shoulder and leaned it against the rock wall still in its carry-case. He rested his butt against the same wall, hands on knees, panting. He was winded but here. Unseen. He reached under the overhang to bring out his tripod and set it up.

He slid his bolt-action model 70 Magnum, made by Winchester in 1951, often called the Rifleman's Rifle, from its worn fleece-lined soft-leather carry case. Its metal was heat-treated to withstand the high temperature of thousand-yard shooting. Already attached was his old tried-and-true Unertl 36-power scope that was nearly as long as the rifle barrel. Already sighted-in.

Finally, he attached the rifle to its tripod. Took out his H & H Magnum shells in .300 caliber with their four-inch-long Sierra 280-grain slugs. He slid a single shell into the chamber. He didn't plan on needing more than one.

Thorne glassed the meadow far below. There were Hatfield's FBI hostage/rescue boys right where they were supposed to be, 750 yards out from the empty podium – facing the wrong way!

And somewhere among those tumbled boulders and sharded granite and twisted pine shrubs above them, between Thorne and the Feebs, was Corwin, prepping his shot. Thorne's self-delusions were gone. He had always known, deep inside, that he would be brought to this. Him or me. Or be Sharon's glass tiger and let the president die.

23

NOT QUITE MUGGING for the cameras, President Gus Wallberg shook hands with Ranger Rick and Sam Jones beside the steel-barred cages that held Smokey and Pooh. He had already chatted and posed with Laura Givens and Sean McLean for the media.

'We'll be opening the cage doors to release the bears when you start your speech, Mr. President,' Ranger Rick explained.

'Wait a minute, wait a minute,' objected Jaeger. 'At the end of his speech, not the beginning.'

Jaeger could just see a pair of grizzly bears charging the podium in the middle of the President's speech and being cut down by automatic weapons fire on the six o'clock evening news.

'We know these two bears really well, sir,' said Rick. 'We'll have to coax them out. The timing will work out.'

Wallberg wasn't so sure. Vicious black deerflies buzzed around them, and he had forgotten that wild things smelled so... well, wild. He gladly started away, encased by a moving diamond of Secret Service agents.

Jaeger had been right. If Corwin was lurking here, he would die. Nothing bad could happen to Wallberg on this day.

Corwin was in the classic prone, the rifle rock-steady on its tripod. He moved his optic almost leisurely across the assemblage in the meadow below. People filled his scope.

The president had just mounted the viewing platform where the governor of Idaho was stepping toward the podium to introduce him. Jaeger waited to the president's right in an almost belligerent pose, Crandall beside him in a similar stance. To Wallberg's left, slightly behind, were his wife and Quarles.

Corwin was in the zone: as he waited for Wallberg to approach the podium, his pulse dropped into the low sixties that he knew from a lifetime of experience gave him his best shots.

This was the shot of that lifetime.

Thorne's only edge was that the most deadly shot, the head-shot, was also the riskiest. The head was highly mobile and the brain was protected by a great deal of bone. Any slight movement, and a high-velocity round fired at distance could ricochet, even miss altogether. Corwin wouldn't risk it. He wouldn't shoot until Wallberg had started his speech, and then it would be a body-mass shot.

But when in the speech? Think, dammit! Of course. Corwin would wait until Wallberg made the gesture any politician on earth made at least once during a speech: turning and raising an arm to shoulder height to gesture. This would expose his underarm. A shot into the underarm vent of the Kevlar protective vest would rake the chest and explode the heart.

And where was Corwin? At 950 yards? At 1,195 yards? At 1,210 yards? Or at some site Thorne had never even considered? As Morengaru had taught him, he closed his eyes to look through the tracks to the animal he was stalking. Here, he was stalking himself. Where would he fire from?

He opened his eyes. If he had Corwin's genius behind the gun, he would take his shot from 1,210 yards out.

Thorne scrambled down through the rocks, rifle in hand, striving for speed and silence at the same time. He was staking everything on a tumble of boulders about a hundred yards above the 1,200 yard ravine where he now believed Corwin was hidden.

Corwin's breathing slowed. He moved his scope across the assemblage one more time, then back to his target. Everything fell away. Against all conventional wisdom, he would shoot just as Wallberg started his speech, and it would be a head shot.

*

The rangers slid up the steel barred cage doors. The bears were suspicious. Yes, over there was the forest, and freedom, but what if this were just another of the humans' tricks?

Jaeger stared out over the crowd, but saw only Nisa Mather. His sexual obsession hadn't ended with her death. Sharkey in L.A. would find him a woman who at least superficially resembled her, a woman he could possess phsyically, repeatedly, could bend to his will as he never could bend Nisa while she was alive.

Gus Wallberg looked out over the meadow, over the bears in their cages at the edge of the forest, over the faces upturned below him. But he saw only the millions of people at their TV screens that night. He felt the same surge of power he had felt when giving his acceptance speech, in his gut and in his groin, felt what sex was supposed to give him but never had. He lusted for their power, they offered it, he took it. Now it was his.

'My fellow Americans, today we begin a grand journey...'

Thorne dropped to his right knee, brought up his rifle, released the safety, sat back on his right foot and braced his left elbow on his left knee, his upper arm jammed into the kneecap just above the elbow. He began taking controlled breaths to slow his pulse. He looked through the optic. There he was!

But Christ! In the scope, Corwin was taking up trigger slack! He was going for the head shot even as Wallberg started speaking! Thorne's finger contracted ever so gently against the six ounces of slack in the trigger pull. The rifle bucked in his hands, and even before it steadied again he knew he had made his shot. But in the exact micro-second he had fired, Corwin's rifle also had recoiled. He had gotten off his shot, too.

As Corwin's rifle recoiled he was struck a great blow in the side. No pain, not yet: just the dizzying sensation of a giant fist swung against him. He had felt it all before, eighteen months ago. Then, Mather.

Now, the tracker, not dead after all, had done him. So what? He had seen the red mist. The halo of blood around the ruined head. Nothing else mattered.

He crawled in a half-circle like a stepped-on landcrab, to face the rear of the V and the life-saving torrent. He was already going into shock, but he would make it. The stream would carry him down, far away from all pursuit forever.

Thorne paused to momentarily scope the scene below. Men shouting, women screaming, Secret Service agents springing to the platform. Smokey and Pooh, terrified by the noise, smashing out of their open cages and charging toward the forest and freedom.

The forest Rangers were making motions as if to draw their sidearms, but by presidential fiat they were unarmed this day. The students were slapping high-fives: the bears were free.

People were milling on the platform around the man lying on the planks with little of his head left.

Corwin was in the burn again on that icy November night, crawling for the cabin a thousand feet away. Blood stained the earth beneath his turtle-slow body at each movement. Dark, rich blood. Arterial blood? If so... No. He would make it. Get into the icy water so it would stop the bleeding...

Dead men. So many great shots. So many dead men.

Terry. Laughing with him in front of the fireplace on Marshall Avenue while Nisa, age ten, lay on the floor swathed in a blanket, watching TV cartoons.

Nisa, an adult, dead herself. No! No...

Crawl. Would the tracker get to him before he could get to the rushing torrent? His vision dimmed. Tired. Drop your head into the dirt. No. Crawl. Arm. Leg. Again. Again. He was trying to float up out of his body. No! Just a few feet now... He had done it all before.

Thorne covered the last twenty yards in one sustained rush and slide to drop down into the sniper's nest, like running the half-frozen scree on Mount Kenya far above the tree line. Corwin's gun was still in place. Away from it, going toward the stream, crawl-marks etched in blood. Like the scrabble of just-born turtles in the Seychelles, heading for the sea once they had broken from their shells and crawled up out of the warm sand.

At the very point of the V was Corwin, an arm moving feebly, a knee flexing, pushing. Trying to reach the stream. To escape. Except that he was already dead.

Crunch of boots. The tracker. Corwin found the strength to turn his head. He could see the man looming over him even though the light was dimming. No matter. He would soon be away, free, where they could never touch him.

Thorne knelt down, leaned in so his face was close. Corwin was deathly pale, dirt and blood were smeared across his features. He was trying to speak. A murmur. A whisper.

'You, me… we are…' The voice trailed off. Then, another great effort. '…the same man…'

Thorne said coldly, 'I didn't murder my daughter.'

'I…' Corwin stopped, his voice choking off.

Dead? No, Goddammit! Thorne had a sudden cruel need to take everything from Corwin, to send him on his way shorn of any smallest shred of triumph.

'Corwin!' he barked. The eyes opened. 'Here's something for you to take with you through the wall. You missed.'

Blood dripping from Corwin's slack mouth outlined his teeth in red like the teeth of a Halloween warlock. Then, he grinned.

And asked, very distinctly, 'Did I?'

He thrust with a foot, rolled over into the rushing water. Thorne caught a boot heel for a microsecond, then it was jerked from his grasp by the stream, and Corwin was gone. He stood up slowly, exhausted, silently mouthing Corwin's final words.

Did I?

Thorne's world had just been turned upside down.

PART TWO

Thorne

It is no crime to lose
your way in a dark wood.
Ovid, *Metamorphoses*

24

WITHIN HOURS, THE headlines would shout it: WALLBERG
SAFE CHIEF OF STAFF KURT JAEGER KILLED WOULD-BE
PRESIDENTIAL ASSASSIN SHOOTS WRONG MAN

Gustave Wallberg and First Lady Edith Wallberg sat side-by-side
in their luxurious aisle seats on Air Force One, unabashedly holding
hands. For security reasons, there were no accompanying newsmen,
thus no one to make public their private closeness.

For Edith, it was easy. Gus had cheated on her with Nisa Corwin,
but she had stifled her anger and hurt and jealousy and had never
spoken out, and the affair had ended. Now he was for her alone,
alive, to become one of America's great Presidents.

For Wallberg, not so easy. He had been terrified and was still
shaky. It was only because some mountain wind had blown a tiny
hurtling bit of lead a couple of feet off course that the shot meant for
his chest had exploded another man's head.

Beyond any normal survival guilt was the fact he was relieved that
Kurt was dead. He had been forced to make Jaeger his Chief of Staff,
and next term would have had to make him Secretary of State.
Because on election night…

He could see the two of them vividly, knee-to-knee in straight-
back chairs in the disused ballroom on the roof of the Beverly Hills
Marquis. Like that famous photo of Jack and Bobby in a similar
pose. Kurt was talking, using his hands.

'Corwin must already be on his way to the Delta.'

How had Corwin even found them? Wallberg wondered.

'What if we do nothing? That might solve—'

'True, they wouldn't be around to talk to the media, Governor. But
Corwin would be.' He leaned closer. 'I know a man here in L.A. who
can make all of this… go away.'

There it was: his bargain with the devil that had put him in Kurt Jaeger's ambitious hands. But what else could he have done? Sometimes individual deaths had to serve the greater good.

'Mr. President? I have that preliminary report.'

Shayne O'Hara was sliding into the seat across the aisle from him. Just as quickly, Edith slipped by her husband's knees.

'I'll just leave you men to it.'

When she was out of earshot, O'Hara said, 'The FBI and my Secret Service agents have initiated a security sweep of the survivalists and ranchers on the list of those vocally opposed to the release of grizzlies into the Bitterroot Wilderness Area.'

Wallberg had to remember that the conventional FBI and the Secret Service were paddling around over there in the lilypads, chasing terrorists domestic and foreign, not knowing that it was no terrorist, but Hal Corwin, who had tried and failed.

'Our other main focus is of course Al-Queda. They could have used a mercenary from some former Iron Curtain country as their assassin. If they did, we'll quickly vector in on him.'

'Ahh… Who's handling the on-site investigation?'

O'Hara leaned back; for the first time, his heavy red features were almost relaxed. The buck was about to get passed.

'We know the shot came from up on the eastern rock face. Hatfield insisted that he and his Hostage/Rescue lads cover it. It makes sense. They are highly trained, and they were already up on the mountain.'

Out of shape from all of those Washington months, Hatfield hauled himself up, panting, to an open rocky V that was shielded from below by scrub pines. Just another possible site, this one impossibly far out. He jerked his Glock from its holster before realizing that the man squatting with his back against the smooth rock wall was Thorne, not Corwin. Thorne looked exhausted, drained. His hair was wet, as was his shirt down to mid-chest. A Winchester Model 70 rifle rested butt-down on the ground between his knees, the muzzle pointing up past his left ear.

Hatfield's voice was squeaky with adrenaline.

'What in the fuck are you doing here?'

'I've been on site since I left D.C., but what difference does it make? Wallberg is still alive, no thanks to you.'

'My men were in place seven hundred-fifty yards out—'

'Facing the wrong way. You assholes maybe, just maybe, if any of you can shoot for shit, could have killed the bears from there. You sure as hell couldn't have killed Corwin. I did.'

'Where's the body?'

'In the stream.'

Hatfield was enraged. He wanted to smash Thorne over the head with a gunbutt, but refrained. Refrained from calling in the rest of his team, too. At the moment, only Thorne – and soon, he – would know what had really gone down here. He wanted to keep it that way if he could.

So he went looking, prowling the little V-shaped ravine, noting the rifle on its tripod, the laborious blood trail back to the noisy torrent rushing by. A lot of blood. It looked arterial to him. But still…

He returned to Thorne. 'Again. Where's his fucking body?'

'I told you, in the stream. He looked dead, but when I started to check his vitals, he rolled into the water.'

'So you don't know he's dead, you just think he's dead.'

For the first time, Thorne showed emotion. 'He's dead, dead, fucking dead, Hatfield. And I killed him. Another five years of lousy dreams.'

'We'll bring in the bloodhounds—'

'Bring in whoever you want. Maybe they'll find him. Or maybe' – he gave a grim chuckle – 'those bears they just released will find him first. I took him in the chest cavity – what the Rangers call a target-rich environment. There's so much in there to mess up. Heart, kidneys, arteries – hit any of them, the target suffers an immediate and catastrophic loss of blood. Same with the liver if my shot took him lower down. Unconscious in ten seconds, dead in fifteen.'

Hatfield was stubborn. 'He got to the stream and went in.'

'So, a lung shot. It would incapacitate him but might not kill him right away.'

Hatfield wanted to show his own expertise. 'Sometimes they survive a lung shot even without treatment.'

'Maybe so, but hypothermia would kill him before the stream took him a hundred yards.' Thorne repeated, 'He's fucking dead, Hatfield, and I wish he wasn't.' He made a weary gesture. 'Fuck it. Wallberg's alive, so I'm getting out of here and—'

'You're going into federal custody to face a board of inquiry into why you didn't fire a warning shot when you realized Corwin was here on this mountain.'

'You sure that's what you want, Hatfield? Right now, nobody knows I was here except you. If I keep my mouth shut, who is to say who took out the man who tried to kill the president?'

Hatfield hid his elation. The damn fool was going to hand it all to him. He asked casually, 'Where have you been staying?'

'The Super 8 in Hamilton. Under my own name.'

'You've got some balls, I'll give you that.'

Thorne pushed himself erect against the rock face. 'I've still got to hike up over this mountain and down the other side before dark. I left my rental car there.'

He started away, but Hatfield caught his forearm.

'You weren't here today, get it? You aren't in Montana. You're in Fort Benning. Just go to your motel in Hamilton and stay there.' He let go of Thorne's arm. 'I'll make my report to the President at Camp David. If there are no leaks of your presence here in the meantime, I'll send you a one-way ticket, coach, to Nairobi. Do we have a deal?'

'Deal.'

'Leave the rifle.'

He wanted it to match up with any slug they might find in the ravine, but Thorne said, indifferent, 'Sure, except how do you explain Corwin's having two Model 70s on site?'

He left with the rifle. Hatfield called his team to come up and join him.

When they arrived, panting, Baror asked, 'Where's Corwin?'

'Dead. I shot him just as he shot at the President. He crawled to the stream and rolled in just as I got here.'

'Should we bring in the bloodhounds?' asked Perry.

'You bet. We want that body. Now let's secure the scene.' He took Franklin and Greene aside. 'I just got word that Thorne flew into Montana this afternoon. He's staying at the Super 8 Motel in Hamilton.'

Walt Greene squawked, 'I thought he was at Fort Benning.'

Hatfield looked quickly around. Nobody else had heard.

'Go to a motel close to his where you can monitor the shit out of him. Where he goes, what he does, who he talks to. He's driving a rental car, I don't know what kind. Ray, I want a GPS transmitter on that vehicle soonest. Walt, I want his phone bugged and miniaturized transmitters in everything he's not wearing – his luggage, his clothes – everything.'

Franklin asked, inevitably, 'Personal surveillance?'

'Electronic only, for now. We don't want him to have any idea we're monitoring him. Don't go cowboy on me, guys.'

'Shit,' said Franklin. 'He walks away free and clear?'

'Flies away.' Hatfield couldn't help grinning at them. 'But not free and clear, believe me.'

25

Did I?

The voice whispering in Thorne's memory brought him up from a light and troubled sleep. The covers were swirled around his waist, he was pouring sweat. Christ, the dead Corwin couldn't come crowding into his nightmares along with the dead Alison and the dead Eden. Just couldn't.

He sat up against the headboard, squinted at the green digital numerals of the bedside clock. Four-thirty a.m. For the first time he regretted registering at the motel under his own name. But still, if there were no leaks that he was here in Montana, he could be on a flight to Kenya within a few days.

Hatfield would have his glory, Thorne would have his bad dreams. A lousy exchange, but back in Tsavo, with time, the dreams would cease. He'd have his small life back. He had killed yet again, and Jaeger was also dead. But the president was still alive. Mission accompolished. Sort of. Except…

Did I?

Thorne pulled a chair over to the window, sat staring out.

Did Corwin mean that literally? Or, dying, just did not want to believe that he had missed, that Wallberg was still alive? It made no sense that Corwin would want to kill Jaeger.

A bulky man carrying a small valise was silhouetted by the street light as he crossed the parking lot toward a Ford sedan by the office. A mongrel with an ear flopped down over one eye like a beret crossed in front of him. The man aimed a boot at it. Yipping, the dog avoided the kick, a matador avoiding the horn.

Thorne let his thoughts slip into the void, as Myamoto Musashi, the great Samurai swordsman, had called it. Could Corwin conceivably have survived as Hatfield had feared? It had been a steel-jacketed bullet, not a hollow-point, it might have passed right through his body, missing all the vital organs...

No. The man was dead. Thorne's own bad dreams told him that. Hatfield would come through with the airplane ticket, and official confirmation that Thorne was free to go back to Kenya. He told himself that's what he wanted: to be well out of it.

Hatfield was driving his golf cart from the Camp David heliport to the President's cabin when his pager vibrated. He pulled over, punched the number into his cellphone.

'Hatfield.'

Doug Greene's voice said, 'The phone bug is in place, and the transmitters are in Thorne's clothes and luggage.'

'What about the GPS?'

'Ray put it under Thorne's rented Cherokee before dawn this morning. At eleven a.m., the vehicle became stationary at a family-style restaurant on highway 93 five miles north of town.'

'Okay. Good work, both of you. Keep it up.'

Getting out of the Cherokee, Thorne stopped dead. The motel parking lot, 4:30 that morning, the asshole who tried to kick the dog on his way to a Ford Crown Victoria sedan. And the Crown Vic's interior light had not gone on, an old security trick to keep anyone from seeing the driver's face.

Thorne had not parked beside the blank back wall of the Bounding Elk Restaurant because he wanted to hide his presence there, but because tradecraft died hard. If Hatfield had bugged his car, he had to know, without Hatfield knowing he knew. Just in case something deeper than Hatfield's paranoia was going on.

Thorne got his flashlight out of the glovebox, found a flattened cardboard box in the dumpster, and laid it on the ground beside the Cherokee as a makeshift mechanic's Rollerboy. Using his heels, he slid himself under the car.

His flashlight found two small, square devices, lashed together with duct tape, attached by a magnet to the car's frame below the driver's seat: a satellite receiver, and a CelluLink transmitter with a snub antenna for the monitoring station's connection. Strung along the undercarriage to the back of the vehicle, a power wire for the GPS antenna. Thorne had studied a similar device ten years ago while training at the Farm.

He slid back out. He had been under for less than two minutes. It took him another minute to spot the miniature wafer-thin GPS disk antenna set behind the rear bumper. It would be in a direct line with a communications satellite above.

A bug on his car meant a bug on his motel room phone, too.

The usual suspects were seated around the table in the spacious front room of the presidential cabin at Camp David. Hatfield, there to report, Wallberg, his yes-men Quarles and Crandall, and, hovering in the background, Johnny Doyle.

Wallberg said, 'Let's all bow our heads for a minute of silent prayer for Kurt Jaeger, a brave man who gave his life for his country.' He soon raised his head and intoned, 'Amen.'

Hatfield stood up, thankful for the prayer. He wanted to subtly invoke Jaeger's specter: He is dead, Mr. President, and you are alive, because of one man: me, Terrill Hatfield.

He began his report.

'Halden Corwin took his shot at twelve-hundred yards out from an improvised sniper's nest on the eastern slope overlooking the meadow.' He did not remind them that Thorne had originally proposed this scenario. 'I killed him before he could kill you.'

Wallberg had dropped ten years. 'The details, man!'

'I caught a glint of metal at the narrow mouth of a V-shaped ravine, so I worked my way up within a hundred yards of it. And there was Corwin, just about to shoot. He got off his round, Mr. President, but my simultaneous body-mass hit knocked his aim off. He had just enough life left in him to roll into a mountain stream rushing down the hillside behind his sniper nest and be swept away.'

'Enough life left to roll into the stream!' There was a rising note of rage, perhaps mixed with panic, in the president's voice. 'Without a body, you don't know a damned thing!'

'Mr... President... he... is... dead. I made the standard take-out shot, under the arm and into the chest cavity. The crawl trail to the creek showed heavy blood-loss. Preliminary FBI Lab DNA tests confirm that it is Corwin's blood. Coupled with the wound, the shock of the icy water killed him within minutes, perhaps seconds.'

'You don't know that! What's the usual procedure here? Infra-red fly-overs, a massive sweep... manpower...'

He paused. He was a politician, not a manhunter. Hatfield slid into the silence easily.

'In this kind of situation, Mr. President, bloodhounds. They miss nothing. And I already have them on site. I'm sorry I wasn't in time to save Chief of Staff Jaeger, but Hal Corwin is dead. The bloodhounds will find his remains.'

He paused, wanting to dissipate the tension in the room, then took a chance, and stole Thorne's off-hand remark.

'Unless Smokey and Winnie the Pooh find him first.'

There were several chuckles around the table; even Wallberg had to crack a smile.

It had worked. He had gotten past the fact he had no body to offer to the president. And he knew that once Gus Wallberg got back behind his desk, the issue of Corwin's body would soon fade from the man's memory even if they never found it.

Victory Number Two: Brendan Thorne was not even mentioned.

Thorne took a stroll around Hamilton, killing time until he heard something from Hatfield. When he got back to the motel, he checked at the desk for messages. None. The toothpick he had lodged between the frame and the bottom edge of the room's door was still there. Since finding the transmitter, he felt as if he were living in a glass house with the interior spotlights turned on. He lay down on the bed. In stasis.

*

'Shit,' said Ray Franklin. The QuikTrak historical data file showed that Thorne's Jeep Cherokee hadn't moved since he had gotten back from breakfast. Right now, Thorne was being a good boy: but he had a nasty surprise waiting for him. Hatfield had promised them that.

The phone interrupted his thoughts. It was the front desk. A package had just been delivered by messenger.

The fist Thorne had been awaiting pounded on the door. It could only be Ray Franklin – and was. Behind him was a short, chubby agent with avid killer's eyes who had to be Franklin's partner, Walt Greene. It would have taken both of them to bug his car and his phone as quickly as they had. He let none of this show in his eyes.

'I hope you guys have something for me.'

Greene was darting his own eyes around the room, like maybe he hoped to find Thorne hiding a scantily-clad underage girl there. Franklin thrust a bulky sealed envelope at Thorne.

'Yeah, Special Agent Hatfield instructed us to give this to you.' He paused. 'Meanwhile, from me, fuck you.'

Thorne didn't answer. Just took the envelope and closed the door. Inside the envelope was his severance paycheck from the FBI, and a one-way ticket, Dulles International to Nairobi International, in four days' time.

He lay back down on the bed in a totally different mood. Tomorrow he would reserve his D.C. flight; they hadn't bothered to include a reservation for that. Fine by him. Gave him time to maybe get down to Fort Benning for a quick goodbye meeting with Victor Blackburn. In D.C., he could see Sharon Dorst and tell her how it had all worked out.

Because he wasn't planning to ever return to the States from Tsavo. Tsavo! The nightmares would gradually slack off as they had done seven years ago, his life would resume as he had wanted it to.

Then why did going back feel like some sort of defeat?

26

AT MIDNIGHT, A yawning Thorne turned into North First. He'd overpoured, as airline stewardesses used to say when they'd had too much to drink. He wished it had been Tusker beer – or better yet, pombe, home-made from maize, that packed a kick like a mule. But Miller had done the job: it had made him realize that even though he had his life back, he didn't really care.

Did anybody? Hey! Squealer Kemoli, the magistrate who had been so reluctant to sign his deportation papers, he cared. Morengaru, he cared. Thorne checked his watch. Mid-morning in Nairobi. He found a payphone beside a closed gas station, and used the phonecard he had bought when he'd realized his motel room phone was bugged. Squealer Kemoli himself answered his office phone on its second ring.

'Arthur Kemoli.'

'Squealer! I'm flying to Nairobi in a few days and—'

'No. You are not.' Kemoli switched abruptly to Swahili. 'They will be at the airport waiting for the rhino-horn poacher.'

Thorne went into his room without bothering to check for intruders. In a way, they were already inside. It was over. He was out of options. He stripped, took a long hot shower, ended with cold, as cold as he could stand it, then sat down to stare out at the parking lot.

Then he got it. Hatfield had put out the word. They were just waiting for him to go back to Nairobi, where he would be arrested, convicted, and jailed on the phony charges Hatfield had set up. In an African jail, he'd have the life expectancy of a fruit fly. He would never get a chance to change his mind and tell anyone he had killed Corwin and saved the president. Neat and nasty.

What if he didn't go back? Then they would gather him up and fold him away in some terrorist-detention cell of Hatfield's choosing in the sacred name of National Security. Or worse yet, stick him in some mental institution.

He got into bed, still maybe a little drunk. His eyes drifted shut. Against their lids, Tsavo's old bull elephants browsed and trumpeted. Morengaru squatted by a trail, grinning as he pointed out a shifta's footprint in the dust.

A cammo-clad drug dealer lay face-down on a jungle path in Panama, blood pooling around her. He turned her over. She was Alison. Dead. Underneath her was Eden. Dead.

He looked down at the dying man and said, 'You missed.'

Corwin's teeth were a warlock's, outlined in blood. He asked, 'Did I?'

Thorne came bursting up from sleep yelling, 'DID YOU?'

He sat on the edge of the bed, panting, shivering even though sweat was pouring off him. His only defense was to find out what Corwin's last words had meant. Who had Corwin been? Not what some file said, but who had he been? Why had he done what he did, why had the president's men from the git-go so desperately wanted him dead?

Where to start? Easy. Find the motel where Corwin had been staying. There were just a few little towns in the semi-wilderness country on the Idaho side of Trapper's Peak. Corwin would have written down his vehicle description and license for the clerk. A vehicle he would have hidden for a quick getaway somewhere within, say, a five-mile radius of the valley up which he had gone to kill Wallberg. The car would still be there. If Thorne could find it, maybe something in it would point to the truth about who Corwin really had been.

Some knowledge that might give Thorne a razor-thin edge.

Lemhu. Tendoy. Baker. Salmon. Shoup. North Fork. Gibbonsville. Tiny Idaho towns within striking distance for Corwin. But only Salmon had any accommodations listed with Triple-A. Of Salmon's three choices, the Motel Deluxe, the cheapest of them, was downtown, with access to cafes and shops.

If Thorne's motel-room phone was bugged, anything not currently on his person by now would have miniaturized transmitters planted in it also. The Cherokee was transmitting its location constantly. If Thorne removed the equipment they would know it. But during his stroll downtown yesterday, he had noted an old clapboard house with its garage converted into a one-man auto-repair shop. Just the kind of place he needed.

Today, he took half an hour to wander those few blocks, using store windows to check his backtrail. Nobody behind him. Parked in the driveway was a new Chevy Silverado with a pair of deer rifles on the rear-window rack. Inside the garage, a husky blond kid in his mid-twenties pulled a grease-smeared face out from under the open hood of an '02 Ford F-150 pickup.

'I need transportation,' said Thorne. 'Something four-wheel and offroad.'

'They got a Hertz and an Avis here in town.'

'I don't like car rental outfits. I don't like credit cards. I like cash.' Thorne took out his roll. 'Like this.'

Up close, the kid smelled of sweat and motor oil and cigarette smoke. He kept wiping his hands on a greasy red rag he took from the back pocket of his coveralls, over and over again, staring at Thorne's roll as if mesmerized by it.

'I've got a '94 Dodge Dakota four-wheel out back. Thirty-a-day, $500 security deposit, pay for your own gas.'

'Five-hundred? A ninety-four?'

The blond kid grinned. 'Three-fifty.' He paused. 'Back country. Off-road. It ain't hunting season, and some terrorist fuck took a shot at the President of the United States down by the Bitterroot ridge a couple of days ago. Wouldn't be that you're some sort of journalist, would it?'

'Wouldn't be.'

The kid stuck out a hand. 'Andy Farrell.'

'Brendan Thorne. I'll tell you tonight whether I'll need your Dakota tomorrow too.'

'I usually eat dinner at The Spice of Life on Second Street. You can get me there. They close up at nine o'clock.'

Thorne turned in at the Motel Deluxe on Salmon's Church Street. He flashed his badge and commission card with the FBI seal on it at the dark chunky woman behind the desk. Although they now were outlawed, his 'creds' worked like a dream. He asked the woman about any man who had stayed there for a week or so, maybe left before dawn two days ago.

She already had the old-fashioned sign-in register open flat on the desk and was turning pages. 'You got a name?'

'Hal Corwin?'

'No Corwin. We did have a guy reserved for two weeks, then checked out early.' She turned the register, pointed to an entry. 'Hal Fletcher. As in arrow-maker. My people know about fletching arrows. He the loony tried to shoot the President?'

'A person of interest,' said Thorne.

'He sure wasn't any sort of an Ay-rab. He seemed a nice guy, too. In his fifties, lean, sorta tall, looked like he spent a lot of time outdoors. Had a limp.' She smiled at a memory. 'He played catch with our son in the parking lot every evening.'

'What was he driving?'

She checked the register again. 'Nineteen-ninety 4-Runner. California license 5-c-w-d-o-4-6. I 'member it as dark green.'

Andy Farrell was having a beer at a table by the window when Thorne got to The Spice of Life. The blond hair had been washed, he'd switched to slacks and a sport shirt and a windbreaker and was having a cheeseburger and fries and a Caesar salad. A skinny twenty-year-old waitress with hair dyed bright scarlet and a ring through her lower lip was flirting with him. Thorne slid into the chair across the table from him.

'They only got beer and wine here,' said Andy almost apologetically, as if he were the host and Thorne was a guest.

'All I need is a cup of coffee.'

Andy waved at the waitress. 'I eat here because they use organic greens and veggies, and their burgers are damn good.'

Thorne grinned and jerked his head toward the waitress.

'And here I thought maybe she had something to do with it.'

Andy's face flamed almost as scarlet as the girl's hair. When she came with Thorne's coffee, Andy asked for apple pie a-la-mode for dessert. Thorne did too. After the table had been cleared, Andy leaned across it to speak in a low voice.

'I been thinking, you ain't no newsman.'

'Said I wasn't. Maybe I'm one of those alphabet-soup guys from the government. You're a hunter, right?'

'How'd you know that?'

'The gunrack in your Silverado. Since you hunt, you must know the back country around here pretty well.'

'Try me.'

'Okay. Below the western side of the ridge above the meadow where the President gave his speech, there's a sub-alpine valley. Do you know it? I need to find a—'

Andy exclaimed, 'Jesus Christ! The bastard went up that valley to the massif, didn't he? He wasn't any Muslim, he had to be a local who knew the terrain.'

'Knew the terrain, yeah. Local, no. Now, if he needed to stash a four-wheel SUV within a five-mile radius of that valley so he could get out of Dodge quick, where would he put it?'

Andy stood up, said, 'Be right back,' and left the cafe. He came back with a topo map from his truck. He opened it out on the table-top, tapped a finger on one of its squiggles.

'See that minor national-park road right there? I'd look up any one of those little dirt tracks going off of it.'

'You should have my job.' Thorne stood up. 'If I'm not back with the truck within a couple of days, you'll find it hidden under that stand of fir trees at the mouth of the valley. The keys will be on the left front tire. Will the security deposit cover going over there and getting your truck back?'

'Christ yes, more than. But...' He paused. 'I'd sure like to be in on whatever it is you're doing, Mr. Thorne.'

Thorne shrugged and grimaced. 'I wish you could, Andy. I'd feel comfortable with you covering my back. But...'

'I know,' said Andy, crestfallen. 'National Security.'

Thorne scattered too much money on the table. 'My treat.' He stuck out his hand. They shook. Before he knew he was going to say it, he added, 'I kill people for the government, Andy.'

'I figured maybe you did,' said Andy solemnly.

Walking out of the place, Thorne thought, Maybe that'll be my epitaph: he killed people for the government. Maybe, in this case, the wrong person?

Corwin's 4-Runner was the key to everything. If Thorne couldn't find it, he'd painted himself into a corner and would just have to flat-out go on the run. He had to believe that if he found it, he would find something to point toward something he could use as leverage against Hatfield's scheming.

In the morning he walked up the street for breakfast, came back, and used the room phone to make a reservation to fly Northwest from Missoula to Minneapolis the next night, then on to D.C. Give the Feebs something to chew on.

For the same reason, he drove the Cherokee and Franklin's GPS transmitter to the Ravalli County Museum in the old county court-house on Bedford Street. If they bothered to track him there, they would figure he was just killing time.

He let a collection of American Indian artifacts fascinate him for an hour, then went out the ground-floor men's room window, leaving it unlocked, and went shopping. To buy more time, he needed to give Hatfield something tough to explain away.

In a variety of stores, he bought underwear, shirts, socks, a water-proof pouch to use as a wallet, two pairs of pants and one warm jacket, shaving gear, a pair of shoes and a pair of ankle-length boots, a belt. He also bought a wood rasp, Providene-Iodine 10% topical antiseptic microbicide, gauze bandages and adhesive tape, and thin opaque medical gloves. At the last minute, he bought two more $10 phone cards. They could be traced but it took time. He paid cash for everything. At the bank, he cashed the FBI's severance check, and drew out his day's limit of cash on his ATM card. After today, his money belt would have to see him through.

Everything fit into two grocery shopping bags he left under the men's room window at the museum while he hauled himself back up inside. He walked sedately out the front door, drove around to pick up his purchases, and went back to the motel. No messages on the phone. No intrusions into the room. He hadn't expected any. They were so damn sure of him, like his FBI taggers in D.C., that he felt only contempt for them. And anger.

He paid through the next day, telling the room clerk not to bother making up the room in the morning, and put out the DO NOT DISTURB sign before going to bed.

27

THORNE ROLLED OUT at four a.m., silently tore up the bed, laid a lamp on its side, and tipped over a chair. His cash was in his money belt, his money clip was on the dresser with a few bucks in it, along with his keys and watch, the FBI badge, and the wallet that held his i.d. and driver,s license. His passport was hidden in his suitcase where they were sure to find it.

He left the clothes he had worn the day before tossed over the room's still-upright chair, left his shoes with yesterday's socks stuffed in them under it. He also left all his old clothes in the dresser right where they were, and left his suitcase in the closet. He would carry no miniature bugs away with him.

He put on new socks and the new boots, then dropped the shopping bag with his new shaving kit and his extra new clothes on the grass below the rear window. With gloved hands, he quietly broke the glass inward and artistically scattered shards of it around on the floor.

Only then did he draw the wood rasp across his forehead and let blood splatter around the room and on the window sill. After he disinfected and bandaged the cut, he put on his money belt and dressed from the skin out in his new clothes.

A two-step run, and he dove through the glassless window, tucking and rolling as he hit the grassy slope behind his room. He waited. No window opened, no lights went on, no pale blob of face looked out at him. When they came to clean the room the following morning, they would find what looked like a murder scene, and call the cops, who would be all over the crime-scene before Hatfield could close things down.

Thorne went through the woods to Andy's Dakota four-by-four parked two blocks away. In his waterproof pouch was his new i.d.:

driver's license, social security card, library card (expired), and three unemployment benefit payment stubs. All of them legal and valid, all identifying him as one Benjamin Schutz: Benny the Boozer's full and real name. Also in the pouch was his FBI commission card. He hoped he wouldn't have to use it. Not because someone would challenge it – how many civilians knew what FBI credentials looked like? – but because eventually it would get back to Hatfield that the card was in play. Once that happened, the noose would tighten.

The wood rasp, bandaids, disinfectant, and surgeon's gloves went into three different dumpsters on his way out of town.

An hour later, he ran Andy's Dodge Dakota in under the firs at the mouth of the valley, and left the keys on the tire. Carrying his shopping bag, he walked northwest on the national park service road Andy had pointed out, checking out the dirt tracks going off on either side. No vehicle passed him, not one.

Four miles north of the valley, he followed a barely-visible abandoned logging trace. A quarter-mile in, he found a single truck tire track in a patch of hardened mud. No more tracks, but a heavy vehicle's passage was marked by broken twigs and matted-down grass for another quarter-mile.

In the thick underbrush under the pines, where it would be well-hidden from the road and invisible from the air, was a dark green 4-Runner. He pulled away the fragrant fir boughs and checked the license number: California 5 CWD 046. A current registration-month sticker on the license plate, a previous year's sticker under that. It was Corwin's car.

The keys were stashed in front of the left rear tire. It had a full tank of gas and fired up immediately. He rifled the glove box. Maps and a flashlight, the manual, paper napkins. Then he remembered that in California, a vehicle's registration and insurance papers were usually stowed behind the sun visor on the driver's side. They were there, and they were electrifying.

The truck was registered to a Janet Kestrel, c/o Mrs. Edie Melendez at an address in an L.A. suburb. A woman could explain the months when Corwin dropped out of sight. A lover, travelling with him? An assassin who helped him plan the Delta murders?

Whoever she was, she was the real, solid lead Thorne had been hoping for. If he could find her. He got back to Highway 93, then drove north toward I-20 to get out of Idaho as soon as possible. At Spokane, Washington, he would get another interstate that would take him south toward California.

Crandall laid the Hamilton *Daily News* on Wallberg's desk in the Oval Office, folded so the pertinent below-the-fold headline was prominent: MYSTERIOUS DISAPPEARANCE FROM LOCAL HOTEL

Wallberg read the article as if the newspaper were a poisonous viper writhing toward him across his desk.

'When did this happen?'

'Two days ago, Mr. President. It cycled routinely to Shayne O'Hara because of the town's proximity to the attempted assassination site, then routinely from his office to us.'

'Set up a meeting with Hatfield, ASAP.'

'Talk to me,' snapped the President.

Hatfield was literally on the carpet, standing at attention in front of the President's massive hardwood desk in the Oval Office. He had not been asked to sit down.

'Mr. President, as you know, when we dismissed Thorne at Camp David he was to await further orders at the Mayflower Hotel. Instead, he left word that he was going to Fort Benning, Georgia, to spend a couple of days with an old Ranger buddy.'

'Did he know his return to Kenya was all arranged?'

'I sent the ticket to the Mayflower myself.'

'You checked on the Fort Benning angle, of course.'

'A room had been reserved in the BOQ by his buddy, but Thorne never showed. Victor Blackburn is career Army, he would not jeopardize his pension by covering for Thorne. They haven't seen each other for ten years. In fact, he's just pissed off.'

Wallberg frowned. 'What have we learned in Montana?'

'Franklin and Greene have taken over the investigation from the locals. Everything of Thorne's was left behind. Everything. Rental car, keys, his FBI badge, his money clip with cash in it, his wallet, shaving gear, i.d., clothes, luggage. We found his passport hidden behind the lining of his suitcase. The room's rear window was broken inward, and a great deal of blood was splattered around. Our lab is rushing the DNA testing, but it almost certainly is Thorne's blood.'

'Could it have been… Corwin?' It was a half-whisper.

'Mr. President, Corwin is dead.' Hatfield leaned across the desk, ebony features intense. He had practiced this move in the mirror. 'But Thorne is alive. It was a non-lethal amount of blood spattered around. Non-lethal, Mr. President. And one vital piece of identification was not recovered from that room.'

Wallberg was staring at him. 'Which is?'

'His commission card with the FBI seal on it. Don't you see, sir? He left his badge behind but took the card.' Hatfield let the tension build, then sat down abruptly, unbidden. Franklin's quick work had given him time to force his tame psychiatrist, Sharon Dorst, to give him the ammunition he needed. 'The psychiatrist who did Thorne's inital fitness evaluation noted a strong identification with Corwin. They are a generation apart, but as you know, their profiles are extremely similar.'

Wallberg was shaken. 'Meaning that the identification is so strong that Thorne is going to start stalking—'

'No chance, Mr. President. His aversion to killing is too deep, based on a devastating personal loss for which he feels responsible. But he feels a need to understand Corwin. He couldn't do that from Kenya, so he went to Montana instead.'

Thorne tunnelling back into Corwin's life might be almost as dangerous for Wallberg and his ambitions as another sniper stalk. He slapped his hand on the desk in time with his words.

'Find him. Corral him. Rein him in. Shut him down.'

Hatfield had gambled on there being something real between

Corwin and the President, something that Wallberg didn't want to come out. What could it be? Was there any way he could uncover it? Meanwhile, feeding on it, using it, whatever it was, he had turned what looked like a disastrous setback into a victory!

He could hunt Thorne down and take him out with impunity. The man would just disappear, and the secret of who actually had saved the President's life would disappear with him. Forever.

'Full National Security powers, Mr. President?'

'Whatever it takes, Agent Hatfield.'

28

IT WAS A warm day of smoggy sunshine in the L.A. suburb of Carson. Through the open windows of the 4-Runner came the faint stink of petroleum from the world's largest oil refinery a few miles away, huge as a nuclear disaster site. Grace Avenue, running off Carson Boulevard, was a racial layer cake, black and brown with white frosting. Much of the street was projects, rabbitwarrens set back behind narrow strips of lawn.

The address given on the 4-Runner's registration for Edie Melendez was a small, not-quite-run-down bungalow. The door was opened by a woman of about thirty, obviously not Latina, with the square body and strong face and piercing eyes of an American Indian. But she brought with her to the door the mingled aromas of refried beans, tortillas, tacos, frijoles, salsa, hot peppers.

'Mrs. Melendez?' He had decided against using the FBI credentials. He held out his hand. 'My name is Brendan Thorne.'

'Glad to meet you.'

'Um... do you know a Janet Kestrel? She used this—'

'You are a friend of hers? You know where she is?'

Dead end. Thorne said, regretfully, 'I'm sorry. I'm trying to get in touch with her myself.'

'She is my little sister. I hoped...' She made a flustered gesture. 'But please, come in, por favor.'

They sat on a sagging sofa in the small living room. All the furnishings were old, worn, but everything was scrupulously clean. She said her sister Janet was *muy guapa*.

'Our birth name is Roanhorse, we are of the Hopland Indian clan up by Santa Rosa. When she became a blackjack dealer in Reno, she started calling herself Janet Amore.'

And after Reno, she started calling herself Janet Kestrel. Why, when her birth name was Roanhorse?

'She just drove up here one day last fall, and said she was gonna live with us while she looked for work. But she was only here two days, then she saw something in the newspaper and got real excited. She said she had something she had to do. My husband, Carlos, he was glad when she left. He didn't like her because he said she didn't know her place.'

She put her hand on Thorne's forearm, as if he was an old friend she had known for years. Her face was sad.

'After we got married, I found out real quick that Carlos, he didn't want me, he just wanted his green card.' A sudden spark animated those big, dark eyes, made her momentarily vivacious. 'Before she left, Janet told me I should leave him, and we'd go to Reno and she'd teach me how to deal blackjack.'

'Sounds like good advice to me,' said Thorne.

'You think?' she asked seriously. Then she shook her head, as if at an impossible dream. Her face became sad again.

'The night she left, she got beat up, real bad. The cops found her in an alley behind some fancy hotel in Beverly Hills.'

What had Janet Kestrel seen in the newspaper? What did she feel she had to do? Who had beaten her up? Corwin? Why?

'The hospital, they called me. My husband says, Wha she doin, guy had to beat her up?' She was a good mimic. 'He wouldn't drive me, so I rode the bus up to see her. The hospital was real fancy, up by Beverly Hills. Cedar's-Sinai? She looked awful. She couldn't remember anything about what happened to her.'

'Did the cops talk to you? Or to her?'

'Not to me. And I only saw Janet the once. She was asleep from all the pain medication they had her on, but she woke up all of a sudden and told me where she'd parked the 4-Runner. She asked me to get her duffle bag from the truck and give it to a certain nurse. I did, a hefty black lady who was real nice. She said she would smuggle it into one of the hospital lockers for Janet, and put the key in Janet's clothing.'

She paused and sighed, very expressively.

'Carlos wouldn't let me go back up there for three days. When I finally could, Janet was gone.'

Dead end indeed. 'Ah... when did all of this happen?'

'It was in November, early – like around election day.' She put out her hand again, like a trusting child. 'If you find her, you tell her Edie is ready to go to Reno with her and learn how to deal blackjack. Promise?'

'I promise,' said Thorne.

If he found her. But wait a minute. The hospital wouldn't let her check out without making financial arrangements.

Cedar's-Sinai was a hulking state-of-the art medical facility on Beverly Boulevard between Robertson and Doheny, across the street from the Beverly Center. Thorne went in after visiting hours: they would be settling into their nighttime routine, maybe they would cut him a little slack.

But he ran up against an iron-faced, iron-haired night supervisor named Marlena Werfel, who took no prisoners.

'If an ex-patient named Janet Amore is missing, it doesn't concern this hospital. Or you.'

Regretfully, Thorne shoved his FBI commission card under her nose.

'Yes it does. I need to know when she checked out, what her financial arrangements were, and the name of her physician.'

She stared at the credentials for a moment, her little pig eyes snapping with indignation.

'Patient information is confidential. You'll have to come back tomorrow when the administrator's office is open. And I'll be reporting your unprofessional behavior to your superiors.'

If he'd been a real FBI agent, he could have forced her to go into the computer and get him what he wanted. But he didn't want her to carry out her threat to call the local FBI office. If it got into the system, it would get back to Hatfield.

'Sorry if I seemed rude, Mrs. Werfel. Just doing my job.'

'Badly.'

As a frustrated Thorne stalked down the corridor toward the elevators, a rotund African-American nurse carrying a tray full of items covered with a towel fell into step beside him. She spoke out of the side of her mouth without looking at him.

'Doctor Walter Houghton. You didn't hear it here.'

She turned in at an open doorway and was gone. Thorne kept on walking without any reaction. But he could feel Werfel's BB eyes drilling into his back down the length of the corridor.

Hatfield spent the morning at the firing range, focussing on requalifying with the Hostage Rescue team's various weapons. He barely qualified because he couldn't get Thorne out of his head. The man seemed to have dropped off the face of the earth. Since Corwin couldn't have come back from the grave to do him in, then just as he'd told the President, it had to be a setup engineered by Thorne himself. But why? Hatfield suddenly cursed aloud in sudden comprehension.

Someone had leaked to Thorne what would be waiting for him when he got back to Kenya. Not any of his men. Even if they'd known exactly what he was planning, they wouldn't have said anything about it. They were a close-mouthed lot.

So, someone in Nairobi. Maybe one of Muthengi's men. Or maybe that magistrate, Kemoli. Told Thorne his arrest was planned. That's why he had disappeared! He was going to try to get to the President in person to tell him who really had stopped Hal Corwin.

Hatfield had to find him first. He went out to his car and from the spare tire well got the throw-down piece he'd taken off a dead bank-robber the year before. It was a World War II Colt .45. Back on the firing range, he fired a clip through it, leaving it uncleaned so ballistics testing would show it had recently been fired. He returned it to the trunk of the car.

When he walked into his office in the Hoover Building, his phone was ringing. He snapped into it, 'I told you, no calls!'

'Didn't tell me,' said a male voice in a twangy, down-home accent straight out of Maine.

Sammy Spaulding. They'd been classmates at Quantico. Hatfield had qualified for Hostage/Rescue, Sammy had ended up as AIC of the L.A. Field Office. Adrenaline shot through Hatfield. An hour after he had left the Oval Office, he had e-mailed a BOLO marked HIGHEST PRIORITY to major FBI FOs around the country:

Be on the look-out for any use of temporary credentials
issued in the name of Brendan Thorne.

'Talk to me, Sammy. Tell me you've got something I need.'

'What I've got is an irate call this morning from a night administrator at Cedar's-Sinai Hospital. Seems some guy claiming to be one of our agents interrogated her last night concerning a former patient. She thought the i.d. was fake, so she memorized the number on the commission card. A real pain in the butt.'

'Yeah, yeah, yeah,' said Hatfield impatiently. 'Whose credentials were they?'

'Your buddy's. Brendan fucking Thorne's. She shined him on to the day people, but he never showed. You want me to—'

'No!' In a quieter voice, Hatfield said, 'I'm under orders to handle this one personally. I'll be out there tomorrow a.m.'

'I'll lay in some barbecue ribs and grits and watermelon.'

'Up yours,' said Hatfield.

Thorne got a room for the night in a run-down motel below the Sunset Strip, next door to a bar that closed at two a.m. and opened again at four. When he did get to sleep, sometime around three a.m., he woke from his already horribly familiar nightmare, drenched in sweat and yelling, 'You missed,' with Corwin's reply, 'Did I?' following hard upon it in his memory. He had to stand under a cold shower for twenty minutes before he could face the day.

Walter Houghton, M.D., had his practice in a medical office building on Doheny a few blocks from Cedar's-Sinai. Thorne told the receptionist that his name was Brendan Thorne. 'I don't have an appointment, but if the doctor could spare me just two or three minutes…'

But she was already nodding brightly at him through the sliding glass panel separating her from the waiting room.

'Have a seat, Mr. Thorne. Doctor will see you directly.'

He sat down, alarm bells ringing. Houghton had the sort of upscale practice that usually meant days or weeks before getting an appointment. Had Werfel phoned the doctor an early-morning heads-up? Was the FBI on its way? He had to chance it. He didn't have anything else.

Ten minutes later, he was shown into the crowded office of a handsome, lean, erect black man of about his own age. Houghton had beautiful liquid eyes and stern features. His white smock was crisp and he had a stethoscope around his neck.

As he shook Thorne's hand, he said, 'I hear the dragon lady over at Cedar's worked you over pretty good last night. The nurse who gave you my name put in a good word for you, but I feel protective about Janet. She was brutally beaten with feet and fists. At least no knives, clubs or soda bottles. Ended up with a broken arm and broken collarbone, a cracked shin, a permanent metal pin in one wrist, two cracked ribs, and a bruised but not ruptured spleen. If you're bringing her more trouble…'

'I just want to ask her about a friend of hers.'

'Can I believe that?' asked Houghton almost to himself. 'Well, we'll see. If your friend was involved in any way…'

'No friend, I've never met him. I'm just looking for him.'

They locked eyes. Houghton looked away first.

'Okay. All the evidence of sexual assault was there, but no oral, anal, or vaginal penetration took place. She was gutsy and stoic at the same time. Never a word of complaint. Not even a groan out of her. She just took it. A couple of days later, a quiet, tough outdoorsman in his fifties talked with me at the hospital. He said he'd like to kill the man who did it. I asked if he was a tough guy, and he said No, just an angry one.'

'Did he give you a name, address, anything?'

'Nothing. I never saw him again. He left a cash deposit here when I was at the hospital that more than paid for her medical and doctor expenses. He's even got a refund coming.'

'Did Janet leave an address with you?'

He evaded a direct answer by saying, 'She checked herself out of the hospital before she should have, saw me twice here at the office, then never came back. Thanks for stopping by.'

Dismissal. Without even thinking, Thorne said, 'There's a psychiatrist in D.C. named Sharon Dorst.' He rattled off her number. 'Call her. Ask her about Thorne.'

Houghton hesitated, then handed Thorne a card with his office phone and fax on it.

'Give me a day to think about it,' he said.

29

THORNE KNEW HE should get out of L.A. as soon as possible. Right now the FBI could be putting an intercept tap on the doctor's phone. But he couldn't leave empty-handed. Janet Kestrel was who he was looking for. He had no other possible leads. Maybe Houghton had believed him. Maybe he even would call Sharon Dorst.

So, a day for Houghton to think, a day for Thorne to kill. He decided to start at the Los Angeles Main Library at Figueroa and Flower, a venerable place with mosaics around the interior of the rotunda depicting the founding of the city by Spanish priests. At the main reference desk on the second floor, he paid five dollars for access to one of their computers, used a key word search to call up the post-nomination press coverage of Wallberg's campaign that he'd barely glanced through before being forced to abandon it at the Mayflower Hotel.

He found a filler item he'd missed in D.C. A man had tried to rob one of Wallberg's media consultants in the gift shop at the El Tovar Hotel on the south rim of the Grand Canyon. The consultant's name was Nisa Mather.

Since Flagstaff and Phoenix were the population centers closest to Grand Canyon National Park, Thorne brought up their papers' coverage of the event. The candidate, Gus Wallberg, was hiking down on the canyon floor when a grey-haired, uniformed man mopping the gift shop floor spoke to Nisa Mather for a minute or so, then tried to grab her purse.

She screamed for security, the man fled with what one fanciful reporter called a wounded-wolf lope, and jumped into a dark green SUV driven by a woman. Another Wallberg aide, Kurt Jaeger, ran after the 4x4 but couldn't get the license number.

Corwin? Asking why she betrayed him? Maybe threatening to kill her husband? So she screamed for security, then said he'd tried to snatch her purse. In a way, gave him enough time to escape, with Janet Kestrel driving the get-away vehicle?

Back in the *Post*'s coverage, he found an even more provocative item. Two weeks before election night, Wallberg was relaxing for a day at the posh Desert Palms Resort and Spa in California's Mojave Desert. While taking a midnight dip alone in the spa's natural hot springs pool, he was accosted by a naked man. Secret Service agents fired shots, the assailant fled.

The man being naked, far from branding him as a nut in Thorne's eyes, suggested that the intruder had been Corwin. At night in unknown terrain, you could move much more quietly naked.

He Googled the Desert Palms Resort and Spa, then used one of his phone cards to make a one-night reservation for Benjamin Schutz. Yes, mid-week, they had a single available.

Uniformed guards checked his i.d. at the resort's front gate before letting him through the high enclosing adobe wall into the compound. Supposedly the place had been built by Al Capone; there was even a Capone suite hewn out of the native rock, all antique furniture and art deco, where Wallberg had stayed when he had been there.

Thorne's room was in a tamarisk grove down by the picnic area. There was a tennis court surrounded by rare California clump grass; there was an exercise pool flanked by ornate teaberry bushes; there were 'sun bins' designed for solo nude sunbathing. The gambling casino of Capone's day had been converted into the Casino Restaurant, with plush draperies, a huge fireplace, and a chunky refectory table that should have been gracing a medieval monastery. Perhaps it once had.

He bought swim trunks at the gift shop, draped a big woolly bath towel over his shoulders, and padded up the walk past the mud baths and sauna and massage rooms to the hot pool. It was a blue, smooth-bottomed concrete cup, going from one foot to five feet in depth, shielded by decorative rocks and shrubs. At one end, the hot natural mineral water boiled up at regular intervals to spill down a man-made cliff into the pool. The closer to this overflow, the hotter the water.

Thorne drifted in the hundred-degree velvet half-darkness, waiting for just the right security guard to stroll by. Had him! In his fifties, with a lined, leathery face, hard eyes, thinning sandy hair, a flawless uniform, and a military bearing. Perfect.

'Vietnam?' asked Thorne, dog-paddling to the side of the pool. 'You can always tell a guy who's seen action.'

'Twenty-five years as an M.P., stateside and overseas.'

'Ex-Ranger myself. Panama. Desert Storm.' He shook water out of his eyes and hauled himself up on the side of the pool. 'They were telling me about that crazy nut jumped the president last fall. Were you working here then?'

The guard glanced around, then sat down on a lounge chair.

'I gotta tell you, there was something screwy about that whole thing. Hell, this naked guy, he was just talking with Wallberg, and then the feds showed up. He shoved Wallberg underwater and took off. They started shooting. They found blood but didn't find him.' His thin, hard lips curved in contempt. As Thorne had hoped, this ex-M.P. had no respect for civilian security forces. 'They couldn't find him, so they claimed he crawled off into the desert and died.'

'Did they even hit him?'

'Hell no. That guy took off like a scalded-ass ape. No way did he take a round. I think he scraped his head on the rock deliberately to give 'em the blood. I didn't see his face, but he was about the President's age. Rangy and quick even though he had a limp. Wouldn't surprise me if he was ex-military.'

At seven a.m. the next day, Sammy Spaulding met Hatfield at the unobtrusive corner of LAX where the FBI landed its jets. He whistled softly when he saw the Gulfstream.

'And you thought I was blowing smoke,' grinned Hatfield.

'I thought you were covering your ass on some screw-up.'

'Never happen, my man.'

Sammy was one of the few people outside his own team whom he actually trusted, but Hatfield drove alone to keep his appointment with Marlena Werfel at Cedar's-Sinai. She met him behind her bastion desk in the admin office.

'First,' he told her, 'I want to apologize for any inconvenience or distress our man might have caused you.'

'He was extremely rude.'

'He has that reputation.' Hatfield focussed on her. 'You see, he's supposed to be undercover in Chihuahua, Mexico. That's why I flew out here from D.C. to talk to you in person.'

'I knew it! He was asking inappropriate questions about a patient we had here last November. Janet Amore.'

Who the hell was Janet Amore? But if Thorne wanted her, Hatfield wanted her. 'What was Amore being treated for?'

'She was mugged and beaten badly in an alley.'

'And you couldn't give Thorne an address for her?'

'Could have. Didn't. Her sister's. But she's long gone from there. He also wanted to know what sort of financial arrangements she made with the hospital, and her doctor's name.' A satisfied sniff. 'I wouldn't give him either one.' She lowered her voice. 'But he might have gotten the doctor's name from one of our nurses who's a talker and a trouble-maker.'

'You're a true patriot, Mrs. Werfel,' said Hatfield.

He phoned Houghton's office and ordered the receptionist to have the doctor awaiting his arrival. In Houghton's crowded cubicle office, Hatfield flopped his FBI credentials on the desk.

'Special Agent Terrill Hatfield. I have just come from an interview with Marlena Werfel at Cedar's-Sinai—'

'I know Mrs. Werfel. She is an… efficient lady.'

'More than efficient. A patriot.'

'Spare me,' said Houghton.

He was just the sort of black man Hatfield despised: smooth, suave, polished, self-assured, with manicured nails.

'Last November you treated a mugging victim named Janet Amore. Everything you have on her, including current address.'

'If I ever treated such a patient—'

'Oh, you treated her, all right.'

'If I ever treated such a patient, her medical records are protected by law, Agent Hatfield.'

'Not from me. How would you like a handcuffed ride to the Federal Building?'

Houghton stood up so as to be eye to eye with him.

'I came up from South Central, Hatfield, the first one in my family to finish high school, let alone go to medical school. I make a lot of money and I have a lot of clout – my bedside manner with this town's movers and shakers is impeccable. So take your best shot – boy.'

Hatfield was quivering with rage, but it was he who looked away first. Unlike Dorst, Houghton was unfazed by threats. The President would not want a public squabble over Hatfield's right to see the patient records of a woman whose name he had just heard for the first time an hour before. He switched tacks.

'Has a man named Thorne, maybe posing as an FBI agent, been to see you? Since he's not one of your patients, you can't hide behind doctor privilege on him.'

'I never hide behind anything, Agent Hatfield. Since you won't believe whatever I say anyway, I have no information.'

Getting into his car, Hatfield thought, Fuck him, I'll get to Janet Amore from other sources. Or maybe Thorne was there, and Houghton's covering his ass for some unknown reason.

He'd better put a bug on Houghton's phone. If necessary, hack into his computer, burgle his files, intimidate his staff. One way or another, Hatfield would get what he wanted. He had the President of the United States in his pocket.

30

'*YOU MISSED.*'

'*Did I?*'

The exchange had added weight and meaning now. Driving back to L.A. with the easy noontime traffic, Thorne mulled over what he had learned at the Desert Palms Resort. Corwin had confronted Wallberg face-to-face, had even talked with him – about what? Could have killed him, and hadn't. Just ducked Wallberg under the surface of the water so he could escape. Did this mean he really had meant to shoot Jaeger after all?

Thorne left the Hollywood Freeway at Vine, went west on Sunset, then south toward Houghton's office. By now, The FBI surely would have interviewed the doctor and would have a tap on his phone whether he had been cooperative or not.

Doubtful they'd have a tap on Houghton's fax machine. Thorne found a Kinko's, parked beyond it, walked back, sent an unsigned message to Houghton's fax number: Your day is up. From a coffee shop across the street from Kinko's, he watched and waited for half an hour. Nobody resembling a Feeb appeared. He went in, asked if there was a reply to his fax. There was. The Taco Bell a mile from my office. 2:30 p.m.

Thorne got there at two to monitor the fast-food outlet from the adjacent gas station's mini-mart. No Feebs. When Houghton arrived at 2:25 in a silver BMW-7 luxury sedan, Thorne opened the rider's-side door and slid in.

'Let's just ride around.'

Houghton wore dark glasses that gave his strong-boned face an actorish cast. 'I'm glad you faxed instead of phoned.'

'So someone came around.'

'A most unpleasant specimen, Special Agent Terrill Hatfield.'

Houghton chuckled. 'Accusatory. Bullying. Threatening me with all sorts of dire things. I don't like bullies. I don't threaten easily.'

'I was counting on that.'

'I was on the knife-edge about helping you or not, but Hatfield took care of that. As soon as he left, before he could get a warrant for a tap on my phone, I called your psychiatrist friend Sharon Dorst back in Washington and left her the number of my health club.'

'Friend?' said Thorne, mildly surprised.

'Oh yes. Definitely a friend. She was cagey at first, but then she opened up, a lot. I think I understand a great deal more now.' He stopped at a red light, looked over at Thorne. 'The man who paid Janet's medical expenses, someone named Halden Corwin, is the man you're trying to track down.'

'With good reason.' Now Thorne chuckled. 'I think.'

'What I didn't tell you yesterday is that Janet checked out in the middle of the night and had to leave behind a beautifully tanned bearskin. One of the nurses hid it in a hospital locker for her and gave her the key.'

'Corwin's. He must have given it to her.'

The light changed, the BMW glided down the street. 'Janet sent my nurse the key at the end of January and asked if we could get the bearskin to her without the hospital knowing. We did.'

He pulled the BMW into the gas station next to the Taco Bell and stopped. Full circle. He took a folded memo sheet from his inside jacket pocket and handed it to Thorne.

Thorne unfolded it and read: JANET ROANHORSE General Delivery Groveland CA 95321.

'I'll cover as long as I can,' said Houghton, 'but Hatfield will find out about that bearskin from someone on staff at Cedar's-Sinai and then bring a lot of pressure on my nursing staff. I can't ask them to sacrifice their careers for this.'

'I wouldn't want them to.' Thorne shook Houghton's hand and opened his door. 'Many thanks, doctor.'

'He pissed me off,' said Houghton, and drove off laughing.

*

Hatfield was fuming. There had been no calls from Thorne on Houghton's phone, there was nothing to indicate he had ever gone to Houghton's office.

So he called Quantico. He couldn't really use the FBI full-bore, because nobody except his team knew about Corwin, or about Thorne. But the President was behind him, so he could have his Hostage/Rescue team flown out to L.A. with their equipment. Special training exercise, some bullshit like that. Several trained men looking for Thorne was better than one trained man. He knew he could count on his team to get the job done and, within reason, keep its collective mouth shut.

Waiting for them to arrive, he put the name Janet Amore out on CLETS and the National Crime Index, e-mailed the DMVs of all fifty states, Googled her, all without any results at all. No credit history, no driver's license in that name. As if she didn't exist. He planned to go interview the sister, Edie Melendez, but by her name she was probably a stupid beaner without a thought in her head.

First he would take his ally, Marlena Werfel, out to lunch. A modest meal at a fancy place with a reputation, like Spago's in Beverly Hills, would impress her. She could maybe even see a star or two and dine out on the experience for years.

He didn't mention business until they were on dessert and coffee. It turned out she had something worth a $125 lunch for him. Potentially, something big.

He started out, 'I spoke with Houghton. If Thorne went to see him, the doctor is stone walling. Patient confidentiality and all that. He's doing the same thing on this Janet Amore. Is there anything you can think of that might help me find her?'

She started to shake her head, then paused. Her eyes widened, she exclaimed triumphantly, 'The locker!'

'What locker?' he almost snapped.

'That nurse I told you was a troublemaker was seen sneaking something into one of the hospital lockers and giving the key to Amore. The nurse who saw her mentioned it to me. None of my business, of course. But then Amore sneaked out in the middle of the night and had to leave everything behind. I just bet whatever it was is still in that locker.'

If Amore had left something behind – clothing, letters, photos, personal belongings – it was sure to give Hatfield some sort of clue to who she was and where she might have gone, and why Thorne was looking for her.

'Let's go take a look at that locker, Marlena.'

But when they opened the locker with a master key, it was empty. Hatfield's always volatile temper was bubbling up.

'You mean someone just took it? How could they do that without the key?'

'Amore must have given the key to someone,' said Werfel. 'They could have sneaked in, opened the locker, and emptied it.' Her eyes gleamed. 'But my troublemaker will be on shift tonight. She'll know who took it, and why. I'll get it out of her.'

'You sure it wasn't Amore herself?' demanded Hatfield.

'If she'd been around, I would have known about it. I'll have the anwser by morning.'

Probably it was the sister, Edie Melendez, who had taken it. If it was, she would have an address on Amore. And she would be easy to break down, her being a beaner with a green card that was probably bogus. Hatfield wouldn't wait for morning.

Dusk was approaching when he fought his way through the rush-hour exodus from L.A. to Grace Avenue in Carson. No one was home. A half-hour later a yard man's beat-up old truck pulled into the driveway and a handsome Latino with liquid eyes and black hair in a '50s pompadour got out. Obviously the hoosban. Hatfield intercepted him between truck and house.

'We want to talk with your wife, Melendez. Right now.'

The man turned quickly, warily, retreating to the safety of the racial barrier. He whined, 'Wha' you want with her, man?'

Hatfield flopped his credentials open before Melendez's startled eyes. 'Special Agent Terrill Hatfield, Federal Bureau of Investigation. Now start talking.'

The change was remarkable. The diffidence was gone. 'Day after your other man was here, I come home, Edie, she gone. Nobody cook me no meals, nobody wash my clo'es. Took off with all the dinero in the house.' He stepped close. He reeked of beer. 'You gotta get her back for me, man!'

'This other agent? He have a name?'

'She never even tell me he was here.' He jerked a thumb at the house next door. 'Neighbor, he tell me after she gone. A gringo, he say, with black hair. Thass all he know.'

Thorne. Looking for Amore in all the wrong places.

'We actually want your wife's sister,' said Hatfield. 'Janet Amore. We know she's been staying here with you and we know she had her sister pick up a package at the hospital after she was discharged.'

'Package? I don' know nothin' 'bout no package.'

But the resistance had disappeared at mention of Amore.

'She was here, si, but she gone,' he said eagerly. 'Is always trouble, tha' one. She's nothin' but a puta, man. Look for her where the whores walk the streets. She got beat up cause she did bad things. Of that I am sure.'

A whore. 'Gone where?'

'Doan know, doan care. Maybe Edie, she know. But Edie, she gone too.' His belligerence returned. Obviously his green card was in order. 'She lef' cause of FBI, now wha' the FBI gonna do to get her back for me?'

'We're not going to do anything,' said Hatfield. He handed Melendez a card. 'But if your wife gets in touch with you, or her sister does, you call this number, pronto. Or you'll be back in Mexico so fast your fucking huaraches will be smoking.'

31

THERE WERE TWELVE of them waiting for the bus at Groveland, an old goldrush town in the Sierra foothills on the way to Yosemite National Park. It was their first river raft trip, and they were charged up. The bus pulled up. They filed aboard. The driver stood in the front, counting noses.

'It's about a fifteen-twenty minute ride to Casa Loma,' he said. 'Then five miles of really bad road to the Put-In Spot on the Tuolemne River. I'm glad to see you're wearing warm clothes. This early in May, the river is still pretty darn cold.'

A slender woman with streaked blond hair and smile lines at the sides of her mouth gestured at the equally slender fifteen-year-old boy beside her.

'Can Jimmy sit up front behind you?'

The boy looked embarrassed. The bus driver chuckled.

'Sure can. He'll like that ride down the hill. By the way, in case any of you are worried, the rafts almost never get tipped over. Even if one of 'em got holed by a sharp rock, there's no life-threatening danger. But just to be on the safe side, AQUA River Tours furnishes wet suits, life jackets and helmets to all our clients.'

He didn't add that anyone going into the river would get bruised and scraped, maybe get a cracked rib or two, because that's not what the clients were paying to hear. Instead, he fired up the bus. Snorting diesel fumes, it lurched forward.

At just eleven a.m., they were at the water's edge, where four guides were holding three rubber rafts in place against the steep earth bank. The clients crawled enthusiastically to their places, and were pushed out into the swirling current.

*

Thorne had driven hard well into the night, had checked into the Groveland Hotel, an 1849 adobe wedded to a 1914 Queen Anne Victorian. Two story, white with red-brown trim, with pillars all the way around. While he was checking out in the morning, he asked where the post office was. The clerk, a middle-aged man with silvery hair, faraway blue eyes, and turtle-wrinkles in his thin neck, smelled faintly of mothballs.

He nodded with little jerks of his head. 'Street behind the hotel, up the hill. Along there a ways.'

Groveland had a population of 1,500, which doubled on the weekends during the summer months. The AAA Tour Book said the town's main recreational activity was white-water rafting on the Tuolemne River a few miles distant.

Thorne found the post office easily, an ugly modern brown building with what looked like a corrugated iron roof and inset doorways and a somehow incongruous blue mailbox at the foot of the gleaming concrete front steps. Inside, behind the counter, was a round, rosy-faced woman in a blue uniform with a nametag, ROSIE, pinned to the front of her shirt.

'A few months back I sent a package from L.A. to a Janet Roanhorse at General Delivery,' Thorne beamed. 'I was wondering if you have any record that she ever received it?'

Rosie didn't have to look anything up. 'Sure did. Roanhorse, that was her daddy's name. Her folks had a little cabin in the woods a few miles out of town. They died a few years back. She came back to take the place over, and calls herself Janet Kestrel now.'

'I'm just in town for the day, and I was really hoping I'd get a chance to see her... '

Rosie shook her head, making her curls dance, and beamed confidentially at him. 'We can't give out folk's home addresses. But you can catch her at work, AQUA River Tours, at a little spot called Casa Loma. Right on highway 120 north, you can't miss it. The only building there is called the River Store. It's set back on a little knoll. There's a cutout of a big blue coffee cup on top of it.'

He thanked her and left. It was just nine a.m.

*

Janet loved it on the river, narrow, twisting, fast, here dark and deep and swirling, there white and shallow and boisterous, throwing up spume and leaping over sharp half-submerged rocks with joyful exuberance. It took great skill to keep the rafts from hitting anything.

But the letter had come from the Sho-Ka-Wah Casino. Today was her last ride down the river as a guide. Tomorrow, she would catch a bus to Hopland and find a place to live and start work at the casino as a blackjack dealer. She felt a sadness at leaving the river-rafting she knew and loved for an indoor casino job dealing blackjack, something she also knew but had never loved. But it paid better than rafting, and she had to start building a new life. At least this would be at a casino run by her own people. And she might never get that call on her cellphone from Hal to go retrieve her 4-Runner.

They stopped for lunch at one p.m. at a pre-arranged spot that in another month would be sun-washed and toasty. No more snow lingered in the steep mixed oak and pine forests flanking the river, but in here under the trees it was still chilly. They lit fires and ate their sandwiches around them.

Jimmy, the fifteen-year-old boy who couldn't get enough river lore, attached himself to Janet. As they ate, he kept plying her with questions about rafting and about what seemed to him the wilderness they were passing through. He ate quickly, so after they finished, she walked him around, naming the various trees and bushes. He reached out for a red-leafed vine curled around one of the oak trees, and she grabbed his arm.

'That's not sumac, Jimmy. It's poison oak.'

He jerked his hand back. 'That stuff gives you a rash.'

'I'll tell you a secret.' She picked one of the leaves. 'There's a way you can develop immunity for it.' She ate the leaf. 'You do that for a while, carefully, and pretty soon—'

'Oh wow! That's way cool.'

'But don't you try it,' she cautioned. She suddenly giggled, in the boy's world. 'Your mom would hunt me down and kill me dead if you did.'

*

Thorne parked the 4-Runner on the blacktop in front of the River Store and checked out the other vehicles: a white van with a big metal luggage rack on the roof, and a pale green camper with a dark green plywood box on top to hold belongings. There was also a three-year old Suzuki and a '94 Chevy Astrovan. Inside, he was greeted by the rich smell of espresso and a big old man with a grey handlebar mustache and a long grey ponytail.

'Sam Arness,' said the man. 'What can I do for you?'

'A cup of coffee for starters. Is Janet Kestrel working today?'

'Yep, and nope. She's working, but she ain't here.' Arness gestured down the store to a door in the back wall. 'AQUA Tours. She's a damn good white-water rafting river guide for them, one of the best. AQUA does class four trips – toughest is class five. They're off down the river on a one day trip and'll be back after dark.' He squinted at the store's electric clock. 'Might catch 'em at the Put-In Spot down on the river, but I doubt it, they're usually on the water by eleven.'

'I'll drive on down. I'm just waiting for Janet anyway.'

'Hope you got four-wheel, road's mean as a damn snake.'

Sam Arness was right. Thorne needed the four-wheel all right on the incredible five-mile dirt track to the river thousands of feet below, a narrow slanting cut down the steep side of an immense brown tree-covered slope. The hillside rose on one side, fell away into infinity on the other. Roll your vehicle here, and you'd still be rolling at sundown.

Around the next turn he braked sharply. A golden eagle was in the road, a jackrabbit clutched in its talons. It flapped away in wide-winged, indifferent dignity. As he neared the valley floor, the air got cooler. He could hear the distant rush of the river. The road levelled out and there it was, the Tuolemne, its banks overarched with pines and angled hardwoods.

He found a tiny park area with a gently-sloping earth ramp down to the river. The Put-In Spot. As Sam had warned, the rafters were long gone. Just rustic restrooms and a signboard posted with pet-leashing and fishing regulation notices, and a stern red-edged warning about hazardous, turbulent waters and sharp edged rocks beneath the surface and WEAR YOUR LIFE JACKET.

A quarter mile downstream he sat down on the grass between the road and a leaky old boat, minus oars, hidden in the bushes, leaned back against a tree with his eyes shut, and listened to the rushing water.

Just how much jeopardy might he have put Janet Kestrel in by trying to track her down? Hatfield would ferret out her address in Groveland from Houghton's office staff, would know Thorne was ahead of him, and would come rushing down Thorne's backtrail trying to find her – probably with his ball-breaker Hostage Rescue/Sniper Team in tow.

Marlena Werfel was bursting with news and enthusiasm.

'The package was taken from the locker by one of Dr. Houghton's nurses. Mary Coggins.'

That lying bastard! Hatfield had just known Houghton was holding out on him. But it was easy to go around him.

'Outstanding!' he exclaimed. 'Just one more question, and I'll let you get back to work. Does Dr. Houghton have afternoon rounds here at the hospital today?'

Werfel checked the schedule. 'He does. At three o'clock.'

'Oustanding,' Hatfield said again, this time softly.

It was 3:15. There were two patients in Houghton's waiting room, and two nurses behind the glassed-in check-in desk.

'Mary Coggins?' Hatfield demanded.

The petite brownette he remembered from last time looked up. He pushed through the door beside their cubicle and as it closed behind him to shut them off from view of the waiting patients, he grabbed her arm, half-dragged her down the hall to an empty examination room and shoved her inside.

She started to protest, but he slammed the door and snapped, 'You're in a lot of trouble, lady. Federal trouble. Aiding and abetting a possible terrorist fugitive fleeing to avoid prosecution.'

'I did no such thing!'

'You unlawfully removed a package from a Cedar's-Sinai locker and sent it to Janet Amore. She's a federal fugitive, so your action is aiding and abetting. You'll be detained at the Federal Building in Westwood, in the morning you'll be arraigned in federal court...'

'I've got a five-year-old daughter at home!'

'Leaving a child alone is a criminal offense—'

'She's not alone. My mother's with her. You can't—'

'Can and will if you don't tell me everything.'

She was frightened now, crying. 'We... I didn't know anything about a fugitive warrant. So when she called and asked if we... I... could get her bearskin and send it to her—'

'A bearskin?'

There were tears on Mary Coggins' face, but he could see her deciding to go all noble and protect the doctor and the rest of the staff. He didn't care what she did, as long as he got what he wanted.

'Yes, a bearskin,' said Coggins. 'Janet said on the phone that she needed it for some sort of ceremony. That is not a federal offense, not in the United States of America.'

A ceremony, he thought? What the hell did she mean? He said, without much force, 'I can make it one.'

She raised her head proudly.

'Go ahead, then! I did it. Alone. Nobody else helped me, not the doctor, not the other nurses. They didn't know anything about it.'

If anybody called his bluff, Hatfield knew he couldn't make anything stick. Not against her, not against anyone else. Better to get what he had come for and get out, before Houghton returned from his hospital rounds and made an official complaint.

'All right. Just give me the address, and I won't have to file a written report on this.'

She took the offered way out. 'Janet Roanhorse, General Delivery, Groveland, California.'

Janet Roanhorse? A red Indian instead of a Mex?

'I thought her name was Amore.'

'She wanted it sent to Roanhorse.'

32

THEY GOT TO Ferry Bridge just at four p.m., as scheduled. The guides splashed into the knee-deep eddying water to pull the rafts up onto the earth bank so the passengers could get out. Using supplies from the guide house tucked up under the bridge, the guides turned into cooks. The clients sat around eating crackers and oysters and veggie dips while the guides worked to turn out a surprisingly complete dinner.

Jimmy's mother abandoned the appetizers to approach Janet where she was using stainless steel tongs to expertly turn the chicken breasts grilling on the propane stove. The woman had a quizzical expression on her face.

'Jimmy said you eat poison oak leaves. Do you? Really?'

Janet gave her an almost sheepish grin, and nodded.

'Yeah, from time to time, to keep up my own immunity on these trips. It does work, but I don't usually tell any of our passengers about it. But Jimmy was so curious, I just showed him. He's a great kid. He's so observant and interested that he got the other passengers really seeing what was around them. It was great having him in the group today.'

Jimmy's mother leaned close. 'I think he's in love.'

After dinner, they brought out the guitars and more wine. Everyone felt fine and mellow, but for Janet it was bitter-sweet. A high point, but of what was her final trip as a guide down the river that she loved.

Hatfield was on his cellphone with AIC Sammy Spaulding.

'I'm on my way to the Burbank Airport to meet the other members of my team. I need a smaller plane that can carry all six of us and our weapons up to a little town called Groveland, not too far from Yosemite.'

'Christ, I can't do that, Terrill. The red tape—'

'This afternoon, Sammy. I don't want to pull rank, but this is a National Security issue and I'm under direct orders from the President. How about in your report, you just say it's a Hostage/Rescue deep-cover training exercise?'

There was a long, stunned silence. 'That might do it.'

'Two more things. Lean on the Groveland postmaster to get the address of a woman named Janet Roanhorse. They'll sure as hell have it, a hick town like that. And have a couple of rental cars waiting for us wherever the pilot sets us down.'

He could hear the muted clicking of Sammy's computer keys.

'That'll be the Pine Mountain Lake Airport a few miles out of Groveland. The cars'll be there waiting.' He added, trying to get back a modicum of control, 'You owe me bigtime, you bastard,' and hung up.

It was nearly dark when the party finally broke up. The bus was waiting to take the clients back to Groveland. There was a lot of loud talk and laughter; it was cold enough so their breaths sent puffs of vapor into the air. As they were filing aboard, Jimmy turned back to shake Janet's hand, very formally.

'I want to come back every week this summer,' he said.

She didn't say anything about this being her last trip. But as Jimmy boarded the bus, she gave him a little hug and a peck on the cheek. His mother embraced her; then they were gone.

For the next hour, the guides were busy deflating the rafts and lugging them and all the rest of the gear up to the edge of the road. When the truck arrived, they stowed everything aboard and climbed aboard themselves for the trip back to Casa Loma. Everything Janet did had an end-of-summer flavor to it. An ending. But she reminded herself it was also a beginning.

On the flight to Groveland, Hatfield planned his strategy.

He needed that girl, whatever her name was, because he needed to know why Thorne was looking for her. And he wanted her before

Thorne found her. When Thorne did, Hatfield wanted to be there frst. If she was an American Indian, native-born, he couldn't play the green-card game with her, but he could pressure her as he had pressured Mary Coggins: by using the threat of arrest as a security risk.

Franklin came up the aisle and leaned over him.

'When do we get briefed on what's up, boss?'

Hatfield slid over so Franklin could sit down beside him. It was always good to give his team the feeling that they were all in this together.

'We're trying to track down a woman named Janet Amore or Janet Roanhorse, take your pick. From the Roanhorse I think she's at least part Indian, but I'm not sure. We want her because someone else does. And we want her first.'

'Who wants her? Why?'

'I don't know why. That's what I want find out. As to who...' He paused, savoring what Franklin's reaction would be. 'Brendan Thorne.'

'That prick!' exclaimed Franklin. 'I'm gonna enjoy this.' He slid out of the seat. 'I'll give the guys a heads-up.'

Hatfield thought about what he'd told Franklin. Yeah. He was sure he was right. Thorne had crossed the woman's tracks somewhere and was looking for answers just as they were. But answers to what? There was still too much he didn't know. Did it all go back to the California Delta? He had been there himself, but he still didn't know what really had happened there on election night.

Jaeger had been there, and Jaeger was dead. Corwin had been there, had killed them, and Corwin was dead. Thorne was trying to find out some of the same things Hatfield was, but Thorne would soon be dead, too. Did it really matter that much what had gone down before he had arived at the scene?

What did matter was finding Janet Amore before Thorne did.

Under one of the Casa Loma store's night lights, Thorne leaned against the big spare tire mounted on the back of the 4-Runner, his arms crossed, deliberately obscuring the vehicle with his body. He watched the guides unload the rafts and equipment.

He instantly identified Janet Kestrel. She was a tawny-skinned mid-twenties, full-bosomed and lithe, her warrior blood unmistakable: it was there in the strong nose, the high cheekbones, the deep-set liquid eyes with their predator's fierce gaze. No physical effects seemed to remain from the savage beating she had sustained five months before. A fit companion for the much older Corwin, whatever their relationship had been.

As she talked animatedly with the other guides, Thorne could see that her eyes were the only jarring note in that Indain warrior look: they were the clearest, most crystalline blue Thorne had ever seen, glacier-deep.

After the four guides had shut and locked the shed, the other three crowded around Janet, hugging her in turn, as if she were going away and these were their goodbyes. He was glad he had pushed so hard and fast to find her.

Finally she and the other woman broke away from the men and started for the camper with the plywood box on top. As they walked by, Kestrel's glance passed casually over Thorne, then did a double-take at the 4-Runner. She paused.

'Why don't you just go on, Flo? I think I know this guy, I can get a ride home with him.'

They embraced again, briefly, then Flo went on to her camper as Janet strode over to Thorne, her face set with anger.

'Okay, Jack, start talking. How did you get my car?'

'We don't have time for that now,' Thorne said, a rough, urgent edge on his voice. He needed to get her out of there, quick. 'My name is Brendan Thorne. A really nasty FBI agent named Terrill Hatfield is on his way here right now, and he's coming after you.'

Astonishment momentarily froze her anger.

'After me? Why? How?'

'He wants to ask you a lot of questions about the attempted assassination of President Gus Wallberg in Montana.'

'That's ludicrous! I've never been to Montana in—'

'It was Hal Corwin behind the gun. Hatfield has connected you with both the man and the event.' He didn't say that his own search for her had triggered Hatfield's interest. Time enough for that later, when he had her safely out of there.

His words had struck her in the chest like flung rocks. Oh God! Hal had tried to kill the president! But how had some FBI agent connected her with Hal? And how had this Brendan Thorne ended up with the 4-Runner?

'Hatfield probably doesn't know you're going under the name Kestrel, but by now he'll have connected up Janet Amore and Janet Roanhorse through that hospital administrator – Werfel – and Doctor Houghton's office staff. He'll have pressured Houghton's people to find out where they sent the bearskin, and he'll get your address from the post office in Groveland – that's how I got it. If you want to talk to him instead of me, fine. But you don't have any other choices.'

'I can run. I'm good at running.'

'Not from Hatfield and his men. Not alone.'

She had been hit with a series of stunning blows, but she recovered quickly. She just put out her hand. 'Gimme the keys.'

'They're in the 4-Runner.'

She ran around to the driver's side and he got in beside her. As she fired up the engine, all she said was, 'I need some things from the cabin.'

Thorne was filled with admiration. If she had been riding shotgun for him, it was no wonder that Corwin had kept ahead of everybody for so long.

33

HATFIELD HUDDLED WITH his crew near the rent-a-cars at the Pine Mountain Lake Airport. Their breath went up in plumes on the cold, high-country air, so different from L.A.'s smog-laden offering. Their faces were pinched from pumping adrenaline: they wanted action. It was what they lived for.

'Okay, guys, listen up. Roanhorse is in her twenties, black and blue, maybe part American Indian. She's living in a shack off one-twenty. I don't think she's armed and dangerous, but I'm not sure. We either take her tonight or stake out her place until she shows. Only I will interrogate her, because only I have been given the guide-lines.'

'We got you, Chief,' said Eisler.

'I've got directions, I'll drive the lead car with Franklin and Greene. Perry, you drive the second car. Any questions?'

Baror asked, 'If she resists, how hard do we push?'

'No shooting. It's vital that I get a chance to talk to her. If she's packing, it's going to be a woman's gun. A .380, something like that. Stopping power of a mosquito. You've got your flack jackets. And hell, you're big tough guys.'

He couldn't tell them Thorne was the real target here, that he wanted Thorne isolated so he could shoot him down. They were loyal to him, but they still were federal agents: they wouldn't stand still for a flat-out execution. He doubted Thorne could have beaten them to Roanhorse, but he had to brief them on the possibility, however remote.

'I doubt we'll get so lucky, but she might be accompanied by the guy we brought back from Kenya, Brendan Thorne. Turns out we might be talking a major terrorist here.' Franklin and Greene knew Thorne was no terrorist, but not even they knew he had killed

Corwin, not Hatfield. If it comes to grabbing Roanhorse or taking down Thorne, take down Thorne.' He paused. 'Anybody have anything?' No one spoke. 'Then let's saddle up.'

Baror exclaimed, 'Hi Ho Silver, and away-y-y-y!'

It was their usual battle cry. Grinning, they headed for the cars. The prospect of action, as always, had them hyped.

As she drove, Janet kept casting covert glances over toward Thorne. He reminded her of Hal: much younger, but the same self-containment, the air of physical capability, the hawk eyes.

He asked, 'Is there a back way to your cabin?'

'Aren't you being paranoid? He can't be here already.'

'You don't know Hatfield. I do.'

'How do you know him?'

'Later.'

'How did you get my truck?'

'Later.'

A mile from the cabin, she swung the vehicle into what looked like a hiking path through the pines. They bounced over roots and rocks, branches banging against the sides of the car.

She was getting edgy. 'We can circle around and leave the 4-Runner a quarter of a mile from the cabin.'

'Good. This was your folks' place, right?'

How did he know that? She said, 'Yes. My place now,' then felt compelled to add, 'The old man got drunk a lot and beat on my mom and my sister and me. Then mom died and it was just Edie and him and me. Edie sneaked away to L.A. and married a Mexican. Soon as I was eighteen, I took off. Anywhere was gonna be better than here, with him. When he died, the cabin came to me. So I came back. Wood stove, no electricity, but it suits me fine during the warm summer months when I'm a river guide.'

'How about during the cold winter months?'

She wrenched over the wheel to avoid crushing a fender against a rough-barked Ponderosa.

'Then I spend most of my time in Reno, dealing blackjack.'

'Is that where you met Corwin? Reno?'

'Later,' she said, aping him.

'Fair enough.'

She thought, Why did I tell him all that? She had to get away from him as much as she did from Hatfield. It sounded to her like the FBI was after him, too, so after she found out from him where Hal was, she could use him to ditch the feds.

She drove the 4-Runner in a tight circle to face back the way they had come, then cut the engine and lights. They sat in silence until the high country silence that was no silence at all had again closed in around them. A nighthawk gave his cooing chuckle somewhere in the middle distance, throwing its voice, as always, so she couldn't be sure just where it really was.

Thorne surprised her by quietly opening his door and getting out. He stood beside the 4-Runner and gestured toward the cabin, speaking softly through the open window.

'It's too silent over there. No wildlife sounds. Hatfield and his crew have the place staked out, waiting for you or me or maybe both of us. We'll split up here, I'll create a diversion. Where do we meet up if things go wrong?'

'Meet up? Uh – Whiskey River.' She said it before she thought it through, then knew it was the right thing. At Whiskey River she would be among friends. She wanted to lose Thorne, but she had to find out from him about Hal first. 'It's a biker bar in Oakdale, down the hill a ways.'

'Since the Feebs are here, they'll have your real name from the Groveland post office.'

'You're saying I should lose the 4-Runner?'

'Yeah. It might lead them to you.' He tapped a hand lightly on the window frame. 'Give me five minutes.'

He melted into the undergrowth, as silently as she had ever seen anyone move, even the reservation Indians of her childhood.

Hatfield put his team in place in the woods between the highway and the cabin, took the driveway himself. If the woman was alone, his men would hold her while he waited for Thorne to show. If Thorne didn't appear, he'd interrogate her alone. Why was Thorne looking for her? How did she fit into things?

If Thorne was with her, he'd let his team take her, then tell Thorne they had to talk. Kill him, make it look to his men like self-defense. He went into a comfortable crouch in a grove of western hemlock beside the track into her cabin, his .40 Glock semiauto resting on his right knee with his forefinger very lightly touching the trigger.

He tensed. Someone was walking cautiously up the gravel drive behind him. How in hell…

Thorne's voice was a hoarse whisper.

'Hatfield? Has she shown yet? Do you have her?'

Hatfield came slowly erect, the gun still out of sight beside his thigh, sure that he would be able to see Thorne on the open driveway by the light of the gibbous moon.

'We're waiting for her,' he said in soft tones that wouldn't carry to his men. 'I sent you the tickets to Kenya, why in hell did you fake your own death?'

'Because I've seen the inside of a Kenyan prison.' Thorne gave a low laugh. 'No thanks. But why did you plan to set me up? I told you I didn't want credit for Corwin. Told you all I wanted was out. Why didn't you just let me go my way?'

Hatfield peered through pale moonglow at the figure just visible on the far edge of the drive.

'I was under orders to make sure you stayed out of the country for a few months.' He was slowly raising his Glock, keeping it where no vagrant ray of moonlight could touch it. 'Then you'll be released and you can go back to Tsavo…'

He pumped round after round at the shadowy figure. It was blown sideways, spinning into the thicket of heavy juniper bushes beside the road with a long, loud, strangled cry. A moment of thrashing, then silence. He'd got the fucker! Now, just seconds to cover himself with his men.

With a gloved hand, he pulled out the old Colt he'd pushed the rounds through at the firing range in D.C. The perfect throw-down piece, untraceable, exactly the sort of illegal weapon Thorne would carry. He fired three times into the air and threw the gun into the bushes where Thorne had fallen.

'Over here!' he yelled. 'I need lights! I need guns! I need men! Now!'

Like her father before her, Janet had wrapped her money stash in waterproof plastic that she had buried near the rear corner of the cabin only eighteen inches down in dry soil. She dug it up with her pocketknife, then moved silently up the side of the cabin toward the door. At the flurry of gunfire from the driveway, she jumped two feet in the air.

'Over here!' an unknown voice shouted. 'I need lights! I need guns! I need men! Now!'

Hatfield's men sounded like a cattle stampede as they abandoned their posts to rush to the aid of the shouting man. Hatfield? Had he shot Thorne? Killed him?

She ran to the door, slipped in, grabbed up her cellphone, jerked the bearskin off her bunk-bed, threw a couple of armloads of clothing into a backpack, was out again within ninety seconds. Her Reno wardrobe in the closet might hold them there, making them think she just hadn't gotten home yet.

She drove slowly, cautiously away, without lights and without even thinking of waiting for Thorne. He would make it or he wouldn't. She would wait for him at Whiskey River for... three days. Longer than that, he wouldn't be coming.

Hatfield was waiting impatiently by the heavy thicket of juniper bushes where Thorne had gone down. He said to his men, 'Thorne! He came up behind me and started firing. No warning, no words, nothing. He's in that thicket. I don't have a flashlight...'

They went in, Franklin in the lead. 'Here's his piece!' He took a knee, and, without touching it in any way, sniffed the barrel of the throw-down .45 that Hatfield had planted there. 'Yeah, this baby's been working all right.'

They worked their way through the thicket and congregated on the far side. They had found the gun. They had found heavy blood splotches. But they hadn't found Thorne.

Hatfield had a sinking feeling in his gut. But, hit like that, bleeding like that, Thorne couldn't get far.

'Listen up.' They stood in an exhausted circle around him, adrenaline leaching from their bodies. 'He's hit, and he's hit hard. Throw a perimeter around this wooded area until first light, then beat the bushes until we find the bastard's body.'

'Cops?' asked Eisler.

'We don't invite the cops in, ever. You know that. If you spot him, shoot first and shoot to kill. Treat him like a Texas rattlesnake. By sunup, I want him in a bodybag.'

34

THORNE SAW HATFIELD coming up with the Glock and threw himself sideways into the cover as he had done with Corwin up on the mountain, yelling to make Hatfield think he was hit. But Christ, he was hit. The bullet smashed his side like a wrecking ball, accelerating the twist of his body so he went down hard on his side in the undergrowth, stunned.

He was bleeding heavily. Good: give them something to puzzle over. Bad: lose too much blood, the body would go into a defensive mode, pull blood in from the extremities, shut down everything not needed for sheer animal survival, and he'd go into shock. If the shock didn't finish him off, Hatfield would find him and finish him off. Move. Now.

Things were going in and out. Essential to stop the bleeding now, so they would have no blood trail to follow. He ripped his sodden t-shirt apart and stuffed a long strip of it right through the wound, closing off both entry and exit.

That was when the pain started. Good. Pain meant he might not go into shock. But he had at least one broken rib, maybe two. Did he have bone splinters driven into his lungs? In his head, he heard Hernild's voice:

The bullet entered and exited at an angle... fragmented the seventh rib... glanced off rather than penetrated... rib bone driven into the chest cavity but not into the lungs themselves... crawled a thousand feet to his cabin... saved his own life...

Hit as Corwin had been hit. Now he was going to have to save his own life, also as Corwin had done. Using all his woodcraft, he managed a silent crawl to the side of the thicket away from the searchers. Somehow found his feet, his balance, staggered away.

Hatfield must have planned to kill him all along. So why the ticket to Kenya, why the elaborate charade? None of it made any sense...

He fell down. Had let his mind wander. Forget Hatfield for now. Just keep ahead of him. He struggled to his feet, went on. From lodgepole pine to lodgepole pine, from subalpine fir to subalpine fir, from white spruce to white spruce. Finally into a stand of poplars where the going was faster. Plenty of tree trunks to hang on to as he lurched along, and they grew thickly, almost like bamboo, so it would be harder for anyone to see him moving through the grove.

Just before moonset, he looked back the way he had come. No blood trail. He was going to make it! He was going to beat that bastard Hatfield at his own game. Whatever that game was.

His whole life had been fight or flight. Usually fight, but now, flight. Flight where? And just like that it came to him, the whole thing. The Loma Vista store. Call it two miles. Food. Clean water. AQUA River Tours. Medical supplies. Antibiotics. Hope someone on an overnight camping trip had left a vehicle parked there. Surely he could jump the ignition and get it going. He was a Ranger wasn't he? Well, ex-Ranger...

He jerked his mind back. He had wandered out onto Highway 120. He got back onto the shoulder. Bent to pick up a fallen branch for a walking stick, and fell down again. Idiot! Keep the head higher than the heart or he'd end up as dead as Corwin.

Corwin! That was it! Hatfield wanted him dead because he, not Hatfield, had killed Corwin and thus had saved Wallberg's life. If Thorne was alive, even in a Kenya jailhouse, he could keep telling people all about it. Eventually, someone might listen. And talk. Talk to important people who might believe, and talk also, and Wallberg might hear about it... Far better for Hatfield if Thorne were dead.

Ahead, in the just beginning pre-dawn, he saw the Casa Loma store. And the '94 Chev Astro minivan that had been parked there yesterday morning. Detach the wires under the dash to bypass the ignition switch... And what? Drive as far and fast as he could? Hope he got to Oakdale and Whiskey River and Janet Kestrel before Hatfield caught up with him?

To his wandering mind, Janet seemed to have all the answers he needed. She'd give him two or three days before she moved on. He would have to get to Whiskey River before then. He'd have to tell her that Corwin was dead – and that Thorne was the one who had killed him. Then somehow, despite all that, get her to work with him on finding the answers he sought.

But first things first. He needed food, water, antibiotics to stave off incipient infection. Already he was getting feverish. If he went goofy, he was lost indeed.

He threw a rock through the store window.

As the sun began to shine through the notch of the Tioga Pass beyond Yosemite, Hatfield had to admit that Thorne was gone. Or that his men had missed the body. They should be expanding the perimeter of the search, but they didn't have the manpower for it. He was operating outside the FBI action structure, and at this point, he couldn't call in the cops or the sheriffs. Because if Thorne was found alive, he knew Thorne would talk.

The girl hadn't shown, either. His search engines had been useless: he'd been looking for Amore or Roanhorse, not Kestrel.

He ransacked her cabin. What looked like all her clothes were there, and her personal papers. Missing were her i.d. and purse and money and car keys, but she would have needed those…

Car keys!

He checked his watch. Eight a.m. He didn't remember Sammy as a workaholic, but he called the L.A. FO and asked for AIC Spaulding. Sammy was in!

'Terrill! I couldn't sleep all night. How much trouble am I in with the big boys back in Washington because of you?'

'None. We missed our man. But I need you to run a Janet Kestrel, that's K-E-S-T-R-E-L, for a California driver's license, any vehicles registered to her, any wants and warrants.'

'That sound you hear is my sigh of relief. Okay, Kestrel. I'm feeding her into the computer right now. Anything else?'

Hatfield paused, could see no downside to going ahead.

'Yeah. Put out a Seeking Information Alert on her.'

'An SIA? That's terrorist shit, Terrill.'

'I keep telling you this is coming from far up the food chain. I need to ask her about a possible associate.'

'Got you. Ah hah! Janet Kestrel. Valid California driver's license and a valid Nevada driver's license. She holds legal title to a 1990 Toyota 4-Runner, dark green, Calif Five, C-W-D, Zero-Four-Six. Registration and insurance are current, no wants or warrants. I'll keep digging, but—'

'Put out a BOLO on the 4-Runner as well.'

He hung up, elated. They didn't have Thorne – yet. But he'd soon have the girl. Had she and Thorne ever hooked up? Did she connect with Corwin in any way? Was that why Thorne was looking for her? He'd wring her dry, then decide whether he had to keep her on ice, probably in the FBI's secret detention cells at the Federal Building in Westwood. The post-9/11 anti-terrorist laws gave him plenty of authority to do that.

With the BOLO out on her 4-Runner, and the SIA out on her, it was just a matter of hours until he had her in custody.

Janet was already in Oakdale with the 4-Runner stashed in Kate Wayne's garage before Hatfield got out his BOLO. Kate had been a fellow blackjack dealer with her in Reno, but three years before had married a biker who was part-owner of Whiskey River. They had a daughter, now aged two, and a good marriage until he was killed in a motorcycle crash. Kate took over his share of Whiskey River, and now worked there as night bartender.

Janet got Kate's spare key from the fake rock beside the front door, looked in on Lindy, Kate's two-year-old sleeping daughter, and fell into bed in the made-up spare room of her modest California bungalow two blocks from Whiskey River. She went to sleep, hard, without even remembering to wonder whether Thorne was dead or alive.

35

ALIVE. SORT OF.

A half-feverish Thorne drank water and ate trailmix, then treated his gunshot wound with antibiotics taken from one of the AQUA Tours first-aid kits. He bandaged it and wrapped the bandage in plastic bags for waterproofing, and stole a life jacket. Before staggering out to hotwire the Chevy Astro, he left a hundred-dollar bill on the counter by the cash register.

This night drive down the tortuous dirt road to the Tuolemne River – the track Arness had called mean as a snake – seemed much more dire than his drive down the morning before. It was just a blur of never-ending twists and turns ahead of his high-beams, no barriers to a precipitous tumble to the valley floor and the ribbon of river, more daunting because imagined rather than seen in the obscurity of night.

When the track finally leveled out by the Tuolemne, he stopped the car and rolled down his window to hear the rushing water. It was not a soothing sound. Even through his medicated haze, he shivered slightly.

He left the keys in the ignition, put on the life jacket, and half-slid down the grassy bank to the leaky old boat hidden in the bushes. With his last strength, he wrested it from its bed of weeds, shoved it into the water and crawled in. Bent over and clutching the gunnels, he worked his way forward to the bow of the boat. The stern lifted, slowly swung around.

Facing forward, he watched the water seep up between the boat's dried-out planks, chills running through him even as sweat stood on his face. He let the river take him.

Kate Wayne looked more like a cowgirl than she did a biker. She rolled her own cigarettes and wore plaid shirts with leather loop ties, tight faded jeans and embossed high-heeled cowboy boots, and a Stetson hat over her streaked-blond hair.

Right now she was pouring coffee, her shrewd brown eyes, set in a lean fox face, examining Janet seated across the kitchen table from her.

'Don't try to bullshit me, lollypop. You only act this way when you're scared shitless. Remember, I knew you when.'

Janet chuckled and bit into her third toasted English muffin slathered in butter.

'You're right, I'm in trouble. Because of Arnie. You remember I worked in Reno last summer to pay for a new roof for the cabin. Anyway, mid-July, Arnie and I were in the Golden Horseshoe after my shift. I was trying to watch Wallberg accept the Democratic Presidential nomination on TV, Arnie as usual was trying to turn me out, with him to protect me – and I got pissed off. So I started flirting with this old dude on the next stool. Then Arnie got pissed and slapped my face, really hard.'

'Arnie was always good at that. Why you let that turd—'

'Next thing I know, he and the old guy are taking the place apart. Arnie had a knife, the old guy a bottle. The cops came in the front while I was dragging the old guy out the back. I got him into the 4-Runner and started driving. I figured Reno'd had enough of me for a while. His name was Hal. We traveled together 'til November. The best four months of my life.'

'That's the goddamndest story I've ever heard.'

'He got me away from Arnie. He... valued me. Made me value myself. We never made love. I tried, at first, but he couldn't do it. His wife had been killed by a drunk driver years before, and he still felt guilty about it.'

Kate asked, 'It's because of him that you're in trouble?'

'Yeah. Him and Arnie. The FBI is looking for me.'

'What the fuck did you do?'

'Nothing. I lent Hal the 4-Runner in January and haven't seen him since. A man named Thorne showed up at AQUA Tours last night, driving it. Said the federales were after me.'

'How did he get it?'

'I don't know. But he was right – the FBI was waiting at my cabin. Thorne held them up so I could get away. I told him to meet me here, but then I heard shooting at the cabin. I don't know if he's alive or dead. I have to know.' She smiled wanly. 'And I have to ditch the 4-Runner. So you've got a built-in babysitter for the next few days.'

'What I've got is a lot of trouble right here in River City.' Kate was on her feet, a glint in her eye. 'You can trade Fat-Arms LeDoux pink-slips, even-up, your 4-Runner for one of those Harley clones he always has around.'

Still no sign of Kestrel or the 4-Runner. Ray Franklin had gone through her place again, and had torn it apart looking for a paper trail. He found one item: a letter from the Sho-Ka-Wah Casino north of Santa Rosa, offering her a job dealing blackjack.

'You think that's where she went?' Ray demanded eagerly.

'We'll check with them, but I doubt it. I think she heard the gunfire by her cabin, and drove hard all night to get away. She could have been in Mexico before we got out the BOLO. Easy for an Indian to hide in Mexico. I'll ask Spaulding to see if her 4-Runner was logged through the border near Tijuana.'

'Why is she so important?'

'Because she was important to Thorne.'

An hour later, the Seeking Information Alert for Kestrel under any of her names came up with something. Kestrel – under the name Amore – had, for the past three years during the winter months, been a licensed dealer at one of the casinos in Reno. No negatives on her from the casino or the cheap rooming house on South Virginia Street where she lived.

She had also worked in Reno for part of the previous summer, and in July was 'present' at a bar brawl in a joint called The Golden Horseshoe. A hardnose named Arnie McCue had been beating her up and some old guy rescued her. Both she and the old guy had disappeared, presumably in tandem, just as the cops arrived, and hadn't been seen since.

On the surface, nothing. But McCue's interview was provocative: 'He was just an old fart, drunk at the bar. Had a limp, but he sure could move quick. Quicker than me.'

Old guy. A limp. Moved quick. Corwin. Had to be.

Hatfield had his connection. Amore had been running with Corwin from July until the Delta murders in November. No wonder she had changed her name to Kestrel. Somehow Thorne had found out about her, and had gone looking.

None of it helped much. He didn't know where Kestrel was. He didn't know where Thorne was. Or even IF Thorne was.

Thorne was. Barely. He had never been so cold and wet as he was right then, shooting the Tuolemne in a disintegrating rowboat without any oars. Not even as a kid when he and his best friend Wally would shoot the Chino River in a rubber raft when the ice went out in the spring and took all of the Fairbanks bridges with it.

The rowboat kept riding lower and lower in the water, until just the gunnels were out, but it was keeping afloat. Then the sodden craft hit a jagged rock broadside and flipped over. Thorne got ten minutes out of clinging to the largest piece of wreckage before he was knocked loose. It was like getting caught in the surf in Panama; he didn't know which way was up, tried to grab breaths when his face broke water, kept curled up like a shrimp to avoid shattering his limbs on the rocks.

One foot struck gravel. He tried to bury his fingers in the shifting bottom, but was ripped away again. More rocks. More foaming white water. Pebbles! He belly-flopped into foot-deep water on a sloping stony bottom. Crawled up a few feet onto the beach where the eddy had thrust him. There, the rushing river couldn't catch his legs and drag him back again.

The sunlight through pine boughs felt warm on his back. His clothes started to steam. He shut his eyes. He slept.

Walt Greene burst in. 'Old guy runs the Casa Loma store had a break-in last night. Also at the AQUA River Tours facility in the same building. The perp stole dried food and water and first-aid stuff. He also stole a car an overnight camper had left parked by the store.'

'How far is it from Casa Loma to Kestrel's cabin?'

'Couple of miles.'

'Shit! Did you get out a stolen vehicle report?'

'Didn't have to. We found the car abandoned by the Tuolemne River with the keys in it, down five miles of the damndest road you've ever seen. That's the spot where AQUA River Tours puts in their river-rafting rubber boats.'

Hatfield demanded sharply, 'Why is that significant?'

'Janet Kestrel is a river-rafting guide with AQUA. Arness says Thorne came around yesterday morning looking for her.'

A major screw-up. In their rush to get Kestrel's home address, they hadn't asked the Groveland postmaster where she worked. Thorne had. That's how he could have beaten them to Kestrel – if he had. He could have waited for her at AQUA Tours, alerted her to the fact that the FBI was looking for her.

'We took Arness down to the river to look around. He said that a half-stove-in rowboat was buried in the weeds there for a couple of years, and now it's gone. No oars, but even so…'

'Okay,' snapped Hatfield. 'First light we start searching down both sides of the river. We'll have to use the other river guides, and the local police and sheriffs, too. If they find Thorne alive, we push the National Security button to keep them from starting any interrogations of their own.' He paused. 'Meanwhile, I'm authorising an affirmative on Compromise Authority for Thorne for everyone involved.'

Compromise Authority: shoot on sight. Shoot to kill.

36

IT WAS MID-AFTERNOON when Thorne was awakened by the chill. The sun was low in the sky so its rays no longer warmed him. He moved his arms and legs, checking to make sure everything was working before staggering to his feet. His side ached abominably, but ribs eventually healed themselves. Just don't breathe deep.

For the moment, his fever had disappeared. But his meds and food also had disappeared, with the boat. So his fever might return. He started working his way downriver toward Ferry Bridge, walking on stone or gravel that would take no footprint, resting often against a tree, sitting on a rock. He ripped his stolen life jacket with his knife, draped it off a dead, half-submerged aspen, then plodded the sun down the sky to dusk.

Hatfield would discover the abandoned car. Tomorrow they would search the riverbanks, with luck find pieces of the missing boat and the life jacket. The river emptied into Don Pedro Lake, where a body could easily disappear for weeks. He could only hope that's what they would think happened to him.

Janet might have driven straight for Canada or Mexico before they had time to get out a BOLO on the 4-Runner. But he had to assume she would be in Oakdale, waiting.

Shadow fell across him. He looked up. He was under the bridge. He waited until full dark and beyond, when there would be no traffic on Ferry Road. Scuffing out his tracks as he went, he used the bridge supports to haul himself up the steep earth slope. Get to Big Oak Flat five miles away, crawl unseen into the back of a truck at the gas station, and get taken away.

At first light, Hatfield was in a raft on the Tuolemne, wearing the wet suit, life jacket, and helmet given him by the guides. The sheriff's men conducting the search of the river banks had found a part of the rowboat, a curved piece of wood they said was a strake, part of the boat's keel outside the gunnel. But it wasn't enough for Hatfield. He needed Thorne's body, or some semi-kind of proof that he was dead.

'Tag it and bag it and leave it for the recovery team.'

Then they found the life jacket impaled on an aspen branch.

Adrenaline surged. 'Don't touch it!'

They were two miles from Ferry Bridge. The ripped life jacket swirled back and forth in the foaming white water like someone waving for help. No body was found, but there was no indication that he had climbed up from under the bridge to the road. Hatfield looked up at the ring of solemn faces.

'This man is a major National Security risk. We have to be sure he doesn't get away. Does anyone believe he is alive?'

They looked at one another, then away. Then shook their heads. That was enough for Hatfield. They were the river search experts. But even so, he told them, 'Search the river banks for another ten miles tomorrow, just to be sure.'

Later, he told his Hostage/Rescue team that they could abandon the search.

'Thorne is dead. Close the book on him. Make Kestrel our priority now.'

They did. But several hours later, Perry could only report, 'No sighting of her anywhere. Indian casinos are under a lot of scrutiny in California these days, so the Sho-Ka-Wah will notify us if she shows up. They want to cooperate.'

'Don't hold your breath on that one,' said Hatfield. 'No reports of border crossings into Mexico or Canada?'

'None,' said Baror, 'but she could have walked across.'

Corwin was dead. Thorne was dead also. The 4-Runner had not shown up. Kestrel had no paper life, and was probably in Mexico. Maybe it was time to figure out a way to somehow report all of these negatives as positives to the President.

At the outskirts of Manteca, where east-west 120 hit I-5 running north and south through the great central valley, Janet parked the

4-Runner beside Fat-Arms LeDoux's no-name gas station. Fat-Arms was 350 pounds, six-eight, hack boots, blue work shirt with the sleeves cut off to show his fat twenty-two inch upper arms, a red bandanna around his head like a pirate of the Caribbean.

He walked around the 4-Runner under the lights, glowering.

'Somebody heavy looking for it, could get my nuts creamed.'

'Looking for me,' said Janet. 'Not for the 4-Runner.'

'I got a Suzuki thumper, we trade pink slips even up.'

An entry-level bike, but its single-cylinder, four-stroke engine had a hefty 600cc displacement. After they traded pink slips and Janet had roared away, Fat-Arms chortled aloud. He had stolen the Suzuki in Sacramento the week before, dummied up a pink, and switched plates with a totaled Yamaha V-Max. When she renewed the registration, the VIN would come back hot. Janet would get busted.

'Stupid, fucking, stuck-up bitch.'

Served her right. She'd turned him down once, hard, when he had come onto her at Whiskey River.

Whiskey River was long and narrow, with an L-shaped bar along the left wall, a couple of tables along the right. In back, it opened out to a small dance floor with a bandstand for Friday and Saturday nights. But this was the usual slow mid-week night, just the way Kate Wayne liked it.

On the juke, Willie Nelson was grating out Whiskey River, their virtual theme song. Three wannabes she knew drove Harley clones were drinking draft beer at the bar. At one of the tables a guilty-looking couple, probably up from Modesto in separate cars for illicit sex, were having a drink before heading back to their respective dreary spouses.

A stranger shuffled in, paused to scan the room with deep-set, bitter chocolate eyes sunk deep in his face. Coal-black hair filthy and matted, ripe clothing. A three-day beard on his lean, feverish cheeks. He looked like a train wreck, but managed to climb onto a bar stool.

'What'll it be?' asked Kate.

For answer, he put his head down on the bar and passed out.

Kate punched out her home number on the bar's phone, whispered to Janet's cautious voice, 'He made it.'

Thorne woke to a pair of warm brown expectant eyes staring into his face from a foot away. A shorthair black-and-white mongrel was sitting on his chest, wagging its tail on his belly. His side, bandaged, hurt; his ribs, taped, itched. He had no idea why he was flat on his back with a dog on his chest. The dog lifted a front paw. They shook, solemnly.

'His name is Jigger,' piped a voice from beside the bed.

Thorne could just see the top half of a tiny girl's face beyond the covers. She had big solemn dark eyes and cornsilk hair. Maybe two, about the age of Eden when...

'I'm Thorne,' he said, quickly stifling memory.

'Lindy,' she said. 'Me'n Jigger wanted to say "hi".'

'Hi.'

She whirled and ran out of the room. She wore a pink frilly dress. Jigger jumped down and trotted busily after her.

When Thorne opened his eyes again, Janet was there. She wore jeans and a blouse and a sheath knife on the outside of her right boot. Her arms were crossed over her breasts in what could almost have been a defensive stance.

He gestured at his wrapped ribs and bandaged wound. 'You?'

'Jigger's vet. He won't talk. You got to Oakdale night before last and stumbled your way into Whiskey River and passed out. My friend Kate called me, we brought you over here. This is her house. Lindy's her daughter.'

Thorne steeled himself. 'We have to talk.'

'Not here. Not now.' She gestured after Lindy. 'After hours at the bar. I'll leave the back door unlocked.'

37

THEY WERE IN the conference room under the White House. Just the two of them. No aides, no notes taken. Hatfield had to use smoke and mirrors to spin his essential lack of results to his utmost advantage.

'Mr. President, we are concentrating on a blackjack dealer and casual prostitute named Janet Kestrel. She hooked up with Corwin in Reno in July, travelled with him until the election, then disappeared. I have a BOLO and an SIA out on her.'

For Wallberg, somebody new to worry about. With Corwin dead, he'd thought Thorne, snooping around in the past as Hatfield had said, was his only concern. But this Kestrel woman also sounded like trouble. This was dangerous ground; Hal Corwin might have remembered things and told them to her, things no one else could know about. With Kurt Jaeger gone, Wallberg knew he had to find someone new to trust. Probably Hatfield, but not yet. For now, dissemble, act as if Kestrel was of no importance to him.

'So she traveled with Corwin. Corwin is dead and gone. Thorne is our priority here.'

'Frankly, Mr. President, we want the Kestrel woman because Thorne was looking for her. Since we can't ask Thorne himself, it's vital to catch her and find out what he wanted from her.'

'Can't ask Thorne himself,' snapped Wallberg. 'Say what you mean, man. That you can't find Thorne.'

'Can't ask him, Mr. President,' Hatfield persisted. 'We have every reason to believe that Thorne is dead.'

Wallberg kept his face and voice impassive. 'Indeed?'

Hatfield spun his tale. Thorne exchanging fire with him, and, wounded, trying to escape down the Tuolemne. Water-logged rowboat, wreckage, life jacket. Absolutely nothing since.

Hope leaped up in Wallberg's chest. 'I find it symbolic,' he intoned sententiously when Hatfield was finished, 'that both Thorne and Corwin found their quietus in icy, rushing water, as if trying to cleanse themselves of their sins.' He stood up. 'Good work, Terrill. But find this Kestrel woman. Confirm that Thorne is dead. I need closure in this matter so I can get on with the business of running this great country of ours.'

'Closure you will get, Mr. President.'

Alone, Wallberg felt a rising excitement. Corwin was dead, Thorne was probably dead, no longer able to pick at certain forty-year-old knots in the fabric of his life before the presidency. Hatfield would find Kestrel, extract whatever information she had, tell it only to him. The man was proving his dedication to the Presidency – and to Hatfield's own ambition: to become the Director of the FBI. As Edith had said on New Year's Eve, no one could stop Gus Wallberg now.

Walking the perimeter of the Whiskey River lot, Thorne felt surprisingly good. The vet had done his job. No real pain. In front of the bar, no vehicles. In the dirt parking lot out behind, no bikes. In the wall he faced, no windows. A good place for a talk. Or a take-down.

He drifted the door open. Smells of beer and booze; this being California, none of cigarettes. Janet was sitting at a small round table across the dance floor, nothing in her hands, a bottle of whiskey and two thick-bottom shot glasses in front of her. He slid the deadbolt shut, sat down across from her.

'Okay,' she said, 'now tell me about Hal.' Her eyes were hot, intense on his face.

'I'd better tell you about me, first. It's relevant. I grew up in Alaska, did a lot of hunting and trapping. I joined the Rangers, when I became an ex-Ranger, the CIA hired me as a contract sniper for a CIA front in Panama. Seven years ago I lost my wife and infant child, about Lindy's age, to a drunk driver. I vowed to my wife's memory I would never kill again, and became a camp guard in Kenya at a fancy tourist lodge. Any of this sound familiar? Like a parallel to Hal's life?

Anyway, Hatfield framed me so I would be deported back to the States.'

'Sure, I see the parallel. But I think I hear violins.'

'This isn't a sob story. Hatfield framed me to get me back here to hunt down Corwin for the president.' He outlined for her the presidential pressure to find Corwin, the way he had done it, the cat-and-mouse with Corwin, blind chess – in Minnesota, in the Bitterroot Mountains.

'So you're saying Hal shot at Wallberg and hit Jaeger.'

'That's what I'm saying. From twelve-hundred yards out.'

'That's what I can't believe. Hal wouldn't miss. Not even from twelve-hundred yards.' Her eyes were chips of blue ice, glacier-cold. 'I think he meant to hit Jaeger, and that's enough bullshit about how and why. I want to know where. Goddamn you – where is Hal Corwin?'

Thorne's own personal Rubicon. 'Dead. I killed him. I know it's not worth anything, but I'm sorry he's—'

She came across the table at Thorne, knocking him backward out of his chair, landing on top of him. Her left hand was a claw that scored his face with long bloody parallel grooves. Her right hand was jerking the knife from her boot. She stabbed downward at his throat. He knocked the blade aside. The knife buried itself two inches deep in the hardwood floor.

Thorne swung an elbow against the corner of her jaw. She sagged. He threw the knife away. It hit the bandstand with a clang. He got up, panting, righted his chair, retrieved the bottle and unbroken glasses. He sat down heavily, hunched over with pain from his ribs, watching her like a hungry hawk.

Her eyelids fluttered. She moved her head, pressed a hand against the side of her jaw, yelped. Her eyes opened, filled with malice. She measured the distance between them.

'Don't even think about it,' he said.

After a full minute, she sighed and got to her feet and went around him to her chair and sat down. She poured herself a drink, held up the bottle. He nodded. They drank, set the glasses down. He resumed as if she hadn't tried to kill him.

Their stalk of each other down the mountain. Firing at the same time Corwin fired. Corwin's crawl to the stream. She didn't interrupt, just kept her eyes on is face.

'I told Corwin, "You missed." He said, "Did I?" and rolled over into the water and was dead and gone forever.'

To his surprise, the story seemed to calm rather than incense her further. She just said, 'I repeat: he must have meant to shoot Jaeger instead of President Wallberg.'

'I thought of that. But he had a history with Wallberg, none with Jaeger. It just doesn't make sense, unless you know things I don't. You can see why I had to find you, why I hope we can work together to find out the truth. What were you to Hal? Lover? Co-conspirator? How did you two meet? What did he tell you about him and Jaeger? Him and Wallberg?'

'If I said he told me nothing about anything, then what?'

'If that's the truth, then we're both screwed. Hatfield isn't going to stop. I thought he just wanted me in a Kenya jail. Instead he tried to kill me. If I was dead, I couldn't tell Wallberg that it was I who saved him, not Hatfield. So now he has to kill me. It's not urgent with you, but he thinks you might have some knowledge he wants. He'll get you, then he'll stick you away somewhere until he has your story.'

She poured them each one more shot, as if needing the time to make her decision. They sipped, then she sighed and said, 'First, you have to tell me about that night in the Delta.'

'Everything? You won't like it.'

'I have to know. Tell me anyway, even if some of it's… awful.' He did. She blanched fish-belly white at the state of Nisa's body, but didn't stop him. When he was finished, she said, 'I spurred Hal on. I said that if I was his daughter, I'd kill my husband for trying to kill him.'

'So you knew his story. How did—'

'We met in Reno. He saved me from a beating by a guy who

wanted to turn me out with him as my pimp. Hal and I left that night and traveled the west together. There was never anything sexual between us. He became the father I wished I'd had, I became the daughter he wished he'd had. When we heard on the TV that Wallberg would be at the Grand Canyon, I told Hal he had to talk with Nisa because I knew it was chewing at him, what she did. She told him that Damon shot him for Wallberg. He didn't believe it, because Wallberg had once been his best friend.'

'So why did Nisa yell for security?'

'What she said made him so angry that he said he was going after Damon. She panicked. But then she just said he had tried to snatch her purse, to give him time to get away.'

'Were you there, too?'

'Outside. I was dressed up like a squaw girl to be inconspicuous. But Jaeger saw me and came on to me. He told me they'd be at the Desert Palms Resort in California later that month, and wanted me to meet him there. Said he'd show me a good time. Instead, I told Hal about the Desert Palms, and talked him into going over the wall to find Damon Mather. I waited for Hal in the 4-Runner. But neither Damon nor Nisa was there. Hal saw Wallberg alone in the mineral pool and tried to get the truth out of him. He got nothing except shot at.'

'So he didn't go there to kill Wallberg.'

'He didn't even go there to kill Damon Mather, though I thought he did. He just was going to get the truth out of him. That night the two of us ended up in a little desert motel halfway back to L.A., drunk. I was in a rage at what all of those people had done to him, and that's when he said it was Mather who pulled the trigger and that he didn't care any more, he was going to quit, get on with his life.' Her eyes were miserable. 'I left while he was asleep. I abandoned him.'

'Not much else you could do at that point,' said Thorne.

'I should have stuck with him. When I read in the L.A. newspapers that Wallberg would be at a Beverly Hills hotel for the election, I saw a way to make up for it. I conned my way into Jaeger's room as the stupid little squaw girl from El Tovar, and saw Nisa's name and a phone number and 'Terminous' on the pad by his phone. I pretended I hadn't.'

'Something's missing here. You ended up in the hospital.'

'I just remember bits and pieces about that. I was in a maid's cart… two black guys were dumping me in an alley… When I woke up in the hospital, Hal was there. I told him about Terminous and the phone number. Seeing me all beat up must have made him change his mind about Mather, made him decide to go kill both him and Nisa. If I hadn't told him where they were—'

'Did you ever think that maybe Jaeger wanted you to get that phone number? Two black guys dumped you in the alley. Two black guys were with Jaeger in the Delta. Maybe he wanted Hal to go there so that he and his men could kill him.'

'They were there to kill Hal?' Her eyes were wide with surprise. 'Not to save Nisa and Damon?'

'That's one of the things I need to find out.'

'Hal is dead. Nisa is dead. Damon is dead. Even Jaeger is dead. There's nobody left to ask.'

'There's the two black guys. I think they're from L.A. If I could get down there without Hatfield spotting me…'

For the first time, she smiled. 'I can do that for you.'

38

ON FRIDAY MORNING, five bikes drove south through the pre-dawn darkness from their rendezvous at Whiskey River. All of that wild-and-free-on-your-chopper stuff was, well, just stuff. Motorcycles at best have five-gallon tanks. You might stretch it to two hundred miles with a tailwind, but you'd be bone dry. Then there were breakfast and lunch stops, bathroom and coffee breaks.

Leading them was burly, bearded Worf the Klingon, riding a 1998 Harley Dyna Wide Glide with a customized paint job, ape-hanger handlebars and lots of chrome. With his bandanna under his neo-Nazi pot, and a bunch of decals sewn onto his leather vest, he was the sort of outlaw who was a magnet for law enforcement. Just what Janet needed to avoid, but she hadn't said that to Worf. Because the others, despite wrap-around shades, leathers, and American flags on their backs, were nine-to-fivers. The black-leathered mamas up behind them on their bikes were their wives. None of their bikes smacked of the outlaw chopper: two customs, a standard, and Janet's thumper. Multipurpose bikes, good for a round-trip to the high Sierra or to commute to work on Monday. Law-enforcement would-n't waste time on them.

With his uncut, unkempt hair, and a good start on a beard, Thorne, up behind Janet on the Suzuki, fit right in. Their first chance to talk, besides shouted comments over the thunder of the engines, came as they ate hot dogs and guzzled non-alcoholic beer at a rest-stop south of Fresno.

'Let me get this straight,' said Janet around a big bite of hot dog. 'We're after an L.A. pimp named Sharkey who used to supply Jaeger with whores. Just how do we go about finding him?'

'We don't. We let him find us.'

'Then what do we do?'

'We make him tell us what really happened in the Delta.'

That's when Worf bellowed, 'Let's saddle up.'

Ninety-nine cut over to I-5, which took them up over the Grapevine and down into the L.A. basin. At Santa Clarita the others cut off west on Cal 126 toward the Los Padres National Forest for their weekend encampment. Janet and Thorne kept on toward L.A. They would rendezvous with the others on Sunday for the ride back up to Oakdale.

The Gaylord Arms was a shabby hot-sheet motel on Santa Ana near the Watts Towers. Thorne took two rooms on the first floor with separate entrances and separate room numbers but with a connecting door in between, giving the check-in clerk too much money and hinting at a weekend drug buy or a bootleg porn shoot. Janet didn't register.

'What makes you think Sharkey will show?'

'Putting out Jaeger's name with the low-life element will make him come to us. Maybe tomorrow.'

She almost hoped Sharkey wouldn't come. What might a man like Thorne do to make him talk?

'Mind if I take the bike while you're spreading the word?'

'It's all yours.'

Thorne hit three pick-up bars and two strip-joints, leaving the same message everywhere: 'A man named Jaeger told me to see a man named Sharkey to get me some girls for a beat-up-your-ho video I'm making. My name is Thompson and I'm in room 121 at the Gaylord Arms.'

Bread upon the waters. But finally it was too much for him, and he returned to the motel. Janet was not back yet. An hour later, someone playing rap music on his cell-phone paused outside the door. Thorne stood on a chair to peer down through the slats of the window blind without being seen himself. The man was black, 30, shaven-headed, wearing a yellow FUBU shirt with a pimp's gold rings on his fingers and in his ears, and a pimp's gold chains around his neck. Sharkey? This soon?

Seemed like it was. He called softly through the door. 'Yo, I be Sharkey. Lookin fo a man calls hisself Thompson.'

Thorne returned the chair to its place, opened the door, and stepped back so the man and his rap music could come in. Something struck him very hard on the back of his head. Going down into the twilight zone, he thought in disgust:

rap music coming through the door to cover Sharkey himself coming in from the connecting room... thought Sharkey'd want to talk first... stupid... stupid... stu-p-i-d...

A voice said, as through gauze, 'Me'n Horace gonna hurt you bad, sucker. I likes to hurt 'em, mos surely do. Dudes or bitches, don't make no mind...'

Thorne was gone from there.

Janet rode north, then west on Century Boulevard to the vast sprawl of LAX, twice around oval World Way past the endless array of passenger terminals, then back east to Century again. Approach avoidance. She finally stopped at an all-night cafe for a bowl of chili and countless cups of coffee.

She couldn't be part of this. Because of Thorne, the Feds were looking for her. Thorne had killed Hal, now planned to torture Sharkey to find out what the man knew. She stopped with her cup halfway to her lips. She had lousy taste in men.

Arnie McCue, her one-time boyfriend in Reno, had wanted to make her into a prostitute. To get away from him, she had gone off with Hal Corwin, a man old enough to be her father. Who had Hal been, really? A mercenary. A man who murdered his own daughter and desecrated her body. At her urging, at least the killing part of it. Now she had gone off with Thorne – after trying to kill him because he had killed Hal.

This was not who she was, urging a man to kill people, trying to kill someone herself. Hal and Thorne had infected her, the pair of them, with their own madness. She had to let go of both of them.

The time had come for her to build a real life for herself. Start by embracing the racial heritage she had always rejected because her father had been an abusive drunk, and go deal blackjack at the Sho-Ka-Wah Casino. Build on that. Yes! She smiled to herself. For once she was making the right decision.

But when she turned the bike back into the Gaylord Arms parking lot, her light swept across two black men supporting a stumbling, head-lolling Thorne. Without thought or hesitation, she goosed the bike. The man in front, a deer in the headlights, skittered. Bad choice. The bike hit him in the chest. He flew backwards into a parked car.

The roar of the bike got through the haze in Thorne's head. Then the sound of impact. Janet! Saving his ass! Even as he thought it, he was falling backwards and flailing his legs. Woozily, not with his usual snap, but doing it just the same. His foot whapped the gun out of Sharkey's hand, his leg took out Sharkey's knees. He rolled over, gave Sharkey an elbow to the throat that had just enough on it.

'The street,' he croaked to Janet, tossing her the car keys Horace had dropped.

He leaned against a car for a moment. He couldn't have done it alone, but he was coming out of it fast, now. He dragged Sharkey into the room and dumped him on the floor. No door opened, no head was thrust out. Three rooms that were lit went dark. A $50,000 black Lincoln Town Car pulled up. Janet sprung the trunk. Together, they dumped Horace in and slammed the lid.

Sharkey was tied with wet towels to a chair in the middle of the room. Sweat gleamed on his shaven head, there was drool at the corner of his mouth. Thorne sat in front of him, monotonously slapping his face with a wet wash cloth. Then Thorne took out his Randall Survivor. The blade gleamed.

'C'mon, Sharkey. Wake up. Pain time.' He tipped Janet a quick wink that she didn't catch. 'Turn on the TV and wait in the other room, honey. I know you don't like to see blood.'

Leaving, she hit the remote. It was an old movie. The Dirty Dozen. Before she could get the connecting door shut, she heard Thorne say, 'First a finger, then an ear...'

*

As the door closed behind Janet, a memory from the Rangers overwhelmed Thorne's mind. Victor had been ambushed by a rebel patrol in Colombia. They'd cut off his pinkie finger before Thorne could get there. Victor hadn't even groaned. Thorne had killed three rebels with his Randall Survivor, the others had fled. He'd carried Victor over his shoulder five miles through the nighttime jungle back to base. Later they got very drunk and laughed about it.

He had known then that he could never be a torturer. But Sharkey didn't know that.

Thorne snapped him contemptuously under the nose with his middle finger, very hard.

'I think I'll start with the nose,' he said.

Sharkey wet himself.

'Okay, Sharkey, Horace is already dead,' said Thorne, 'but you've still got a chance – just one. Why did Jaeger take you and Horace to the Delta on election night?'

Sharkey wanted to lie, but this sucker would off him in a second like he had Horace. It was in his eyes. A life-taker.

'To take out some dude,' Sharkey said. 'Me an Horace, we stayed up on the levee, couple hundred yards off from this houseboat. Jaeger had balls, he went down there alone to check things out, wasn't even packin' no heat. It was real foggy, we couldn't see shit, couldn't hear shit. After a while, Jaeger, he come back up, say the dude ain't there yet. Say, when the dude come, you wait an whack him after he goes inside. Not before.'

'So you waited.'

'Yeah. After a while, dude show up, tall, kinda old, had a gimp. We move in.'

A gimp. Corwin's limp.

'Dude goes aboard, Jaeger yells, 'Now!' We start poppin caps at the houseboat, old Jaeger he breaks out his mufuckin cellphone! Starts yellin fo the heat, says we takin fire.'

'Were you?'

'Dunno, man. The fuckin fog, we couldn't see nothin, couldn't hear nothin, so we was shootin at nothin. The heat comes, Jaeger tells us to cut out. That's it, man.'

'Did Jaeger do any shooting himself?'

'Tole you, man, cat hadn't got no gun. Anyway, he was a executive type. Never got his mufuckin hands dirty, not that way, anyhow. Now, with some bitch…'

Thorne wasn't listening, was thinking. Jaeger had gone aboard, had found Nisa and Damon dead. For some reason, maybe something he saw on the houseboat, he figured Corwin would come back. When he did, Sharkey and Horace would kill him just before the sheriff's men arrived. The lawmen would find just what Jaeger wanted them to find: Corwin and his victims. Three dead bodies. Pretty much as Thorne had thought it must have been.

He groaned his way to his feet. Now all of his ribs were sore, not just the cracked one. His jaw was swollen, one eye was almost shut. His kidneys were a new agony. The best that he could hope for was just to piss blood for a few days.

He threw Sharkey's car keys on the bed. At the moment, he didn't know if he was more disgusted with Sharkey or with himself. Sharkey, for who he was. Himself, for who he was in danger of becoming. He said, 'Horace is in the trunk of your car. Alive. He'll need patching up.'

39

JANET WAS SITTING on the side of the bed with her hands knotted in her lap. She had heard nothing from the other room except *The Dirty Dozen*, Telly Savalas going psycho and getting his. She started to her feet when Thorne came through the connecting door in an agonized shuffle.

'Is he…' she began breathlessly. 'Did you…'

'Is he what?' Thorne collapsed into the hard-back chair by the writing table. Then he got it. 'Is he dead? Christ no. Guy like him, you give him a little nudge, he knows what he'd do to you if he had you tied up. His imagination does the rest.'

'What does a little nudge mean, exactly?'

'I snapped him under the nose. Once.' He demonstrated. 'Go look. Right now he's trying to get those towels unknotted. He'll square it with the night-clerk, get Horace to a doctor – don't worry about him. He's a pimp and he kills people.'

'So do you kill people.'

'Not for money. And not any more. But maybe I should have messed him up a little. He sure messed me up.' He groaned his way to his feet. 'Let's get out of here. You're driving.'

She did, Thorne clinging to the back of the Suzuki like a damaged limpet. It was a long ride, north on the 405 to La Cienega and all the way to Sunset. She stopped at an all-night convenience store for a bottle of Ibuprofen, then Thorne checked them into a twin-bedded room under his Benny Schutz identity. It was the same run-down motel below the Strip where he had stayed before he saw Walter Houghton, M.D., for the first time.

He ate six pain pills, lay down on one of the beds, fully clothed, to stare at the ceiling. It was after two a.m., so the bar next door was closed. It would open again at four, but for now there was relative silence.

'We gotta talk while I still can,' he said. 'You know, you saved my butt back there. They were going to kill me and dump me off the edge of Mulholland Drive.'

Janet sat on the other bed as she had sat on the bed in Watts, her hands white-knuckled in her lap. She said nothing. Thorne sighed. She wasn't giving an inch.

'Okay. It's just what we thought. Jaeger wanted Hal to kill them both so Sharkey and Horace could shoot him just before the police got there. It would have been a perfect frame, the murderer and his victims, dead together. But Hal got away.'

'Until you came along,' she snapped. Then she added, in a softer voice, 'I'm going to get some coffee. You want any?' He just shook his head wearily. She nodded. 'Okay, I'll put up the DO NOT DISTURB sign when I leave. G'bye, Thorne.'

'See you in a little while, Janet.'

'Sure.'

But when he woke in the morning, Janet was gone. She'd left Thorne flat, just as she'd left Corwin. How could he have expected anything else?

She'd also left a note beside his head on the pillow, written on the back of an all-night coffee shop menu.

Thorne:
Sitting in that hotel room last night thinking you were
torturing Sharkey, I knew I had to end it. I really didn't
know Hal at all, and I really don't know you. I need
my own life.
Goodbye. Good luck.
Janet.

Saved his life, then dumped him. He'd thought his capacity for emotion had died with Alison, but reading Janet's message he'd realized what a given she'd become in his life. He'd started to feel things he hadn't felt in seven years. How stupid could he be? How could he expect that she could ever forgive him for Hal's death?

When he woke in the morning, Fat-Arms LeDoux didn't know where he was. He felt dead. He squinted, realized the stripes down the wall were bars. He was in jail.

He sat hunched up on the edge of the bunk, his head in his hands, trying to remember. He'd finished stripping out Kestrel's 4-Runner, had ridden up I-5 to to celebrate and to drink his fill at Chopper's Roadhouse near Lodi, a biker-friendly and colors-welcome saloon where outlaws of every stripe could hang out.

Which made this the Lodi jail. A line from the old CCR song came back to him: Oh Lord, stuck in Lodi again.

He'd dropped a lot of crystal meth, so when Dangerous Dan spilled beer on his new Tony Lama ostrich-skin cowboy boots, Fat-Arms called him a peckerwood. Dan went for him. They flailed around on the filthy floor until Dan jumped up and laid a size 12 Timberland against the side of Fat-Arms' head.

Yeah, he remembered now. Bouncing up himself, jerking his Buck knife from a pocket of his vest, sticking the serrated blade into Dangerous Dan's gut. Then somebody cold-cocked him.

And here he was, in a cell. Was Dangerous Dan alive or dead? Not that he gave a rat's ass, but if he was dead, Fat-Arms was looking at a world of hard time. If Dan made it, Fat-Arms maybe had himself some wiggle room. If he could think of anyone he could sell to the D.A. in return for a plea-bargain.

Then he remembered Janet. Somebody heavy looking for her, not for her 4-Runner. Not cops. Not crooks. Which left…

He went to the front of the cell and yelled for the trustee, Mitch, a skinny con with close-set eyes and a wispy mustache. Fat-Arms was an outlaw biker of the meanest sort, which made him a local jail-house celebrity.

'Hey, Mitch, how's Dangerous Dan?'

'Word is, he's hangin on. Prolly gonna make it.'

'Good. Then tell the D.A. I wanna talk to the Feds about a broad owns a dark green 1990 4-Runner.'

When Thorne tried to get up to go to the bathroom, he ended up kneeling on the floor with his upper body on the bed, like a kid saying his nighttime prayers. Slid further, down onto all fours. Tried to pull himself up. Couldn't.

His bladder let go. Bloody urine all over the floor. He grovelled around in it, finally was able to drag himself back up onto the bed. He lay there on his side, panting. Thank God for DO NOT DISTURB signs. This was the lowest moment of his life, worse than the worst moments in Panama. There, he'd still been in control of his own body. Here, all he could do was wait until his strength came back. Wait. Rest. Maybe pass out again.

At noon on Sunday, a tall, hard-faced, very fit-looking black guy in a white shirt and a Brooks Brothers suit and a dull tie walked into Fat-Arms' cell in Lodi like he owned the place. Fat-Arms was unfazed: he'd stomped plenty of niggers like him.

Hatfield looked at the disgusting blob of suet on the bunk. He'd put away plenty of redneck peckerwood bikers like him.

'Hatfield, FBI.'

Fat-Arms' guts churned. The nigger was The Man! He held all the aces with the joker as his hole card. A tremendous belch burst from Fat-Arms. The Fed laughed in his face.

'You've got three minutes, LeDoux. Then I'm out of here and you're in here – twenty-to-life, no parole.'

Fat-Arms talked so fast that spittle flew from his lips.

When he was finished, Hatfield went outside to lean against his Crown Vic and call Ray Franklin on his cell-phone.

'Get a flatbed and a warrant for LeDoux's garage in Manteca. Kestrel traded the 4-Runner for a Suzuki thumper, even up. Gather up all the parts of the 4-Runner and haul them out of there. Impound them. Kestrel doesn't know it yet, but LeDoux traded her a stolen bike for her vehicle.'

Franklin was gleeful. 'We got her for receiving stolen property! Any idea where she is now?'

'Stake out a biker bar called Whiskey River in Oakdale, east of Manteca on highway 120. Also stake out the house of a Kate Wayne. Kestrel went with a bunch of bikers to L.A. for the weekend, and should show up at one or the other place tonight.'

'Search warrants for the house and bar, arrest warrant for the Wayne woman?'

'Search warrants, yeah. But don't execute 'em yet. Don't get spotted by anyone. Don't talk to anyone. Arrest warrant for Wayne, no. She's a single mother, we don't need the grief. When Kestrel shows, notify me and get her on a plane to L.A. soonest. I'll meet you at the Federal Building in Westwood.'

'Thorne?'

'LeDoux never heard of him. Thorne is off the board.'

Janet waved goodbye to the other bikers and cut off toward Kate's house. She wanted to take a long hot shower, eat a big bowl of chili, and play with Lindy and Jigger. When Kate got home, Janet would recount her weekend and then hit the sack.

Getting off the bike under the sycamore tree beside Kate's house, she groaned aloud. Over a thousand miles on that snarly little beast in the last three days. She ached all over.

Whenever she thought of Thorne, tears came to her eyes. For a while she'd started to think they could have some sort of relationship when all of this was finished. But dammit, she'd had to leave when she did. She'd get over it.

She wheeled the bike into the garage next to Kate's little Toyota Echo. Edged her way back out again, closed and locked the door, turned – and was surrounded by four men in street clothes.

'We have a warrant for your arrest,' said one in a cold voice.

Hatfield's men! How…

Two of them twisted her arms up behind her back, cuffs were going on even as they were herding her around the garage toward the street behind Kate's where they'd parked their car. She tried to protest.

'There's a little girl in there I have to take care of—'

'We've already talked with Mommy,' said the hard-bitten muscular one in a sly, almost insinuating voice. 'Mommy's not going to go to work tonight after all.'

40

ON WEDNESDAY MORNING, Thorne was able to get off the bed like a normal human being. His ribs were every color of the rainbow, but finally he looked worse than he felt. He stood under the shower for 45 minutes, hot as his bruised body could take. He hadn't had anything to eat since Saturday, but he hadn't been hungry. Had just crawled to and from the bathroom to drink water from the faucet and piss it out again. This morning, for the first time, his urine was clear of blood.

He dressed in his last clean clothes, opened the windows to let out the stench of blood and urine, and left three $20 bills for the maid. After tossing his soiled clothes into the motel dumpster, he went to the coffee shop down the street to order eggs and bacon and sausages and hashbrowns and sourdough toast and orange juice. He planned to drink a gallon of coffee, too.

On the mend, definitely on the mend. But for what? His quest was finished. Sharkey's story had nailed it all down...

He paused with his first forkful of sausage and egg halfway to his mouth. Sharkey's story.

Sharkey and Horace started shooting as soon as the mid-fifties limping man went into the houseboat. Jaeger called the cops on his cellphone to say they were taking fire and returning it, so the sheriff's men would find Corwin dead beside his victims. But had Corwin really returned their fire, or had he just slipped away as Deputy Escobar had speculated?

That's when Thorne's forgotten fork spanged off his plate to hit the floor with a metallic clatter.

Returned their fire with what? The Magnum had been emptied into Nisa and Damon, all right. But not by him. He hadn't been there before. He had just arrived for the first time when Sharkey and

Horace opened up at the houseboat. No time to kill and reload, let alone time to befoul Nisa's body.

Thorne dropped too much money on the table beside his untouched food, gulping half a cup of tepid coffee on his way to the door. He knew what had happened. He just needed to get proof. He owed that to Janet. And much more besides.

Janet remembered the midnight plane flight from Oakdale. She remembered being shoved down a dimly-lit corridor, being stopped in an open doorway while the cuffs were taken off, then being shoved in, hard, before the door slammed shut behind her. She was in a cell. But where was the cell?

It had a head-high window of one-way glass in the door so they could look in but she couldn't look out. A knee-high bunk was bolted to the floor, with an inch-thick mattress and a single thin gray blanket. A sink and toilet were built into the wall facing it. In one upper corner of the room was a camera lens: they could be taping her even when she went to the bathroom. They fed her at irregular intervals. Bland institutional food.

The interrogations, in a room down the hall with a table and two chairs and the ubiquitous camera behind one-way glass, were always the same. How long had she and Corwin traveled together? What had they done? Where had they gone? She told them only what she was sure they had already learned elsewhere.

Only Hatfield asked what Corwin might have told her. And about Thorne. To him, her replies were unvarying: Corwin had told her nothing. She had never heard of anyone named Thorne.

'We have recovered your 4-Runner.'

'I owned it free and clear. I had the right to trade it for a motorcycle if I wanted to.'

'Not a STOLEN motorcycle,' Hatfield said in nasty triumph.

And she knew how they had found her. Fat-Arms LeDoux.

Sammy buttonholed Hatfield outside the interrogation room, where he obviously had been waiting. A company man, unlike Terrill.

A bureaucrat. Afraid to bend the rules when they needed bending.

'Ah, Terrill, we've gotten whatever we're going to get from her. What do you want me to do with her?'

'Let her rot,' Hatfield said.

'I read the transcript of LeDoux's statement. She was driving a hot Suzuki thumper she didn't know was hot.'

'Lighten up, Sammy.' God, what a pussy! Hatfield clapped him on the shoulder. 'We're the good guys. Don't you want to be Assistant Director?'

Sammy sighed. 'Has the D.A. up in Lodi sprung LeDoux yet?'

'LeDoux is slime. Let them bury him forever.'

Watching Hatfield strut away down the corridor, Sammy Spaulding saw his old pal in a new light. This wasn't why he had become an FBI agent. He wanted to catch the bad guys. He didn't see any bad guy in this scenario. Only a lone, scared woman.

But... Assistant Director. It could be his. With the President behind him, Terrill was going to become Director. He would take Sammy with him up the ladder.

Unless Terrill came up against someone who was even tougher and more driven than he was. Little chance of that.

'Only Superman can stop a train with his bare hands,' chuckled Walter Houghton, M.D. 'Take off your clothes.'

They were in one of the medical examination rooms at Houghton's office. Thorne said, 'I'm not that kind of guy. And I didn't come here for a physical.'

'You're getting one. Get naked, my man.'

Thorne stripped. Slowly and carefully. Houghton gave him a routine physical: took his blood pressure and pulse, peered into his eyes with a bright light, hit his knees with a rubber hammer, held a stethoscope to first his back, then his chest, while having Thorne breathe deep. His strong, delicate fingers poked and prodded, getting grunts and one yelp. He re-dressed the gunshot wound, retaped the ribs.

'Any advice?' asked Thorne.

'Eat more.'

'Thanks for the check-up, but I didn't come for medical reasons.'

Houghton, watching him get dressed, asked, 'Then why?'

'You told me Janet Kestrel was raped, but there was no oral, anal, or vaginal penetration. So what's the evidence of sexual assault as opposed to just a beating?'

'Oh, the assault was sexual, believe me. Punching and kicking her gave the assailant an erection, so when he was finished he could manually ejaculate on her face and body.'

Thorne nodded. 'And if someone sent you a semen sample, could you match its DNA with that of Janet's attacker?'

'Of course.'

'Hold that thought,' said Thorne.

Houghton sighed theatrically. 'Enigmatic to the very end.'

Thorne rode a series of city buses way out Sepulveda into the Valley, looking for just the right setup. Finally, in the back of a mall parking lot in Mission Hills, he spotted a beat-up 1998 Isuzu Trooper LS with a FOR SALE, $850 sign in the driver's window and a phone number written in soluble paint on the door.

The paint was peeling, the trim around the left headlight was gone, the front bumper was mashed down on the left side. But the rubber was good, a like-new spare was mounted on the back, and scrawled on the FOR SALE sign was '153,411 mi, runs great, power windows and steering and door locks, full tank of gas'.

He was reminded of his ancient Land-Rover, back in Tsavo. He shook off the memory, and called the number. When he asked about the Trooper, a squeaky-voiced teenage girl exclaimed, 'Matt'll be there in ten minutes. Don't go 'way!'

Matt was a community college student, thin and earnest and eager to make a sale. Thorne took the Trooper around the parking lot and out into the hustle-bustle of Sepulveda, with Matt beside him, stopped back in the lot with the motor running.

'Seven-fifty. Right now. Cash.'

Twenty minutes later, Thorne was on the 405 north to its merger with 1-5 in the Trooper, the signed pink slip over the visor. Whenever he stopped for gas, he bought candy bars and corn chips. Seven hours later he checked into the Microtec Inn and Suites at the cloverleaf where east-west 12 intersected north-south 1-5. He ate everything in sight at Rocky's across the interchange. Back in his room he left a message for Deputy Escobar at the San Joaquin County Sheriff's Department. No name: just a phone number, room number, and two words: CALL ME.

Escobar called back within a half hour. Thorne said:

'Lunch is on me tomorrow, same time, same place.'

Escobar took just a moment to place the voice. Then he said, 'Check,' and hung up.

Thorne went to bed and slept hard, without nightmares.

41

'Deja vu all over again,' said Thorne when Escobar entered the Sunset Bar and Grill at the Tower Park Marina off California 12. The deputy did indeed look exactly the same, right down to the minia-ture purple heart and mid-East service bar pinned above the ESCOBAR nametag on his impeccable tan Sheriff's uniform. He chuckled at Thorne across the table.

'Not you. You look like you need to swear out an ag-assault com-plaint against somebody.'

The place was crowded with tourists and day-sailors. A blonde waitress came to take their order. Cheeseburgers, fries.

'You ought to see the other guy,' said Thorne. 'That's not the best part of it. Now the Feebs are looking for me as hard as they were looking for your perp last time around. You can win a promotion by turning me in.'

A grin softened Escobar's features. 'I knew that relationship wouldn't last.' He turned his coffee cup idly. 'I saw by the TV that Jaeger ate a bullet for the President up in Montana. You know any-thing about that?'

'Yeah, a lot. Listen, you told me you took fluid, blood and tissue samples at the crime scene here in the Delta – including semen samples from Nisa's body, right?'

'Right. And the Feebs threw me off my own case and then stonewalled the evidence. No DNA results, no autopsy results, no tox screens. Never told me if the Magnum was the murder weapon, or even who it was registered to. So I forgot to tell them about my samples. I've got nothing to compare 'em with anyway.'

'The Magnum was Damon Mather's.' Escobar's eyebrows went up in surprise. 'Yeah, intriguing, isn't it? And here's something else.

Back in November, a doctor down in L.A. had a rape victim who was connected with this case. Intimately. Her attacker ejaculated on her face and body after beating the shit out of her. And the doc's got the perp's semen samples.'

Escobar's eyes gleamed. Thorne had been right: getting shut out of his own murder investigation had cut deep. Escobar was waggling his fingers before Thorne even finished speaking.

'Okay, c'mon, give. The doc's address. I'll overnight my semen samples to him as soon as I get back to the office.'

For the next two days Thorne marked time, exploring the Delta's twisting waterways in a rented boat, hiking along its levees and studying its bird life. He wanted to call Janet at Whiskey River, just to hear her voice; but he figured he had nothing to tell her that she would want to hear.

On the third day, unable to contain himself any longer, he sent a three-word fax to Houghton: Yes or No? Twenty minutes later, he got back a one-word reply: Tomorrow. The next afternoon brought another one-worder: Yes.

Thorne drove to Lodi to drink beer and think. Johnny Doyle had laid it all out for him that night at the Hard Times Cafe, he just hadn't been listening hard enough.

Kurt fuckin' Jaeger, our wunnerful Chief of Staff, had th' hots for Nisa... She turn'd 'm down cold...

Not understood by Doyle, but now understood by Thorne: she turned Jaeger down so hard he suddenly found he had trouble getting it up with any woman. That humiliation quickly led to obsession, to beating women for sexual release. Thorne felt as if he had raised a rock and found something slimy underneath it.

So he got a black pimp in L.A. named Sharkey to fin' 'im hookers din't mind gettin' beat on...

When Janet Kestrel turned up at Jaeger's hotel in L. A., he left Nisa's name and phone number and 'Terminous' on his phone pad for her to see. He had glimpsed a woman driving Corwin's get away vehicle at the Grand Canyon, and thought Janet was she. But in L.A., she played him so skillfully – while he was playing her – that he was deceived into thinking she was just a stupid little squaw girl after all, with no connection to Corwin.

So Jaeger had followed his usual M.O. with any attractive woman at his mercy. He had beaten her to get sexually aroused, then had masturbated on her unconscious body.

But at the hospital she passed on to Corwin what she had seen on Jaeger's phone pad: Nisa's name and number and the word Terminous. On election day, Corwin called Nisa, but she hung up on him before he could say they had nothing to fear from him. Then she called Jaeger, terrified, thinking she needed protection because Corwin had found them. Jaeger's plan for revenge was back on track.

That night at the Delta, Jaeger told Sharkey he was going to 'scout around' the houseboat. He went aboard, maybe saw Damon's gun, said something like, 'For Chrissake, gimme that thing before it goes off.' Of course Damon did: Jaeger was there because Nisa had pleaded with him to come rescue them.

Instead, he killed them. Six shots, muffled by the fog, five into Nisa. Then he ejaculated on her body. Murder: the ultimate sexual frenzy and release all in one package. With Corwin to take the rap. But Corwin survived.

No wonder that Jaeger had dragged Thorne out of Kenya when the computer said he was the best man to find Corwin. Jaeger had murdered Corwin's daughter and had befouled her body, and had blamed it on her father. Who was still alive. Jaeger was terrified, in fear of his life.

But he was also ambitious. And Corwin had been smart enough to know that the best way to get him out in the open was to make all of them think that Wallberg was his target.

Where Wallberg went, Jaeger went. When Wallberg was exposed, Jaeger was exposed.

End of Jaeger. But end of Corwin, too, thanks to Thorne.

Nothing to do now except tell Janet what had really happened on the Delta that night. He used his phone card.

Kate's voice said, 'Whiskey River.'

'This is Thorne. Tell Janet to be proud of Corwin. Tell her that he was not psychotic, just a man bent on vengeance. Tell her that he didn't do anything ugly or dishonorable.'

'I can't. A week ago that fucking Fat-Arms LeDoux rolled over on her for immunity on an ag-assault charge. Hatfield's men took her away in handcuffs.' Her voice brightened. 'At least, Hatfield reneged on their deal. LeDoux's going down, hard.'

A week. His heart sank. It wouldn't have happened if he hadn't gone looking for her. Janet didn't have anything they wanted, but Hatfield would never believe that.

Thorne felt his face grow hot. For a moment he thought it was an adrenaline rush, then he recognized it as rage. The same rage that had so often carried him safely through his Ranger years, suppressed since Alison and Eden had died.

Now he welcomed it. Red, cleansing rage, as he had felt at the Colombian rebels who had cut off Victor's finger. But this rage was directed at Hatfield.

The fucker had gone too far. Despite what he knew, despite what Hatfield had done to him, Thorne had been planning to creep meekly away, find a way to get back to Africa. But this! The Ranger mantra flashed through his mind: *Rangers don't leave Rangers behind.*

For right now, Janet was a fellow Ranger.

And she had saved his life, as he had saved Victor's.

They had taken her watch, but Janet came awake with a start and knew it was the middle of the night. Her edge was that she had nothing to tell them except that Thorne was alive. And she would never tell them that. She had deserted him, sick, in the middle of the night, but she knew that if he learned where she was, he would try to get her out. He would fail, but he would try.

Thorne had the Benny Schutz identity, so he could move around freely. Hatfield thought he was dead. He had the Trooper, a clean vehicle with no connection to Brendan Thorne in anyone's data base. He knew what Jaeger had done on the houseboat. No one else living did.

There had been something between Wallberg and Corwin from forty years ago. When Wallberg got that inaugural day message meant to get Jaeger into the open – CONGRATULATIONS TO A DEAD PRESIDENT – he had instantly accepted the idea that Corwin wanted to kill him. Thorne was going to find out why.

For Janet. For the dead Hal Corwin.

He had a lot of driving to do. Tomorrow was Memorial Day.

42

MEMORIAL DAY. GUS Wallberg sat in the old easy chair that had been his father's, staring out of his study window at the blue and sparkling water of Lake Minnetonka. The kids were up for the weekend and had the sailboat out, heeled over with the wind, slicing through the waves. He could almost hear their shouts and laughter through the thermopaned glass. Edith was supervising in the kitchen: in two hours they would have a backyard barbecue under the big oak trees that would go on until well after dark.

Just six months ago, he and Edith had sat here together on New Year's Eve, looking out over the frozen lake from this very window, discussing his upcoming presidency. What a difference those six months had made! Corwin's inaugural-day letter had not yet been written. Thorne had not been brought in from Africa at Kurt's urging to try and find Corwin and stop him. There was no hint that Kurt would die by Corwin's hand, no hint that Corwin would die by Hatfield's hand.

No hint at all that Wallberg's poll numbers would soar as a result. The American people thought their President had almost been assassinated by some Muslim fundamentalist terrorist or some right-wing survivalist fanatic, and had rallied around. What would they think if they knew that countless millions of their tax dollars had been wasted by the Justice Department to find an assassin who didn't exist? Well, they would never find out.

Only Wallberg and a tiny handful of his most trusted aides knew that it had been someone from the President's past. Terrill Hatfield had killed the killer, thus freeing their President of the dark burden he had carried for forty years.

Almost freeing him. He sighed. Even here, even for just a weekend, he could not escape the pressures of his job. A hardcopy of the first draft of his Fourth of July speech was lying unedited on his lap. Looking at the clock on the mantel above the huge stone fireplace, he felt a tightening in his chest. In one minute, Hatfield would be calling on the secure scrambler phone with his final report on the search for Thorne and that woman, Janet Kestrel. Depending on what Hatfield had to say, Wallberg might truly be free of that dark burden.

The phone buzzed discreetly. Wallberg lifted the receiver from its cradle with no visible tremor in his hand.

'Terrill, happy Memorial Day.'

'Thank you, Mr. President,' came Hatfield's unmistakable tones. 'I hope you are being allowed to relax with your family.'

'I'm on my way to a backyard barbecue right now. You have news for me?'

'I have closure for you, Mr. President. Janet Kestrel is in custody. A week of sleep deprivation, no privacy, and interrogations around the clock. We have wrung her dry. I can assure you that Corwin did not pass on to her any dangerous knowledge of any sort.'

'Outstanding!' But Wallberg still had concerns. 'When you release her, Terrill, won't that leave us with a new problem? If she goes to the media—'

'I am arranging for her permanent commitment to a mental institution as an incurable psychotic. She will have daily psychiatric counselling sessions that will be taped without the doctor's knowledge. The more she insists on her story, the more apparent her psychosis will seem. If anything does surface…'

Wallberg's burden was lifting, lifting.

'How soon will you be able to get it done, Terrill?'

'Within the week. Both parents dead, her father was an alcoholic, so I ordered the Los Angeles AIC, Sammy Spaulding, to work up a psychiatric history starting in her pre-teen years, fabricating a pattern of sexual abuse from age two on into her teens. I went through Quantico with Sammy, he's a solid company man, and I've instructed him to make sure that the paperwork is bullet-proof.'

Wallberg nodded his unseen approval as he listened to Hatfield giving him his life back. The man was worthy of his trust. But even with any threat from Kestrel neutralized, he still had to ask. Thorne was surely dead, had never met Corwin, but still he had been digging into the past.

'Did the Kestrel woman have any information about Thorne?'

'None. We know he was looking for her, but we found her before he could. She had never even heard his name until I questioned her.'

'Any old Ranger friends he might have contacted? Those elite military types tend to stick together.'

'His only Stateside contact was Victor Blackburn, that Ranger stationed at Fort Benning. We have been clandestinely monitoring his phone calls, letters, e-mails and faxes, twenty-four/seven. Nothing. Since Thorne disappeared into the Tuolemne River, he has reached out to no one, I mean no one. No contacts, no sightings. Mr. President, Brendan Thorne is dead.'

The final weight fell from Wallberg's shoulders. All possible vestiges of anything Corwin might have known or recalled was gone from the face of the earth. Anyone he might have passed anything on to was dead. Or incarcerated as insane. He cleared his throat sententiously. He loved this part of being President: the chance to reward the loyal service of his underlings.

'I know how fervently you want to serve your country, Terrill. Serious lapses by the current Director of the FBI will soon be brought to my attention. I think you will enjoy my Fourth of July speech.' He paused. 'Mr. Director.'

'I…' There was a catch in Hatfield's voice. 'I thank you from the bottom of my heart, Mr. President.'

'You have earned the position, Terrill.'

Both men hung up simultaneously, each in his own way elated and transported by the conversation. Dreams really did come true. The good guys really did win out in the end.

It was the first of June, two days after Memorial Day. Brendan Thorne had gotten to Rochester, Minnesota the night before, coming north on 52 after driving east on I-90 non-stop from Rapid City, South Dakota. Just after midnight he had checked into a modest, anonymous motel called The Highway near the junction overpass of 14 and 52 west of the city.

Tired as he was, he had known it would be a mistake to stay at one of the big downtown hotels like the Kahler. The Feebs checked places like that. The Highway Motel was neat, cheap, and clean, just blocks from St. Mary's Hospital and about a mile from the Rochester Public Library on Second Street, S.W.

The library was an old-fashioned tan limestone building with a warm and welcoming air. In a glass-fronted display case were artifacts from the massive tornado in the last century that had devastated Rochester and led to the eventual establishment of the Mayo Clinic and St. Mary's Hospital. One was a piece of wood with a straw driven through it by the force of the wind.

When the silver-haired and bosomy woman behind the counter finished checking out a stack of bright-jacketed kids' books for a soccer mom, Thorne approached her. She had a severe Irish face but a pleasant smile.

'That straw through the plank!' he enthused. 'Amazing!'

'Good often comes from ill. The tornado was the making of this city.'

'Well, it's a fascinating display.' He paused. 'I'm hoping that your library has the *Rochester Post-Bulletin* newspapers from the Vietnam war era on file.'

'Have you tried the *Post-Bulletin* itself?'

'I'm much more comfortable in a library setting, ma'am.'

She gave him a warm smile. 'I know exactly what you mean. We don't have those newspapers on computer yet, not that far back, but we do have them on microfiche.'

Twenty minutes later, Thorne was threading film through one of the three reading machines in a small musty windowless room hidden away behind the library stacks. There was even a photocopy machine that turned out white-on-black thermal copies.

He worked with a great sense of urgency. He had to get the leverage to break Janet out before they drained her dry and stuck her away in some mental facility where he could never find her.

The year he wanted was 1966, the day was January first, New Year's Day. He started turning the crank of the microfiche reader. When he left two hours later he had a thin sheaf of thermal copies from his research. He paid for them, carried them out to his Trooper, and drove back to his motel.

A warm breeze billowed the lacy curtains out into the room, then sucked them back against the screen. Diesel fumes from the highway mingled with the enticing smell of broiling meat from the steakhouse down the block. Thorne settled down with Chinese takeout and the photocopied news stories.

Thirty-nine years before, a fifteen-year-old girl named Heidi Johanson had been struck and killed by a Buick Skylark sedan driven by an eighteen-year-old boy named Halden Corwin. An anonymous caller reported that there was what looked like the body of a dead girl on a narrow snowy road off Highway 52 north of town, a half-mile from the Rainbow dance hall.

The Sheriff responded, and found the dead girl. Just as a call came in reporting a Buick sedan had been stolen, he found the car, run into a tree two hundred yards further down the road. Corwin was behind the wheel. He was taken to St. Mary's Hospital ER with head lacerations. Heidi Johanson was taken to the morgue.

Heidi was a farm girl who had been two years behind Corwin at Rochester High School. She was seen at the Rainbow earlier that evening, dancing, perhaps intoxicated, perhaps with Corwin. Nobody was sure. Her injuries were devastating, instantly fatal.

Corwin had been arrested at the hospital the following morning. There had been many New Year's Eve accidents for the ER to deal with; by the time his blood-alcohol level was tested, too many hours had passed for the results to be admissible in court. When he showed up for Heidi Johanson's memorial service four days later, he was thrown out bodily by the dead girl's big brother, Sven. All good, tear-jerking, small-town paper stuff.

Thorne leaned back and stared unseeing into the night. Corwin had turned eighteen just before the new year, so he had been charged with vehicular manslaughter as an adult. There was one small item about an upcoming hearing, but after that, interest in Corwin was as dead as the girl he had killed. The *Post-Bulletin* didn't cover the fact that he had been given a choice by the judge to volunteer for Vietnam or face a stiff jail-sentence, and had chosen Vietnam. Yesterday's news.

Was there any way, after all these years, to get a look at the Olmsted County Sheriff Department's accident report? Sure. Parade in waving his FBI commission card. He had no doubt he'd get a copy of the report. Even less doubt that he'd have Hatfield's men dragging him from his bed by dawn the next day.

He made notes from the newspaper clippings on the few facts he could explore, the few people he could try to contact.

The first and best source of information would be Heidi's father, Oscar Johanson, but if alive he would be at least eighty now. Her brother Sven, probably around sixty, maybe still around.

Harris Spencer was listed as the ER doctor who had treated Corwin on the night of the hit-and-run. Retired? Moved away? Dead?

Time was passing. Tomorrow, hit the library to initiate internet searches for Sven Johanson and Harris Spencer.

43

THE FARM WAS on narrow blacktop highway 42 near the tiny town of Elgin. Pastures, green grass, grazing cows, corn fields. Thorne got the number off the mailbox beside the highway, and turned up a gravel road leading to a white house and a red barn with a pond down behind it.

Redwing blackbirds gently bounced on the cattails flanking the pond, their musical calls filling the air. Chickens pecked industriously in the dirt, pigeons studded the barn's roof-line. A golden retriever came bounding down from the house, tail wagging and tongue lolling, to thrust a wet nose into Thorne's palm with a golden's unquenchable optimism.

The only sour note was the strong-looking sixtyish man, who would have been blond when he'd had hair, working on a tractor near the chicken coop. He straightened up and wiped the sleeve of his blue workshirt across his brow, glaring at Thorne from angry eyes. Chronic dissatisfaction calipered his mouth. He spat out a long dark-brown jet of tobacco juice.

'Whatever you're sellin', I ain't buyin'.'

From six paces away he smelled of sweat and the snoose he was chewing. Probably Copenhagen: a round can distorted the pocket of his shirt under his old-fashioned bib overalls. He looked like a man who would have thrown Corwin out of his sister's memorial service.

'I've heard you can give me some information on a man named Halden Corwin.'

'The bastard murdered my sister!'

'I heard it was an accident.'

'Yeah, well, you heard wrong.'

But Johanson's gaze faltered. He wiped his forehead again with his sleeve. Leaned back against the tractor and crossed his arms on his chest as if protecting his ribs.

'Heidi, she was a sweet thing. Mebbe not too bright, but she was lead cheerleader at the high school.'

Thorne said nothing. Johanson's face darkened.

'I told Pappy it was a mistake, lettin' her cheer-lead like that. She liked the boys, an' all them big athletes from the football team come snufflin 'round like she was a bitch in heat.'

Thorne prompted, 'Boys like Corwin.'

'Yeah, Corwin. Mind, he had a girl in his own class was sweet on him, Terry Prescott, but over that Christmas they'd had a fight and broke up. Corwin musta started chasin' Heidi. Had her with him in that Buick he stole, didn't he?'

This was a new idea for Thorne. 'I thought he hit her by accident.'

'Mebbe, mebbe. But what would she've been doing out there alone on that road in the freezing cold on New Year's Eve?'

'Okay, tell me how you see it.'

Johanson recounted his own highly-colored version of the hit-and-run as if it all had happened the day before. It was obvious his sister's death had consumed his life, but even so, he recited essential-ly the same facts that Thorne had gotten from the *Post-Bulletin*'s accounts.

'The newspapers never said whose car it was Corwin stole.'

'The mayor's,' said Johanson. 'Justin Wallberg. He insisted on paying for Heidi's funeral expenses an' everything.' Sudden pride flooded Johanson's face. 'His son has ended up being the President of these here United States.'

Driving away, Thorne kept turning it over in his mind. Nothing made sense. If Heidi had been in the car with Corwin, how had she ended up in front of it? If Corwin and Terry Prescott had broken up, and he'd been chasing Heidi Johanson, why had Terry married him in mid-February, just before he shipped out for Vietnam?

And that thing about Corwin stealing the Wallberg Buick was also sending prickles up Thorne's spine. Why hadn't he just borrowed it? Why weren't he and Gus Wallberg out catting around together on that New Year's Eve?

*

Harris Spencer's modern but modest Rochester home was on Northern Heights Drive, N.E. The contrast with Johanson's farm couldn't have been greater. Walking up the concrete drive from the street, Thorne could hear laughter and splashing from behind the house. Obviously the Spencers had a pool, kids, grandkids.

A pretty dark-haired woman about Thorne's age came up the side of the house from the back yard in flip-flops and shorts and a faded blouse with ruffles at the sleeves. There were laugh-lines around her eyes. She had a tall cold wet-beaded glass of lemonade in each hand, shoved one at Thorne as she joined him.

'I saw you drive up. I bet you want Daddy.' Without waiting for a reply, she turned to the open door of the house and yelled, 'Daddy, there's somebody here to see you.' She turned back to Thorne. 'He's in his study, first door on the left.' Then she was gone again, back to the pool-party.

'Come in, come in,' called a voice from down the hall.

Harris Spencer was just standing up from an easy chair near the picture window, shoving reading glasses up on his forehead. A hard-back book was tented open on the chair-arm. He looked a vigorous seventy, with dancing blue eyes in a narrow, mild face.

'I see my daughter as usual has bullied you into taking a glass of her lemonade.' He held out his hand. 'Harris Spencer. Glad to meet you.'

'Brendan Thorne.' They shook.

Spencer gestured him to the couch across from his easy chair. He sat back down. Thorne sat on the couch.

'I'm retired from the Clinic, the freezer is full of walleyes and mallards, and you can play only so many rounds of golf. So these days I'm catching up on all the reading I missed over the years. Do you like to read, Mr. Thorne?'

'Anything I can get my hands on.'

'Good man. I read a lot of mysteries, all kinds. But especially medical mysteries. I'm addicted. But I'm rambling. How can I help you?'

Thorne opened with, 'You must have seen dozens of drunk-

driving accidents over the years. I'm sort of snooping into one par-
ticular one that happened on New Year's Eve, 1966. A boy named
Halden Corwin—'

'Ran over a girl named Heidi Johanson. Damn!' Spencer slammed
a fist on his chair-arm for emphasis. 'I've been waiting forty years for
that other shoe to drop!'

Thorne set his lemonade on the arm of the couch. 'What other
shoe?'

'I was only twenty-nine at the time, doing my very first tour of
night duty at St. Mary's ER. Life and death. Heady stuff. You remember your first one.'

Thorne could vividly remember his first night patrol in the
Panama jungle. He'd been nineteen. Nothing had happened.

'You probably know the basics. Corwin had always been a sort of
wild kid, but not a bad one. He was underage, but that night he'd
been drinking at the Rainbow, then went out and stole a car, and ran
over the Johanson girl by accident on a nearby country road. He
plowed the stolen car into a tree a couple of hundred yards beyond.
The sheriff's men brought him to the ER.'

'I didn't know about him drinking at the Rainbow.'

'He was out cold when they brought him in to us, but after he
woke up he told me the only thing he remembered was being at the
dance.' He leaned forward, face intent. 'His blood alcohol level
seemed to me too high for him to be able to drive a car. Somehow he
did. That bothered me. Still does.'

'I thought no alcohol tests were run until too late.'

Spencer gave a little half-laugh. 'I told you I was young and eager.
I ran 'em myself and didn't tell the police when he was arrested
because I hadn't recorded them so they couldn't be used in evidence.
Besides, I felt he had enough trouble.'

Thorne sipped his lemonade. It was good. The sounds of summer
carried from behind the house. Spencer cocked his head.

'The wife, kids, grandkids. God bless 'em, every one.'

Thorne said slowly, thinking it through, 'If he was so drunk he was
passed out, how did he remember the Rainbow?'

'He wasn't passed out – knocked out. His head hit the steering wheel when the car hit the tree. No seatbelt, of course. Twenty-two stitches. Retrograde amnesia, common with severe concussions. Sometimes part or all of the events shortly before the blow comes back, sometimes none of it ever does.'

Amnesia. In Corwin's case, apparently permanent. Again the prickle up Thorne's spine that he had felt leaving the Johanson farm.

'What did he think happened?'

'He had no idea. Even when he was all patched up and awake, he didn't remember much beyond the Rainbow. Something about someone helping him into a car...' He shrugged. 'Maybe a false memory, maybe Heidi herself. I guess we'll never know.'

Thorne said, 'He and Gus Wallberg were teammates in football and hockey, and great buddies off the field. Why would he steal the car of his best friend's old man? He could have just borrowed it. And since he and Terry Prescott had broken up, why weren't Corwin and Gus Wallberg out together that night?'

'Who knows? Maybe Gus had a date of his own.'

'Good point. But then wouldn't he have been driving his dad's car?'

Spencer nodded. 'It never came out, but some other kids claimed the two of them were drinking together at the Rainbow.'

'Both of them drunk?' mused Thorne. 'Corwin maybe more so? You said he was a wild kid in those days. Maybe he was even already passed out in the car when they left the dancehall.'

Spencer kept it going. 'And Gus Wallberg is driving—'

'Hell yes,' said Thorne eagerly. 'It's his father's car. Wallberg goes roaring down the little country road, Heidi pops up in front of him, he hits the brakes, too late... WHAM!'

Spencer was really into their hypothetical reconstruction. 'So it's Gus who's in a panic and runs into the tree.'

'He's the mayor's son,' said Thorne. 'Maybe he's already planning a life in politics.'

'Even if no criminal charges are brought, his career ends right there, before it even starts. So...'

'So his buddy Corwin is out cold on the seat beside him. Comes from a lousy family, indifferent student at Rochester JC, probably'll flunk out and get drafted for Vietnam anyway. So Gus slides Corwin into the driver's seat, hikes back to the Rainbow, calls his old man... Good old Dad is a politician...'

Thorne ran down, stopped. Spencer was nodding.

'Yes,' he said. 'Here's where it always falls apart for me, too. I just can never quite buy it. Gus would have had to run the car into the tree deliberately, so Hal would be blamed – his best friend. Even if Gus would do that, I can't see Mayor Wallberg saying to him, "I'll report that my car was stolen, son, and say you were home with your Mom and me all night."'

'Not enough heat for the mayor to do it,' agreed Thorne, remembering that the man who had killed Alison and Eden lost his license for a few months, that was all. 'Wallberg was mayor, a politician himself. He would have known that a drunk-driving hit-and-run charge wouldn't stop a young man's later political career, especially not in those pre-MADD days. Remember Ted Kennedy and Mary Jo Kopechne? And that was years later.'

Spencer gave a low chuckle.

'We started sounding like Kennedy-assassination theorists there for a minute, didn't we? In reality, I can't see Gus Wallberg letting his best friend take the blame for the accident, and I can't see his dad letting him get away with it if he tried. Mayor Wallberg felt so terrible that it was his car killed the girl that he paid for Heidi's funeral, her memorial service, everything. He didn't have to do that. He even paid the family compensation for their loss. They bought that farm out near Elgin with the money.'

'An unusual gesture, don't you think? Like maybe there was some guilt mixed in?' Which gave Thorne an idea. He asked, 'Were any blood tests run on Heidi to see whether she had been drinking that night?'

Spencer looked surprised.

'I'm sure not. She was the victim, after all. And she was only fifteen. And she was already dead.'

'How extensive were her injuries?'

'Terrible. Almost like she'd been run over deliberately. Couldn't have been, of course. Corwin was too drunk to formulate such a plan. I was bothered enough by it that I attended her autopsy, but...'

'Was there anything to support that idea?'

'Only thing would be that the poor girl was three months pregnant at the time of her death. So two lives were lost. And there were whispers that it might have been Hal's child. But three months before, he had been very involved with Terry Prescott, was going steady with her. Plus the fact that Heidi was two grades behind him. That's a huge age-difference for kids in high school.'

'And Terry married him before he went off to Vietnam. So obviously she didn't think he was the father of Heidi's child.'

Thorne's tickle wouldn't go away. If Terry believed Corwin was innocent of getting Heidi pregnant...

'They didn't have DNA testing then, but if Heidi's body was exhumed, even now, could they run tests to determine—'

'The point is academic,' said Spencer. 'She was cremated.'

44

THORNE PACKED HIS meager belongings. Sleep tonight, leave first thing in the morning. Again, a lot of driving to do. He felt his rage trying to rise again. He ruthlessly suppressed it. It didn't serve him here. Not yet, anyhow. He didn't need it.

Heidi had been carrying Gus Wallberg's illegitimate child, and would have been demanding marriage – the mayor's son was a real catch. That New Year's Eve was just about as Thorne had pictured it – except the hit-and-run wasn't by Corwin and wasn't a hit-and-run. It was deliberate murder.

Three months pregnant. Wallberg would be frantic by then. Call Heidi up secretly, tell her to meet him on the country road near the Rainbow at midnight. We're going to elope, don't tell anyone. Get his best friend Hal – who he was maybe jealous of? – really drunk. Maybe dope his drinks. Get him into the car, at midnight speed down the country road – wham! Heidi's gone.

And it worked better than he could ever have hoped. Hal Corwin not only had been passed-out drunk and couldn't remember anything, he had ended up with retrograde amnesia from a concussion. Or was it just Wallberg's good luck? Thorne wished he'd asked Spencer if the blow to Corwin's head could have been deliberate, not just from accidentally striking the windshield. When Hal was arrested for vehicular manslaughter he didn't fight it. He accepted that he must have killed the girl.

The mayor knew what his son had done. Knew that Heidi was carrying Gus's baby. He not only paid for Heidi's funeral and memorial service, he bought her family off with a new, prosperous farm so they would agree to Heidi being cremated, along with the fetus she was carrying. It would have been the mayor, also, who made sure

Corwin got a chance to choose Vietnam over jail. They wanted him in a war zone where he would probably get killed.

But Corwin wasn't killed in Vietnam. He thrived. Became a hero. Later, became a mercenary. But then his wife Terry was killed by a drunk driver – just as he believed that he, drunk and in a stolen car, had killed Heidi. All he could do was retreat to a hermit's life in the big woods.

Meanwhile, for the Wallbergs, him becoming a mercenary was almost as good as him becoming dead. He would never return to Rochester, would be as absent from Gus Wallberg's life as Heidi was. Here was where, to Thorne, it got grotesque. After he became governor of Minnesota, Wallberg initiated a long-term affair with Hal Corwin's daughter. Physical infatuation? Love? Or a subconcious further destruction of Corwin?

Thirty-nine years later, Wallberg got presidential ambitions and broke it off with Nisa. But that wasn't enough. What if Corwin's memory returned? What if Corwin realized his buddy Gus had made a girl pregnant, had murdered her in a panic, then had set up his best friend Hal to take the rap for it?

Wallberg voiced his fears aloud, mostly to himself, just once. But Damon Mather, with his ambitions, was there to hear it. The wheel started to turn. Mather tried to kill Corwin.

Now they all were dead. Gus Wallberg was safe. He was President of the United States. If Thorne went to the media, the administration's spin doctors would get going. It's all lies. It didn't really happen that way. Where is your proof?

His proof was cremated in Rochester. His proof was dead on a mountain in Montana. Thorne couldn't touch Wallberg.

But Terrill Hatfield didn't know that, and Hatfield was Thorne's real target. He could be manipulated through his own ambitions. It would be enough. It would have to be enough.

One more debt to pay. Thorne called Whitby Hernild's clinic in Portage. Hernild himself answered the phone.

'Clinic.'

'This is Thorne. Hal Corwin is dead.'

There was a long, unexpected pause, then Hernild blurted, 'My God! That's terrible? When? How?'

'When he killed Kurt Jaeger.'

Still strangely subdued, almost detached, Hernild said, 'I was… afraid it might be Hal behind the gun.'

'I shot him just as he took his own shot. But even so he hit who he aimed at. He wanted to avenge his daughter's murder. He was no psycho. But he should have been after Wallberg, too.'

'What an extraordinary thing to say. I don't understand.'

'Because I've pieced together what Wallberg did to Hal on New Year's Eve forty years ago.'

'Hal had amnesia. He could never remember that night…'

Thorne told him. All of it. Hernild was almost wistful.

'Is there anything you can do about it?'

'No. Even if Hal was still alive, he couldn't do anything. There's no proof for any of it. So Wallberg gets away with it.'

Thorne hung up feeling, not purged as he had expected, but oddly unsettled. But he had done what he considered his duty to the man he had been manipulated into killing. He had cleared Corwin's name with those who mattered – his best friend, and the woman who had thought of him as a surrogate father.

Except that Janet was still a prisoner.

Jennifer Maplewood was fifty-eight years old and lived in a gated community with armed guards. But she was sure she was going to be murdered in her bed by rapists. After one of Jennifer's thrice-weekly sessions, Sharon Dorst always badly needed her twenty-minutes downtime before her next patient.

She wasn't going to get it this day. She had just closed the outer door behind Jennifer when it opened again to admit someone else. She turned, irritated.

'I see patients only by appointment…' She ran down. It was Thorne. She grabbed him and hugged him, then stepped back, red-faced. 'I was… ever since you…'

'Me too.' He squeezed her shoulder. 'I know you felt you let me

down when Hatfield got hold of your session notes. You didn't.
We're square. But I need a favor from you.'

'Anything.'

'Hatfield is doing to another woman what he threatened to do to
you. I need his home address. You have FBI connections. Can you
help me?'

'Give me two hours,' Sharon said. Her face tightened. 'And call me
when… when you've made her safe.'

Because she knew that then she would make more phone calls to
her FBI contacts. Calls she should have made weeks ago.

Driving home to his temporarily empty house well after dark, Terrill
Hatfield was a happy man. His imminent accession to power had
turned his wife on in ways he hadn't dreamed possible. Yesterday
Cora had read coy remarks in a *Washington Post* column to the effect
that Terrill Hatfield would be announced as the new Director of the
FBI in the President's Fourth of July speech. Last night she had given
him the best sex of his life. This morning she had packed her bags
and had flown down to Atlanta to lord it over her mother and two
sisters.

The best of both worlds. Great sex, and now she wasn't here to
start nagging at him as usual. Life was sweet.

He parked his Crown Vic in the driveway, went in the front door,
deactivated the alarm, and turned on the single dim light over the
wet bar in one corner of the living room. It was soothing after the
fluorescent glare of his office. He poured three fingers of Wild Turkey
into a squat heavy cut-glass tumbler and added a single ice cube.

Standing at the picture window and looking out, he thought, Cora
was right. This place is too small for us. We need to be further out,
with at least an acre. Room for a horse. Room for two horses. We can
ride together on Sunday mornings. After Wallberg's announcement
of my appointment as Director of the FBI on the Fourth of July, we'll
go house-hunting…

That's when a hand came over his head from behind, curved
fingers hooked into his nostrils and jerked his head back. An icy

point of steel touched his throat. He could feel a drop of his own blood running down from the broken skin as he was duck-walked awkwardly backward into the room, away from the window.

He had been trained for situations like this. He would…

'Reach across your body, nice and slow, take out your Glock with two fingers, and drop it on the floor.'

Thorne! Alive! All of Hatfield's training deserted him. He could barely breathe, he felt like he might pass out. He dropped his Glock on the floor as directed.

The fingers on his face went away. A hand touched his ankles, checking for a backup piece, went away also.

Hatfield turned, warily. Thorne was leaning against the sideboard Cora had bought last fall during their swing through the New England antique shoppes, his arms crossed so Hatfield's own Glock pointed up at an angle toward the ceiling. Like the Sean Connery pose in those old James Bond movie posters. The pose was deliberate, Hatfield was sure.

'How…' His voice came out in a croak. He hated this display of weakness in himself. 'How did you know where I…'

'Friends in high places,' said Thorne.

Hatfield frantically ran the people who knew his unlisted address through his mind. How could Thorne pressure any of them into giving him up? A threat to their children, maybe?

'I know all the secrets. Jaeger's. Wallberg's. Yours.'

Had Thorne somehow discovered whatever it was that Wallberg had kept hidden from everyone? The thing Hatfield ached to know himself, to give him some ironclad hold over the President?

'Jaeger's dead,' said Thorne, 'so his secrets don't matter. What I know about Wallberg may not be enough to take him down without proof. If I went to the press, I think he'd survive the charges. But you—'

Hatfield tried bluster. 'Don't be so sure I can't—'

'You lied to him about me being dead, you lied to him about who really shot Corwin and saved his life, you threatened Sharon Dorst with illegal detention, you ran illegal surveillance on Victor

Blackburn down at Fort Benning, right now you're illegally detaining Janet Kestrel. Wallberg obviously knows all of it – except about me. All I have to do is let him know I'm alive and you'll be gone in the flick of an eyelash.' He paused, very deliberately. 'Or...'

Hatfield couldn't help it. He burst out, 'Or what?'

'Or at noon tomorrow, California time, Janet Kestrel walks out of the Federal Building in Westwood a free woman.'

'Noon? Tomorrow? I can't possibly—'

'If charges were filed against her, expunge them. If any surveillance tapes were made, destroy them. If anyone follows her, if anyone tries to grab her again, I go to Wallberg. Free her, leave her and Dorst and Blackburn alone, countermand the order to arrest me if I go back to Kenya, and I'm gone. Wallberg keeps on being President. You become Director of the FBI.'

'What guarantee do I have that you'll honor your—'

'None. But it's the only deal you're getting. All you have to do is go back to being the sort of FBI Agent you swore to be in the first place.' He stepped closer, lowered his voice. 'Are we clear on all of this?'

'We... we're clear.'

'Make yourself a new drink. You dropped your last one.'

Hatfield made his drink. As he did, he saw the room reflected in the picture window. Thorne was gone. He knew with a bitter certainty that even as Director, he would never again cross the man in any way. He didn't have the stones for it.

He was Sharon Dorst's glass tiger.

Friday night, Whiskey River was jumping. The TV was blaring, in the back room their weekend rock band was warming up its instruments for the night's work. Kate had even managed to not think about Janet for over an hour. The house phone shrilled. She grabbed the receiver from under the counter with one hand while pouring a shot of vodka with the other.

'Be waiting across the street from the Federal Building in Westwood at noon tomorrow. Jet Blue has morning flights out of Oakland to Burbank that will get you there in time.'

She recognized Thorne's voice. Someone was shouting in her face. She stuck a finger in the ear without the receiver to it.

'Janet will walk out at noon sharp. Just get her away from there, quick as you can. Take her wherever she wants to go.'

'That Indian casino in Hopland offered her a job dealing black-jack. But she'll want to see you and talk to you, Thorne.'

'Tell her I'm like... a kestrel. In the wind.'

Janet was doing pushups on the edge of her bunk when she heard the familiar sound of her cell door being unlocked. It swung wide. Framed in the opening was her chief interrogator. She didn't know his name. None of them ever gave her a name. He was holding something out to her.

'Here is your watch, Ms. Kestrel.' It was the first time he had addressed her by name. 'It's eleven-forty a.m. on Saturday, June eleventh. You are free to go. All charges against you have been dropped. I'm... I'm very glad it worked out this way.'

He was gone. Another man stepped in with the clothes she had been wearing when they had grabbed her. All of the items had been freshly washed and ironed.

Ten minutes later, Janet was squinting against the dazzling noonday sunlight outside the monolithic black tower of the Federal Building, sucking in huge gulps of free air, dazed, totally disoriented. Someone called her name. She looked quickly about, saw a familiar figure far across the weekendempty parking lot.

'Kate!' she cried, and was running toward her friend.

Sammy Spaulding stood at his office window watching Janet Kestrel and the other woman, trying to imagine Janet's feelings. He was still stunned by the phone call from Hatfield he had received at home the night before, ordering her release. But as he had told her, he was glad she was free.

In fact, he felt as if he too had been set free. Free from Terrill Hatfield's insinuating presence, free from the dazzling heights of power Hatfield had implied would be his. He took me up on the mountain, Sammy thought, and showed me what could be mine. Assistant Director of the FBI. Any Agent's wet dream. But now the spell had been broken. It was so simple when he thought about it. Just be the FBI Agent he had sworn to be when he had graduated from Quantico.

Just blow the whistle on Terrill Hatfield.

45

Fort Snelling National Cemetery, where so many of Minnesota's dead heroes were buried, lay between the Minneapolis-St. Paul International Airport and Highway 5. It was the Fourth of July, and in the adjacent Fort Snelling State Historical Park, President Gustave Wallberg, Edith at his side, was taking his ease in a picnic area under a stand of elm trees a hundred yards from the Minnesota River. They were surrounded by his entourage, which in turn was encased in a cocoon of Secret Service agents.

It felt wonderful to be the centerpiece of an old-fashioned birth-of-our-nation VFW picnic. The speech he had been working on a month ago during the Memorial Day weekend was now finished. And damned good it was, hitting all the right patriotic notes.

He checked his watch. Almost show time.

Twelve-hundred yards away, Brendan Thorne was literally up a tree. A week earlier, before the unobtrusively elaborate security preparations had begun, he had climbed thirty feet up into this huge old oak to jam a three-foot one-by-twelve board between two branches to form a makeshift sniper's platform.

He had also cut a keyhole in the foliage so he could scan the picnic grounds through his spotter scope. He wore shooter's gloves, and an earphone radio so he could listen in on the speeches.

Hatfield was honoring their agreement. Janet was free, Dorst and Blackburn were no longer under even clandestine surveillance, and he had talked with Squealer Kemoli in Nairobi. The Kenyan arrest order had been rescinded. So he, too, was honoring their agreement. Distasteful as he found it, he would do nothing directly to hamper Hatfield's rise to power.

*

The veterans and their families were already drawn up around the bunting-bedecked platform to hear their President speak. There was one important amendment to the speech that no one knew about except Wallberg. He would not be announcing Terrill Hatfield's elevation to Director of the FBI as previously hinted to the press corps. He had received signed e-mails from two high-ranking Bureau officials, each alerting him to, and giving him the details of, separate pending investigations of misconduct by Hatfield.

He had expressed his thanks and his profound shock at Hatfield's actions, and had assured each of them that Hatfield's name would be withdrawn. True, Hatfield had saved his life by shooting Corwin at the critical moment in the Bitterroot Range. True, everything the man had done, including the unlawful detention of Janet Kestrel, had been done on behalf of Wallberg and with his knowledge.

But there was no paperwork to that effect. Wallberg had made sure of that. Whatever wild charges Hatfield might make as he went down, President Wallberg had deniability. And it wouldn't hurt his ratings that he would be seen as taking an ethical stand: no breaking of the law in the Wallberg administration. But justice would be tempered with compassion. Hatfield would resign from the FBI without jail time.

Just as well. Hatfield was ambitious. In time, he might have become another Jaeger, trying to uncover secrets best left buried, seeking influence with the Oval Office.

Gus Wallberg sighed and put aside his bottle of beer – Leinenkugel Honey Weiss, a good Minnesota brew – and got to his feet. A pity. The national good could demand heavy sacrifices: three people had died on election night, so now it was Hatfield's turn to pay a heavy price for his country.

'Time to earn my keep, people,' he said to his entourage.

There was hearty sycophantic laughter. He blew Edith a kiss and started off, encircled by young, hard-eyed, highly-conditioned men speaking to their wrists or to the collars of their sports shirts. He shook hands, waved, grinned, tossed out greetings as they opened a pathway through the crowd for him to get to the podium. He was in his element. He was the future, Terrill was the past. As was Corwin. And Nisa. And Thorne.

Thorne, in his sniper's nest, following Wallberg's progress with his scope. The president's clothes were carefully casual: a Solumbra sun hat, slacks, and a gaudy short-sleeve sport shirt. In his left hand was a fried chicken leg. A man of the people. He stepped up to the podium where his speech was laid open for him. No one up there to introduce him. He wanted the platform all to himself.

Watching from a distance of twelve-hundred yards, Thorne realized how much he despised this man. Ten years ago, he would have tried the impossible shot and would have lost his own life in the attempt. On this day, Thorne planned no mayhem. He had his sniper's nest but he had no sniper rifle. He was here to feel just a little of what Corwin must have felt in Montana, sighting in on a hated target a dozen football fields away. This was Thorne's final bloodless bow to the man he once had been. Soon he would disappear without anyone ever knowing he had been there.

Wallberg looked out over the throng, drawing his power, as always, from their numbers, from their rapt attention, from their devotion to him. And from the dozens of media cameras pointing at him to help bump his ratings ever higher. He had planned to talk about himself a good deal, knock the accomplishments of the previous administration, but Edith had advised him that it might sound petty, self-serving; better to just praise America.

'My fellow Americans, we are gathered here today to celebrate the birthday of this great nation which has given so many blessings to all of her citizens. Beyond the beer and the potato salad...' he raised his arm above his head to wave around his chicken leg, '...beyond the fried chicken...' The well-rehearsed but seemingly spontaneous gesture drew wild applause from the crowd. '...we honor all of those brave men and women who gave up their lives on foreign battlefields so that we might enjoy the fruits of their sacrifice. From the shores of Tripoli to the trenches of the Ardennes, from the death march of

Corregidor to the jungles of Vietnam, from the mountains of Afghanistan to the deserts of Iraq...'

Dammit, thought Thorne, it isn't right. This man is a murderer, not a president. Thorne's finger crooked around the imaginary trigger of the rifle he didn't have. If it had been real, he would have squeezed off his shot and to hell with nightmares. Instead, he could only extend his arm and point a rigid forefinger...

'...To Gettysburg, right here at home, where another great American President once said...'

...and whisper, 'Bang, you're dead!' and...

...see Wallberg's head explode in a bloody froth of brain and bone and flesh, the red mist that every sniper knew marked the perfect head shot. It was almost as if Thorne had fired the fatal round himself.

But he hadn't. He was already half-climbing, half-sliding down the side of the tree away from the distant speaker's stand. He dropped to the ground and strolled away along the river bank. In his ear was the familiar pandemonium of death by assassination that had become all too familiar to the modern world.

Thirty minutes later he was driving his Trooper sedately out the Old Shakopee Road, which would lead him to a bridge across the Minnesota River and eventually to 101 West, which would take him... where? No fixed destination. Just away from there.

As he drove, he tried to assess what he had seen. Before speech-day, even though he planned no shot, he had scouted the area as any good sniper should. Apart from his tree, the only site offering a clear shot at the podium was the roof-tower of one of the old stone battalion buildings at Fort Snelling. He had dismissed it out of hand: it was fifteen-hundred yards out. Threequarters of a mile. There was only one man who could have made such a shot, and that man was dead.

The rather gaunt, mid-fifties man, unarmed except for a sheath knife, slipped silently through the sunlit early morning forest. He looked like someone recuperating from an illness or a dangerous accident. There was a hesitancy in his movements, a hitch in his step. Still, no twig crackled, no grass swished. He passed out of the trees and into the burn by a fire-blasted spruce, walking so silently under a blood-red cardinal on a branch above that the bird was not even aware of his passage. He still was the ultimate woodsman.

A voice froze him in mid-step.

'A doctor out in L.A. recently gave me a physical after I had bled out a bit, and his medical advice was, "Eat More."'

The gaunt woodsman looked at the younger man who had appeared out of nowhere, like morning mist through the trees.

'I don't have a lot of appetite. Some bastard shot me.'

'Guilty,' said Thorne.

'How did you know I would be...' Corwin paused, nodded. 'Of course.

'Where else would I be?'

'Yeah. Still hiding in plain sight.'

'I'd better change my M.O.' He made a slight gesture. 'There's fresh coffee back at the cabin. Do we have time to...'

'All the time in the world,' said Thorne.

Half an hour later, they were sitting across from each other at the hand-hewn table, at ease in one another's company. Corwin was right: the coffee was fresh, and damned good. No food; Corwin's appetite hadn't returned yet.

Thorne stood, took a turn around the cabin's single room.

'I was up a tree twelve-hundred yards out when you took your shot at Wallberg,' he said. 'I was there just to watch the bastard and wish there was something I could do to him. But for me, anything beyond about five-hundred yards is pure fantasy. I've always been more assassin than sniper.'

'You're talking about that big oak by the riverbank?'

Thorne shook his head. 'Dammit, Corwin, you're good.'

'I considered it myself, but I knew I wasn't nimble enough these days to climb down and be away before they came looking.' Corwin's craggy face was almost serene. 'Fort Snelling itself was better by far. There, I could have a car waiting.'

'But – fifteen-hundred yards out.'

Corwin made a gesture. 'It was that, or forget about it.'

'A car with a driver,' said Thorne. Corwin looked at him sharply. Thorne ignored the look. 'What I want to know is how you survived in the Bitterroot Range. Was it a lung shot?'

'Yes,' said Corwin. 'Anything else I would have gone into shock and bled out.'

Thorne sat down again.

'I once entertained – and rejected – the idea that if it was a lung shot you might have survived it.' He waved a hand. 'I'd already decided that you were just about the toughest goddam guy I'd ever gone up against. If you could avoid hypothermia, maybe the icy water could stop the bleeding like the icy air of the Minnesota winter did after Mathers shot you.'

'You were right. It could. It did.'

'But I had to figure, what then? You crawl out of the water, there's nobody around to help you… So, you die. End of story. So how…'

'Cellphone,' said Corwin. 'In a waterproof case.'

'A cellphone. Yeah. The missing piece. Of course. You'd need it with you to call Janet as soon as Jaeger was dead, wouldn't you? So she could tell you where to leave her SUV.'

Astonishment flitted across Corwin's face before he could quite close it down. 'How do you know Janet?'

'I found the 4-Runner, registered to her. So I found her.' Thorne shrugged. 'A long story. She can tell it to you herself. At the moment, she's still mourning you as dead.'

Corwin was silent.

Thorne said, almost musing, 'But you didn't call her, you called Hernild. He's a pilot, he flies out and gets you and flies you back to that private clinic of his without hesitating a second. Then he nurses you back to health again, like he did the last time.'

'You've got that all wrong,' snapped Corwin, tight-lipped. He half rose. 'Whitby had nothing to do—'

Thorne waved him back down.

'Bullshit. He had a mighty strange reaction when I called to tell him that you were dead. Now it makes perfect sense. Hell, he knew that at that very moment, you were right here, safe in your cabin in the woods.'

Corwin settled back down as if exhausted.

'And here I would have stayed,' he said, 'except your phone call laid out exactly what Wallberg did to me all those years ago. It jogged my memory, it all came back. The fucker stole the life of poor sweet romantic little Heidi Johanson, and that of her unborn child – his child, too. To say nothing of what he stole from me.'

'Your shot at a normal life,' said Thorne. 'So you got yourself another rifle, and another scope, and enlisted Hernild as your driver, and…' Thorne held up a hand. 'Don't try to tell me he wasn't. And then you went hunting.'

'That's about it.' Corwin stood up. 'I'm through running away and hiding, I'm through killing. I just want to live a hermit's life. If you'll let me.'

Thorne was also on his feet. He chuckled.

'Two burned out cases with all the killing behind them. That's for younger men…' and he paraphrased a line he'd read, maybe from Shakespeare, 'whose consciences have not yet made cowards of them all.'

'So what happens next?' asked Corwin.

'I'd like it if you'd shake my hand,' said Thorne. 'Then I'll be on my way.' He caught himself using yet another poet's words. 'Miles to go before I sleep.'

Corwin stuck out his hand, thought better of it. Instead, he closed his arms around Thorne in a fierce embrace. A warrior's salute after a long and bitter struggle that had finally come to an end for both of them.

46

BECAUSE THE Sho-Ka-Wah Casino was on tribal land, the five-member tribal council of the Hopland band of the Como Indians made all decisions concerning how it was run. They had poker, blackjack, slots, Keno, and single-ball roulette that was really just bingo in formal dress. No craps: it didn't pay off enough.

Janet Kestrel was on her final break of the day in the cafeteria, drinking coffee, when Herb Runningwolf, head of security for the casino, came in and headed her way.

He was a tough, square-faced, thirty-year-old Indian wearing a blue suit and with his hair in a ponytail. His main job was to stop trouble before it started. Little did. Since there was a $200 table limit, card-counters didn't come. And since the most a player could make in a day was about $800, few high-rollers bothered, either. Mostly, all he had to deal with was drunks.

Herb laid a hand on Janet's shoulder.

'I just wanted you to know that your sister started her training and orientation courses this morning. She's smart and she's eager, and I think she's going to work out just fine.'

'Thanks, Herb. And thank the council for taking her on.'

'Blood is blood, sister.'

He patted her shoulder again and moved on.

She returned to the casino proper to replace Charlene at Table Four for her final twenty minute stint. At Sho-Ka-Wah, instead of the shoe, they used a shuffler that handled five decks of cards at a time. The decks lasted six to eight hours, then were retired from rotation. During each of her daily eight-hour shifts, Janet spent twenty, forty, or sixty minutes at a blackjack table, got a twenty-minute break, then moved on to a new table. The short stints discouraged connivance between dealers and gamblers.

Janet was popular with the players because, like them, she was just there for the cards. She dealt 'em, they played 'em. Ten minutes into her shift, a new player sat down at the one empty seat at her table. She seldom looked at faces, just at hands. These newcomer hands put down a stack of chips. She dealt two rounds of cards. The hands flipped up their hole card. It was an ace, as was his up-card.

'Double-down,' the owner of the hands said.

The voice jerked her eyes from the cards to his face. Brendan Thorne. He winked at her. She dealt the next round, went busted when she took the dealer's mandatory card at sixteen. Thorne got blackjack on both hands.

'You beat the house, sir,' she said gravely.

'Calls for a celebration,' he said.

'I'm off in eight minutes.'

He nodded and picked up his modest winnings and left the table. As her hands automatically flipped out cards, she could see him making his way toward the front door. Looking good! Recovered. Rested. No thanks to her.

She stopped at the ladies' room to wash her hands and throw water on her face and run her fingers through her long black hair. Butterflies in the stomach: how was she supposed to act? She had abandoned him to save herself, he had refused to abandon her. But she couldn't feel just simple gratitude toward him. She had to feel either much more – or much less.

When she came out into the cool, deepening dusk, he was leaning back against the side of a beat-up old Isuzu Trooper with his arms crossed and a bemused expression on his face. Exactly as she had first seen him, only then it was her 4-Runner outside the AQUA Tours office a compressed lifetime ago.

She simply said, 'Thank you for what you did – however you managed it. And thanks for what you told Kate about Hal. It helped me a lot when... while Hatfield had me.'

He took both her hands in his. His hands were as warm as hers were cold. He looked into her face, very serious.

'Hal is alive,' he said.

'Alive?' Her eyes got huge.

Even as he said it, he knew that he hoped she wouldn't want to go to Corwin. It was all jumbled up in his mind. What he saw as his duty to a man he had wronged versus emotions he had thought were forever dead.

Janet rescued her hands from his. She lowered her head so he couldn't see the tears in her eyes. She realized with a thrill that he was as confused as she was.

'Hal assassinated President Wallberg, didn't he?'

'Executed him,' said Thorne. 'Wallberg was a murderer.'

She felt something let go, something composed of unshed tears and loss and loneliness and a longing to find out who she really was. And to make that gradual discovery with someone she could maybe love, someone who could maybe love her.

'So is Hal,' she said. 'You aren't.'

With a sort of astonishment, Thorne realized she was right: he had never killed except in self-defense, or as what was his duty. Corwin had been a true mercenary, no matter what he was now. It made a difference somehow.

They got into the Trooper without speaking further. Neither knew where it was taking them, but they both knew they wanted to go there. To find out. To know.

The long rains had come at last to East Africa's vast Serengeti plains, almost a month overdue. Just the day before there had been pitiless sun and choking dust over the red land. Then at dawn the heavy, black-bellied clouds began advancing inexorably across the veldt, dropping their hard, straight, unyielding rain.

Morengaru sat on top of an isolated termite mound, his tightly-curled hair uncovered to the pouring rain, his meager clothing plastered to his skin, his shotgun slanted up from between his knees and past the side of his head. Champagne corks rescued from the trash bin at Sikuzuri Safari Camp were stuck in both barrels to keep them from getting scaled with rust inside.

Morengaru walked here every year for the start of the long rains.

It was the only miracle he had ever seen and the only one he would ever believe in.

On the flat plain's furthest horizon a thin line of green appeared, advancing toward him under the blessing of the rain at about the pace of a man very slowly walking. The grasses were racing through the few short weeks of their cycle: renewal, rebirth, replenishment, before the dry season dropped them back into dormancy again. Within days, they would be knee-high, and millions of migratory grazing animals would be spreading out across the green and verdant plains. Behind the grazers would come the inevitable, necessary predators.

Morengaru's remarkable ears picked up automobile sounds. He stubbornly refused to turn his head from his miracle, but he knew that a four-wheel drive vehicle was approaching across the plains behind him. He listened to it the way a classical music lover listens to a Mozart symphony: with his whole being.

A Land-Rover. He listened even more intently as it drew up behind his anthill. A venerable 1960s Land-Rover, in fact, one of the ancient ones with the canvas top and the short wheelbase. He fought it, but the beginnings of a slow smile made his teeth gleam in his ebony face.

The Land-Rover stopped. When the engine was cut, the rain made a thrumming sound on its stretched canvas top. The engine kachunk-kachunked two or three times before it died. It needed tuning. Had not been driven in a long time. Several months, in fact. In his pocket was a key to it that he had never used.

The doors opened, slammed shut. The sounds of two people getting out, swishing through the wet but still dead grass around the termite mound. Two? He almost turned, but disciplined himself. They climbed up and sat down, one on either side of him. Peripheral vision showed him a man and a woman, wazungu, white people, wearing already-soaking safari jackets and widebrimmed safari hats tipped back off their heads so the rain could pelt their faces as it did his.

Only then did Morengaru turn from the advancing grasses he had come all this way from Tsavo, afoot, to see. He looked gravely at the woman first. She was in her late twenties, tawny-skinned, shapely, beautiful, with very long gleaming black hair and startling blue eyes. She met his scrutiny unblinking.

He turned to look at the man. He was forty, also black-haired, dark and quick-looking. But also drawn, as if he had been through many things that had seasoned him. The man hooked two bent fingers toward Morengaru's eyes, then toward his own.

'Tatuona tena,' he said solemnly, repeating it from their last meeting. We shall see each other again.

'Ndio,' replied Morengaru, equally solemn. Yes. Then he added, 'Uso kwa uso.' Face to face.

The woman held out a hand to Morengaru and greeted him. 'Jambo, bwana.'

Hello, sir. 'I am Janet Kestrel.'

Morengaru took her hand in both of his and bowed very slightly. 'Memsa'ab.' Madam. 'I am Morengaru.'

Then of one accord, all three of them turned to face the pounding rain and the advancing line of green that they all had come to see. It had deepened, broadened now, from a line on the horizon to cover half the veldt in front of them. For a long time they watched its progress. No one spoke. No one had to.

When the growing grasses had almost reached their termite mound, soon to surround it and pass on, Morengaru stirred and spoke, without turning his head.

'Since we three landless rogues, maybe we go hunting now.'

They laughed, three people lost in the vastness of the Serengeti plains, drenched by East Africa's life-giving long rains.

Acknowledgements

As always, my wife Dori, first in my heart, is first in these acknowl-edgments. She accompanies me through the endless hours of writing and revision of all of my novels, brilliant and sensitive and tough-minded in her insights and suggestions.

Otto Penzler, the mystery field's greatest editor, historian, and publisher, who invited me to join his new mystery list at Harcourt. I find myself a pygmy among giants.

Henry Morrison, my agent, who over the years has never ceased to amaze me with his wit and intelligence, his editorial and creative suggestions, his understanding of the publishing field and its dynamics.

My foreign agent, Danny Baror, a bulldog in securing foreign sales for his writers, securing excellent advances, and in protecting our rights in other countries.

Bill Corfitzen, who patiently drove Dori and me all over Washington, D.C. and environs, and gave us an insider's description of the Department of Commerce cafe and courtyard.

Jane Lepscky, who took us around the Georgetown docks and marina, and who suggested the Alexandria tour boat as a colorful and tricky way to get my man Thorne to and from Old Town.

Several old friends from my years in Kenya, especially John Basinger and Edgar Schmidt, who shared many adventures with me. Also the late Neil MaCleod, John Allen, Errol Williams, and Joe Stewart, ex-Headmaster at Kakamega Boys Secondary School. Others embedded in my memory are the real Morengaru, Arthur 'Squealer' Kemoli, Elijah Muthengi, Mbalilwa, and Prabatsingh M. Mahidi.

Olga Shezchenko gave me detailed descriptions of the Tuolemne River white-water rafting trips for which she was a singularly skillful guide. Olga also told me the colorful way to build up immunity against poison oak.

Retired Army Colonel William Wood shared detailed knowledge about military tactics, arms, explosives, what snipers face, and the things they must know for their strange and deadly work.

Movie producer Paul Sandburg, for his unflagging delight and enthusiasm for all of my projects, his wisdom about the ways of La La Land, and his suggestions about L. A. locations.

The wonderful staff, especially Theresa McGovern, at the Fairfax Branch of the Marin County Public Library system, for their dedicated pursuit of obscure reference material for me.

All of the people at the Sho-Ka-Wah Indian Casino in Hopland, California, who gave Dori and me access to their operation. Especially the Hopland Tribal Council; Sho-Ka-Wah's general manager, Don Trimble; the Sergeant of Security for the day shift, Mike Hatfield; and Herb, the security man who took us around.

Warf the Klingon, for insider information on outlaw bikers and the Harley cult.

Last, but not least, the good folks at Whiskey River in Oakdale, California, for good drinks and good talk and truly funny barroom jokes over a long Thanksgiving weekend.